GW01319736

Allies

Kaylid Chronicles Book 4

Mel Todd

Bad Ash Publishing

Atlanta, GA

Bad Ash Publishing
Atlanta, GA 30127
www.badashpublishing.com

Book Layout © 2017 BookDesignTemplates.com
Cover by Ampersand Book Covers
Allies/Mel Todd. -- 1st ed.
ISBN 978-1-950287-02-4

To all those who don't look like anyone else.

I searched for you from the other side of the galaxy.

—RARZ GOLDWING LIRYLINE

CONTENTS

Chapter 1 - Visitor 1

Chapter 2 – Meet the Family 9

Chapter 3 – Going Home 17

Chapter 4 - Shifted Perceptions............................. 27

Chapter 5 - True Colors 35

Chapter 6 - Talking It Out 43

Chapter 7 - Small Talk... 54

Chapter 8 -Getting Personal 62

Chapter 9 - Bombshells 68

Chapter 10 - First Domino 78

Chapter 11 - Meet the Troops 87

Chapter 12 - From here to there 96

Chapter 13 - And Back Again 105

Chapter 14 - Planning Stages.............................. 113

Chapter 15 - Whirlwinds...................................... 123

Chapter 16 - Practice 132

Chapter 17 - New Toys 140

Chapter 18 - Suck it Up.. 149

Chapter 19 - Confrontations 157

Chapter 20 - Cloth of Humanity 166

Chapter 21 - Alien Ships...176

Chapter 22 - No Plan Survives..188

Chapter 23 - Step One of Many 198

Chapter 24 - Losses 207

Chapter 25 - Ladder of Success..214

Chapter 26 - Hope Realized 223

Chapter 27 - Revelations...233

Chapter 28 - Taking Command 238

Chapter 29 - Heavy is the Head 246

Chapter 30 - Paths Forward 254

Chapter 31 - Complications 262

Chapter 32 - Gift Horses 270

Chapter 33 - Planned Downfall..279

Chapter 34 - Hail Mary...284

Chapter 35 -Line in Granite...290

Chapter 36 - Kamikaze 301

Chapter 37 - Impact...308

Chapter 38 - Falling to Earth 317

Chapter 39 - Coming in Hot 328

Chapter 39 - Survivors 339

Chapter 40 - Blood 347

Chapter 41 - Goodbye 355

Chapter 42 - Aftermath 361

Epilogue.. 366

Chapter 1 - Visitor

With the invasion focusing on densely populated areas, people are fleeing to more remote areas and overloading the infrastructure there. Reports from areas as diverse as Nebraska and Scotland and Iceland mention the sudden influx of people fleeing the attackers. Their presence is causing life-threatening issues as the support system can't handle the influx. ~TNN Invasion News

McKenna kept sneaking glances at the being sitting next to her in the Humvee as they raced back to their headquarters. The president and others needed to be notified and that could only be done from there. They didn't carry their phones with them. There was too big a risk of it going off at the wrong time, and besides, even with a phone on silent they made noise when they vibrated—too much noise. This wasn't a call she wanted to make out here anyway.

~What is he? Is this a Drakyn?~ McKenna tried not to stare even as she asked in the mindspace. The weird feeling of someone in her mind had faded, but she could feel everyone's rapt attention on their guest.

~You could just ask me your questions. I am here to help both our peoples.~ The rich vibrant voice filled the mindspace and it took everything McKenna had to not squeak in surprise.

She whipped around to stare at him and noticed Perc and JD doing the same thing. While surprise was hard to read on Kaylid warrior form faces, the echoes of emotion down the mindspace let her know they had the same reaction she did.

"How did you do that?" The Humvee drowned out her voice but the Drakyn tilted his scaly head.

~You were talking so I did not think it would be rude to reply. Was it?~

~How can you speak English?~ Toni blurted out the question even as McKenna had to brace herself when the Humvee swayed sharply. Some of the soldiers drove the vehicle like it was a sports car. It wasn't, and the bruises proved it, though at least their bruises faded fast—the soldiers weren't so lucky.

~It would do me little assistance if I could not speak the language of the ones I hoped to offer mutual aid. We obtained examples of your speech and some of my people have made the effort to learn them. Most were gleaned off your streaming networks. As I speak it and hear it, my own skill becomes more accurate. It is an odd language. There are many conflicting ideas inherent in the words. I think I prefer the ones called Spanish and Italian. They have more of an eloquent sound and flow, almost like music.~

McKenna checked to make sure her jaw wasn't hanging open. This just seemed too surreal. She wanted to ask so many questions, but the swirl of confusion in the mindspace told her she wasn't alone.

~Wefor?~ She had no idea if this stranger could overhear that too, but almost didn't care. Almost, so she did try to make it private.

[Yes.]

The AI's voice had a weird, wary note to it.

~Is he, it, telling the truth?~

[There is no information on a living Drakyn in accessible databases. Anything you learn will be new information for the databases.]

~In other words you have no clue and are flying just as blind as we are.~

[That may be another way to put it.] The AI almost sounded aggrieved, which was just amusing.

A shudder shook the vehicle as it came to a halt. The engine shut off and the silence seemed a physical thing.

"Let's get our guest inside." Lawson said, he sounded tense and McKenna gave him a look. His eyes were wide and skin pale as he stared at the Drakyn, flinching a bit as the dragon man flexed his wings in the confined space.

"Can we make sure to let people know what we're bringing inside? I really don't want him or us to get shot." McKenna looked at Lawson meaningfully.

Lawson stared at her blankly for a moment, then shook himself. "Oh, yeah." He stepped out of the vehicle and walked a few steps away, flipping on his radio and talking. McKenna didn't bother to listen, she trusted him after the last week or so. And all of them knew how fragile this hope was. Instead she focused on the Drakyn, cycling through all the things she wanted to say.

~How come you can hear us, when we are talking in our minds?~ This was Cass, and McKenna got the impression she was waiting on the other side of the door, acting as protection and backup for both sides.

~I do not understand the question. You are talking. If you did not want me to hear, you would have put it on a private wave length instead of a public space.~ The rich voice sounded confused and his body tilted its head a bit looking at McKenna.

~Silent? Public? Wefor?~

[There is no information to address your question.]

The Drakyn flinched back, his flexible nose wrinkling. ~What is that? It spoke before.~

Interesting when Wefor spoke just to me it was private. Or he didn't react.

3

~Wefor, the AI in my head.~

~Ah. Yes. That information had been passed along. Though I did not expect a separate intelligence.~ The Drakyn flexed his wings again, the tight constraints of the vehicle making it an aborted motion.

McKenna had a burning need to know what else had been passed along and by whom. How much did this Drakyn know?

"Okay, you're clear. Guaranteed no one is going to pull a weapon. I talked to Captain Alfonso, he's waiting. We'll call the right peeps." Lawson called back. He sounded a bit calmer.

"Ready? We have people you need to meet." She glanced at the Drakyn and really wished she had some idea about how to read their facial expressions or body language.

All that training we got and nothing that would be useful now.

She ignored the thought that the training had been provided by people who treated these beings as their worst enemy. And they had no idea how accurate some of the details would be.

He came out after her, and yes, she knew it was a male, something. Everything about him screamed male. His huge red wings flexed in the open air. McKenna sucked in a breath. There was an aura about him that just took your breath away. Perc and JD followed, and she realized again how huge the Drakyn was. The reds and yellows of his scales reflected light, casting colors on the back wall of the strip mall. The soldier posted there drew in a sharp breath but didn't move or draw his weapon. McKenna took that as a positive, even if his eyes were wide and breathing rapid.

The Drakyn titled his head scanning the bland building and the two men looking at him.

"Your buildings are so blocky." It came out almost as a question but not quite.

McKenna shrugged. "It works. There are more varieties in other places." She shifted her attention to Lawson. "Alfonso ready for us?"

"Yeah. I don't think he believes, but he's waiting and has the landline connected and with a dial tone," Lawson replied, looking at at the alien standing there. Some of the junction boxes had been taken out and even cell phone service was spotty, but everyone figured it wouldn't occur to the Elentrin to tap into the landlines. With an odd look on his face Lawson shook himself and turned, pulling open the door. "Let's show off the dragon."

McKenna took a steadying breath as the aforementioned dragon tilted his head a bit. "I am called a Drakyn, not a dragon."

"Old name, mythology, stuff like that. I hope it doesn't matter but expect people to call you that. Probably a lot," McKenna told him, resisting the urge to tell him anymore.

Oh, the media will have a field day with this when they get a hold of him.

"As you say." It took him moving sideways through the door to be able to enter and they walked into a room of people gaping at him.

~I knew what you said, but I still didn't expect that. Holy moly.~ Cass's thought held a touch of awe, not awe of his beauty, but of the power and something else this creature embodied.

It creeped McKenna out.

The Drakyn stood, seemingly unaffected by everyone looking at him, a mix of fear and wonder in their eyes.

"Alfonso in his office?" she asked, wanting this done and over with. Maybe then they could get back to a normal life. If that even existed anymore.

5

"Yeah. Waiting for you." Lawson stayed outside, shutting the door even as he spoke. "Go ahead and take him in. He's waiting." The door shut.

Coward.

She sighed, recognizing that everything had been dropped on her. Fighting back the irritation, she darted a look over at her friends. JD and Cass stood together, Cass leaning into his furred form. Perc leaned against the wall, watching her, his black whiskers laid back tight against his muzzle.

"Come on then." She waved at the Drakyn and led the way to Alfonso's office. The huge being following her with his wings folded down against his back. She really wanted to inspect those wings. They were fascinating. But he made the already small hallway seem tiny. Glancing back, she noticed he blocked most of the light as she knocked on the open door.

I really hope he's on our side.

Mark Alfonso looked up and paled, blinking rapidly. "Holy fuck. It's a dragon."

"So everyone keeps saying. I am a Drakyn and here to help in your, well, our fight against the Elentrin." His voice clearer than it should have been with that mouth formation.

Maybe partially telepathic? Or maybe he's just practiced? Or maybe I know nothing about them?

Alfonso cleared his throat. He started to wave them to a seat but thought better of it with a second glance at the bulk of the Drakyn.

"I know you've got an in with the people at the top, Largo. Do you want to call them?"

~Wefor, what's the SecDef's number?~ She had no idea, it had been a contact on her phone and she had left that with Toni, just in case.

With calm precision Wefor rattled off the number and she dialed it, setting the phone on speaker with everyone

6

watching everyone else. All in all she'd really like to have just crashed. The emotional whiplash of the day had drained her. In sleep there was the chance of happier things.

"Burby. Who is this and how did you get this number?" His voice snapped out, harsh and tired on the third ring.

"Doug, it's McKenna Largo. I have a situation." It was the nicest way she could think of to put it.

There was a pause then a heavy sigh, and she swore she heard liquid pouring into a glass. "McKenna, not that I don't enjoy your company, but every time you call my hair gets grayer."

"You're bald," she pointed out, voice dry. Alfonso looked at her with his eyes wide and face pale.

"You're talking to the Secretary of Defense," he hissed, his voice so low she almost couldn't hear him. But she did and rolled her eyes at him.

"I shave because otherwise I'd look like Santa or a Monk, neither of which is appropriate. So what is it now?"

She didn't know how to interpret the odd tone in his voice and frankly didn't have the energy to try.

Either that or I'm getting lazy knowing how the people in my head feel. That might not be a good thing.

"We have someone here that has offered to help us." She started off slowly, not sure how to say this.

"Someone? What type of someone? Why would the Russians or the Brits come to you? They have their own problems and I doubt they care about ours." A curiosity and exasperation mixed together in his voice. She should have felt sorry for the bombshell she was about to drop. She didn't.

"Our possible ally is a Drakyn." She almost added the sir, but right now she didn't feel all that respectful. He wasn't out here risking his life like they were. Watching people they liked die.

7

"A what?" The screech had her pulling back from the phone, glad it hadn't been up to her ear.

"You heard me. A Drakyn has shown up and offered to help."

There was silence then a flurry of noises, keys clicking as he typed and a muffled shout of "Get in here now," to someone on his side of the line.

"We'll have someone headed your way to pick him, her, it up. Where are you?" She could tell he was trying to find something to write their address down on. Before either Mark or she could reply, the Drakyn spoke.

For some reason both she and Alfonso were startled. He took so much space, but had stood so quietly his presence had disappeared from her awareness. That was distinctly uncomfortable.

"No. I will only deal with McKenna Largo and her family unit. They are the ones I will interact with. They watched me arrive as a part of her, it is only fitting they are my liaisons." That same musical quality of the voice echoed through the room and vibrated down to her bones, but this time it felt like unmovable granite making a statement.

Chapter 2 – Meet the Family

In most urban areas of all states, the garbage companies are also collecting bodies. The dense metal of the trucks makes them the ideal collectors. All telecommunications companies have worked in concert to set up an 800 number that routes you to the nearest collector to call in for dead Elentrin on the street. More rural areas are asked to either take the bodies to the local crematorium or dispose of them individually. Note that this only applies to aliens, for any other body type the police will be dispatched. ~ TNN News

Captain Alfonso swallowed and looked like he would have rolled away if he had the room, instead he just sat up a bit straighter and his hand dropped beneath the desk.

"Don't you dare," McKenna snapped out and he flushed a bit pulling his hand out.

"Dare what?" Burby asked on the other end of the line. "And why would he only deal with you?"

"Like I know. Ask him." She waved at the Drakyn who crossed his arms across his chest and just gave her a level look.

I hang around JD and Perc, arms the size of my thighs should not intimidate me.

"He's just staring at me and not answering, so I'd say it's not negotiable," she finally said when the Drakyn just looked at her.

"Fine, whatever. I'll get someone down there to get you guys. But be aware, it's getting worse out there. China? Yeah, let's just say China may never be a power again."

"We will meet at her family unit residence. It is proper all of them are involved." The voice rumbled again, and McKenna heard choked sounds from the hallway as well as squeaks of excitement from kids who were eavesdropping in her head.

That made her realize she had been channeling everything into the mindspace, something that had become automatic. And it meant this dragon could feel them.

"No. I have children, I won't put them at risk by your presence." The words slipped out and she didn't even try to moderate them, just glaring at this being who could probably break her in half if he wanted.

Hell, he could probably break Perc in half.

He pulled back, scales around his nose and eyes flaring slightly as his eyes widened and for a second the swirl of colors sucked her in.

"I would never put nestlings at risk." He deflated back down to his normal. "But I understand your fears. However, it is important that I meet all of your unit, even the nestlings. It is proper."

~Why?~ Toni's voice had a sharpness to it that hurt. But McKenna didn't even attempt to gainsay what she asked. She needed to know the answer also. In fact, she could feel everyone's awareness pulling at the space as they all paid very close attention, even Nam.

The being blinked at them. She realized he had two sets of eyelids like most reptiles, but he was close enough she could feel his body heat. So not cold-blooded? So many questions and not enough answers.

"You are the ones I will be working with. You will be the leaders for your people. You have the information you will need to make this, already loaded into your memories. It is only proper you are involved in the saving of your people. You are the leaders."

McKenna frowned at him. "No, we aren't. The president is the leader. I'm just a police officer that got an AI stuck in my head. I don't have the power to do anything."

His brows furrowed. "You are the leaders, you will be. It will be you who decide what comes after. You have the knowledge and ability to make the correct choices. If I work with anyone else, they will lack the knowledge needed." His hand, with three fingers and the thumb, and scaled with sharp claws where nails would be, reached up and rubbed his left eye ridge then jerked his head up, his ridges rising up.

On a human she would have interpreted it as an 'Oh, yeah' reaction.

"Ah, I had forgotten. I was instructed to say certain words where all could hear them. Without speaking them, the knowledge would not be accessible." He cleared his throat and said slowly, both out loud and pushing through the mindspace. "Stars of Alara find justice for the ashes of Alara."

McKenna wondered if their new ally was insane, but a cry of pain or surprise came from outside the small office and inside the mindspace.

~What the hell?~ the words exploded from her in mind and out loud as she took two steps and looked down the hall. Perc, JD, and Cass all leaned against the wall, grabbing their heads, panting.

~Oh shit, that hurt. Kids?~ McKenna could hear a frantic tone to Toni's thoughts and the impression of movement.

~Charley? Are you okay?~ She asked as she headed down the hall towards the others, who were shaking their heads slowly and standing up straight again. Though the slowness in their movements reminded her of the poison that had wreathed through them not so long ago.

11

~That hurt.~ There was a hint of a whine in his voice, and Charley almost never whined.

~What hurt? What happened?~ She tried not to panic at his tone, but Toni and the kids were so far away from her. Trying to tamp down the feeling of everything spiraling out of her control, not that she had ever been in control, she headed over to Perc. JD was already checking Cass out, his large clawed hands gentle on her fragile skin.

"You okay?" her voice came out raspy as she got close to Perc and she didn't like it.

"This is my fault. I had been warned there might be pain involved. I forgot." McKenna whipped her head towards the dragon, glaring at him.

"What did you do to them?" Accusation and frustration coated her tone, but the being only shrugged.

"It's okay, Kenna." Perc rasped out, dropping his hand from where it had been grasping his head. "Remember the dreams we've had? Well, apparently we had a bunch more that were blocked from us. All that info got dumped into our brains at once. It was a bit intense to say the least."

"Intense? I swear for a second I expected Minerva to burst out of my head," Cass muttered it, but she didn't sound amused. "My brain now feels gorged and over-stuffed. As if I'd eaten too much information."

~Yes that,~ Toni chimed in.

~My brain has a tummy ache,~ Jessi contributed and McKenna had to close her eyes and fight the desire to be home, hugging her kids and protecting everyone.

Though I'm curious why this didn't hit me too.

"It was necessary." The rumble of words was musical. But they set McKenna's teeth on edge. She spun, ready to attack this invader. Her stomach churned, body wound tight enough to break.

"Kenna, no." JD's voice reached her at the same time Perc pulled her back against him. In warrior form he still had a decent amount of height on her. She fought for a second, then calmed down. Closing her eyes, she concentrated on breathing in and out, all too aware of the audience.

I always have an audience these days.

She let her eyes slip back open and looked at her friends. ~Explain, please.~ She moved it to mindspeak, not wanting to let everyone know what happened until she could get a handle on how dangerous.

~Ash has been giving us training. Information to help defeat the Elentrin. It was locked until just now. Maybe to protect us, maybe him, but it's information we needed. It'll just take a bit to get it all unpacked and figure out what we know.~ JD's voice was calm and steady, as always. Her rock.

~Truly. I did know it would hurt, I did not realize the level of pain that would be involved. If I had known, I would have spoken the trigger words in a much less public space.~ The Drakyn glanced around at all the soldiers surrounding them, many with weapons ready to jerk up at the slightest wrong move.

JD shook his head, straightening up to his full height. "Chill out, people. Just a headache. Not like I got shot or tazed or something." A round of snickers ran through the room at that. The stories of McKenna's misadventures had provided humor when it was sorely needed.

For her part, McKenna rolled her eyes, her tension fading, and turned back to the small office. Captain Alfonso stood there, face a bit pale and eyes wide. "You didn't expect this job to be boring, did you?" she said, trying to lighten the mood.

Mark tried to smile and gestured to the phone. "The secretary of defense is still on speaker." He almost squeaked it out, and she sighed, walking back in.

"How much did you hear?"

"Enough to know I'm headed back to your place. Anyone else I should bring?"

"You get a new joint chief yet? If this helps the way we hope, we'll need someone who can order military types around besides you. Someone that might have an idea of tactics? Otherwise, since I don't know how he can help, I can't answer what's going to be the right people to bring."

On the other end, Doug sighed. "You're never what I expect. Meet you there this afternoon. I hope this works. We're taking heavy losses in dense urban areas. At this point I can guarantee you every person currently in office won't be re-elected."

McKenna snorted. "Am I supposed to care? This has nothing to do with politics, it's about survival. If I honestly thought that anyone in office could have stopped this and didn't, I'd skin them alive. Slowly. But as it is, we'll suffer through."

A burst of laughter from the other end and Alfonso flinched. "I'd join you. You're right though, most voters won't care. Oh well, if we make it through this, I'm done. I will have served to the best of my ability. After this I'm retiring and going to work on forgetting aliens exist." The words were meant to be humorous she thought, but she flinched, knowing they were the aliens now.

"Okay, bring food. We'll be more comfortable in human form and will need the calories. You can get the good stuff better than we can at this point."

"Understood. See you in a few hours." The line clicked, even as she heard him start to give orders on the other end. Rubbing behind her ears, it really did feel good and relieved stress, she looked at Mark.

"Can you get us a vehicle and escort? We're about thirty-five miles from here. More of a suburban area. I suspect the level of Kaylid is lower there because, of all the shuttles I've watched not many have gone there, and my people there have kept a very low profile. I'll probably need some snipers, people that know how to fight. If they attack us there, they'll do it en-mass, assuming they have any idea what's up. They might not."

"If they know I am here, they will bombard your planet, and focus on this area. It would be best if they had no idea." The Drakyn's voice rumbled behind her, and she flinched. It was his voice. Wefor's created an odd dissonance in her mind. His hit every primal reaction she had. Much like when that lion roared. She wanted to run, hide, kneel, worship, all wrapped up in one emotion. It created an odd reaction she didn't like. And it made her cranky.

"Well, we aren't going to broadcast it. They don't seem to communicate much. So we'll get you to our place, but if anyone sees you, you'll cause a stir. You aren't exactly inconspicuous. But we'll try."

"Ah. Hmm. I assume you all look like this being here?" He indicated Cass and Alfonso with a wave of his hand.

"Well, yes. Variations of colors and stuff. Granted Cass is a female by gender, while Alfonso is a male, if that makes a difference." She replied, her arms folded across her chest as she glared at him.

The corner of his mouth turned up, the scales pulling slightly, but he didn't reveal any teeth, which made her oddly comforted.

Stupid primal brain. He's here to help.

It didn't help, she still saw an apex predator and had to fight to NOT run away.

"I had assumed. While my people do not nurse, so we have no mammary glands, it is not an unknown aspect of female genders. Though you do not have neutral genders, correct?"

McKenna blinked and didn't know how to answer. What was a neutral gender?

"No. While there are a few species on our planet with either both sexes or neither sex, humans are either XX or XY chromosome-based. If that answers your question," Cass

15

responded, her sharp blue eyes fascinated. McKenna could see her fingers twitching, as if taking notes by typing on an invisible keyboard.

"Yes, thank you. Interesting. My people are able to choose more what they want, if they want a gender, as we have triad chromosomes. But for now that will suffice."

"Suffice for what?" McKenna stared at him, all of this just seemed so odd. Aliens, invasions and now dragons. Even a movie would have had more logic than her life at the moment.

"To make myself less obvious." He rumbled and closed dark red lids over those swirling eyes.

"And how—" she broke off in shock and took a step back, pressing into Perc as the Drakyn started to change.

Chapter 3 – Going Home

Who will win, the animal or the human? More and more people are asking these questions after a few more attacks by rabid shifters. If you shift will you de-evolve into your animal form? What does this mean for the protections that were rushed into law? People are starting to wonder if this new ability might come with more downsides than just invading aliens. ~TNN News

In front of her stunned eyes the scales faded, drawing into the skin even as they smoothed out. A weird feeling struck McKenna again as if she had a visitor in her head, but it felt familiar, so she didn't worry about it. What was happening was more incredible.

McKenna couldn't take her eyes off his wings as in slow motion, yet still faster than she could countenance, shrank backwards and were pulled into the body, until she could hardly even tell where they had been. He condensed, shrinking down to be about the height of Perc, while his shoulders and body slimmed down to something approaching human norms. The colors of his reds and yellows, smoothed out to be more normal, though his skin tone tended towards a red clay color that she'd never really seen on people.

When he opened his eyes, they were the only part still-fully inhuman. They swirled with colors almost opalescent and pale compared to the vivid colors they had been. His fully humanoid hands tightened his robes with quick efficient movements to handle his sudden loss of mass.

"What? How?" the words burst out of multiple mouths as they looked at a man who seemed human in most respects. About six-feet-tall, and weighing maybe 250 pounds, with reddish yellow hair, and smooth skin. With sunglasses on, no one would have given him a second look if they passed him on the street.

McKenna struggled with the realization he had weighed close to 500 when he got in the Humvee. The damn thing had tilted. It only shook a little when JD or Perc got it, and it sank when this being climbed in.

The stranger tilted his head looking at them, blinking. Even his secondary eyelids had disappeared.

"You did need me to pass as a member of your species, correct?"

"Well, yes. What I don't understand is where the mass went. How do you weigh less now? I mean I'm assuming you weigh less because you're physically smaller. If not, your mass would be insane. Most vehicles won't be able to support you." Cass's voice bubbled out and McKenna was glad she had said it. Her mind still couldn't get around the absorbing wings.

A long beat of silence then he shrugged. "I do not believe I could explain it right here. Besides, if you can utilize that method it might come in useful. But will this appearance work?"

Was he avoiding? Hiding something from them?

The questions ate at her, but lately nothing ever seemed to get answered to her satisfaction, so she just let it go.

~We okay with bringing him home?~ McKenna asked even knowing he would hear. This wasn't something she'd decide. They all had too much on the line, even though she didn't see any other choices but to go with his whims. Right now she felt like she was being backed into a corner and she wanted to hiss at the sensation.

~I want to see the dragon.~ Nam's voice was so soft, almost timid, but she had strength there, too, that McKenna had to smile at.

~You do?~ She knew her tone had softened, but the little girl was too damn cute.

~I do, too. I never met a dragon before,~ Jessi interjected before any of the adults could respond.

~That would be because they don't exist. You can't have dragons, the math doesn't work.~ Jamie's dismissive voice would get Jessi's temper up in thirty seconds. Luckily Toni stepped in before it could escalate.

~If you two want to squabble fine, but do it in your own mindspace not this one. Shoo. Yes, that's fine, Kenna. I'll get coffee and stuff going. I assume bigwigs are coming with you?~

~I think Doug Burby and others will be showing up there, yes. I told him to bring food, if it helps,~ she offered even as some of the tension had faded with the completely normal squabbling of the kids.

~Yeah. Since we stocked up, we're still good on meats, but fresh stuff is pretty low, and trucks are hit and miss. Going to be some very hungry people by the time this is done.~

~I know. We'll need to shift but we can eat the calorie bars and do it slowly to use the least amount of calories. See you when we get there.~

She turned and looked at everyone. The pure humans looked confused at the silent staring. Though the soldiers they worked with had gotten used to it.

"Take it you need an escort to your place?" Alfonso said wryly. He seemed to have regained his equilibrium and she appreciated that. Having him freaked out would create a ripple effect.

"Yes, please. Lawson if you can spare him, but something a bit less obvious than the Humvee if possible," she responded, trying not to smile at the burble of excitement leaking down from the kids.

He sighed and walked back in the office and came out almost immediately tossing a set of keys to her. "There's a Suburban out there. Take it. If you see any place with gas fill it up or you won't be driving it back."

McKenna caught the keys in midair. "Will do." Their cars had been damaged too badly during the firefight that first day to be drivable. Everything useful had been stripped out of them ages ago.

She gave the dragon an arch look. "Then let's get this show on the road."

He furrowed brows at that but followed them out of the back door. Lawson stood out there watching the area, a pensive look on his face.

"Hey, Lawson. You just got volentold." JD said, a grin splitting his muzzled face revealing too many sharp teeth.

Lawson groaned. "Great. What is it is this time? Storm the White House? Rescue the princess? Who's this and where'd the dragon go?"

McKenna jerked her thumb at the Drakyn. "Turns out they can change forms too. He's coming with us. Ready for an off-the-reservation trip?" Even as she talked, she tossed him the keys heading towards the dark gray Suburban sitting in the corner of the lot.

"With you guys? Why not? Not like I thought I'd live to see my pension." He followed her and climbed into the driver's seat. He took a minute to organize his weapons to be easily accessible, but not in the way. JD headed to the passenger side while Perc and Cass climbed into the far back.

"Our place. We're taking this guy to meet the family. Plus the secretary of defense, and whomever else he drags along with him."

Lawson choked. "Shit, Largo. You don't do anything by half-measures." He narrowed his eyes and at her and the now-human alien who looked around with interest. "Don't you have kids at home?"

"Yep. And he wants to meet them." She shrugged and said the thing that had been running through everyone's head. "Not like they'll be in any more danger than they're already in. There's aliens that want them, remember?" Her voice dry and sarcastic.

"True. Well then, saddle up boys and girls and other creatures. Time to go meet the family." Lawson said in a fake announcer voice.

"Don't quit your day job," JD advised. "You'd starve to death trying to support yourself as a comedian."

McKenna caught Lawson's mock glare as he closed the door and she climbed into the back where the others waited. Cass and Perc were in the back row with the Drakyn-turned-human waiting for her on the bench seat.

I can't believe this is my life.

She shook her head and buckled in. She felt him watching her carefully as she adjusted the seat belt. With elegant movements, he mimicked her.

McKenna started to talk but stopped before the words left her mouth. She'd gotten used to saying all the snarky inappropriate stuff in her head and now the person she wanted most to talk about could hear everything she said.

When did I become that person? Or is it I'm just used to having all of them as my sounding board and vice versa, knowing it's a place we can say anything. Make a note that if he's trustworthy maybe we can have him teach us how to lock it down to private so no one else from outside can overhear. Huh, wonder how the kids do it.

The odd silence both in and out of her mind ate at her while JD talked quietly to Lawson giving him directions. It didn't help that Lawson drove the Suburban the same way he did the Humvee, like it was a sports car. The seat belts were mandatory even with almost no traffic.

Lacking the desire to try and make small talk she turned her attention to the scenery. Most of her questions needed to be heard by everyone.

It felt odd to look outside and not have a weapon in her hand. They were heading quickly out of the city and into the dense suburbs of DC. This is where they had run across the most action and her hand itched to hold a weapon. Everyone in the vehicle fell silent and she wondered if they were feeling the same disquiet.

The Elentrin slaves liked to kick in doors and go through houses. They'd found enough tech to prove they could track Kaylid, but they couldn't get it to work for them. Probably the nanobots had a special wavelength or radiation or something. Wefor had suggested it but McKenna's body didn't have any senses that would let her know. But since the commander module could ID Kaylid and have the symbol bounce up in her vision, it only made sense the Elentrin had the same ability.

So many people dead. So many people captured. She'd made a habit of learning not to think and some days she greatly missed the burn and softening whiskey once brought her. Not that she'd had whiskey lately.

~Toni?~

~Yes?~ A tilted amusement in the tone made McKenna wonder what was going on. Either way she'd find out shortly. And she'd get to hug Charley and Nam. That alone made going back to the house worth it.

~You have any alcohol? We've all earned more than a bit of distance.~

~Oh yes, please.~ ~Yes, anything.~ The comments from the rest all tripped over each other and she didn't even bother trying to unravel who had said what.

~Yes. I'll have stuff waiting.~ McKenna didn't ask, just smiled, knowing whiskey would be in her future.

~Tell the bots to cut it back. We don't want to get drunk, but we all desperately need to take the edge off.~ The image of Caroline sagging to the ground filled her mind.

[Understood. New commands will be incorporated by the time you arrive at the house.]

McKenna felt the relief even as the stranger in the vehicle tilted his head looking at her. "The voice of your AI is most discomfiting."

His words fell like bricks in the car as all the Kaylid looked at her and she saw Lawson's frown in the rearview mirror.

"Yeah. But you get used to it. It's part of her, part of us now." McKenna lifted her head in challenge, but rather than meeting the challenge he nodded his head to her.

"I understand. Insult was not intended."

She expected something else, but instead he turned his head looking out the window with every indication of being fascinated by what he saw.

Half a dozen times she started to say something then stopped. A scritching sound caught her attention and she glanced into the back where Cass had apparently found a notebook and a broken pencil. From the odd end and the bits of wood and graphite on the floor McKenna figured she sharpened it with a claw.

"Desperate or something?" her tone teasing.

"Yes," Cass said, glancing up at her, flashing a smile. "So many questions and thoughts, I don't want to risk forgetting any."

The sheer Cassness of the comment made McKenna laugh and for the last few minutes of the ride, everything seemed normal; even the being sitting next to her in the car. The car slowed and pulled into a familiar driveway. Before it had even stopped, McKenna was out of the car and moving up the driveway. The door burst open and a streak of blond hair, pale skin, and boundless energy slammed into her.

Joy swelled within her as she held him tight. "Missed you, kiddo."

Charley just nodded burying his head in her fur. Annoyance swept through her that she couldn't feel him against her skin, and she called her human form forth. Her fur melted away and she felt her bones shift back into her normal form just as a dark-haired missile hit her on the other side.

A smile splitting her face, she kept Charley close to her but grabbed Nam and picked her up. "Damn, I missed you two." Nam wrapped her arms around McKenna's neck and hugged her back just as tightly.

The wave of love and joy washed through her from the two kids and something in her relaxed. She held Nam close, but finally lifted her head to look around. Toni stood at the door, in her human shape, her body tense, but a smile on her face. On the other side of the threshold peeked two dark heads, but they stayed inside.

Behind her McKenna could hear the others getting out of the car, but her attention was snagged by the burn marks on the house and blood on the driveway. Her heart rate spiked as she whirled around looking. The house, the entire area, showed signs of recent battles. She recognized the signs well enough by now.

"You were attacked? Why didn't you say anything?" Her voice too loud on the overly quiet street. Anymore, people didn't even play radios and TV loud enough to be heard. Closed caption had become very poplar.

"Because you couldn't do anything, and it would have only stressed you out. I handled it. We're fine." Toni glanced around the area, eyes sharp. "Though we shouldn't stay out here much longer. People are noticing."

McKenna followed her gaze and saw curtains and mini blinds twitch. She also saw holes in screens big enough to allow rifles to slip through. All the cars were placed in garages and the place hummed with wariness.

Our new reality. But food is getting tight. It has to change, or we will break down.

The bleak thought forced her into action.

"Yes. Everyone inside now. Perc, JD, bring the weapons. Lawson, get the car in the garage. It should fit, barely, but it should fit. Kids, back in the house now." Toni turned and moved into the house even as McKenna turned to see Perc encouraging the Drakyn to get out of the car. He moved slowly as if off-balance from the ride. The kids had darted in as soon as McKenna spoke.

Everyone moved as if the atmosphere had sunk in and no one wanted to be standing in the open. They entered the living room with only kids and the sound of Carina and Toni talking in the kitchen. McKenna sank onto the couch and the kids immediately swarmed her, intent on not letting her go. Missing them had hurt so much and she wouldn't exchange that pain for anything in the world.

The Drakyn stood in the middle of the room, inspecting the place with interest. McKenna watched him, but he just looked, not touching anything.

McKenna raised her voice. "Toni, you have my cellphone?"

"Yeah. Carina, could you give it to her?" Carina came out of the kitchen, the phone in her hand, gave it to McKenna, then headed back in. The smells coming out of the kitchen made her stomach rumble. They'd eaten but nothing like real cooked food. Mostly it'd been MREs, cold canned food, or instant soups.

She shook her head and pulled her attention away from food and the Drakyn. Instead she focused on the phone. It took a minute to power up, but once up she texted Burby.

How long till you get here?

His response came back almost at once.

Another ten. Bringing five people, two are security. Chris is one of those. Have food and questions.

She laughed softly at that, but at least he warned her. Then she blanched. She'd never told Chris about Caroline. Oh, that would suck.

Chapter 4 - Shifted Perceptions

With the lockdown of many cities, food is getting scarce in some areas. Truckers, both shifter and normal, are being offered bonuses to make food deliveries. Most farms are in rural areas and are relatively unaffected by the invasion. They are making sure food is still being delivered to most canneries and are prioritizing fresh food deliveries. At this point all people with CDLs have been federally granted the right to carry weapons across state lines if they hold a concealed carry permit in any state. ~ TNN Invasion News

"Our other guests will be here in another ten. There will be five people, including Christopher." Cass and JD closed their eyes for a minute but nodded. Perc looked at her and there was warmth and understanding in his eyes. "We probably need to get some more chairs in here and make the space wider."

Perc and JD nodded, moving couches and grabbing chairs while Cass went into the kitchen. McKenna looked at the kids. "Okay kiddos, time to head up to your room. We don't know what's going to happen yet."

"But I want to see the dragon," Nam said, her voice soft and eyes wide. "I don't see a dragon here."

Jessi had a mutinous look on her face and even Charley widened his eyes to look at her. Only Jamie didn't look interested.

Oh right. He doesn't believe in dragons.

McKenna had to fight back a smile as she thought about it for a minute and shrugged. While the dragon shifting now or later didn't affect anything, maybe walking in and seeing a huge humanoid dragon would get more across faster. Burby and his people weren't bad, but shock had a value all its own.

The Drakyn was watching her, though he had maintained a decent distance from the kids. Only smart as Perc and JD were usually nearby, their claws still very prominent.

Huh, wonder why Toni's been hiding in the kitchen.

Still watching the Drakyn watching her, she pinged Toni. Trying hard to keep it tight and private. If it was private from the others maybe it would be private from this stranger.

~Hey. You okay? Any reason you're hiding in the kitchen?~

She felt the pause in her mind and turned to gaze towards the kitchen even as she tightened her hold on the kids. They tensed in reaction and she felt their awareness sharpen, but she kept part of her attention on the Drakyn, the rest on Toni.

~I missed you guys. And I'm fighting the temptation to pull all of you into my arms and never let you go again. It hurt not having you here.~ Her thoughts had truth and a bit of embarrassment.

~Good, 'cause we felt the same way. I thought our not being here would keep you safer. Apparently I was wrong.~

~Kenna, no one is safe right now. But I took care of them. Left the bodies in the street and sent a text for a body pickup. Which is the strangest thing ever to say.~

McKenna wanted to follow up on that but could feel everyone looking at her. ~Why don't you and Carina come out and meet the dragon.~

There was an odd pause and for a minute McKenna thought she sensed a whiff of fear run through the other woman, but it was gone before she could decide what it was.

~Sure. Want a cider?~

~Yes, please.~ The desire for that was high. Turning back she noted Perc and JD had set up a wide ring of chairs. Amazing how quiet it was when the people involved could just pick up the furniture and move it.

"I know you changed to make it easier on us to get here. But it will help if the people coming, the people who have power to make decisions, can see your more alien form. And, well, you do look like a dragon in that form."

"Dragons don't exist," Jamie muttered. It was quiet enough McKenna pretended not to hear it, though from the glare Jessi and Nam gave him they weren't so nice.

"Ah. There is no reason why I can not do that," he said. As he spoke his voice reverberated in the room like music. McKenna couldn't figure out how he got his vocal cords to do that. As he spoke, Toni stepped into the living room, two beers and three ciders in her hands.

McKenna smiled at her, took the cider, but quickly moved her attention back to the being. Out of the corner of her eye she saw Toni hand the drinks to the others, then move to watch the stranger. Something about her behavior kept pulling McKenna's attention away, but she couldn't focus on it right now.

He took a deep breath and started to change.

It's a bit different from ours. Smoother and as if he decides what happens.

Her musings were interrupted by the Drakyn speaking again, even though his eyes were closed. "Do you wish wings on this form?"

"Yes!" A chorus of young voices rang out before McKenna could even start to respond. She glanced down to see all the kids had their gazes locked on him, rapt fascination on their faces. Even Jamie.

A corner of his mouth tilted up. "Then wings it shall be. They remind me of my siblings' nestlings when they were still limited to one form."

The comment came across as an offhand remark, but the idea that he had brothers and sisters, that his people had families, made her relax just a little.

As he changed, his hands went to the robe, loosening it as from the back of his body, wings slowly formed and flexed as they emerged. The red scales all but glowed in the muted light through the windows and McKenna could hear the lack of breathing as everyone watched the man turn into a humanoid dragon.

"I saw, but I didn't believe. It is you." Toni's voice was barely a whisper, but McKenna and the dragon turned to look at her. Her eyes were wide, and her face had paled a bit as she stared at the Drakyn, her breathing rapid.

"Toni? Are you okay?" McKenna asked, starting to rise, even with the kids all but engulfing her.

The dragon fastened his eyes on her, those weird swirling colors and Toni sucked in a sharp breath. He seemed to do the same, frozen into a statue of power and grace looking at her.

"I, no, yes, sorry, just." The words came out in a stumbling halt. Cass and JD both moved towards her, but before they could reach her the sound of a vehicle pulling into the drive grabbed their attention.

"You deal with that, I'll be in the kitchen." Toni blurted and McKenna watched in astonishment as Toni fled. Toni Diaz who never backed down from anything, fled. The dragon turned to watch her go.

She wanted to follow her, but already she could hear people getting out of their cars and letting them stay outside wouldn't be acceptable. Standing with Nam still in her arms, the little girl was channeling a spider monkey, refusing to let go.

30

JD and Perc were glaring at the Drakyn even as Cass followed Toni into the kitchen, but McKenna couldn't even talk to her mind-to-mind. She didn't want to take her attention away from what was about to happen.

She walked to the door and glanced through the window to see the stressed faces approaching her. With a resigned sigh, she pulled open the door. Five people stood there, Christopher and Doug she recognized. A new man in his late fifties in a uniform, Marines maybe, another agent, and a woman in tactical cargo pants, a tank top, with a loose cardigan over it. All of them had weapons on them and looked like they knew how to use them.

Is that a good sign or bad that everyone comes armed and you care more about their ability to use the weapon than anything else?

"Come on in." She stepped aside, letting them all come inside. They moved in quickly but almost all of them slammed to a halt as they set eyes on the Drakyn.

"Stars and Stripes. She wasn't kidding." The new military guy said, his hand twitching a bit.

McKenna got the door shut and pushed past them. Kneeling she set Nam down, even though the little girl didn't want to let go. "Time to go, kids. Go play. We'll let you know if anything happens. This is going to boring adult arguing."

"Huh. Dragons." Jamie muttered and headed towards the dragon, his hand outstretched as if to touch the wings. Nam followed a half-step behind him.

"I don't think so." She gently grabbed both of them and shooed them out of the room.

Jessi pouted and looked like she would protest but Charley and Jamie grabbed her and dragged her away. Nam followed with a long last look at the Drakyn. McKenna turned around to see everyone still standing there, staring at their visitor, and her temper snapped.

"Gods, get in here, take a seat. He's here to help and standing and staring at him like he's a circus freak isn't helping anyone." Her voice had a sharp edge and she saw JD cast her a sideways glance. McKenna ignored him. She wanted normalcy and knew it would never happen again.

Doug Burby cleared his throat and moved over to one of kitchen chairs while the agent stayed near the door. Chris stood behind the chair the military guy took, watching everything. The woman, she looked like she had Hispanic in her background mixed with something that gave her grey eyes. She didn't fit, but McKenna couldn't find it in herself to care.

"Welcome everyone. May I introduce our guest?" She turned to the visitor and froze. With a sigh she rubbed her temples. "And I don't know his name because I'm not getting enough sleep, enough food, and the damn AI won't let me get drunk even if we had the alcohol. So there it is." With a frustrated jerk of her hands she sank back into the couch and considered going after the kids. That sounded much better than dealing with all of this.

The woman grinned at her, a flash of coffee-stained teeth, then fastened her eyes on the huge being. The variation of red, yellow, with just a hint of purple in his scales shone in the light through the windows.

His eyebrows moved in a gesture that made McKenna think it was a sign of amusement. Out of the corner of her eye she saw Toni watching from the kitchen, an odd look on her face. Cass hung back, giving her emotional support, while Carina looked at everything, but the dragon kept the majority of McKenna's attention.

The Drakyn looked at her and nodded. "It is expected. You have brought me into your nest, though I still need to be introduced to all your nest members. Disorientation is understandable." He looked around at all of them and performed an odd half bow, half nod. Either way it came across as elegant and refined.

"I am Rarz Goldwing Liryline. I am here as both a warrior and ambassador of the Drakyn. I come both to offer assistance and beg assistance in the battle against the Elentrin. They have declared themselves blood enemies against me and mine, and while we are not blame-free, we have never killed theirs wholesale. As one of the warriors I beg for you to help us and allow us to help you in this fight before you too are destroyed by their hate."

McKenna looked at him, stunned.

That's it? Nothing great or glorious? No "We have magical powers and I'll destroy you if you don't help?" No, "This is what I can offer, how can you help me?" Dang. I think I'm expecting too much from aliens.

She blinked at him, knowing she looked like an idiot. To her relief, Burby spoke up before she could make an even bigger fool of herself.

"And how can you help us? Do you have weapons we can use against the Elentrin?" His eyes sharp as the Marine leaned forward, watching.

Rarz, he pronounced it raw-erz, shrugged. "We do not have many weapons in our culture. The Elentrin are the only enemy we have. We have spent countless years trying to hide from them or make peace."

"How has that worked for you?" The Marine asked, his voice dry.

Rarz bowed a bit, his wings spreading. "As you can see, I am here. Begging assistance."

Doug sighed and looked at McKenna's friends all looking at him. "You never bring me easy stuff, and I don't have time to play the political games."

"You have less time than you think." Rarz said, his voice oddly gentle for a being that looked like he could take out a tank.

"Why do you say that?" Again the Marine asked the question.

Really, I need to start asking names, or demanding introductions.

"Per my source, they are starting to collect asteroids to send at your planet. The last time they did that, the planet was destroyed to the point that over ninety-five percent of all life was killed."

The room went quiet and the woman said slowly. "You mean ninety-five percent of all people?" McKenna winced. She knew the answer to this.

"No. Even the species in the oceans and the insects were destroyed. The only remaining people are ones we rescued, or are slaves to the Elentrin. Most of creatures that lived in that planet only remain as memories to a select few."

Chapter 5 - True Colors

Elentrin have been spotted moving through Rome. Drones being used by various government agencies have been tracking any shuttle not doing straight drops. They often are disgorging a Elentrin who starts to walk around. Already people are coming out to meet the alien. The two original women haven't been seen for a while. What does this mean for the center of Christianity on Earth? ~ TNN News

The first day of the invasion, at least when aliens started dropping to the earth, Raymond Kennedy hid in his apartment, terrified they might sense that he was a creature like them. Even the wonder of the warrior form couldn't get past the loathing of knowing he'd been infected like an animal. The news covered these aliens dropping into cities, shooting people and carting them to shuttles that then took off with their captured prizes inside. The idea of being one of those so callously disposed of locked him in his own home.

But as hours passed, then a day, he realized they didn't know about him specifically. Boredom, more than anything else, kicked him out of his panicked mindset and let him start looking around.

The government had been all but shut down. No congressional meetings, no movers and shakers having lunches together, no passing by staffers in the hall seeing what they might let slip. Raymond hadn't been so frustrated since his teens. Without his ability to gauge people's moods, reactions, to catch the feeling of what was going on in the halls of power, he felt hamstrung, useless. That was not acceptable.

Careful inquires proved the black ops group he'd used to drop off those meddling idiots in the jungle had been deployed to other areas to deal with the threats. Of the six people involved, three had been reported dead.

Just as well, it reduces ties back to me, not that I think it will matter once this is all over. But I'll need to remember to clean up any loose ends. Those shifters have become way too high profile to allow this to stand.

Showered and in jeans and a t-shirt, unusual garb for him, he contemplated going out. He was like most staffers and ate out more than anything else. Which meant his food stores were low to begin with, and shifting into that wolfman form hadn't helped. He was down to rice and flour, and not being a chef, he had no idea what he could make from that other than rice.

The news had listed stores with limited supplies that would be open for six hours today. And some of the small shops were open, though you had to knock for entrance.

Arming himself with his 1911, what real men used, and a small bag, he slipped out. Stepping out on the street, the first thing he noticed was how quiet it was. Normally the area of DC he lived in had a constant stream of car engines, honking, people chattering, heels clicking on the sidewalks, dogs barking, just noise that created a background he never noticed. Now he was hyper-aware of the lack of that noise. Walking down the street he kept swiveling his head, trying to pay attention to everything. He held the drawn pistol in his right hand, and the bag gripped loosely in his left, ready to be dropped at a moment's notice.

I need to invest in a backpack, plebeian as they are. It would be nice to have both hands free right now.

The thought got added to his list of things that needed to change, though that item was much simpler than many of his others. As he walked, his anger grew at the aliens that had forced this great country to this, people hiding in their homes, scared to emerge. He saw blinds move, curtains twitch, but no kids outside, not even dogs. Everyone was hiding.

That stupid bitch and the football player, this is their fault. Even after we win against these aliens, they will still be here, ruining our world. That isn't acceptable.

He only saw one vehicle on the street, an older model truck with a gun rack in the back holding two rifles. The man driving it nodded at him as it went by, but nothing else was said. Raymond just fumed.

I should be sitting at an elegant restaurant, getting information to use against someone and figuring out how to make this country what it should be. Strong, unified, and lead by those with the talent and skill to rule.

The frustration and irritation that arose from that thought caused his spine to stiffen and his pace to pick up.

New goal: Make sure the shifters have no place on this planet and are not a threat to any true human.

The knowledge that he was what he hated got pushed further and further back in his mind. This was just proof that he was better than the rest of them, because he didn't need to change, didn't need to flaunt the unnaturalness to the world. He could control himself and help others control those who weren't as smart and skilled as he was.

He strode to the grocery store six blocks from his brownstone, scanning as he went. As soon as America got back on its feet these aliens would see that regular humans weren't prey.

The doors slid open as he approached. Cautiously he walked into the silent store. The lack of music threw him off for a bit. It had never dawned on him before how much noise they were surrounded with, all the time.

A cashier rose up, rifle in hand, and looked at him. "Prices are as marked, you can spend up to a hundred dollars, cash only. No produce left. There's a guard at the meat section, tell him what you want, and he'll get it for you."

Normally cashiers were young awkward teens, or middle-aged women that looked like they had forgotten how make-up worked and didn't care. This one was in his mid-thirties, fit, and held the rifle like he had no issue using it.

Raymond just nodded. He'd grabbed cash expecting that, but he sneered internally anyway.

If he's so fit, why isn't he out there fighting against these invaders?

Keeping the sniff to himself, he moved farther into the store, then stopped. How barren the shelves were surprised him. Where normally every shelf was full, now the pickings were slim. There was food, but nowhere near as much as what he had expected. Offended on a level he couldn't explain, he started to raise his voice to demand to know where the groceries were, but the quiet movements of the other shoppers stopped him.

Yet another thing these aliens need to pay for.

Outrage coated his entire being as he stalked past the bare shelves. True to the cashiers' word, an armed guard stood at the empty meat freezer.

"Is there any meat?" Even his words sounded overly loud and he flinched, lowering his volume a little. "I'd like to get some, maybe two packages? What is there?"

"Hamburger at five a pound, chicken at three a pound, steaks at six a pound." The guard spoke just as softly. "Everything is one-pound packages only."

Raymond clenched his teeth but had to admit they could have tripled the price and hadn't, instead just limiting what you could buy. "Two packages of hamburger, one of chicken." He spoke the words through clenched jaws, but the guard just nodded.

Spaghetti, hamburger helper, and some chicken alfredo. That should do me for at least a week if I can get some eggs.

The guard came back with the meat and put it in the cart. Raymond found the rest of what he needed, but to his surprise there were lots of eggs at three dollars a carton. He grabbed some processed ham and then headed to the cashier.

Everything together totaled fifty. They were using only round numbers and he didn't care that the taxes had been rounded up too. Change made too much noise. But curiosity made him ask about the eggs.

"Why so many eggs, for relatively cheap?"

"Locals have brought them in to trade and eggs last a long time without refrigeration. So we've gotten lucky and they go far when mixed with other food," the cashier stated, his eyes wary as Raymond finished packing everything in his bag, the eggs on top.

"Good to know." Trying to maintain the façade of caring, he nodded and headed out, his gun at the ready.

He paid closer attention to his surroundings as he walked back towards his home, not wanting to risk being mugged for the groceries. His stomach grumbled at the thought of food soon. Though the eggs were interesting, and the idea of barter sparked ideas deep in his mind of down-the-road possibilities. As he walked, he realized the area was rather nice with the quiet. He'd never realized how loud all the horns and engines were. Raymond almost smiled as he headed back to his house.

He'd just crossed a street and was approaching the end of the businesses where the more residential area started up, when he heard a faint sound. It seemed crystal clear in the quiet of the day.

The screaming got louder, and he looked around for something to get behind. No sense asking for trouble. An alley up ahead with two over-full dumpsters lay to his right. Stepping up the pace he moved into the alley and behind the trash. He set his bag down on the ground carefully, not wanting to break those eggs.

He squatted and looked through the gap between the dumpster and the wall. It placed him far enough back that he had a full view of the entrance of the alley. A woman carried a young kid, probably between four and seven. He avoided kids if at all possible. Babies were only good to get votes.

"Help! Please someone help! They're after me! HELP!"

Idiot. Yelling just tells them where you are.

His thought scornful as he watched her run past, the sound of her hard shoes echoing on the pavement.

And really, if you think you will have to run, wear sneakers.

A moment later a Kaylid came into view, stopping and raising its weapon, a red bolt snapped out of it, and he heard a dull thud and the crying of a kid. The Kaylid paused looking down the alley, right towards him. It lifted its head, then wrinkled its nose as it stood there.

Raymond froze, not even breathing. After what seemed like an eternity, and his lungs had started to burn, it turned and headed down the street. He still sat, not breathing, listening as hard as he could. A whine and the cry cut off. His vision pulsed at the corner of his eyes, but he didn't dare breathe. The same furred beast, its pelt the colors of rotten tomatoes stalked back by, the woman draped over his shoulder. This time it stalked by, not even stopping, and still Raymond didn't move.

Good riddance. The more that are gone, the easier it will be to put them in their proper place, serving their betters.

That thought gave him the strength to keep holding his breath, no matter how his lungs burned.

Ten more seconds, I can make it ten more.

Five

Eight

Ten

He took in a slow breath fighting to not gasp as his lungs pulled in the air that he needed so bad. His mouth tasted metallic from the saliva that had pooled in it. Breathing in, slowly, quietly focused him. A half hour passed before he rose on legs that had fallen asleep, but not even the pins and needles sensation caused him to make a sound. Picking up the bag quietly, he flipped off the safety on the gun. With the gun raised, he crept to the alley entrance then stopped just out of sight, listening.

Nothing. You need to get home.

He stuck his head out and peered in the directions the Kaylid had gone. All the joy at the peaceful day, gone. He couldn't see or hear anything, so he turned and headed at a fast walk to his house. The child lay crumpled in the middle of the street, blond hair a direct contrast to the dark of the pavement.

This is why we need a genetic cleansing. People like that are too stupid to live, and the idea of them spreading their genes to those humans that are worthy to rule them? Unthinkable.

He moved on past the girl, making sure he made as little noise as possible. He lived three blocks past that and turned onto his street with relief. Raymond didn't let himself run, but he headed up the stairs into his brownstone, shutting and locking the door with relief.

Animals. They're all animals. We need to make sure we're protected from them. The very fact these aliens think they're livestock is proof enough that we should make sure their existence can't hurt us anymore.

Raymond put away his groceries and did some cooking even as he thought.

We need to put laws in place to prevent them from ever being in positions of power. This just proves shifters are nothing more than animals. Not only do they change into animals, they're hunted like prey; culled like livestock.

They passed the amendment to the constitution giving them protection, but I can make it so they're shunned. Regardless of the legal protection, you can't force people to hire someone.

He hummed as he cooked, thinking about ways to sway people, riders to put in bills that would make it better to hire humans than these animals.

The court of public opinion. People believe anything if someone they trust says it; then they repeat it and spread it.

A slow smile crept across his face as he sat down to eat.

And I know exactly how to start this campaign. He'll help me, I'm sure.

Chapter 6 - Talking It Out

The new rage is home gardening. For the restricted hours that the local home improvement stores are open, they are reporting that all seeds and vegetable plants are sold out in the first open hour. With it being late summer the growing season is limited, but with proper care many plants can grow and produce food. Also, the countertop plant gardens have been going for upwards of a hundred dollars each. But with food getting tight any bit can help. Across the country waivers for having chickens in back yards has also been granted and hens are going for forty to sixty dollars apiece. This feels like a throwback to World War II, but any food source is valid. Hunting licenses are being granted liberally and even in states where hunting has historically been low, they are having record turnouts of hunters. ~ TNN Invasion News

A ding from the kitchen pulled everyone's attention away and McKenna sighed. "Did you bring food? We're all pretty hungry and this might take a while."

"Oh, yeah. Laurent, would you go grab the food please?" the SecDef said with a weary sigh. The other agent nodded and headed out the door, gun up and scanning before he stepped out. Doug looked at all of them, and then closed his eyes and rubbed his temples a bit. He groaned, an exhausted sound. "Yes, food and drink sounds good." He opened his eyes and looked at Rarz. "This is not the way it should go. You should have a team of diplomats, advisors, and everything else. But right now, that really isn't an option. I can get a few people on the phone and we can talk. The only reason I'm even still in the area when everyone else is bunkered down is I have no family. I'm former military, and enough of the Cabinet trusts me to let me be the forerunner for all this. We're in trouble. The rural areas are holding up well enough but inner cities are a mess. If people figure out we're about to be pounded by asteroids, society will collapse." He looked like he was about to say something else, then shook his head.

"You might want to introduce us before everyone is really confused. Because so far the only person whose name I know is our visitor." The woman spoke with a hint of amusement in her voice.

Doug looked at her and nodded his head. "Probably. It might make me look like less of an idiot." He rose to his feet and gave a half nod-half bow to Rarz. "I apologize for the disorganized way you have been greeted. Our only excuse is an alien invasion is not the norm for us." He paused as Laurent came back in pulling a wheeled cooler, then continued. "My name is Doug Burby, I'm the secretary of defense for this nation. Please be aware there are many nations on our planet, and I can only speak for ours."

Rarz tilted his head at that but nodded.

Doug turned to the Marine who had stood while he spoke. The man wore his dress uniform. That was the only reason McKenna figured he was a Marine. The blues looked like he'd been wearing them for days, and a gun was holstered at his hip.

"This is Gunny Sergeant Philip Roberts, he is the acting Joint Chief." McKenna saw JD tilt his head, his brows rising up. Doug must have seen it as he half-smiled, if that was what the twist of his lips qualified as. "Yes, it's unusual, okay, has never fucking been done, to have an NCO as the Joint Chief. But he's qualified for a few reasons. He's here, he has combat experience, and he has a brother who is a Colonel in the Army, and a sister who's a Captain and a pilot in the Air Force. Giving him a better grasp of what is available than most. That and he's damn good and isn't a bigoted asshole like the last guy." Doug shrugged. "Besides we can't get anyone else in. They're all trapped in their local areas and at this point I just need someone with ideas of how to use the various groups to help. So yeah, he's acting JC."

McKenna turned a laugh into a cough and the gunny shot her a smile that let her know he'd heard the story.

"Everyone," Gunny Roberts said in a soft voice, though he didn't take his eyes off of Rarz.

I wonder how much of that is due to him being dragon and how much is due to him being a threat?

Burby turned to the woman who still sat and just waved at everyone, a bright smile on her face. "This is Blair Lewis. She's a cultural anthropologist and has been advising on how our interactions with the Elentrin went."

"You mean sideways?" JD interjected. She couldn't read his face in warrior form but in the mindscape she got the feeling he hadn't really meant to say it out loud.

"Oh, I doubt I'd use that term. I'd go with screwed from the start. We never had a chance. However, if we can figure how they view the world, maybe we can use it against them. Or we kill them all. I'm fine with either." Her smile showed all teeth and McKenna blinked.

"More bloodthirsty than most scientists I've run across," McKenna commented, all too aware of Rarz listening and paying attention to all of them. Though Toni's continued lurking in the kitchen nagged at the back of her mind.

"My sister was killed in London in one of the first landings, protecting some teens that were shifters. I never was much for pacifistic crap anyhow." Blair said, and focused on Rarz.

Laurent came out of the kitchen, the cooler obviously staying in there. "They said they'd have food out shortly." He kept furniture between him and Rarz, though all of them gave Rarz a wide berth. "Do you have anything you can't eat or don't eat?"

"No. Food is fine. I doubt there is any food on your planet I am not capable of ingesting without incident." Rarz replied in a level voice, as if none of this disturbed him.

In other circumstances McKenna might have dug out hot peppers to test that, but now she removed it as anything to worry about. And the smells from the kitchen were very distracting.

"Sir, if I may?" Gunny Roberts asked.

Doug waved at him. "Go for it. But Rarz?" He waited until the Drakyn had focused on him. "We're desperate, I don't have time for fancy negotiations or anything. I'll promise what I can, but I might be overruled. Know that we are very fragmented now and what I say may not be backed up by our politicians."

Rarz's wings bobbled up and down a bit. "Understood. I am familiar with the ways of politicians from other cultures. My culture doesn't support that type of interaction, but I do understand your structure. Others have had it though, and many of them have also suffered from the Elentrin." He leaned back again, and McKenna arched her eyebrows as his tail created a way for him to balance in an odd tripod way.

I wonder if that's comfortable. It does put him at a height advantage, but I don't have any stools and anything else would either break under him or would be horribly uncomfortable.

She let it be as the woman watched while Doug waved at Roberts. "All yours, Gunny."

"I have a few questions if you don't mind, sir." This time it was clear he was addressing the Drakyn who nodded and paid attention to the Marine. McKenna felt like a third wheel, and took another swallow of her cider, trying to ignore the food smells. It had been a while since they'd had home-cooked food.

"That is why I am here. Ask. I will not be offended." Rarz rumbled, his voice sounding more powerful than it should.

I almost want him to go back to human, just so he feels more normal, but the point was to have him NOT be normal. Why me?

McKenna sipped the cider again and tried to focus. Exhaustion, restricted calories, death, fear, and stress, they all combined to make her want to turn into her cat, curl up in a ball and sleep.

~Could I get some caffeine? Falling asleep.~

~Ooh, yes please,~ Cass and JD chimed in. McKenna glanced their way and saw Cass's head had started to droop, while JD never turned down caffeine.

Rarz head twitched their way, but he didn't turn and look at them. She knew he'd heard.

~Coffee or soda?~

~Coffee,~ chimed all three and Toni laughed.

~Will do.~

That conversation hadn't taken more than a few seconds, and Roberts had pulled out a leather portfolio and a pen, balancing it on his knees with the ease of long experience.

"As you can see our planet is being assaulted at multiple points, but I can only address the military abilities of this country. It's a significant part of this continent, but not all of it." He waited until Rarz responded.

"That much had been expected. But we must work here because McKenna and her group are here." She got sharp looks from the government people, but she just shrugged at them.

"I will address that later. Right now, it isn't relevant." Roberts said. "So we don't have any weapons that allow us to shoot the invaders down coming in via high atmosphere drops. The shuttles are too fast and too small, and when they go back up they usually have captured people in them. They already have too many of our people, and to be clear, by our people I mean humans. At this point I don't care if they're from China, Africa, or the US. They are ours and we do not tolerate kidnapping or slavery."

"Good. That is mostly in accord with the information I had received." Rarz moved his wings, but didn't let them spread out, though he looked around the living room. "Now that the nestlings are gone, is it permissible if I retract my wings? There is not enough space here for them without the risk of breaking things and I tend to move them without conscious thought."

Burby blinked as did the gunny. "You can just remove your wings?" Blair asked, scribbling left-handed in a note-book.

"Remove? I can cause their mass to be stored elsewhere until needed. While I will miss them, I learned many seasons ago how to function in different forms, some without wings. But they do move with my reactions and in this enclosed space I might damage something."

Gunny and Burby shrugged. Rarz turned to McKenna. "Is it permissible to remove the wings while I work in this environment?"

"Uh what?"

Rarz did that strange half bow again. "This is your abode, it would be rude to be in a shape that you do not approve of."

Her mouth worked but no sound came out and Blair cleared her throat. "If I may?"

"Please?" McKenna blurted, still trying to figure out how to say what needed to be said.

"Rarz, in our culture very few people have the right to tell you what to wear or how to decorate your body. That is normally limited to parents. So you are free to remove or add wings as it feels comfortable to you."

"What she said," McKenna commented, nodding her head and ignoring the mental snickers from the rest of her family. Luckily the Drakyn either didn't hear them, or politely ignored them. Either was good with her.

"Ah. Then I shall remove the wings, it will make this space feel less confined."

McKenna didn't know if he intended it or not, but the way he said the word made it clear he felt a bit claustrophobic in here. Then again, his head was only a foot or so from the ceiling, she had a good three feet plus. Heck, so did Perc and JD.

His eyes closed and she caught Toni out of the corner of her eye, peering through the kitchen doorway, fascinated. Carina watched behind her, curious, but not captivated the way Toni seemed to be.

It took a minute, but the wings were absorbed back into his body. It still felt different than how they shifted, but right now it wasn't what she needed to ask questions about. Maybe later, if there was a later, she could find out more. More about why Wefor and the other nanobots were created and why shifting worked the way it did.

"Huh. I've seen shifters change, but that's a new one on me. If things weren't so desperate to talk to you about other stuff, I'm sure I'd ask questions until you were ready to strangle me." Blair's voice embodied everything McKenna felt. She wanted to ask all her questions and address the confusion that surrounded this entire situation, but people were dying and that mattered more right now.

Philip Roberts shook his head and glanced down at his notepad. "Currently we are fighting a war on multiple points, so we don't have any way to know where they'll be attacking at any given point or time. We can't even figure out how they're narrowing in on shifters we have here in the US."

"Oh, I can answer that," McKenna volunteered. All eyes shifted over to her. "The nanobots have a slight isotopic radiation that the proper equipment can pick up. It isn't anything I or other shifters can do, but the people that designed these nanobots would be able to scan for and narrow down to where they are. Plus, clusters of shifters radiate stronger on the equipment than solos. Though from what we've been able to see the powerful scanners are in the shuttles, while the handheld ones seem to be more for narrowing down locations."

Everyone stared at her, even her friends.

"What? I told you I'd been talking to Wefor about it. There wasn't anything we could do to block the scans as we don't have the tech or the time to figure out a way. Telling all shifters to remain alone just puts more of them at risk, especially the kids. And it's not like anyone in the government is talking to me on a regular basis."

Oops, did that sound a bit resentful? Okay, I guess being shuttled back here might have bugged me a little. Oh well.

Burby ducked his head a bit but didn't answer her, everyone else just blinked. Finally, Gunny Roberts cleared his throat.

"Well, that does answer one question of how they're finding shifters. However, they still kill anyone between them and their target and they are rapidly improving their techniques and their weapons. I hate to say this, but they are learning quickly, and getting more deadly."

McKenna sighed. She'd suspected that. It was getting harder to ambush them and that didn't make it easier.

Gunny looked up at Rarz, who still leaned on his tail and legs. It resembled calm patience that reminded McKenna of a hunting animal, content to wait until the time was right to attack.

"So that leads us back to the question. How can you help? Are there more of you coming? What else can you do besides shift? How can we fight them with the resources we have?" Gunny Roberts asked the question in a calm and rational manner, but she could feel everyone tense as they focused even more directly on Rarz.

He shrugged, and she could see how his wings would have moved with that movement. It felt like part of him was missing. But in his human form it hadn't.

"I am unsure. There is me. I might be able to get a few more warriors to assist. If we can make the Elentrin flee I believe we can provide doctors and scientists afterward. But my people have very few that can fight or will fight. I am unsure of your resources, but as their ships are still in orbit above your planet, I assume you have no weapons to shoot them down?"

Doug snorted as Roberts answered. "No. The majority of our weapons capable of making a dent on something the size of their ships have ballistic capabilities. Trying to shoot straight up, or at things coming down won't work. The ships are too far away and our weapons are too slow. We don't have spaceships with weapons. While we could get a ship up there, we'd be lucky to get more than three or four people on it. And this goes for all countries, not just ours."

Rarz blew a long steady exhalation through his nostrils, his equivalent of a sigh she supposed. "I had figured as much."

"So what good are you going to be?" Burby snapped this out, leaning forward and staring at the Drakyn.

"Enough," Blair said, softly laying her hand on his arm.

Burby subsided, rubbing and rubbed his head. He looked like he'd aged a decade in the weeks since she'd first met him. They all did.

"You do have weapons though?" Rarz asked slowly, his head swiveling back and forth between the people there.

"Yes. Nuclear, biological, chemical, and then guns which are a type of chemical weapon."

"We saw these on your media network. However, some of the content we were unsure if it was fiction or reality. It became confusing. For a while we thought you had space-ships and energy weapons. But when we received word you were fighting back only with projectile weapons, we were disheartened."

McKenna watched Blair scribble another note on her pad as did Roberts, but it seemed to be thoughts for later as they just listened.

"But you say you have nuclear weapons and you obvi-ously have warriors." He waved at McKenna and her friends, with Perc and JD still in warrior form. Lawson shrank back, not wanting to garner attention as he enjoyed the luxury of a beer.

"Wait, no. We're not warriors. Lawson is a soldier. Us? We're just trying to protect our people. Our children. Our planet. But this is not what we want to do or are even trained to do," McKenna protested, though lately it seemed all too easy to kill and lead. Easier than she wanted to ad-mit, even to herself.

"Ah. Can all Earthlings fight like you? Or do you have more soldiers to assist?"

Gunny shrugged. "Humans don't like to give up, and most of us put up a fight. But yes, I have soldiers, not hun-dreds of thousands at this point, but I do have them. Why?" His sharp gaze didn't leave Rarz's form.

"There is a technique we have tried before, but we never had the numbers or weapons needed to make it feasible. The warrior who tried died for no gain. But with your assis-tance I might have an option."

"This sounds good, but I can tell people are hungry. Let's eat. Nothing that he tells you is going to turn the tide of this war in the next day or so. Is it?" Toni asked with a strangely assertive look. Not that she wasn't assertive, but there was something almost personal about it.

~Toni, what is going on?~

~Later.~ Her response short and abrupt.

"Give in now. They need the food and the longer they go without it, the crankier they get. One thing I've learned is cranky shifters are not fun." Lawson's voice startled half the people there, he'd been so quiet.

"He has a point. And I'm a bit hungry myself. I can't remember the last real meal I had." Burby sighed and it occurred to McKenna that sending people to their deaths might be harder than killing them yourself.

"JD, Perc, can you bring the chairs to the back deck? I can put the food in here buffet style and everyone can get their food then go out there. It's just as safe as anywhere else. If anything we'll see or hear them coming sooner and have time to react."

It was a measure of their paranoia that everyone came out with weapons and even the agents relaxed with better lines of sight around the back deck. The kids exploded out of the house, still in human form, and expended energy on the play house.

Aware of the people looking at her when she didn't stop the children, Toni shrugged. "If all of us together can't protect them and let them play outside, we've already lost."

The statement made everyone pay much closer attention and Wefor went on high alert.

Chapter 7 - Small Talk

So far, the United States has fared oddly well in this war. Our size, spread out population, and prevalence of gun owners has proved to be a saving grace. At this point reports of shifters being captured in the U.S. has stayed under 200,000, though there are at least a reported 12,000 dead invaders, and over 15,000 dead Americans. But overall we are making them pay for everyone they kill and take. But they are learning. Stay under cover, be silent, don't gather in groups, and if you are a shifter don't go out in warrior form. There are too many stories of killing friends and neighbors by accident. ~ KWAK News

With JD, Perc, and Rarz helping, much to everyone's discomfort, couches and chairs were quickly moved outside and plates of food were in their hands. Real, hot food, that smelled good and tasted better than the canned and MREs they'd been eating for a week. Something that had been crying for attention relaxed as McKenna settled down. With home cooked food in her mouth, and the sound of kids playing surrounded her, she relaxed more than she had in weeks.

I'm home. I missed this.

Even so, the kids didn't scream as loud as they could have, and ears twitched at every sound. Even Rarz seemed to understand they needed to be wary.

After the first rush of hunger had been sated, Roberts sat with his hat neatly on his knee, and his plate balanced over it.

I'd so spill my food and ruin my hat.

"So what do you mean about a technique that didn't work before? At this point if it isn't a suicide run, I think we would be willing try it," Philip replied, setting the empty plate down and reaching for his notebook. Carina flashed him a smile and took it in, her quiet presence soothing. McKenna just rolled her eyes and ate more. The shifters had plowed through the food, but the Drakyn had explored each food item offered him with thoughtful consideration. So far, the only thing he had wrinkled his muzzle at and set aside had been the sliced turkey breast, but the vegetables, beef, and fruit had been eaten swiftly. As Roberts had started to talk, he set his plate aside, though he held the glass of water with careful pressure between his large hands. His head turned to focus on the man.

I wonder how he hears. I never researched reptiles to know how they can hear. But then I don't think he's a reptile. Though for all I know warm-blooded reptiles are possible.

At least her thoughts still remained private as she munched on a piece of steak. The cooked, flavorful food made her feel better. Bland cooking made eating even more of a chore. JD and Cass were working their way through the fruit and while she'd had a piece, it didn't call to her the same way it did them.

"If I understand your term, a suicide run isn't exactly correct, but there are multiple things that must be considered and many possible points of failure." Rarz fell silent, then glanced around at all of them. "How much do you know about how my people travel across the stars?"

McKenna didn't have a clue how they traveled, though the weird hole in space he had stepped out of implied a lot.

"I know how to kill Drakyn. The most vulnerable areas in your warrior and wyrm form. What power to set the weapons at and when to bail." JD said, shrugging his big furry shoulders. Strangely McKenna wished the rest of them would shift back to human. It felt odd being human while three others were in warrior form.

Cass laughed. "I don't know much about the Drakyn, but I know an awful lot about how they store Kaylid. The processes to wipe the minds, the med tech, and suddenly how the nanobots and AIs are programmed. Wefor, at some point we'll need to talk." Her voice had turned serious there at the end and she had an odd look on her face.

McKenna couldn't help it, she glanced at Perc and Toni.

Perc shrugged. "I've got a bunch of info about their ships and technology, how the ships are laid out, but it's still expanding in my brain, so I don't know what I know yet."

Toni focused on her food, not looking at any of them and after a minute Rarz spoke, pulling the attention back to him.

"Then I am taking that as a no, which is a good thing. If they had managed to understand how we travel without mechanics and replicate it, no one would be safe from them." He paused again, popping a bit of fruit in his mouth. "This may come out disjointed but many terms I can not find in your languages. While we accessed some of your scientific data, it is harder to make sure the concepts are being translated and understood correctly without a scientist to discuss it with. You are the first Earthlings anyone has spoken with in a very long time."

"Wait," Blair blurted. "You've spoken to Earthlings before? When?"

"Oh, millennia by the way you tell time." He glanced at Toni then faced Blair again. "But that doesn't matter for the purpose of this conversation though it may explain some of your legends. You have figured out the Elentrin were here once before, right?"

"Yes. Around our Dark Ages we think. The languages provided to the kids and expectations of the population density implied that much. Plus it matches the time lines of stories about werewolves and whatnot." McKenna supplied. That much Charley had helped them figure out.

"Yes, the four-legged canine has always been one of their favorites. Though I have always thought the felines were more deadly." Rarz shrugged. "But that is getting us off topic. My people have had a way to travel to other planets for as long as we have had language that lets us communicate anything. There is a theory your people are calling Entanglement Theory. It has flaws, but the basics are correct. I can find an element of space here and a matching element somewhere else. Between those two parts I connect a path. A tunnel between the two, if you will. I can walk through that tunnel between one place and another."

"How far can you travel?" Roberts asked, making notes rapidly.

Rarz shrugged. "I don't know that there is a limit. The farthest I have personally done is about 250 of your light years."

The adults all froze, various degrees of shock on their faces.

Blair managed to squeak out a comment. "And how long does that take?"

Rarz shrugged, a movement that still needed wings. "About three to twenty steps. Less than five heartbeats for sure."

Everyone just looked at him until Burby shook his head. "While I want to dig into this, and the possibilities it opens up terrify and excite me, I'm not sure how this relates to the question at hand. How do we defeat the Elentrin? What does the way you travel have to do with this situation?"

"Ah yes. We tried a new strategy. The warrior that did it was killed quickly by Kaylid on the ship. But I believe it may work. We can open a portal from the ground here to one of their ships. Allowing people to go through from the planet to the ship. I can keep the portal open even as the ship and planet move with little effort. After two or more of your hours, it will need to be reset, but anyone can use it while it is open."

The sounds of the kids laughing and playing softly on the playset was the only noise as everyone else processed this information.

"I'm sorry. I know I'm not a shifter or anything, but what does that mean?" Carina was the one to break the silence as everyone sat there.

Gunny Roberts, with an odd tone in his voice replied. "It means we get to pull a Trojan horse maneuver, and they don't even need to open the gates to let us in."

Burby leaned back, a half-smile on his face then he frowned. "Roberts. Do you have the latest numbers for how many shifters have been taken?"

"U.S. or worldwide?" Roberts pulled out his phone as he asked that question.

"Worldwide."

A few taps and Roberts replied. "These numbers are very rough, but we think about 1.7 million so far. At least half of those are Chinese where at least a 100,000 just walked onto huge convoy shuttles. But new theories are rising that there are few shifters left that are easily available. The Elentrin are spreading out from the dense population centers of China. Many of the Chinese shifters were located in specific places, which were emptied in the first few shuttles. But the biggest issue is the military is under orders to help the invaders, so Korea and Taiwan look like they are about to be invaded." He paused for a moment looking thoughtful. "Given China's historical xenophobia this says a lot of about how powerful the pheromones work."

Burby leaned back nodding, a frown on his face.

Roberts shook his head dismissing the thought and continued. "Japan is actually pretty safe because outside of Tokyo they don't have a huge population base, though they have lots of fox shifters. Granted we are expecting Tokyo to fall fast. The Elentrin look too much like anime and if they walk in, with no shuttle, and no warning, they'll have them under their command before anyone knows how to stop it. Though more places are adopting shoot on sight orders for anyone in warrior form or an Elentrin. But people affected by the pheromones seem to carry the mesmerizing effect with them for a while. They can convince other people to aid them and the people they talk to can fall under the same spell. Even with distance the effect is hard to resist."

That was news to McKenna, but Rarz nodded. "Yes. It is a molecule that clings and will affect people for hours even after casual contact. It is one of the ways they have man- aged to influence so many planets. My people are immune; as our reproductive systems are not affected by phero- mones, luckily. But if they continue to have issues with larger population planets they will figure out how to aerosol them or simply destroy the planets upon discovery."

"Are there that many worlds with life on them?" Blair's voice had a wistful tone to it and Rarz turned to look at her, his eye ridges raised.

"There are so many planets in this universe, your lan- guage does not have words to express the numbers. Of the small handful we have visited over my race's lifetime, which is," he paused for a minute as if trying to remember some- thing or talk to an AI, "23,241 planets, 15,783 have had life above invertebrate level. Of those 354 have had sentient beings. The Elentrin have only managed to find about sev- enty-five of those planets. Of those, some were immune to their pheromones and the nanobots didn't work on them. Others they have used. But of the planets they are aware of, yours is the most technologically advanced, besides ours and their own."

The shocked stares were getting old, but McKenna felt like bombshells kept being dropped. "There are other species out there that have achieved space flight?" She had to ask. The old dreams of walking on another planet surfaced with a sudden pang.

"Yes. Some are very advanced. But those have been either extremely xenophobic or felt there was no reason to enter what they felt was a private dispute." An odd expression crossed his face. "Though we have noted in the seasons since we shared that information, they have all developed highly aggressive weapons platforms that the Elentrin would not be able to pass."

Burby snorted. "We know a few mindsets like that. So basically no one else is willing to help and you figure since we are involved with this fight, we lose if we don't."

Rarz tilted his head. "If you wish to look at it that way. But you are the first planet with any fission or fusion weaponry that the Elentrin have sent a swarm to. We hoped we might be beneficial to each other. None of the other planets are at a point where even trade for more than occasional food goods or luxury items would be welcome. But you? That is not my area, but I see many things we might be willing to trade, to help each other advance."

"No Prime Directive issues?" Blair asked, then rubbed her forehead. "Sorry, it's a human phrase."

Rarz made a warbling sound that must have been his laughter. "We did run across it. Your Wikipedia is useful. There are many that would pay for your fiction shows alone. No. While there are some in my government that might feel that way, the majority consensus is that all options are available when the Elentrin attack you, yet we can't manage to fight back in any way that has any measurable effect. While I do not have the mindset to be a city manager, I am a warrior. That means I will use any tool, any weapon I can to prevent my people from being killed." He touched his head. "From all beings being killed if possible."

"Be that as it may, the ambassadors and shit can deal with you about that later. Right now I'd like to get back to the plan. Which would be what?" Roberts asked, his entire body focused on the dragon.

"Well, understand I am not a tactician, that is not something Warriors lean towards. We tend more to hit hard then move on or what you call blitzkrieg actions." He bobbed his head and McKenna started to wonder if she was interpreting his body language incorrectly.

~Wefor, do you know how to read him?~

[Not at this time. Information is being collated.]

Well, that's no help.

"Understood. Tell me what you tried, and quit trying to weasel out of it." Roberts's voice snapped out and McKenna saw JD's spine straighten and had to fight back a grin.

In the space after the command JD's and Perc's heads swiveled hard and sharp towards the fence.

"Incoming," JD said in a low deadly voice as he grabbed his gun.

Chapter 8 -Getting Personal

So far, no more news has come out about the US efforts to get weapons into space to disable or destroy the Elentrin ship. At this point we must give up all hope that those taken from us will ever be returned. If we do manage to get weapons up there, there will be no way to differentiate between the victims and the invaders. If we destroy that ship, we will kill our people too. What price to do we pay to end this threat? ~TNN News Op Ed

McKenna spun and ordered the nanobots to her ears, even as she tried to locate what they were referencing. Her ears sharpened and she could hear the sounds that indicated movement. Which meant invaders were close by.

"I can remove them?" Rarz offered, an odd tone to his voice, as he stood going to his full height at over seven feet.

"NO!" Burby's voice barked. "You and the kids inside and if you can get out of sight, do it. I don't want to take the risk of your existence being known."

To McKenna's surprise Rarz looked at him, then her. She made a shooing motion with her hands; his being here could cause issues. He gave a sharp brisk nod and strode towards the house. She felt something brush past her mind, and then the kids, who had frozen at the words, went tearing into the house—no panic, just speed.

Everyone else grabbed weapons as Toni said quietly, "I'll go in and react to any incursion on the inside. I'll yell if I need help." By the time the words finished leaving her mouth she was already inside. McKenna raised her weapon up and boosted the sensitivity of her ears a bit more, letting the bots shape them slightly to pull sound in better.

That's useful even in human form.

"The rest of you inside, too. Leave us out here to deal. You die too easily and are too important." She glanced at their visitors, but the agents were already chivying them back into the house. They'd make sure their charges stayed out of the way, probably in the same room with Rarz or with the kids. Christopher gave her a sharp nod and she realized she still hadn't told him. With a frustrated shake of her head, she moved her attention back to the fence. Now wasn't the time.

~We have to kill all of them, fast before they can communicate with anyone.~ Her mental voice was a sharp flat order. ~If we're lucky, they weren't close enough to hear the words, just that we were talking.~

~They'll smell him. He doesn't smell human.~ JD was right. Rarz smelled like an odd spice with a touch of fire and lightning mixed in with it. It was a recognizable smell. If any of the Kaylid coming after him had ever done a landing on a Drakyn-controlled planet, they would recognize it in a second.

~All we can do is kill them fast. If they find out they're here, they won't wait for that other ship to get here. I'm pretty sure it should be here in the next day or so.~ Her tone grim. ~Let's move toward them and see if we can eliminate them quickly.~

As one they moved out towards the sounds that were only audible with their enhanced ears. The tall fence had nice rails on the back and Perc took two running steps and smoothly landed on the rail of the fence, his clawed feet sinking into the wood a bit as he balanced. His whole body pivoted as he scanned the area, his AR-15 pointed in the direction he looked.

~Clear. Give yourself at least a foot on the other side to miss the bushes. That will put you in the neighbor's backyard. They're coming around from the front of the house.~

That house was directly behind theirs and it made sense if they were trying to approach undercover.

~What did you hear that made you realize they were coming?~ The invaders moved quietly and she was surprised they weren't on top of them already. Over two minutes had passed since JD warned them.

JD turned his head to the side a bit, trapping the side fence in his gaze. ~One of them stepped on something, it broke and it cursed. No one human is going to curse in Elentrin.~

~That would do it. We ready for this?~ McKenna commented, amused that cursing seemed to be a constant among all species.

~Hard and fast,~ Perc affirmed.

McKenna let the men flow over the fence, as she perched on top of the playset scanning the area. While still in human form, she found it easier than ever to move like a Kaylid. Getting to the top and using the vantage point made so she could see the surrounding back yards and watch Perc and JD open fire as Kaylid came around the corners.

In many ways the fact they were so silent let them know they were invaders. Human Kaylid still tended to tromp through, unless they were out hunting like McKenna was or were hunters before they were changed.

Even as the furred head came around the corner, JD's M-16 exploded into sound and a rapid burst of three bullets, then another three, and the body lay on the ground, a mass of red where its head had been. That signified the end of anyone being quiet and the other two burst around the corner, firing as they went.

JD sprang from his location behind a tree even as Perc and McKenna both shot at the two figures coming in fast.

The speed of Kaylid in battle could be breathtaking. Luckily McKenna and Perc were just as fast, and their weapons had a better range.

Perc's first shot missed as the Kaylid bobbed, his second caught it in the shoulder, and it fell. McKenna rose, standing up straight even as Perc had to jump to the ground to avoid being shot. From her angle she put two more three-round bursts into the thrashing Kaylid's body, aiming for the head. It fell still and she pivoted, tracking to where JD and the last Kaylid were fighting hand-to-hand.

She cringed. That was never good. The Kaylid had implanted memories and often had strength over the human shifters, as they weren't running into the calorie conservation issues. From what she had seen, they never left that form. While the last week had made them all good shots, shooting at two people in close proximity wasn't anything she was willing to risk.

~Perc, can you help?~ she asked, even as she tried to listen while pivoting on the top of the play structure in the backyard and trying to sense if anything else was headed their way, while using the noise as a cover.

~On it. Watch our backs.~

McKenna wanted to roll her eyes. If it hadn't been a literal life or death fight, she might have.

~Of course I'll watch your back. What? Like I'm willing to let any one of you get hurt?~

The Kaylid JD fought was one of the more lizardy ones that had been in some of the not-dreams. Not a scaled one like Rarz, but more leathery skin. Lizard probably wasn't the right word, but it reminded her of what they thought dinosaurs would look like at one point. Either way, it had a tail, and claws that made Cass's look almost boring, and it seemed to be vicious. Or desperate.

Maybe there isn't a difference anymore. They have as little choice in this as we do.

The thought hit her with a wave of guilt that she pushed aside. All they could do was their best and the fastest way to quit killing beings, people, who had no choice in this war, was to end it.

Perc had dropped his rifle on a table as he launched himself towards the back of the Kaylid, while at the same time saying in the mindspace. ~Coming in. Don't let him turn you.~

~Got it.~ JD pulled and the Kaylid fell off balance a bit. JD, even underweight, looked like he had twenty pounds on him and at this point it was all muscle and it made a difference. Perc slammed into the Kaylid with claws out, shoving them into its back where the heart would have been in a human.

It screamed. Before, most of the fight had been relatively silent, but now it screamed a high-pitched sound that hurt McKenna's ears and must have been torture on JD's and Perc's.

~Shit, it didn't kill it.~ Perc muttered as he fought to yank his claws back out of the being. JD roared and McKenna saw blood streaming from his side.

The Kaylid's tail whipped up and slammed into Perc from below, lifting him, and she heard him grunt in pain.

~Dammit, finish it guys. Before you get hurt or others come.~

JD growled mentally at her, but her stress and worry as she kept pivoting didn't allow her to feel guilty for the ridiculous order.

As she scanned back to their fight, she saw JD had sunk his huge jaws around the creature's neck, cutting off its airflow. Meanwhile Perc had slammed both sets of claws into the Kaylid's skull. The awful scream had stopped, and it slumped to the ground, a limp greenish-gray bag of flesh, bleeding from multiple wounds.

~You okay?~

~No. I have at least three broken bones and JD has some wicked cuts. But we'll live.~ Perc's mental voice felt gray and dank. It bugged her, but then this entire thing sucked.

A creak of sound had them looking up, muscles tensing, ready to attack again. The back door of the yard they were fighting in had creaked open a tiny bit and an elderly woman, her once black hair streaked with gray looked at them and nodded.

"Take them and dump them out front on the driveway. I'll call a pick-up." She started to close the door then paused, looking back at them, eyes magnified by thick lenses. "Good job." The door shut and it was all silent again.

~Hey, at least not everyone is against us,~ JD said as he stood, blood still leaking from wounds.

~They never were. We'll get the bodies moved, then we'll need some food. I've got my bot working overtime to fix this stuff. Remind me in the future to shoot them from a distance, this close up stuff is brutal and they're better trained than we are.~ Perc sounded distracted as he looked around.

~What he said.~ JD's voice sounded exhausted and in pain, but McKenna stayed where she was, watching and listening as they moved the bodies out front. She didn't get down from her perch until she heard them go in the front door, at which point she dropped off the swing set and headed to the deck, not relaxing, but feeling a bit better. The back door opened before she got there and Doug and Philip walked out, their faces unreadable. They firmly shut the door before focusing on her.

"We need to talk."

Chapter 9 - Bombshells

The fashion and recognition adornments started by McKenna Largo have gone all but viral. Wait times for piercings are upwards of four hours at this point. The gaudier the better is the word of the day. As one shifter put it—"I want you to see me coming a mile away." After looking at her LED flashing neon green earring, we feel her purpose may be achieved. But will it make a difference in the long run? Only time will tell. And that is the one thing Earth seems to be running out of. ~TNN Invasion News

McKenna sighed at the SecDef's words and leaned back against the railing. She could hear Perc and JD talking to each other in the mindspace, as they dealt with their wounds in the house. Cass and Toni were fussing over them and Blair was excited. While normal habit caused them to share spoken words in the space, though they still hadn't figured out how you auto-translated other people's words into the shared space. Wefor just sighed when asked and would launch into a technical explanation that had everyone's eyes glazing over in seconds, except Cass's.

At this point McKenna chalked it up to nanobots and moved on. She was close enough she could easily hear them talking if she focused on it, even through the door and with them in another room. But that took too much effort right now, though she did crank down her hearing a bit.

"About?" her voice wary. The familiar adrenaline drop was hitting and she wanted something to munch on, even if she hadn't expended as many calories.

"Can we trust him?" Burby asked, his voice blunt.

Amusement washed through McKenna. "You realize if his hearing is anything like ours in either form, he can probably hear us clearly out here."

Philip paled a bit and his eyes twitched to the door while Burby rubbed his temples. "Doesn't matter if he can. The question remains the same. Can we trust him?"

"How in the world should I know? I've known him for what, two hours longer than you have? I don't have the slightest idea. But does it really matter?" They had gritted their teeth a bit at her comment, then frowned, looking at her.

"What does that mean?" Philip demanded. He didn't get into her personal space or try to intimidate her, which she both appreciated and it put him a few rungs above General Arnold.

"It means, unless there's a ton of plans being made, we don't have a choice."

Silence from both men met her words and she wanted to beat her head against the wall. "Guys, I listen to the news. I've been out there. You, yourself, told me about the trucks and huge food shortages. We're facing an infrastructure breakdown if we can't get people moving around safely. You heard Rarz talking about them getting the asteroids ready to launch at us and what happened to the last planet."

"How do we know that isn't just a bluff? Something to get us to believe him?"

"One—the person, or whatever, that has been sending us the weird dreams and stuff mentioned they were planning on it. We're becoming too much effort. But they have another ship coming first. They'll try to load it up before doing anything else. Besides, haven't your scientists or astro guys or whatever mentioned the ships are gathering asteroids from the belt and positioning them around Earth?" They looked at each other and Burby pulled out his phone.

A minute later he started to cuss softly. "She's right. They've spotted them heading back and forth from the belt between Mars and Jupiter with objects. But no one put it together."

McKenna tried to remember when she knew about the asteroids and if she had ever passed it on or even mentioned it to the captain. But the mix of memories, dreams, talking in mindspace, and something Rarz had said all blended and finally she shook her head.

"So bottom line, it doesn't matter. If he is tricking us, why? We're losing and have nothing to use against asteroids being flung at our planet. Even if humanity isn't absolutely destroyed, what's left will be pushed back to survival level and we won't have anything we can do about anything."

Philip swallowed hard, and then straightened up a bit more. "Well then. It sounds like we should get to work with our new ally and see how this crazy plan of his might let us strike back." He started to turn to the door and paused. "Sir, why did you ask how many people had already been taken by the Elentrin?"

Burby snorted, running his hand over his head. He needed a shave, McKenna noted. "Because we need to rescue them. If we just blow up the ships with close to a million people on them, the world will crucify us. If we try to rescue them and fail, that's one thing. But if we don't try at all?" He shrugged. "I'm not sure I could live with that either. But we need to stop them and fast." He looked at McKenna. "How long do we have?"

She shrugged. "Not sure. I think the other ship will be here any day."

Philip paled a bit. "I have to figure out how to launch an attack against ships in orbit around us, with an ally we don't know if we can trust, with a technique we can't quite believe, in less than forty-eight hours?"

Burby gave him a humorless smile. "Adapt, improvise, and overcome. We have people to save. But look on the bright side. If it works, we can destroy these incoming ships before they start loading our people on them. Less collateral damage."

McKenna winced. "Doug?"

He turned to look at her and got a wary look on his face. "Yes?"

"Just remember. Most of the Kaylid are slaves. They don't have a choice. And if I'm right, Ash loaded Cass with information on how to break or at least override their conditioning. Besides, if how she's described the containment facilities are correct, we won't know who's from Earth and who's from elsewhere. They're mostly stored in Kaylid forms. We need to rescue as many as we can."

Both men just looked at her blankly and she shrugged. "I know. But could you kill sleeping people who have no desire to do anything but to go home if they could? Not saying we shouldn't fight and kill, just pointing out we'll be rescuing them regardless because we won't always know if they're from Earth."

"What do you mean always know?" Roberts asked, looking at her sharply. She could see the wheels turning in his head and tilted her head back to where they had killed the two Kaylid.

"One of the ones we killed was a reptile or dinosaur-like; leathery skin, no fur with a thicker tail. Not mammal like all Earth shifters that I've heard of. But do you really want to take the time to evaluate each Kaylid you find to decide if they are friend or foe? Knowing that our only real foes look like elves from an anime tale?"

"I'm starting to understand why Burby dreads speaking to you. You complicate everything by doing the right thing." He suddenly grinned and tugged down his uniform. "I always wanted to be Heracles, I guess this is one of my legendary tasks. But the clock is ticking and standing here with our thumbs up our asses won't get it done."

Philip pulled open the door and strode into the kitchen. "Laurent. We're going to need the commanders of the local garrisons. We have multiple bases near here, so we can start pulling in troops. Get someone on the phone and tell them we're going to need people. Details to follow in a few hours, but prepare for heavy, fast loads. We're going to need medics and places to put a lot of people." Laurent nodded and pulled out his phone.

"Stadiums." Toni said, her voice quiet. She stood by the front door looking out it, rifle in her hand.

"Excuse me?" Gunny Roberts looked at her, confused.

"Get a stadium. You can get a lot of people in it, both in the seats and the field. Not to mention the tunnels underneath have lots of rooms, some with places that are almost medical quality."

"What she said. Most people never see the underside of the stadiums, but the professional level ones will have the next thing to surgical suites in them. They're set up to treat lots of injuries and have showers." Perc backed up Toni's comment. "After all, I've been in enough of them."

"Point. Laurent, add that to your list. Now," Philip paused and moved his attention to Rarz. "We need to talk about exactly how this will work."

"You have decided to trust me? Or realized there are no other options?" Rarz's tone remained gentle but there was an echo of laughter that brushed up against the mindscape.

"Told you he'd be able to hear us." McKenna said as she sank into a recliner. Nam climbed up on top of her, and wrapped her arms around her neck, holding on tight.

Rarz glanced at the little girl and his brows drew together, but before he could say anything Philip started.

"We only have a short amount of time. Between the incoming Elentrin and the asteroids, we need to move fast. The stadiums will help, but we'll have lots of confused beings to deal with. And doesn't that just feel odd saying." He shook his head and glanced down at his notebook. "But before we can do anything, I need to know exactly what your limitations are. So we can Trojan-Horse inside? How long can you keep it open? How many people, what are our options?"

Rarz tilted his head all the way back looking at the ceiling.

"There is a story from my past of a Drakyn opening a tunnel between two planets and moving an entire people through it. I have personally allowed two or three to go through, but I've never tested how long I can hold it open. But when I have had others go through, I've never noticed a difference. That is an answer I cannot provide, but I would assume it is a long time and many people."

"If it fails or is disrupted, how long to reconnect or make a new tunnel?"

"Less than one of your minutes."

Philip grimaced. "Which, if you are under fire might be an eternity. What are you thinking?"

Rarz paused and half-shrugged. "This is where I need your assistance. We have no strategy training. Most planets we have interacted with are agrarian, peaceful. We have technology, but we have never used it the way your history shows. In many ways you are the most violent race we have ever seen. You kill each other and fight for sport. Even the Elentrin don't see violence as fun, only necessary. The only reason Ash's people knew how to attack was we had warned them generations ago, but they realized the danger too late and attacking ships in space is harder than we had known."

"Yeah. So we're finding. We make it through this I can promise you every country in the world will be developing a space defense program." Burby's voice was a bit bitter but he shrugged. "What are you thinking, Philip?"

"That we're probably all going to die." He sighed and looked at his notebook, but it was obvious he wasn't really seeing it. "Get a few good SEAL or Ranger teams together, tight squads that know how to work as a unit. Get in, plant bombs, get out. But that leaves the rescuing part."

"There is another complication." Rarz's voice might have been apologetic, almost. McKenna felt herself brace for what he was about to say, her arms tightening slightly on Nam. "McKenna and her group will need to come with us. This will fail without them."

The words fell like bricks in the room and Philip groaned as he turned to look the shifters.

"No offense, but regardless of the last week, you aren't trained for this. You don't know how to work with a team, and I doubt you have any experience with setting bombs or clearing rooms."

"No offense taken. You're right. That isn't anything we know how to do, though I'll tell you fighting in warrior form is another skill set entirely." She looked at Rarz who almost looked sheepish. "Why do we have to come?"

Toni's bitter laugh was a slap across the face and McKenna glanced at her, surprised.

What is wrong with her? I have to find time to talk to her.

"Isn't it obvious?" Everyone looked at her blankly. "The knowledge we were preloaded with. Cass knows how to get people out of the canisters or tubes or whatever. Without her, all the 'people' you want to rescue will probably get killed by their rescuers." She did air quotes around people as she talked. "Perc already said he knows the ship, that means he knows where to go and where the best spots for the bombs will be. Where to disable and where to destroy things." Her smile twisted and McKenna flinched back. "We need McKenna because of the AI living in her head. I'll lay money it can understand most of the systems faster than we can, not to mention the languages and resources. Then there's me." Her eyes had a haunted look and McKenna didn't know whether she should close her eyes to block them out or get up and hug her. "I have all the access codes to the various sections of the ship. And I should be able to register myself as a super user. Somehow, he programmed it to recognize me. So yes. You need all of us. And I have to leave my kids. AGAIN!"

Everyone stared at her and she whirled to look out the window, her body stiff and tense.

~I'm sorry.~ McKenna whispered in her mind, wanting to cry for her friend, her pack.

Toni's shoulders trembled for a moment, then relaxed.

~Not your fault. It is what it is. If we don't do this, our planet will be destroyed. Then my children will be dead anyhow, so at this point it doesn't matter.~

When she turned back around, her face was set, and McKenna squeezed Nam so hard the little girl protested.

~I know we have disrupted your lives. But truly, we were unable to think of any other way. Ash and I tried once before, but we couldn't get the ones we connected with to believe the dreams or me. They were taken before we could convince anyone. You have come further than anyone the Elentrin have faced before.~

Rarz's voice in the mindscape rolled through like a low thrum and she saw Toni's eyes widen a bit. But before they could end their weird staring contest, Philip spoke.

"I don't know if this will make you feel better, but you just became the most important people on the planet.

Which means we're instantly moving you to a secure facility and we're going to start planning the attack as soon as we can get the pieces together. That means you need to work with teams, learning their tactics, and they need to get to know you." He cast a critical eye at Perc, JD, and Rarz. "And we need to get some equipment that will fit you. While you might be able to do that mental thingy that the SecDef told me about, the rest of the team can't. We're going to need to go over the schematics and figure out the types of explosives to take. Either way, we need get out of here and soon. We don't have time and I hope you don't need sleep."

McKenna laughed bitterly. "We do, but we need food and have learned to sleep when we can. But we'll figure it out." She stood up and looked around. "Let's pack up and get out of here."

Carina came out from the kitchen, a worried look on her face as she headed upstairs. Toni followed her to get the kids all packed back up. If it took them more than an hour she'd be surprised. McKenna started to put Nam down so she could go help when Rarz stepped over to her. She stopped still holding Nam in her arms.

Philip and Burby were both talking on their phones in rapid-fire orders, trying to make this work while JD and Perc had headed out to start loading up the car. Lawson went with them, his eyes wide and looking a bit freaked.

Welcome to the big leagues. I wish I could go home. Even the media circus and the drug sniffing seemed easier than this. I never thought I'd wish I was back in that place again, being watched twenty-four seven, but at least then I knew exactly what to do. Now I don't have a clue.

"May I speak with you about the child?" He didn't whisper. His voice didn't sound like it could whisper, but he kept it soft and nodded towards the kitchen.

Thoughts and reactions boiled in McKenna's mind, but she nodded and headed into the kitchen, her body on a fine point ready to attack if he so much as made a move towards the little girl. Nam had turned her head watching him, her gaze intent.

"Is she your child?"

"No. But I won't let anything happen to her."

He tilted his head one way then the other. "That is not my intent. She feels different than the rest of you. Have you noticed?"

Feel, what is he talking about?

"Since you haven't touched her, I assume you mean something else when you say feel."

Nam's voice surprised her. "He's funny feeling. He's all sun and sand and wind. It tickles."

McKenna glanced down at Nam. That wasn't the first comment she'd made that made no sense, but then what did she know about kids? Nam was just a different child all around.

"Thank you, little one." His scaled lips curved a bit, but didn't expose teeth as his eyes, swirling with colors, moved to look at McKenna. "No, I suppose you would not sense it. It will not matter now, maybe not for years, and it will never matter if the Elentrin are not defeated. But she is special. Only a few rare of my people can taste the colors of the mind. They usually become healers or luminaries. She could be one if she wanted. She has the skills." A large clawed hand reached out and McKenna fought to not pull the child away, but Nam reached out her own hand and traced the claw and fingers that looked like they could kill her with a casual wave.

"Be aware she will be more sensitive than most nest-lings. And as she grows she will expand her ability to read and control. I've never heard of a Kaylid developing this, but she has Drakyn in her as do you all."

Wait—what?

Chapter 10 - First Domino

In the five states that have recreational pot sales as legal, every distribution center has sold out. The few people willing to talk all had similar comments. "I have nothing to lose, and if this helps lowered my stress level, why not?" It is interesting to note that while crime has come to a standstill across the board, there has been no attempt by law enforcement to pursue any drug use at this time. And the White House has been unavailable for comment. ~ TNN News

McKenna just looked at him. "We have Drakyn in us?"

"Of course. That is the only reason their nanobots work. At some point our ancestors visited here, bred with your species and time and generations have diffused the effect. But Nam has more than a normal amount. And Toni?" Rarz shrugged. "I always wondered if the Elentrin knew that the only reason their little machines worked was because of our genetic material in their victims. And if ultimately all of this is our fault. Maybe we should have just killed them all that first day."

"Killed who?" McKenna blurted.

"Come on people, we need to get packed and out of here. We have another vehicle that will be here in ten. Rarz, I need to discuss your needs with you before we leave." Philip's voice radiated from the living room with the power of a drill sergeant.

"It is immaterial at this time. This is history so old it lives only in our legends." With another half-nod Rarz turned and went back, his tail following him with an odd grace.

My life is so strange.

~Wefor, is that true?~ She asked in the mindspace as she headed to do a quick pack, not that she had much to do. At the top of the stairs she set the squirming Nam down who raced to help Carina and the others get their stuff all packed up. She could feel the kids' excitement. They still found all this fun. The adults, on the other hand, were grim, and Toni brimmed with helpless rage at the situation they found themselves in.

[There is no reason it can not be true. There is no information in the databases to indicate they are aware of it. Only that they tried it and it would not work on Elentrin but did work on a subject race they had found at one point in their history. One of their ships went back to test it on the indigenous people and the Kaylid were created to fight the Drakyn.]

~I see. Which may or may not be the way it happened. Victors rewrite history a lot. But I guess it doesn't matter. Still doesn't change the situation.~

Pushing that to the side, she headed to where Toni had been sleeping and found the woman shoving things into her suitcase, every move jerky.

"Toni?" At this point talking out loud might give them more privacy.

"I know, I know. This is the best hope we have. That if I stayed, we would probably all die. And by all, I mean all humans. I know that I'm being silly. I know they'll protect the kids to the best of their abilities. I know all of that!" Her voice broke on a sob. "And I still don't want to go. They're changing so fast, becoming people in their own right, not just my kids, and I'm terrified that I'll miss it. I'm terrified something will happen and I won't be here to take care of them, to hold them, listen to them sleep. And I can't do anything about it and I didn't choose any of this."

McKenna pulled on her shoulder gently and Toni turned around, tears streaking her face. With a sad smile McKenna pulled her into her arms and held Toni while she cried. After a minute she joined in, too. Charley and Nam had become so important. And now she was leaving them again, with strangers. She let her own tears come and wash them both clean of some stress. She could feel the kids monitoring them, but they didn't come in, letting them deal with their grief.

After what felt like eternity but was probably only a few minutes, Toni sniffed and pulled back. "Thanks. I guess I needed that. I'll be okay."

"You're one of the strongest women I know. Of course you'll be okay. But that doesn't mean you can't hurt." McKenna pointed out.

"Pot, Kettle?" Toni said with a wry smile. "I know how you feel about Charley and Nam, so don't tell me this isn't killing you also."

"It is. I want to be here with them. She's only six, so I get it. But not being here hurts. However, if I don't try to do something and we then all die?" McKenna shrugged. "I'm torn, so I'm doing what I can."

Toni wiped at her nose. "You're doing fine. Okay, enough emotions. We have stuff to do, then an enemy to kick out of our solar system."

"You sure you're okay?"

"No, but I'll make it. Trust me, compared to Jeff dying, this I know I can handle. I just needed that cry I guess." Toni turned away and started packing again, her movements smoother and more efficient.

"Good. Next question—what's up with you and the Drakyn?"

Toni froze at the question then sighed and turned around. "That obvious?"

"Just weird. You don't usually react like that. So what's the issue?" McKenna started to help her pack up things. They were running out of time and she could hear the others running around, getting things together.

"When I saw him walking out of that portal I almost choked. It was like my dreams had been made real."

"How did you see that? You weren't there." McKenna looked at her in surprise, but remembered the strange feeling at the time.

"No, but we got the comments you made, and I was stressing. I wanted to see what was going on, especially with Perc and JD muttering, like whispers in the mindscape." Toni frowned. "I just wanted to see so badly, and suddenly it was like I was there, but the view was odd. I could see it through your eyes. Everything in color. It lasted only for a minute or two, but I couldn't focus on anything except him."

"We can do that, too," Charley said softly.

McKenna turned to look at him. She hadn't realized he'd been in the hall.

"Do what?" Toni stared at him with the same confusion McKenna felt.

"See through others' eyes. I mean, I can only see through Jessi's. But Jamie can see through hers, also. We haven't tried with Nam. She's too new to us. But yeah, we found that out." He shrugged and looked away from them. "Just heard you talking about it and thought I'd tell you. But it is kinda cool. We're all packed up. So where are we going now?"

He didn't seem too stressed and McKenna wondered how much of his life had been being shipped from place to place.

Is this better for him? Or am I making it worse?

Unable to resist, she snaked out an arm and pulled her to him in a side hug. "You guys okay with all this change?"

"Sure. This is fun. Dragons, aliens, army guys, invaders. It's like being in a movie." He grinned up at her and she rolled her eyes.

"If you say so. Go get your stuff downstairs. I think we're moving to a base."

"Ooh, will we get to stay in barracks? That would be awesome." Charley looked excited at the idea, and Toni snorted.

"Maybe. I'll ask. Now get." She shooed him off and he darted into the nearby bedroom, grabbed a bag and lugged it down the stairs. Jessi and Nam followed with smaller bags.

"I think I'm jealous. They think this is fun. And I don't want to disabuse them of that idea," McKenna commented as she watched them trot down the stairs. "But now," she said turning back to Toni. "Rarz, spill."

"Dammit, I was hoping you'd been sidetracked." Toni didn't look at her as she finished putting things in the bag.

"Not so lucky. Spill, but do it in my bedroom so I can pack." Toni followed McKenna as she began to throw things into her bag.

"So yeah, the dragon walking out of a big shiny portal was a bit of a surprise, but nothing like the fact that I recognized him."

"What?" McKenna looked up, trying to separate dirty and clean clothes. She hadn't even had a shower yet.

"All my life I dreamed of dragons. Both as humanoid and on all fours. Honestly when I shifted, I was surprised I didn't turn into a dragon. But who tells people that stuff? I just pushed it away and focused on being a kid, then being an adult, then a mom. It was silly dreams and not like I had them every night." Toni shrugged as she grabbed stuff out of the closet. "I'd almost forgotten them and I haven't had them for years. The dreams on the ship pushed them to the side, I guess. So when he walked out, I almost choked."

"Huh. What do you think it means?"

"No clue, other than me being weird. But really there are only so many ways dragons can look. I doubt I dreamed about him specifically, probably just a weird parallel thing. I mean a dragon and aliens and shifters." She trailed off as she said that, and McKenna looked at her sideways.

"Personally, I think it would be stranger at this point if they weren't linked. Besides, he keeps looking at you funny also, as if he knows you."

Toni groaned. "I hate it when you're right." She looked around. "That looks like everything." They could hear the people clearing out. "I'll talk to him later. If we survive, it might matter. Now? I'll try to quit freaking out every time I see him. But he looks wrong without the wings."

McKenna grinned. "Agreed. But still. it was getting a bit claustrophobic with them. He uses them the way I use my tail in both my forms."

"That he does. Anything else?"

~Everyone got everything? We good?~ She asked, check-ing with everyone.

~Finishing up the last of the kitchen stuff now. The place will be a bit of a mess, but we don't have time to clean it.~ Cass said.

~Yep, they have another vehicle on the way, and we have the Suburban, the car that was here, and the one Bur-by's crew came in. We're leaving all the bags in the garage and they'll collect them for us. The kids are already in the car; it's the only one with booster seats for the three of them. So we just need to know where we're going.~ Perc had this steady 'everything will be fine' cadence to his voice and it made her feel a bit better.

McKenna cast a glance to Toni who shrugged. They grabbed their bags and headed downstairs. Rarz stood in the living room, out of sight of any person who might be passing by. Philip was giving Rarz a considering look then frowned at Perc and JD.

"Is there an issue?"

"All of you are huge and not inconspicuous and I really don't want anyone to know we have you here. You don't look like a Kaylid, even without the wings." He glanced back at Perc and JD. "Very noticeable especially among a bunch of humans."

"Hey, we're human, too." McKenna couldn't stop the snappish response. Roberts snapped to attention.

"Yes, ma'am. I didn't mean to imply you weren't, ma'am. Just that you are obvious." He stood, not looking at her, his eyes over her shoulder.

McKenna sighed. "I know, but all of us can change back to human. We'll just need to food to replenish the energy. Perc, JD—you okay to change? You have enough reserves for a shift?"

They both stood there a minute then nodded. "Yeah, not going to say I won't need calories to change back. I'm still underweight, but should be fine." JD said, shrugging one shoulder.

"All of you? Wait, Rarz can change, too?" Philip had lost the rigid attention pose.

"Yes. The wings were just too much in that small space." McKenna frowned, then remembered Rarz had changed before the men got there for the awe factor.

Rarz, however, was looking back and forth between them. "Why are you worried about caloric intake? Do you not store spare mass in your quantum spaces?" With his brow ridges furrowed, McKenna figured that was his equivalent of a confused face.

I wonder if all species in humanoid forms have similar expressions? And what the heck is he talking about?

Before she could voice that Perc did. "What are you talking about quantum space? Storing mass?"

Rarz paused, his head moving from one to another looking at them. "Pardon the intrusion, but how do you change now?"

McKenna titled her head, now totally confused. "We have nanobots that do it, and they burn calories to fuel themselves to restructure our cellular structure."

The Drakyn blinked at them, both sets of eyelids closing and opening rapidly.

"That is horribly inefficient and a waste of caloric energy. Why would you do it like that?" His voice sounded astonished and McKenna laughed.

"You think we have a choice? We didn't have a choice in any of this. All we can do is deal with what we've been handed." She paused, looking at him. "Are you saying there's a different way to do this? This isn't how you do it?"

He opened and closed his mouth two times in a row before finally responding. "I apologize. I must think about this. I do not know how to deal with this information and what it implies, much less how to explain to you. Give me some time."

Philip looked at them. "Okay. If that's done, can all of you shift and get back to something no one will look at twice? Besides, I'll need the shifting later to help impress people."

"As long as you have food there to fuel our shift back, it really isn't an issue." JD offered and Perc nodded.

"I'll make a note. Please?" The Gunny actually asked, not ordered.

Points for him.

Her friends shrugged and started to change, flowing back into human, looking grimy and tired.

"Interesting. Yes, much to consider." Rarz watched all of this with sharp eyes then he, too, let himself change.

Once again McKenna noted that he felt different when he shifted. But she couldn't say what felt different. Just that it wasn't like watching or feeling any of hers shift. It felt smoother, like silk against skin. And then a man, dark haired and powerful, but so undeniably human, stood in front of them.

"How do you know our form so well? Or is it that easy for you to change?" Cass asked from the doorway, as Blair Lewis stood next to her. The curiosity in their eyes, matching pairs.

"I have practiced since my majority. The dreams I shared with Tonan Diaz gave me the templates to change into in my later years."

Toni sucked in a sharp breath at her full name and Rarz looked at her.

"We should talk later. Once your world is safe." His words rang deeper and wider than should have been possible, ringing like a bell in McKenna's soul.

"Yeah," was all Toni said as she turned and headed out the door, not looking at anyone.

Chapter 11 - Meet the Troops

Over the last year, micro disturbances have been noticed by a few scientists. But up until now there haven't been more than weird results and most scientists admitted they thought it due to instrument failure. With the appearance of the Elentrin above our world, the possibility that it was real has spiked interest and controversy. But to most scientists' frustration, they can't duplicate the anomalies. There don't seem to be any going on right now. Is this timing or was this the start and maybe something that would have given us some warning had we known what it meant? ~ TNN Science

Philip had asked McKenna to ride with him and Burby so she could share the information about the arrangements with everyone else, even the Drakyn. She agreed mainly because she couldn't sit with Charley or Nam. The booster seats took up the entire row.

"They're arranging space for us at Andrews. Most flights have been canceled anyhow so they're going to set us up there."

"And the kids?" she asked, making sure to pass everything into the mindspace. The space which now held an opal-like button that she just knew was Rarz.

"We're putting them up at the Presidential Inn, along with you. We have the entire floor pulled aside and MPs and agents will be there constantly. Christopher has arranged for three of his female agents to be there and I called in some retired Marines I know to help staff. Note they are retired 'cause they hit twenty years, not because they can't kill someone as easily as they can drain a beer."

McKenna relaxed a bit at that. With that many people, if their kids were hurt no one could have protected them.

"Okay." She sat and listened as he talked, asking questions as they arose, but once again most of the work was on other people. The river of events buffeted her from one side to the other. It annoyed her, but she didn't see anything she could actively do right now except wait.

The trip took over three hours, even with all the vehicles moving at high speed, but the transfer into the hotel, and then the adults to the nearby Jacob Smart Conference Center was smooth. Coffee awaited them and she lunged at it, desperate. At this point it was getting late, and they had been up since early that morning.

Lawson still trailed them, though he'd lost his self-assurance as more and more high-ranking people showed up.

"Should I stay or take back off to my unit?" he asked as an aside.

She glanced around the area and all the strangers coming in and staring at them. "Go. Get back to your people. I just wish we had been able to take a shower." Her voice had a wistful tone and she ran her fingers through hair that felt filthy. JD and Perc didn't look much better and their worn kilts and tank tops looked as rough as they did.

"I hear you. Okay, I'm headed out. And Largo?" Lawson paused, looking at her, a half-smile on his face.

"Yeah?"

"You did damn good for a bunch of spoiled cops." The half-smile grew into a smirk.

"And you weren't too bad for a clumsy ground-pounder," she fired back. He laughed, gave her and the rest of them a wave and headed out.

McKenna sipped her coffee and waited as more and more people in various uniforms and suits filed into the conference room. The five of them found themselves huddled together with Rarz standing slightly apart, yet near them.

~Ever feel completely out of place?~ Toni murmured as she tugged on her t-shirt and jeans.

~Yes, but this is extreme. I feel dirty, like I have the wrong clothes on, and I'm getting tired fast. Even with the caffeine.~ McKenna didn't whine, quite. But she would have given a lot to have met all these people with brushed teeth and hair. Fully rested would have been nice too.

~I think I'd feel out of place here regardless of what I was wearing,~ Cass said, her voice soft. ~This is not my normal group of people. Give me a bunch of people in lab coats and more focused on data than anything else, then maybe.~

~Your culture has such varieties. This world has more cultures and languages than any we have ever seen. I'm surprised more of the luminaries didn't come here.~ Rarz's comment made McKenna turn to look at him. He stood, in human form, his robes made him look like a cosplayer, but he seemed at ease.

~How can you be so calm? You don't know how they will react. You're surrounded by aliens, at least aliens to you. So why aren't you freaking out?~ McKenna tried to keep the accusation level out of her voice, but still, she'd be a nervous wreck at this moment.

He turned and looked at them, all huddled together against the people they would have to face soon and nodded a bit. ~Because this is what I train for. Besides, if they draw weapons I can change to a wyrm or relocate to home in the span of a few minutes. Most weapons are unable hurt me in wyrm form. But you need me. And I need you. This may be the only chance either of us has to halt the Elentrin. If not?~ He nodded his head again, almost like a shrug. ~Then I am unaware of anyone who can stop them. I am a luminary. A finder of new planets, new worlds. I do not know that there is anything else to hope for.~

His words created a lump in her stomach, but it also served to stiffen her spine. This was her world and she'd be damned if she let anyone destroy it without doing everything in her power to stop them. Even Charley and Nam weren't worth the lives of seven billion people.

Taking a deep breath, then a deeper drink of coffee, she looked across the crowd of people and caught Philip's eye. She gave a sharp nod at him. He looked surprised, but then nodded before he started to speak.

"If everyone could please move into the auditorium and take a seat, I'll explain why I've called everyone here." There was murmuring but people moved. Most of them were armed; pistols in holsters at their sides, but a few also had rifles slung over their shoulders. She watched them walk in, they all looked hard, strong, capable. None of them were much over fifty, and they all looked like they'd been in the field for a while.

Once she'd processed this, her dirty exhausted state didn't seem so out of place. She also needed to quit thinking of herself as slightly overweight and frumpy. The last few months between the shifting and her experiences, they all looked like warriors.

She smiled and looked at her friends. Cass and Toni could both pose as models for any swimsuit calendar. The men were cut and huge. They weren't who they had been just six months ago.

"Let's do this. We have some alien butts to kick," McKenna said, putting determination in her voice.

JD arched a brow at her, while Toni and Perc grinned with a fierce expression. Cass smiled at something secret, and from the flicker of emotion across JD's face, she'd said something to him. But all it meant was her friends had her back.

"Ready, Rarz?"

"That is why I am here." He responded, his voice calm.

Most everyone had trickled in, so she followed, walking towards the base of the auditorium where Philip and Burby waited for them. Walking down the aisle, she noted how exhausted the secretary of defense looked. Gunny Roberts looked almost excited and his eyes locked onto them, then drifted over to Rarz, who walked alongside them. In his human form he was notable for his height and size, but with Perc and JD there he didn't look that out of place.

Philip nodded to one side and they took a stance. This time, rather than feeling intimidated, McKenna took the time to inspect the assorted men in the audience. There were only two women that she could see but given who Philip probably pulled in, that made sense. From the sea of colors, between uniforms, patches, skin, and hair colors, it looked like everyone was represented.

Good. We're going to need everything we can get to pull this off.

"Everyone, settle down." Philip's voice caused the room to quiet as he stood up front, confidence in his every line. "Thank you for coming on such sort notice. I know you've all been busy with the efforts to fight against the Elentrin. We have new information about this and an ally has approached us offering to help."

A rumble of soft comments and grunts rolled through the room, but no one asked anything, they just watched. McKenna noted this would be a hard sell. They were men used to fighting, not diplomacy.

Which should make our life easier. We need to fight, not talk to the Elentrin.

"I'd like to ask McKenna Largo to explain who this person is and introduce him."

Wait, what? Great.

She shot dagger looks at Philip who walked off to the side. He seemed immune to her glares as she walked up. Having everyone's attention on her caused her spine to straighten even more, and she had to resist the urge to shift into warrior form to make herself appear stronger.

Where did that thought come from? Interesting. But no time to explore it.

Clearing her throat, she focused on the links connecting her to everyone, and not the sea of faces staring back at her, waiting.

"As he said, I'm McKenna Largo. Many of you have probably seen me on TV both through the video and the press conferences." With reporters she would have expected laughter or teasing, but here, these people just watched her, waiting. "While you know about the warrior forms and the Elentrin, what we never made public, because we didn't think it would make a difference, was how we received the information." She cleared her throat trying to find the right words. "An unexpected ally has been feeding us this information via dreams and sleep training. This ally has also enabled an enemy of the Elentrin to present himself to us."

A rumble of dissent from Rarz vibrated in the mindspace, but she ignored it. Enemy was the best word from her perspective.

"What hasn't been disseminated to the public is why the Elentrin want the shifters as cannon fodder. Their ultimate goal is to eliminate another species from existence. This species is called the Drakyn and the Elentrin have a pathological need to destroy them. I don't know the history and at this point I don't care. I'll take any help that will get these assholes away from my planet." There was a muffled growl of approval at that comment. "With that I'd like to present," she paused, her mind suddenly blank.

~What was your full name again?~ Her voice panicked as she pointed at the opal-like button in her mind.

~Rarz Goldwing Liryline,~ he responded and she almost sighed in relief as he answered her instantly.

"Rarz Goldwing Liryline, a Drakyn." Her words fell into an expectant silence, but as Rarz walked up, you could almost feel the wave of disappointment.

A few murmurs in the crowd, easily heard when she enhanced her ears, indicated their feelings. She glanced at him and shrugged. With this form he did just look like another guy, albeit huge, but he didn't look like the answer to all their prayers.

Rarz moved up to the stage, giving the podium a funny look and then out at the people staring back at him, unimpressed.

~What am I supposed to do now? Is this a social acceptance ritual?~

McKenna blinked at him, and then had to fight laughter. ~Explain to them you are here to help and how.~

~But I do not know how to help. That is why I am here offering help to you, to see how my skills can be used. What I know is small in compared to your experience. The plan sounds valid, but how will it work?~

~I don't know. That's why they're here to find a reason to believe you, to help. To give us the support needed to pull this off.~

The silence held too long as he stood there, the spotlight illuminated on him.

A man stood up in the audience. "What's the big deal, Gunny?" His voice carried clearly, and everyone shifted to look at him. "So you got another shifter. I'll grant you he's a big dude and could be scary in warrior form. But how does that help with ships beyond the reach of our weapons?"

Gunny Philip Roberts stepped up facing the assembled service members. "This isn't just a shifter. This is someone we've never seen. And I have reason to believe that his abilities might give us the opportunity we've been looking for to fight the Elentrin." His words met with a murmur of disbelief, but the man talking sat down.

Philip sighed. "Rarz, I know I asked you to change, but would you mind shifting back?"

"To which form?"

Roberts blinked at him. "You have more than these two?"

"Technically I have four. This form, two legged, what you call warrior, my Kin form, and my wyrm form. The warrior form was what you saw earlier."

McKenna saw Philip's mouth open, and then he snapped it shut. "Later I'll follow up on that. Right now can you change back into the warrior form with wings?"

A half nod of his head and Rarz began to change. As before, watching it was fascinating.

Where is he coming up with the energy? With this many changes in a single day, all of us would be starving for food. Past exhausted.

The question ate at her, but it wasn't anything to worry about now.

In a minute he stood there, the wings moving gently as he held his head up, and a soft whistle of approval from the crowd. But then they fell silent waiting.

Rarz didn't say anything, just stood there, and the crowd started to get restless.

One of the few women stood up, her hair in a ponytail. She looked exhausted and hard. "So he's got wings. My daughter would think it he's cute. That doesn't help us unless he can fly faster than they can land those damn shuttles and destroy them before they take back off. Something we can't seem to do often enough, at least not without killing our own people in them at the same time."

"That is a valid point." Rarz voice seemed to roll across the space like a physical force. "I am awkward at this, but this is not perhaps the best place to demonstrate what I offer. My other form has something of a fear factor, especially for the Elentrin. Then there is the way I can allow you to travel. Is there a much larger space we can move to, perhaps with multiple levels?"

One of the staff for the area stepped up and talked rapidly to Philip.

"I've been told the blimp hangars are close enough and are empty right now with catwalks. Will that do?"

Rarz did his head nod. "I am unsure what a blimp or catwalk is, but we can see."

The gunny sergeant looked at the crowd. "Are you willing to move with us to the hangars?"

"Gunny, you let me take my coffee with me, and I don't care where you lead." A voice spoke out from the crowd. It was met with laughter and general agreement. With resigned shrugs people filed out, the majority stopping for refills on the coffee as they walked the route to the hangars.

Chapter 12 - From here to there

The blocks on China's internet have fallen and for the first time in almost a decade there are no restrictions for information coming in and out, and the reality is horrifying. There are people lying dead in the street, and comments say they killed themselves when the Elentrin left. Snapped images of people in lines to get onto the shuttles have appeared, as well as the instant death by anyone trying to stop them. One of the most memorable pics is of a young man being torn to pieces by others when he trying to grab a young woman from the queue of people leading to the shuttle. Even if we stop these invaders, China may never recover.
~TNN Invasion News

It wasn't a short walk, but the weather didn't make it awful, though the normal laughing and teasing that would have been present was absent. People walked quietly, looking at the skies, their surroundings, and even while carrying coffee in their hands, all of them made sure they could grab their weapons with a second's notice.

No one walked near Rarz, McKenna noted, but they were all very aware of him. His wings sparkled in the lights from the lamps. They'd started their day at seven a.m., found Rarz about two, gotten shipped to DC by seven p.m. and now it was pushing ten p.m. The lights created beacons in the dark, and if the clock wasn't counting down, McKenna would have lobbied to let everyone sleep, shower, and feel capable of thinking. But that wasn't possible. Not when she kept glancing at the sky and wondering when the first asteroids would start raining down.

~I've always loved disaster movies,~ Cass said, her tone somber in their minds. ~But right now all of them involving asteroids, meteors, and comets is playing through my head and most everyone dies except the hero. And I don't think we're the heroes in this story.~

Her words set the mood for the group and ramped up their stress. McKenna saw Rarz glance back at them, his ridges furrowed, but he didn't say anything. He simply kept walking and looking around at the patches of light amid the darkness.

Walking into the huge hangar was both a relief and ramped-up stress again. Here was where their plans and choices would all come into play. Either something would come of it, or all of them would face the fact that the human race just might be doomed.

The echoing cavern of the hangar was lit with huge lights hanging at the top, so much light that the shadows seemed pale and nebulous. Rarz looked at it and his lips twitched, an odd look on his Drakyn form.

"This will do well." He turned to look at the group of service personnel gathered at one side, no one wanted their backs to the huge doors, even as they were being slid closed as he spoke.

"My people have been hunted by the Elentrin for many of your millennia. We are not a race that has many willing to fight. Almost to a one, we are pacifists, but there are some of us that can and will fight. One of the tools we have against the Elentrin is a form called the Wyrm. But we also possess the ability to relocate ourselves from one place to another. After talking to your leaders here, they agreed it might be useful." Rarz nodded at Roberts and Burby before he continued. "You must understand we have had the ability to change shape for as long as our stories have existed." He looked at all of them, his stance wide and easy, his tail motionless, which McKenna's cat side found odd. Tails were only still if you were about to spring.

"We found the two-legged form, the one you saw me wear at first, a long time ago. Then the warrior form, which proved a more elegant way to work with the world around us, allowed us to keep claws and wings." As he spoke, he paced out into the warehouse. Yet they could still hear his voice clearly. He kept walking as he talked; yet they didn't follow him. There was something about how he moved that let them know to not follow.

"But when the Elentrin kept following us, killing us, we were forced to adapt. To change how we had lived. Some of us, the ones that had kept to the ancient ways of hunting, found it easier than most. Over time, many of your centuries, we found a form that strikes terror in the Elentrin and is resistant to most of their weapons. But those of us that can change are few and it takes time to get where they are attacking. But this form is good for surprise and destruction of large buildings or other objects, such as their shuttles or ships the few times they land." By this time he was a good fifty feet away from them.

His path had not seemed so direct, but McKenna frowned when she realized that he was that far away. She resisted the urge to walk towards him. He'd interacted with them enough to know when and how to indicate someone should follow.

Rarz turned and looked at everyone. "While I do not know if this will be helpful with the plans mentioned, you should at least know what a wyrm is."

He undid the tie of his robes and they fell to the ground. Then he reached for the fastening of the belt around his slacks.

~Oh, please tell me he isn't going to strip in front of everyone. I am so glad Jessi isn't here. I swear she'd take this as permission to streak everywhere. 'Well, if the dragon did it, Mom, so can I.'~ Toni muttered in the mindspace.

McKenna had to fight back a wholly inappropriate laugh, but she could see Jessi doing just that. Even in warrior form they still had genitalia. Though the men were more obvious than the females.

The distance, even with the bright light, meant she couldn't see every detail of his body as he did strip. As he let the last bit of cloth fall to the ground, he looked mostly normal. It was the mostly which caused her to frown and try to figure out what seemed off, but the distance blurred details. There was a muffled groan from the people watching and she could sense more than hear their agitation at watching someone strip, but it was overtaken by his next words.

"Wyrm is something else that comes from a time when our ancestors roamed our planet, fierce and terrible. Behold the Wyrm." Even as the words fell from his lips, they changed becoming deeper, and more rumbley. The word wyrm was almost a roar that McKenna could feel in her bones, though it was no louder than anything else he had said.

The shift in air pulled at her hair even as her mind and eyes were locked on what couldn't be happening in the middle of the large hangar. Rarz stood there, mostly human or at least humanoid. The had one head, two arms, two legs, the wings just added flavor. But now his shape shifted and flowed into something else. The flesh and shape bended and flexed, body twisting and flowing, and most terrifying— growing.

By this point McKenna had watched multiple changes, and even the other changes Rarz had done always seemed a shifting of mass or of the body. Making the body restructure itself into a different pattern. What she saw now caused her hindbrain to gibber in panic. She wanted to run, to cower, to freeze in place hoping it wouldn't see her.

The mass of twisting flesh that solidified and took up most of the space was something out of story books. A winged dragon, with scales, large teeth, and claws stood there, colored in red and gold, looking at all of them. From head to tail he had to measure over forty feet long.

He's as big as a whale. That isn't possible.

Her mind protested even as guns snapped up and the military people surrounding her team and Rarz reacted to the threat.

~I really would prefer to not be shot. Though I am not sure your weapons would penetrate my scales, it would still be unpleasant.~ His voice a soft whisper that only she seemed to hear.

Rarz comment kicked her mind back into gear and McKenna cleared her throat.

"Not shooting our alien visitor would probably be a good start to creating cordial relations."

A solid five heartbeats passed as people looked down their weapons at the dragon, then someone sighed. "Point. Besides I have the very bad feeling shooting him would be like shooting a tank. It might ricochet and hit someone I don't really want to shoot."

That got people to lower their weapons and they all just looked at Rarz. His scales gleamed like metal while his eyes swirled with colors.

~I wonder how his pupils and irises work. Not like any animals from this planet, that's for sure.~ Cass's voice had an abstracted quality as they stood and admired him.

He embodied power, beauty, and something lethal. Be it the teeth that were as long as her hand or the claws that made even their warrior forms look tiny, he looked like something to fear. A twitch of motion pulled her eyes to his long, jagged tail that had spikes going all the way down.

I sure as hell never want that coming after me.

She swallowed hard and almost jumped when Toni spoke.

"You do realize you look almost stereotypically like a western dragon from our mythology," Toni said, her voice a hair away from accusation.

~I did mention luminaries from my people visited your planet at some time in the distant past, multiple times to be accurate. That my appearance exists in your mythology does not surprise me to any extent.~

"Holy shit, it can talk in my head," came out of half the people surrounding them; the other half had snapped up weapons and had them pointed back at Rarz.

~It would be rather useless if I could not communicate in this form. But all I can do is project loud enough you hear my thoughts. Unlike other Kaylid, who can speak back to me in a similar manner, I am unable to hear your responses, so you will need to speak out loud.~

Philip had moved out of the mass of people, rubbing his temple and looking at Rarz. Everyone fell silent as the Gunny walked out away from the mass of people but no-where near close to Rarz. McKenna couldn't blame him. Those teeth were intimidating as hell.

"Rarz, I will say this I didn't expect, and while I'm working on not having to get clean shorts," there was muffled agreement to this comment, "I'm not sure how to use this ability. You mentioned something else, about the portals?"

~Yes, but I figured this needed to be seen first, so you understand what is possible. But the relocation is more efficient for what we are trying to do. If you are agreeable, I will move back to your Earth form. This seems to make your people nervous.~

The voice rumbled in her mind and McKenna saw others shudder and rub their temples, though no one turned their attention away from the dragon.

Ha, they should try having Wefor talk in their head. His voice is almost pleasant.

"Please. That might make this easier," Philip replied, and the huge wings bobbed up and down. Rarz lifted onto hind-quarters, his head coming perilously close to the ceiling, then he began to shrink.

How the hell? Where is the mass going?

The astonishment of the shifters watching rippled through the mindspace. There were no words, just intense focus and confusion.

~We need to know how he's doing that. It would make life much easier if we didn't have to worry about energy components.~ Cass's mutter was met with agreement.

~Wefor, you sure you don't know how he's doing this?~

[There is no information to explain this. Conservation of mass is a universal constant. It can cannot be violated and he increased his mass. The air displacement and the way the floor settled verified the mass increase.]

~Add it to our "discuss later" list, I guess. Though starting to seem like all the later things will take years to get through,~ McKenna said as she watched the man pick up his robes and dress again.

He and Philip moved back towards the group and a few people did take a step or two back as he approached.

Philip nodded at him and McKenna realized they'd been talking as he changed, but she had been too busy to pay attention or realize it.

"McKenna, would you be amenable to being my guinea pig?"

His voice startled her, but she looked around and realized no one else could do it. The observers wouldn't trust him, and if this was going to work, she had to trust him. Either she started trusting now, or it wouldn't work at all.

"Sure, what do you need?"

He waved her over and looked at the group. "As I explained to your Gunny Roberts and Secretary of Defense Burby," he stumbled a bit over the titles and she realized they really hadn't told him how to address people. With his command of English they kept assuming he understood how to use it.

That's silly, no one understands English, it's illogical at the best of times.

The thought made her snort even as she tried to relax and not tense up. Glancing back at the others, they were all on edge and she could all but see the desire to shift to warrior form written on their faces. A form much better for fighting than their all-too-fragile human forms.

"My people have a means of travel we call relocating. The best way to explain it is I create wormholes from one place to another that people and objects can travel through. These wormholes can be held open for long periods of time. Also, they aren't physical connections the way you define physical, so they can not be blocked by objects such as planets, though extended interference from suns may make it necessary to drop and reestablish the connection."

Everyone just looked at him and McKenna figured the blankness on her face mimicked the blankness on theirs.

"I'm not sure that makes any sense," Philip said slowly as if he hated to admit he didn't understand.

McKenna didn't have any issue with that. "I have no idea what you just said."

Rarz didn't quite huff out a sigh, but it seemed like he really wanted to. "Are you willing to demonstrate what I am talking about?"

"Sure." McKenna didn't bother expressing her doubts. At this point she just wanted this over, and a bed to sleep in.

His brows wrinkled and he looked at right behind her, then tilted his head up and towards the sky. "There, that should work." As he spoke a glowing circle-portal thing appeared behind her. McKenna jumped back, startled. It felt slightly prickly up close, like static electricity in a ball. It wasn't painful, just prickly so that you knew it was there.

"If you walk through that opening, it will deposit you up there." He turned and pointed. Up on one of the catwalks about thirty feet in the air a similar glowing circle stood.

~Are you insane? You're going to walk into a glowing circle of light? What if you never come back?.~ Toni's protestation cut across the mindspace and McKenna hunched her shoulders in protest.

~Either I trust, or I don't. Do you see any other options? Anyone?~ Silence reigned in the mindspace.

McKenna turned to Rarz, pasting a smile on her face. "Sounds good. Just walk in?"

"Yes. You will reappear up there at the exit area."

"Here goes nothing."

With a deep breath McKenna stepped into the portal. Reality disappeared.

Chapter 13 - And Back Again

"Is anyone out there? I don't know what to do. My name is Jacob Smythe. They came and took my big sisters. They killed my parents and they damaged the doors so they won't open. I'm stuck in the basement and I'm scared. Can someone help? Am I using this right? I'm sorry; it's my dad's radio. I'm not supposed to play with it. But I'm scared and hungry. Can anyone hear me? Help?" ~Intercepted CB radio from somewhere in London.

Colors, sounds, tastes, textures, and even odors, all pulled and swirled through her mind. Not painful, they didn't exist long enough for her to identify any of them, but enough that her mind registered their existence, but couldn't process. She could feel her body moving, walking.

One step

Two steps

Three steps

But she couldn't feel any movement because everything swirled at her and rushed her senses, making her almost dizzy.

Then there was a calm clear space in front of her, something she could focus on. That gave her direction and she stepped towards it and found cool air in her face. The metal grate of the catwalk rang under her boots and a cacophony of voices echoed in her head.

~McKenna what the hell!~ Toni's voice hit her with Perc, JD, and Cass all expressing similar sentiments.

~Where were you? Your light went a funky color. Not the gray of distance, or the black of death, but a weird pulsing silver.~ Cass asked, her voice a bit calmer than everyone else's.

McKenna flinched a bit at the reminder of Caroline's death. A death she still hadn't told Christopher about.

~You are unharmed?~ Rarz's voice rolled through the mindspace and McKenna shuddered a bit. His voice was almost physically there; it felt like a variation of Wefor's.

~I'm fine. That was weird, but I'm fine.~

~It might be advantageous if were you were to wave to show that you are uninjured. Most down here can not speak to you via Speech.~

McKenna oriented herself to look down on the assembled people who were all waving arms and looking a bit excited. She waved at them and the swell of noise grew for a minute, then subsided.

~Would you like to come back via portal or another method?~

McKenna looked around. The catwalk she was on was very high up. With only a long ladder with access, one that had no safety cage. Heights didn't freak her out, but with her exhaustion, and that amount to go down, the ladder didn't seem the best option.

~Portal if you don't mind. Scared I might slip and go splat if I used the other option.~

~One moment.~ A second later a glowing silver swirl appeared beside her.

~I'll be down in a moment.~ With another deep breath she stepped in, a bit more ready this time. The colors and other sensations were still there, but even if she didn't try walk, she realized the peaceful section at the end of the tunnel came closer to her. With amusement she tried to walk backward, but it did no good; the end came to her just as quickly as if she had moved towards it.

Part of it pulled at her mind and she wanted to turn. It felt like she should know how to control, to create, to use it. Something tugged at her again and she tried to turn towards it, but the end kept coming at her no matter how she turned. She couldn't find what pulled at her from a direction that didn't exist.

Stepping out into reality didn't bring peace and quiet this time. Instead, she was buffeted by the sound of people yelling over each other, arguing, and excited jabbering, to the point that she ordered the nanobots to reduce her hearing sensitivity.

"We need to use this immediately. This will give us a chance to get to the ships and destroy them." An older man yelled and Burby sighed.

"Why do you think we're here? But we need to get organized and rescue as many as possible. If we don't make the effort and we live past this, the world would crucify us. Do you really want to start World War 3 with the Chinese after going through this? They maybe be seriously wounded but I have no doubt all their nukes still work, and they won't have anything to lose. We don't have much time, but rushing it will just make it worse."

McKenna sighed. She understood that they would be needed, but for the most part all someone had to do was point them in the right direction. Exhaustion pulled at her like weights around her body, urging her to sleep. That was becoming more important than food.

Philip walked over to her. "You okay? That portal thing didn't do anything to you? It's safe?"

She looked at him and suspected she looked like a drooling idiot. "No, the portal tunnel thing is fine. Why?"

"'Cause you look like death warmed over." He cast his eyes around her small group. "In fact you all look rougher than most the people here."

She shrugged, glancing at JD who just shrugged. He looked tired with circles under his eyes. Of all of them, Cass looked the best. Tired but not exhausted. She also hadn't shifted much, staying in human form.

"Too little sleep, too much stress, and not enough calories. This whole experience isn't easy on anyone." She shrugged. There were lots of people out on the front line. People were dying and worse, people who just wanted to live their quiet lives were being killed. How dare she complain when no one else was getting what she got: food, weapons, protection?

Damn, you're a selfish bitch, Largo.

The sharp self-castigation helped a bit. But exhaustion and a huge hunger for something other than food pulled at her.

"I get that. But none of you are combat trained to know how to deal with this. Besides, from everything that has been said, without you the mission will fail. That means you get the royal treatment." A new man had approached and his words pulled her out of her zone.

McKenna looked at the speaker. Hair buzzed down so tight she could see the dark brown skin under the dark hair. Sun and weather had added lines to his face but with his rich brown skin the color of melted chocolate, she didn't have any idea what his age was. Fit to Kaylid levels, muscles rippled along his body, but he was only her height at 5'7" and about half the mass of either JD or Perc.

"That means you think this is a go, Colonel Sextan?" Philip asked, an odd deference in his tone.

"I think we don't have any fucking choice, so yes it's a go." The man turned to look at all of them. "My name is Geoff Sextan and I'll be helping create the insertion teams.

We'll spend tomorrow morning practicing working together and getting used to your forms. But for now we need to plan, and assign personnel, and try to get people here. These are things you have no skills with and frankly, your input would cloud the matter. I need you rested, fed, and ready to go in the morning. My plan right now is to be attacking by the day after tomorrow. Hell, what's today? I lost track a week ago." His growl sounded frustrated.

"It doesn't matter. Go back to the Inn and get some sleep. If you aren't at the best you can be over the next two days, the planet dies. I'm not willing to accept that." Geoff made it an order, but it was one she wanted to obey.

She wanted to stiffen at that, both in outrage and to assure him she'd do her best no matter how tired she was. But he was right, and she didn't have the energy for outrage.

"I'll take care of it, Colonel," Philip assured him. The man gave all of them, even Rarz who had wandered over, a hard look then nodded once. He executed a militarily precise turn and strode off to intercept another group of people who were just as hard-looking as he.

"Who was that?" McKenna asked, feeling like a bull at full speed had just hit her. No goring, but her worldview felt off-kilter.

Philip took a deep breath and visibly shook himself. "That was Colonel Geoff Sextan, the only living holder of two Medals of Honor, a Ranger. He would have had this position if he'd ever accept a promotion, much less the position. The guy is a living legend like Audie Murphy."

McKenna had heard of Audie Murphy and watched the movie about him. If this Geoff Sextan matched him, he must be pretty impressive. She tracked his movement and noted the way people paid attention to him.

"I see. So what does that mean?"

Philip gave her a lopsided grin. "It means most of the people here will listen to him and go with his suggestions as if they were orders. I'm going to get you back to the hotel so you can be ready to hit the ground running tomorrow." He paused and looked at Rarz. "If you can handle it, we'll need you. Probably ask you to perform lots of portals and answer many questions as we try to work through the logistics of all of this. I hope you can handle another ten or twelve hours of this."

Rarz glanced at the rest of them then slowly shrugged and McKenna had to fight back a laugh.

He's watching our body language and trying to copy it. Smart dragon.

Even as the thought crossed her mind she flinched, then relaxed as no one commented. It got confusing with an AI living in you, people you could talk to via telepathy, and a dragon that apparently could barge in at any time. It made you paranoid about your own thoughts.

"That is acceptable. My species needs less sleep than yours. Our days are longer, and we have the ability to go longer without sleep. Staying awake another hundred of your hours will not be an imposition, though after that I may need to sleep for a significant period."

Everyone looked and at him and he did that slow shrug again. "I am not human, my needs are different."

"Yeah, speaking of which, do you have any needs? You've done a lot of shifting and from what I've learned of shifters they need fuel to replace the calories they burn doing that," Burby asked even as McKenna focused in, interested in the answer. The idea of not being chained to calories would be helpful.

"Food would be appreciated, but is not mandatory. It is apparent that while the small computers you have facilitate the change, they do not provide access to quantum space to store energy and mass in." Rarz paused, a frown touching

110

his face. "I am unsure why you can not do so. Technically you should have the ability; otherwise you would not change at all. But this is something all Drakyn know without teaching. It is part of us, so I am unsure how it would be taught."

Oh well. So much for that thought.

"Good to know. I figure we'll all need sustenance." Philip looked around and waved over a soldier, a sergeant McKenna thought. "Sergeant. Get these five back to the Inn, then get some coffee, sandwiches and fruit over to the conference center. This is going to be a long night, so make sure we're staffed."

"Yes, sir. This way please, sirs, ma'ams."

With efficiency that McKenna had figured out was a hallmark of the service, they found themselves back at the hotel. Walking into one of the group of rooms assigned to them, all with connecting doors, McKenna bleary-eyed, glanced at the clock.

Two in the morning. No wonder I'm exhausted.

Her bags were sitting on the floor and she dug through them, finding clean clothes, and headed to the shower. The long hot shower didn't solve her exhaustion, but it made her feel much more centered and less like a refugee. Tomorrow would come too soon and she felt everyone else doing the same thing. The kids were already fast asleep. She sank into the bed and let sleep wrap her in warm darkness.

~Kenna?~

Toni's voice drifted into her mind as the world turned fuzzy.

~Hmm?~ It was all she could manage to pull out as she listened to Toni.

~I know you're crashing. I am, too. But did you notice anything strange about Rarz? In his human form I mean.~

That caused her to rouse up a bit, breaking the surface of sleep to manage a coherent sentence.

~Like?~

There was a long pause, and sleep started to pull her back down, not that she fought it.

~When he stood out there naked, did you notice he didn't have any genitalia?~

The words weren't enough to bring her to full wakefulness, but they followed her down into sleep. She only replied with a ~Huh.~ before giving into her body's craving for rest.

Chapter 14 - Planning Stages

Attacks in Istanbul and most of that region have slowed as we approach day eight in the siege. Drone and satellite imagery show buildings in ruins, rubble everywhere, and armed figures prowling the streets. The region they attacked is well used to war and after the first day, the Iman for the area declared all humans to stay as human as any in shifter form will be killed on sight. Their response to the invasion has been brutal and there are few reports of any shifters being captured and returned to the ships. But there are more disturbing reports of shuttles landing outside of cities in Europe and lone Elentrin walking in, and leading people back out like the Pied Piper of old. The US government is advising all people to purchase nose filters and wear them at all times. ~TNN Invasion report.

Pounding on her door yanked McKenna up from odd dreams. Nothing from their mysterious compatriot, Ash, but her dreams had been full of weird images and thoughts that faded as she roused.

"Yeah?" Her voice cracked a bit.

I need to drink more water.

She sat up as the pounding started again.

"What?" She raised her voice this time and the person on the other side stopped pounding.

"Ma'am. We've been asked to get everyone up and over to the conference center. Food is waiting. They'd like you ASAP, ma'am." The voice was young and a bit nervous.

"Okay. I'll be out shortly." She didn't move though, weariness still clawing at her.

Coffee, food, water, all of it will help. But you won't get any of it if you don't get going.

~You guys get the same message? You up?~

An assortment of grunts and mumbled answers met her query. Though how you mumbled thoughts she had no idea.

Fifteen minutes later, hair in a ponytail, another shower, teeth brushed, with her spare shifting clothes on, McKenna pulled open the door to her room.

Even though they hadn't talked while she got ready, everyone else must have been moving about the same speed. JD and Cass emerged from one room while Toni stood there, Jamie holding her tight.

Oh, the kids are up.

McKenna changed her direction making a beeline for their room.

Jamie must have told them she was coming because before she reached the door, it had pulled open and Charley and Nam bolted out. Nam leapt at her, achieving a height with that jump that really shouldn't have been possible. McKenna caught her, pulling her tight to her chest even as Charley hugged her like a vise.

"You two okay? Everything good?"

Charley pulled back giving her a look that she had to fight not to laugh at. Wounded pride, contempt, and confusion all wrapped into one.

"Of course. We would have told you if anything was wrong. Or dealt with it ourselves," he muttered, the last part much more quietly.

"Charley, you tell us. People here will help. No more doing it by yourself. Promise me?" She tilted up his chin looking into his blue eyes. "I know adults have let you down. I promise we won't."

He nodded. "I promise. I know. Just, they're mine, you know?" His eyes darted to Nam then over to Jamie and Jessi. At some point she had wandered out and leaned against Toni, too.

"Yeah. I know." And she did. But she was an adult, Charley wasn't. Part of her wished the kids could take warrior form, but for now their animal forms and ability to flee would have to sustain everyone.

She hugged him one more time and nuzzled into Nam's neck. Even their presence made her feel like maybe she could do this. She had to do this; they and everyone else depended on her, so she would do it.

McKenna glanced at the others and they nodded. With one last tight squeeze for both kids, she set Nam down. A wave of love was sent to both of them, on a tight message this time so she didn't affect anyone else. They flushed and smiled at her and she left, hating it but needing to do it at the same time.

A young service woman waited for them in the lobby. Dressed in camos, McKenna glanced at her uniform, Air Force for this person. At this point there were too many people, too many shifting faces, she'd given up trying to track people or branches involved.

"This way please, everyone is waiting." She led them out and hustled them to the conference center.

McKenna had checked the clock as she left and it was only nine, which meant she'd had barely six hours of sleep. And the people they were going to see had been working all night. She'd focus on getting coffee and then figure out how she fit into all their plans.

The crowd from last night had thinned considerably. There were only about three people wandering around the open area where all the food and drinks were set up. Philip was one of them and he headed for her as she filled a cup with coffee.

"Good. We're ready to begin. We think we've got a valid plan worked out, along with a few backup plans in case that doesn't work out." He looked tired but energized in a way he hadn't been yesterday. Yesterday the shadow of defeat and hopelessness had shrouded him.

"You seem upbeat. That mean you think this will work?" McKenna asked, putting her lid on her coffee.

"I think so, assuming everything we know is true. There's a good chance, but an awful lot depends on the information buried in all your brains." He waved at all of them. The others had focused on food and McKenna realized she needed the same. No piles of cold cuts, but there was a decent amount of bacon and bagels, so she set to work making a couple sandwiches with cream cheese, bacon, and mustard.

"Good, then let's see how this is going to work." Coffee in one hand, and two sandwiches in the other, McKenna and the others followed him into one of the large conference rooms.

That this had been become a war room was obvious. Whiteboards had diagrams and notations all over them. Three boxes with a list of names took up one board, and from the half-erased marks you could tell it took a while to get those names aligned.

Philip waved at the tables occupied by five men, plus Burby, Rarz, and Christopher, who stood against a wall watching everything.

She recognized Colonel Geoff Sextan from the previous night. None of the others triggered a memory.

"Please take a seat, so we can explain our plans." Philip said, as most of them started to move towards the tables.

Now or never. You need to tell him.

Grabbing a paper towel from the roll that they had been using to wipe the boards, she set her two sandwiches down and walked over to Christopher.

"McKenna," he said, his voice low as he focused his attention away from Rarz to her.

"I haven't had a chance to tell you, and I'm sorry I didn't try harder to tell you before. Caroline was killed our first day out. One of their shots took her in the chest and she was just dead."

Christopher closed his eyes and he seemed to shrink just the smallest bit before he opened his eyes and locked onto hers. His blue eyes burned into her and McKenna wanted to look away, but she straightened and met his gaze.

"I figured. When she wasn't at the house and you didn't say anything, I guessed that was the answer. Her body was collected?"

"Yes. I made sure of it." She nodded, having made the call herself. Caroline had ID on her, so word would filter back as records were updated.

"Then I'll be notified eventually. I'm the executor of her will." He paused looking away, then back at McKenna. "It was fast?"

"Very. She didn't have a chance to even hurt. She helped a lot, but then we were so out of our depths. If she had lived, by now she'd be as deadly as the rest of us."

Hell if I know if that's the right thing to say. But it's the truth and I'll never forget looking at her, that hole in her chest.

"Thank you. Now go on." Christopher nodded at the tables and everyone carefully not watching them, except Rarz. He had focused on her and Christopher. "You have a world to save."

Those words didn't help make her feel better, or even like she was the person they should be depending on. But it did pull her attention back on what needed to be dealt with right now.

Giving him a sharp nod, she slid into the chair, guarding her bacon and bagel sandwiches. Picking one up, she gave herself a few seconds to put off the inevitable while she chewed on the bagel. The weight of everyone's gazes beat at her like waves against rocks. When the worst of her hunger had been assuaged, she gave in and set down the sandwich. Getting it over with would be better than keeping this up.

"I take it you have a plan?"

Most of the men smiled, or at least they drew back their lips baring their teeth.

"We have one, and we even got the dragon to agree it might work." That smile was definitely a challenge and to her surprise Rarz smiled back, showing teeth a bit whiter and sharper than a human's would be.

"It is a solid plan. Though humans are more vicious than I had realized. Apparently many of your things about peace were only fiction?" He half-tilted, half-shrugged when he said that.

"Oh, probably not. One of the things I've learned over the years, is most people will preach peace and understanding—until they're the one with their back against the wall. Then there are no holds barred. We have a saying on earth; never get between a mother bear and her child. That holds true for most parents. When it comes to protecting those we love, we'll do anything. Most of us have people we love. People we'd die to protect. So yes, we are a vicious and deadly race, and most people—when challenged—take pride in that." She smiled at him and her smile held little humor but a lot of teeth.

"Good. This plan will need that passion." He fell silent and leaned back, shifting his attention to Geoff.

Geoff rose and walked over to the whiteboard, tapping on the squares with lists of names written in them. "As it has been explained to us, the five, well six, of you will need to be the first through the portals to ensure any chance this has of success. As we can figure it, there are three separate missions. The problem is there are four ships and Rarz has said he can only support one tunnel at a time. We're going to hit them one by one, coming back here for refills as needed." He cleared his throat and continued. "We're targeting the ship that's had the most shuttles going towards it and the one we think contains the most Americans." There was a slight rumble in the room. "Listen, I get we want to rescue everyone, but I'll be damned if I leave our people for last. Remember, we still don't know if we'll get anyone out alive. If it works, we'll try for all of them."

That settled people down. McKenna took another large bite of her bagel, enjoying the crunch of bacon and the smooth cream cheese as she listened. At least with her mouth full she couldn't interrupt him.

"Mission one—set explosives to disable or destroy the vessel. We've decided to go with an option that will allow multiple variations. If we can capture the vessel, the rewards for us are staggering. Otherwise we'll destroy it. This group will also provide support and covering fire for the primary group which will be you." He locked eyes with McKenna.

McKenna nodded. Though she had little desire to meddle in politics, with what could be learned, the technology involved in that ship could give them the stars. But she wished it wasn't going to come at the price of so many human deaths.

"The second is to help with decanting the captured and slaved shifters. While we understand that Ms. Borden needs to operate the machinery, we're hoping she can show us how to do it. If what Rarz has said is accurate, there may be multiple chambers to control the containers."

"There are." Perc confirmed. "Per the schematics in my head there are at least ten different ones, and a few specialized sections. Each section only has access to its corresponding sections of storage tubes."

Geoff fixed him with a laser stare. "As soon as this debrief is done, I want you to go with Yeoman Kyle and recreate all the schematics you can. If you have a way to download it, I'll take anything."

Perc shook his head sadly, and Wefor didn't offer any options, so McKenna stayed quiet. Her head wasn't full of secrets others needed. Well, at least she didn't think so.

When no one else spoke up, Geoff continued.

"The third group will be escorting captured people out and getting them to the staging ground. We've taken over the M&T Bank stadium. Even as we speak people are getting it ready to receive wounded, incapacitated, and even hostile prisoners. We have a separate area for the hostiles. We're planning on keeping them sedated until we can undo the programming the nanobots have enforced."

Geoff turned his stare on Cass. "I'm told you will have the key to doing this?"

A squeak slipped out of her, and McKenna turned to look at her and saw the woman visibly still herself and straighten up.

"An hour ago I would have said no. But yes. I think I can, but it won't be fast and there are some supplies I'll need from the ship." She chewed on her lip for a minute then squared her shoulders. "I think the best plan would be if you had at least one shifter on the team involved in the decanting. I should be able to teach them how to go through the process, then we can leapfrog through all of them. We'll need to gather the supplies to short circuit the programming of the nanobots. Though until we have McKenna back and able to assist, keeping them asleep or even in stasis would be the best bet. But this is me guessing. I have no idea what I'll be able to do or what supplies will be available." Her confidence grew with every word and McKenna smirked a bit at the rapt attention JD paid her.

"Already done. There's a shifter assigned to your team, assuming we can get her here fast enough. She's a few states away at the moment." Geoff paused looking at McKenna. "Why do we need you here before we bring them out of stasis?"

McKenna felt like a deer in the headlights, mouth full as she shrugged.

Cass snorted. "Because there's a chance most of them won't speak English and at this time, she's the only person I know that will be able to speak Elentrin to them." ~Though we should be able to speak it soon? Right, Wefor?~

[Affirmative. But it will be slow and halting. McKenna may be best for that.]

McKenna relayed to the humans in the room what Wefor had said, even as she considered if the AI could replicate itself. Anything would be better than feeling the focal point for all their needs.

"Valid. I'll update orders with that information, but anything you can do to make all of this less impactful would be greatly appreciated."

Cass nodded and grabbed one of the many pads of paper littering the table and began to scribble notes. McKenna glanced, wondering what she was writing but Cass's scribble wasn't decipherable from this distance.

"Then if everyone is agreed?" Geoff looked around the room, but no one protested. "Good. McKenna, I want you and your teams to meet the people you'll be working with. For the next five hours you and the teams are going to be training and practicing. We're not expecting seamless merging, that would be something we would work towards over weeks of training. We have only five hours. I just want you to be able to move with them, understand the signals, and the roles each of you will play. Any questions?"

McKenna had a million, but none of them needed to be answered right now. She figured she'd either get the answers she needed, or in the end the questions wouldn't matter. With the bagel turning into something thick and heavy in her stomach, she shoved the last bite in her mouth and stood.

"Let's get going then."

Chapter 15 - Whirlwinds

Many military meetings are being held about how to combat the Elentrin invasion, but nothing has been given to the press on anything more concrete than 'shoot to kill' from our military leaders. While the abrupt firing of General Arnold Murphy caused ripples, in the wake of the invasion, most command has devolved down to the major or colonel level. All we can do is hope our armed forces, police, and neighbors shoot accurately and help protect all of us in this most trying of times. ~OpEd piece SacWasp.

A whirlwind of issuing clothes and weapons ensued. They had new, heavy canvas kilts for all the shifters, with a ton of pockets, most of them already full of various supplies. There were ration bars, ammo, first aid kits, knives, and more. When you added the belt securing the kilts, the entire thing added another ten pounds to them.

They were given a quick training with the new weapons they were assigned. The military decided that in their warrior form they should be strong enough that all of them could handle the heavier guns. They were issued a M240B, which fired 7.62 millimeter rounds. It was bigger than the AR 15, but with their strength in warrior form it didn't seem too unwieldy for any of them. Another two hours at an indoor range got them up to speed firing it.

Over the last week they'd gotten very good at adapting to weapons and even though these rifles, while they had a decent kick, they didn't have any issue stabilizing it. Cass chose not to change, keeping to a P90. Her shortness in warrior form made the gun too long to be comfortable. Besides, of all them, she was the least aggressive and had other duties.

Toni on the other hand took to it like a bear to honey. She carried the weapon with ease and hit headshots every time she pulled the trigger in their practice.

I wonder if she sees the people keeping her from her kids behind every target.

McKenna focused on keeping everything straight in her head, and not letting Wefor's grousing about the primitiveness of their weapons get to her. They might not have the fancy energy weapons the invaders did, but give them six months and they would. Besides, these shot farther.

Breaking for lunch, all of them tried to pack in calories for later, piling up huge plates. As soon as they had their food, they were pulled to various tables.

Perc was grabbed by two young earnest servicemen with a large tablet. They had him at a table with notebooks piled high. They pulled out the schematics of the ship and entered data as fast as he could pass along the information.

Cass had her notes and worked with another two people creating lists of what she needed. She made arrangements to move the drugs she grabbed out of the various parts of the ship to the staging areas.

Meanwhile Toni was being quizzed about how the systems on the ship worked, there were people taking notes as she talked in between bites of food.

JD and Rarz were over at another table talking with three hard-looking men. They all carried themselves the way Geoff Sextan did.

"McKenna, over here."

Turning, a plate of food in her hand, she narrowed in on Burby who waved at her from a table with Philip and Christopher at it. Though Christopher looked uncomfortable seated instead of standing against the wall.

She headed over and took a seat, glancing at the organized chaos around them.

"You think this is going to work?" She sat down and began to eat with focus, urging the bots to store the calories away as fat until she burned them in a bit.

Philip shrugged but Burby nodded. "It has a better chance than anything else. Believe me, I've been involved with a lot of the communications between other countries. Right now, only the arming of citizens and praying they live has had any success rate. At least this is at least a plan." He waved at the people around them. "You can tell they think it might work, because they aren't depressed. You can see there's a spark of hope. That tells me more than anything else."

Something tight in her unwound a bit. "Good." She ate another few bites, then looked up at Christopher.

"You mind if I ask you a question?"

"Feel free, but be aware I might not answer it." Christopher said, but he had a smile on his face.

"I thought the Secret Service only protected the president and vice, with only a few exceptions. How come you're hanging with Burby here?"

"Ah. Valid question. When all this started going down, the president declared him a national treasure and did an Executive Order assigning one agent to him at all times. I volunteered because I was closer to all that's going on, and it gives the president a non-political viewpoint of the current situation."

McKenna frowned but before she could follow up at how odd that sounded, Burby interjected.

"I approved it. Christopher is damn smart, and the president needs to know what's going on. Since Christopher doesn't really have any agenda, it gives the president a much more factual overview than he'd get from any of the political appointees."

"Besides, after Caroline changing I felt like I needed to do more than hide with the president." Christopher added, finishing his meal. Not sure I'm ever going to be able to go back to a normal life after this."

The way he said that made McKenna wonder if something had been there between him and Caroline, but she didn't ask; instead she focused on eating.

"Everyone, please finish up. We're on a short clock and need to get going. Largo, you and your people meet me in the entranceway." Geoff stood as he talked and various people around the room reacted to his actions, ending their conversations and starting to store gear away.

~Looks like it's showtime. You guys ready?~

~No. But we don't have time to waste, so I guess now is as good as ever,~ Cass said, her voice wry, and JD chuckled in the mindspace.

~I'm ready. I want to do something. I don't want to die, but damn these guys are hurting too many people,~ Perc said his voice resolute, it helped to steady McKenna.

The news had been full of stories of families ripped apart. Which was one of the reasons McKenna avoided the news of late. Each story layered guilt on her though she didn't know what else she could have done.

~Agreed, I'm tired of playing defense. I'm ready for some offense.~

McKenna snorted at Perc's comment. ~Miss the football field?~

~Well, yeah. People were only trying to knock me down on that, not kill me. But I agree. It's time to take the fight to them.~ A low growl filled the space vibrating in her mind. But mostly she agreed.

Finishing her last bite of food she bussed her dishes and headed over to where Geoff stood at the door talking with another earnest young servicewoman who trotted off as McKenna reached them.

"We're as ready as we're going to be." She glanced and saw the others approaching, JD munching on an apple as he walked over. Rarz followed, still seeming separated yet a part of their group, it bugged her on a visceral level.

"Good enough. Let's get you to the teams," Geoff stated as they walked out of the conference center and headed back towards the hangar where Rarz had done his little show and tell. It had been set up with cubicle walls everywhere and looked like a maze.

He must have called ahead because as they walked into the open hangar door, three groups of people stood there waiting for them with a small group of people all in black BDUs behind them. The people varied in age, though McKenna didn't really see anyone much older than their mid-forties, height, skin color, and from what little she knew, which service they belonged to.

Geoff didn't hesitate as he strode to the position at the front of the three groups. He stopped and waited until McKenna and her people had clustered loosely behind him.

"I'd like to introduce the groups, but there are too many people, so I'm introducing you to the commanders and their team names. If we all survive, you can get to know each other on a first name basis, but right now we don't have time, and no one is going to remember."

He pointed to the group on his right. A lean Hispanic man snapped to attention as he pointed. "This is Alpha group. They will go by Alpha One, etc. Their leader is Master Chief Miguel Zhen." The man nodded at all of them, sharp dark brown eyes tracing over each person in turn. "His group is mostly composed of SEAL personnel and will have two functions, to protect you and get each of you to where you need to be, and plant explosives at the best locations. All explosives will have a timer, but they can also be remotely detonated."

Miguel stepped forward and nodded to them. "We'll do some training runs to make sure we can work together." He nodded again and stepped back.

Geoff pointed to the next group, a woman headed it this time. McKenna scanned it and realized this was the only woman, or at least the only one she could see. She stood almost six feet tall, corded muscle that McKenna could tell she had earned the hard way, with blond-brown hair cut in a short-clipped style that only made her look more feminine. With brown eyes, skin a dark brown, and multiples cuts and energy burns on her arms, McKenna could tell she'd been out there fighting until lately.

"This is Sergeant Major Elaine Zimmer. She's our med expert and is the lead of team Bravo. They will be working with Ms. Borden to learn how to decant captured shifters as well as how to help keep them alive. She's a registered nurse, and her team is composed of Pararescue personnel. Trust me when I say they are very good at their job. Ms. Borden, the shifter was unable to get here. But trust me the Sergeant Major is one of the best. I'd rather have her working on me than most doctors I know." He said this last directly to Cass, whose eyes lit up.

The Sergeant Major nodded at them, but her eyes looked on Cass and then she gave another brief nod, and a hint of a smile at her lips.

Geoff turned to the last group. A tall man, with pale red hair and a sunburn still stood. He reminded her of those lanky fighters, looking laid back and almost bored until they moved, and you were decked before you realized it.

"This is Captain Sammie Willis. He's leading group Charlie." McKenna half flinched from the name, but Geoff didn't seem to notice. "His team will be responsible for helping Bravo and getting people in and out of the portal to the staging area here on Earth. Rarz, while we understand you need to go back and forth with the Alpha group as we move through the ship, Captain Willis will be in direct communication with you at all times via radio channels. You have assured us you can open and close the portals outside of your field of vision without issue, correct?"

Rarz frowned; his expression appeared stiff and somehow not quite right on his human face.

"True. Though I have never connected one without Speech between me and the being I am opening the portal for. And at least one end must be a place I have already been."

"Well, sorry, but I ain't much for fur, if you get what I mean." Sammie spoke in a soft drawl that sounded jarring after the non-accent of California and the nasal sound of the north.

"Surely that matters not?" Rarz paused and McKenna felt an odd tension in the air, pressure similar to going up in a plane, but all mental rather than physical.

"Odd. I had not realized. I had assumed we spoke in words so those not already a part of your mindspaces did not need to be invited. I did not realize that none but those inflicted with the nanobots had the ability." He sounded actively upset and McKenna saw Toni reach her hand out as if to touch him before she dropped it and took a half step away from the Drakyn.

"Then that will be something else to practice." Geoff's voice had no give to it.

"Yes, sir." Captain Willis saluted, and the lazy tone had disappeared.

"Then get to it, people. We don't have much time before this operation launches. You all know the importance of these civilians. Keep them alive, accomplish the mission, and just maybe your names will go down in the history books."

A snort of derision met his comments and McKenna got the feeling she was missing an inside joke. But the way they held themselves told her they were deadly and competent, and that was the only thing that mattered.

"Tick tock, time's a-wasting." Geoff's words came out as an order. He gazed at them once more before pivoting on the balls of his feet and striding out the door.

McKenna looked at the people all staring at her and wanted to protest. She barely knew what the plan was, much less what they should do now. To her relief Chief Miguel Zhen stepped up.

"Bravo, Charlie, grab Miss Borden and work with her for the next ten minutes. I want to get with the others and work out how to move as a team. We also need ear pieces for all of them."

Captain Willis turned and nodded to one of the men behind him. The man took off at a quick trot out of the room. "On it."

"Ms. Largo, sirs, if you will step over here with me while Ms. Borden works with Sergeant Zimmer." As he spoke Elaine Zimmer had pulled Cass to one side and her team had gathered round her. Cass had her notebook out and McKenna could hear the familiar tones of science talk bubbling out of the group.

JD cast a long glance in Cass's direction, and she saw his hands twitch, but he moved easily over to where Chief Zhen had indicated.

"I've been assured you know how to handle yourselves in a firefight and that you are decent shots. Normally I'd still make you prove it to me, but we don't have the time, so I'm taking it on faith. I don't like taking things on faith, so if you don't know what I'm talking about, don't know how to do something, or need something explained, fucking ask. I'd rather tell you something a dozen times than make the assumption you know and find out you don't. We don't have time to get seamless together, so we're going to do what we can." Zhen's voice was harsh with no humor or friendliness in it.

He waved towards a rack of weapons outside the odd cubicle farm. "This should match what you've tested out on. They're all loaded with blanks. We're going to practice moving through the ship we've built to roughly match the specs Mr. Alexander provided. I need you to trust my team and my team has to trust you." He smiled a dark smile that had no humor in it. "After all, we need to save the world."

"That we do. But please just call us by our first names. We don't have time to deal with this misses and mister crap. McKenna, JD, Perc, Toni, and Cass. You already know Rarz." McKenna said, pointing to each person in turn. The mister-miss stuff would drive all of them crazy if they kept it up.

He introduced the five people behind him, but then just shrugged. "Look, you don't have time to learn our names, and when it gets hectic you aren't going to remember. I'm Alpha 1. McKenna you're Alpha 2A, JD - Alpha 3A, Perc - 4A, Toni 5A. Rarz is Alpha 6. Cass will be Bravo 2A as most of the time the sarge will be watching out for her. Each one of my men will be paired up with one of you. Alpha 2B, 3B, etc. Just call for your assignment and change it to B. Got that?"

It made sense to McKenna if a bit inhuman overall, but no one protested, so she answered for them. "Makes sense."

"Good, then let's get going."

Chapter 16 - Practice

Most of the European union has declared a state of emergency. Even though the fashion of wearing earrings in ears has taken hold of Europe even more strongly than in the US, leaders are asking all shifters to not morph into any form. Please just stay human. Anyone killing a shifter while in non-human form will not be charged unless there is evidence of premeditated murder. Officials say they will not press charges against people for attacking anyone in the warrior form. ~ TNN Invasion News

Miguel grabbed them, assigned their weapons, and set up their order.

"This is how it works, I go first, Perc, Rarz, Alpha 2B, McKenna, Alpha 3B, Toni, then Alpha 4B, with JD and 5B bringing up the rear."

McKenna shrugged, it seemed valid. Even though Perc had done his best to get the schematics out for them to use, he was the only one that actually knew them, so he needed to be up front. Then there was Rarz. She still didn't know anything about him, other than he and Toni seemed to have an odd connection they were both avoiding.

The next hour they spent learning signals, and while not becoming a true team, they were at least getting better at moving together and probably wouldn't shoot each other.

The hardest part for McKenna, and she suspected for the other shifters, was learning to talk in a low whisper that the headsets would pick up and pipe into their ears. She kept slipping into their mindspeak, though the term Rarz used of Speech had gained a bit of traction.

The shifters all flowed into their warrior forms. Since they wouldn't be able to spend the time or calories when it was time to leave, getting into that form now and making sure they were comfortable with the vests and weapons had priority. They decided to have Rarz stay in human form though.

"I fear if I enter in my warrior form, as you call it, I would cause a panic and alarms to go off. While you may disturb them, there is a margin of confusion that you may be able to use to your advantage. "

"Point. How long does it take you to change if you need to do it fast?" Miguel asked and McKenna frowned at him, then realized he probably hadn't seen the show and tell earlier.

"Which form?" Rarz asked, focused on the man with a strange intensity.

"Um? What do you mean?" Chief Zhen seemed thrown off balance for a moment.

"Well there is this human form, which I am in now, my warrior form, which is similar to the ones you see McKenna and her clan in." He nodded at the four of them standing in their warrior forms, it had become second nature by this point. "Then there is my animal form I think you call it, and my wyrm form."

"His wyrm form won't fit in most of the ship without crushing us, walls, or himself." JD interjected, a wry note in his voice.

Miguel looked at all of them as if he expected there to be a joke, but no one laughed. He shook his head and looked back at Rarz. "Your warrior form as you call it. Without the wings. That I heard about."

Rarz tilted his head from side to side. "If I push it, about twenty of your seconds."

"Huh. Okay. I'll keep that in mind. Now let's get geared up. We need to make sure you have the tools you need." Zhen decided Rarz didn't need a weapon, keeping him near the front when Rarz assured him he was tougher than he looked and very fast.

It took a bit to get everything strapped to them. Apparently, these forms were different enough that it created fitting issues with some the equipment Miguel Zhen wanted them to wear. They hadn't worried about vests or much else when they were on the street. The energy rifles the Elentrin forces carried didn't slow down at bulletproof vests.

They practiced moving through the maze, clearing areas, and occasionally having people jump out at them, though she had no idea how Miguel had set that up. They got better and McKenna made herself remember to speak out loud in that low, almost sub-vocal voice. It reminded her of police training, so she and JD didn't have as much issue. Toni and Perc took a bit longer, but need got them going through it in good time.

"How are they doing?" Geoff asked as he walked up. They'd taken a break going through how to handle certain situations and McKenna reminded them they'd all need to wear nose filters to handle Elentrin pheromones.

Chief Zhen shrugged. "They'd fail my classes, but given the situation they're passable."

"Good. Because it's time to go and I don't need to tell you there aren't any other options."

Miguel rubbed the back of his neck as his eyes locked onto McKenna's. "Then let's hope they're the answer."

McKenna snorted, but no one did more than give her a sideways glance. Cass headed their direction as people started loading things into vehicles. Per her norm, she headed right to JD, but looked at all of them.

Allies

"You okay? I've been cloistered with Elaine Zimmer. Woman is scary smart. I think once I show her everything, she'll be fine picking it up. But I'm not horribly sorry I won't be in your main attack teams."

JD hugged her to him, her human form oddly frail compared to his furry bulk, even if he was shorter than normal.

"Neither am I." McKenna was glad her face in this form didn't show emotions as easily.

"If you're all done. We need to get you loaded up and to the launch point. Rarz, I'd like to talk to you please?" Geoff didn't quite sound diffident, but he did sound respectful in a way he wasn't to anyone else.

Huh, wonder what that means? Though it might just be that the blasted dragon creeps him out.

She didn't have time to wonder about much else as energy bars were handed to them, their blanks were exchanged out for live rounds, and their vests were filled with extra ammo and bars before they were ushered into the back of a covered truck. It was packed with supplies and other members from the Bravo and Charlie teams. Rarz didn't join them, nor did the leaders of the other teams, so she figured he'd be in a different vehicle.

The noise made normal speech impossible and she slipped back into Speech.

~Wefor, is there any way to just spread the ability to talk without changing someone?~ It was wistful thinking on her part, but she missed the speed and relative privacy.

[Not that the database has listed. It does not mean it is not possible.] Wefor's voice rattled in their shared mindspace.

~You know, I think there might be, but it's buried. Something I might be able to come up with based on the information that got loaded into my head.~ Before McKenna could get excited Cass continued. ~But it's research project level, not anything I can whip up in the next few hours. We're talking months to years to figure out how to reprogram and guide the nanobots to create the trans-harmonic frequencies and allow non-augmented minds to handle the interface without infecting them.~

McKenna started to ask what she meant about the augmented minds part, but decided she didn't want to know. One more bit of information to creep her out that she couldn't change and it didn't matter right now.

When did you become such a coward?

Her own thought had wry humor to it especially as she knew it was more information overload than anything else. She still had issues sometimes with the idea of how integrated Wefor was with her body, so finding out more was just too much.

~I guess we'll need to work on our radio etiquette then. Cass, what exactly did they have you doing?~

That was enough of a prompt and Cass started to bubble about everything, creating a warm stream of conversation that McKenna could enjoy and let the others interject as she just tried to not think about what was to come.

She had almost dozed off, a half-eaten bar in her hand, when the vehicle came to a jarring stop. It didn't feel like a smooth stop that a driver would have made if they reached their destination.

The window between the cab and the back slid open and words were shouted at them. "We have incoming. Two shuttles coming down and another following. Time to rock and roll people." It dawned on her that was Geoff's voice even as she grabbed her rifle and double checked the ammo and safety.

She jumped out of the back of the truck, and rolled across the pavement to the shelter of bushes on the side of the road as she assessed where they were. Cass, still in human form, clambered out and went under the truck. JD must have told her to do that. Toni, looking like a demi-god with her snarling white fangs against the coal black fur, used the truck for cover as McKenna focused on the shuttles.

~Why are they~ McKenna broke off the thought and talked through the coms they all had. "Why are they focusing on us?"

Silence met that question until Rarz replied. "The odds are the concentration of shifters here, or maybe they have discovered my presence. I do not know everything about their technology. It is possible they have realized a Drakyn is on this planet. They would do anything to kill me. They are quite unreasonable about our existence."

McKenna glanced over to where Rarz had appeared from one of the transport vehicles following them. He stood in the open, watching the shuttles come down.

"Rarz, get down, idiot. They'll shoot you." Miguel barked out over the headsets.

"They have no weapons on the shuttles. Only devices they need to assemble and what they use when they attack."

He made a strange figure, standing there in human form, watching the approaching shuttles with no expression on his face.

~He looks like a blasted movie poster. Idiot.~ Toni's thought was scathing and Rarz turned to look at her, a funny look on his face.

~I apologize if I seem melodramatic. They have always already been on the ground when I have made it to their invasion points. I can see the attraction in their lines, but it seems odd to me to fly under the power of a machine.~

Even as he finished that thought, the shuttles landed and the silver doors began to flow into the ramp specification.

Rarz moved, so fast even McKenna had to blink as he appeared behind the truck they had come.

"Fire as needed. Remember those shuttles can leave without a pilot, so don't get in them." Zhen's voice snapped out over the coms and McKenna winced. The same reaction from the others filtered into the mindspace. She ordered her bots to lower her hearing sensitivity a bit.

After that she focused on the ship about thirty yards from her, its hatch facing her as the back wall melted and started to reform into a ramp.

The moment the opening was large enough, five figures dove through it, hitting the ground in a controlled roll. McKenna had to admire their smooth skill. They almost moved in unison, but instead she focused on sighting in on the first creature.

One of the large lizard-like beings with the smooth leathery skin rose up from a crouch. Its tail seemed less strange now, but it came across as more dinosaur and less dragon after Rarz. The M240B was a bit heavier than her AR-15 and even after the practice there was a difference between targets and firing at sentient beings.

Her focus narrowed down to the skull of the being and she squeezed the trigger gently. She'd braced correctly, so the kick of the weapon didn't faze her, but the shriek of pain and annoyance as a bright line of blue- red blood welled along the side of the creature's skull told her she had missed. It turned and fired. She had to roll to not be hit by the beam of the weapon.

"Fuck, their range has increased. He just hit where I was at over thirty yards. Be aware guys." She snapped out over the coms and in the mindspace. Before at a distance of twenty-five yards, the energy would dissipate, at worst leaving you with a bad burn. From the smoking ground where she had just been, it would have cut right through her.

The spurt of adrenaline narrowed her focus and even as the creature tracked her movement, she pulled the trigger and saw the head explode.

Once there would have been sorrow or maybe a sense of relief, now she didn't feel anything but weariness and a desire to have this all be over. She heard others yelling, and the sharp retort of weapons fire around her, but all the lights in her mind were bright, and that was all that mattered at this point.

Crawling out a bit to get a better view, she scanned the area. One of the advantages of warrior form was the pattern of your fur let you blend with your surroundings, and the Kaylid didn't usually wear too much armor. She'd been so focused on the lizard she'd lost track of the others and it took her a moment to find one.

Almost a moment too long.

Chapter 17 - New Toys

Europe, China, the Middle East, Britain, Brazil, and Mexico have all seen a huge upswing in shuttles descending to capture shifters. While the resistance in the US is well organized, other countries are not faring as well and the world lives in a state of fear never seen before. Even the cold war didn't shut down schools and churches. Wariness and avoiding public places has become the norm. Will Earth recover from this attack? ~ TNN Invasion News

[ROLL!] Wefor screamed in her mind, and McKenna just moved, not even asking which direction, though there was only one way to head. She whipped her body over and over, holding the rifle tight to her. Heat seared the fur on her arm and leg, and she landed in a prone position aiming in the direction the bolt had come from. She had a sense of fur and movement, and she fired, knowing none of her people would be shooting at her, and not with that weapon.

McKenna fired a quick burst of three shots at the figure behind the edge of a second shuttle she hadn't been actively focused on.

Her bullets slammed into the chest of the being firing at her and it crumpled into a splash of dark limbs on the asphalt.

The surrounding sounds died, and all she could hear was her own rapid breathing. Too aware of their hearing capabilities, she stuck to Speech.

~Everyone okay? Anyone hurt?~

~Mom?~ Jessi's voice followed on top of hers, and McKenna wondered how much she had gotten of the sudden violent firefight.

~Yes?~ Toni sounded calm but McKenna looked around for more danger. She'd never forgive herself if anything happened to any of them.

~Is everything okay? Your lights turned a weird color.~ McKenna could sense, more than hear, Jamie, Charley, and Nam listening very carefully.

~We're fine, Jess. Just a bit busy at the moment. I love you very much, but right now don't bug us. It might distract us at the wrong moment.~

~Okay, Mom.~ There was a wave that hit the mindspace and McKenna was glad she was lying down. She saw Toni stagger at the edge of the truck. It was love, worry, stress, need, and trust from all four kids at once. McKenna didn't know if she wanted to cry or laugh. She swallowed and continued to look for any other invaders.

Two more lay crumbled on the sidewalk, and Miguel stood up from a planter he'd been crouched behind.

"Sound off!"

McKenna struggled to remember her code. "Alpha 2A, here." The proper radio etiquette had also been drilled into her head, so she knew at least she had responded correctly.

They all sounded off. A pall settled as one Bravo person and a Charlie didn't respond. McKenna rose and walked around the truck, looking at the three shuttles. She counted thirteen bodies.

"I see thirteen dead, five came out of the shuttle I was watching. Are we missing two?" She kept her voice low and wished she could crank up her hearing sensitivity without having the coms blast her out. Turning slowly, she panned the area, trying to listen and think.

"Only four came out of the one near me," said a voice she didn't recognize, but a wash of a recognition from Cass told her it was probably a Charlie team member.

"There were five on this one far to the right," JD offered and McKenna did her weird mental grid check to make sure they weren't talking about the same shuttle. They weren't.

"We're missing one." Her voice dropped even lower as she said that, and she pivoted in a slow circle.

~Wefor can they raise the sensitivity on my left ear but not my right?~ She asked as she fought to see or find this last threat.

[Of course, would you not think they could?]

McKenna sighed and tried to tell them to increase only her left ear not her right. A moment later sound increased and she listened, feeling slightly lopsided at the difference in sound. She closed her eyes and concentrated. Even as she did, she could hear others talking, whispering in the distance, yet they were as clear as if they were next to her.

If this keeps up for too long, we need to get a way to do this via the Speech, because even with coms I can hear them clearly.

~Get everyone to shush, we're making too much noise.~ She said it in the general mindspace and heard the sounds fall away slowly, though people still moved and breathed and they all seemed impossibility loud.

She kept pivoting even as everyone went silent, but she couldn't tell. The sounds of an Elentrin Kaylid versus a human Kaylid weren't obviously different.

What else? Think!

Her eyes widened and she had the nanobots pull her ear back to normal and she inhaled, sorting through the scents. Her friends whispered across her mind, comforting and familiar. Even the men she'd been training with for the last few hours came in as friend. But a strange scent drifted across the breeze, somehow stale, with weird smells she couldn't place.

~JD?~ She kept the connection as tight as she could, still not sure how Rarz had stepped into their mindspace.

~Yes?~ He came back almost instantly on that same tight connection.

~Where're you located? In reference to me?~ The three convoy vehicles had stopped in the road when the shuttles landed in the intersection. She gazed out at the four-lane road, with two lanes in each direction, the last truck had stopped at an angle, blocking the road. The shuttles formed a half arc, one of them partially on the sidewalk, with their ramps all facing the halted convoy trucks.

She had ended up next to a line of bushes, on the side of the road that had a commercial for sale sign on it.

~Behind the second truck, passenger side.~

She turned and focused and there she could make him out. He would have the breeze directly hitting him where he was.

~Use your nose. Crank it up. Can you smell that strange smell? I think it's part ozone, part things I've never smelled before. Can you locate it?~

She felt his concentration via the link and didn't say anything, giving him the space to focus. Their noses had been useful, but with all the invasions and everything else, she'd fallen back into the habit of only relying on eyes and ears.

~Got it. Yes, that's a weird smell. Best I can figure, it's laying under the ramp closer to Perc than either of us.~ He put this into the mindspace and she could feel Perc follow what they said.

~I see him. Going.~

Before McKenna could say anything, the spotted form of Perc dashed out from where he'd been and tore towards the shuttle JD had mentioned.

MEL TODD

Before with everyone shooting, she hadn't had time to get scared or even think about anything else other than trying to not die right at that moment. Now? Her heart raced and she felt her breath catch in her throat as she watched him run towards an enemy that had proven themselves all too willing to kill.

Movement from the shadows and a bolt of visible light exploded lighting up the darkness, streaking towards Perc.

He dove, but not fast enough and the scent of burnt fur and flesh assaulted her nostrils.

The image of Caroline's corpse flashing in mind again. They'd had a few die in the days of fighting, but none of her people or the soldiers they worked with. Bullets didn't create scorched flesh.

Before she could even cry out mentally, a rapid staccato of bullets chattered out of where Perc had fallen. A few created a resounding ting as they hit metal, but the majority of them made a wet thud. She heard a short cry, then silence.

~Are you okay?~

"What the hell was that, Alexander?" Miguel all but shouted into the coms and McKenna flinched, telling the bots to lower her hearing ability in the right ear another few decibels.

"Getting the last of the attackers. And damn that hurts." His voice sounded tight and McKenna moved towards him, seeing Cass out of the corner of her eye headed that way also. Perc stood and she saw a bright red gash, with at least an inch of flesh missing, between his neck and shoulder.

"You realize if that had been even half an inch closer to your neck, or you were a bit less overly muscled, you'd be dying right now." Cass's voice had a sharpness to it that McKenna totally understood. She wanted to rage at him. but that would be counterproductive. And she refused to address her own terror at the idea of losing him.

144

"Yeah." He glanced down to look at where she pulled the wound open and checked that it was mostly clean. The nice thing about their weapon was it burned through, not leaving much in the wounds. "I've already got the bots working on it. I'll need some calories, and maybe one shift and it should be good enough."

Miguel came storming up to them, his brows furrowed and cheeks flushed to almost red, impressive on his olive yellow skin.

"What in the hell did you think you were doing? That kind of stupid heroics gets people killed!" He didn't shout, not quite, but his tone cut and McKenna didn't know whether to jump in and protect Perc, or let Miguel chew him out like she so badly wanted to.

The idiot, he could have gotten killed.

The thought made her throat tighten and her chest seize with pain. Perc glanced at Miguel, the blood leaking sluggishly from his wound. That meant the bots had already gotten to work or it would be bleeding a lot more. That helped relieve some of the fear that still raced through her system.

"I was thinking that I knew where he was, had a chance of moving faster than he could, and that I was the most disposable as you've gotten the basic schematics of the ship. Besides, we can't afford to be delayed here anymore than what we've already been." Perc glanced at the hole in his shoulder. "Besides, I can heal, your people can't."

Miguel glared at him, but Perc didn't flinch until something in Miguel gave and he sagged a bit. "Fine. Everyone back in the vehicles, we need to step on it. If they know Rarz is here, we need to get you on those ships ASAP." He turned and looked like he was about to start shouting orders as most of the people had gathered around, watching the show.

"I was thinking," Toni said slowly, looking at the dead body lying on the ground.

Everyone paused and looked at her. She'd been so quiet of late that any words meant you stopped and listened.

"Everyone talks about how bad it is to fire a gun in an airplane. I can't help but think that firing one in a spaceship isn't any more intelligent. But those," she nodded at the gun laying on the ground, "we know we can use. If what Charley told us was correct, they can be set to stun, not kill. Besides, aren't we supposed to be rescuing these people? Not killing them because they've been enslaved?"

Miguel moved over to look at the gun, and then his eyes scanned to the rest of the fallen aliens and the weapons lying next to them. "It isn't a bad idea. But can you configure them so anyone can use them? We'd still take our weapons with us but using these first would be much quieter and give us less dead bodies. You sure you can modify them to not kill?" He directed the question to Toni, but McKenna took the lead.

~Charley? Can you tell us how to modify the weapons to stun only? Maybe even disable the ability to kill?~ McKenna asked even as Miguel looked at her waiting.

A few heartbeats of time before he responded, almost as if he had to find the information in his mind. ~Yes. Though it will take you a bit on each one. But I can show you how to alter them.~

She looked at Miguel. "The answer is yes, we can modify them."

He looked at her, with narrowed eyes, then at the weapons. "Do it. Everyone collect the weapons and anything on the bodies that looks like it might be associated with the weapons." He moved his attention back to her. "Update them, make my people and yours watch, so we all know how to do it. And I'll want to test fire one first to make sure we aren't killing people."

McKenna felt her heart stutter at that thought, who would they possibly test it on.

"Got it."

"Then get going people, we need to get this show on the road, the clock is ticking down faster than we can afford." Everyone jumped to it, and in five minutes McKenna found herself back in the troop transport with people watching her and looking at the pile of weapons on the floor.

With a jerk, the vehicle started to move and McKenna braced herself near the cab to be able to work.

~Okay, Charley, now what?~

~It would be easier if I could see what you are seeing.~ He muttered in her head and she felt a weird pressure like a bubble in her mind. Something slipped into place and her brain felt funny for a split second. ~Oh that's helpful. Jess, you were right, I can do it with Kenna.~

~Told you.~ The smugness from the little girl came through just fine and McKenna had to fight back a smirk.

~So you can see what I'm seeing?~ It felt odd, but at the same time didn't feel like anything at all. At some point she'd have to follow up on it, but now she didn't have time.

One more thing to ignore until I can't anymore.

This avoidance of hers was starting to cause issues, but she didn't know how to deal with all the things that kept coming up, so she pushed everything she could to the background until she had to deal with it. Lately though that was biting her in the ass, not that she knew what difference it would have made in the long run.

~Yes. Now pick up the one nearest to you, and turn it over.~ Charley walked her through it slowly, where the settings were, and how to swap out the energy packs. People asked questions as they rode and slowly, the others in the back with her started making the same updates to the weapons they had picked up. There were multiple people working changing the settings. It was slow, delicate work, though the tools most of the soldiers had with them helped. A quiet camaraderie spread through the back as the truck roared to their destination.

~Your people are like what we saw in your records. There were multiple arguments that they were all fiction, stories told to make you feel better in the dark times.~ Rarz sounded thoughtful even as his own flexible fingers worked on a weapon.

McKenna closed her eyes and tried not to laugh. ~They probably were movies, but we have our own heroes. And most heroes tend to be based on someone. Audie Murphy, Alvin York, Paul Revere, heck Lewis and Clark. We aren't perfect, but there are an awful lot of people who will risk their lives to save others. We get reminded of that every time there's a natural disaster and they show the people who risk their own lives to save others. Are all of us willing? No. Are some of us? Absolutely.~

~You are a weird and wonderful species. I hope we survive this so I have the opportunity to learn more about your people.~

~I think we all hope that. We have families to go home to.~ With that, McKenna sent a ping of love and worry to the kids, all of them. She almost cried as they responded back fourfold with their own love. From Toni and JD's reactions, the only two she could see, they sent it to everyone. Charley had dropped out of her eyes when it was obvious she had it down on how to alter the weapons, or at least they hoped they had it. They wouldn't know if it worked, or if they were still as dangerous as ever until they tested them.

But whom are we going to shoot at?

Chapter 18 - Suck it Up

Word has leaked out of DC about a secret mission from DC. No details, but what has been gleaned sounds like a plot from a bad World War II movie. There are rumors of a way to sneak onto one of the ships and try to rescue some of the captured shifters. No one can say how they will get on, or how they will get back, much less with as many people as have been captured, but we can only hope this, like most Hollywood endings, is a happy one. ~TNN Invasion news

The truck slowed to a stop and the engine shut off. This time she figured it was planned as she heard people talking. Stretching a bit, her muscles and body just ached from being bent over and on the floor. The nanobots weren't worried about her low-level pain at this point, or so Wefor had informed her. They were still trying to repair and build up muscle and fat stores. The lactic acid in her muscles wasn't important right now.

Seriously, I've got this wondrous thing in my body and I still get stiff and sore. Oh well, can't say I'm missing my period at all.

Stepping down out of the back of the truck, she almost fell as it registered what was going on around her. The truck had stopped at one edge of a huge stadium, the seats stretching up into the sky. All around her tents were set up, military personnel were running around, and piles of supplies were on pallets.

"You going to just stand there?" JD asked, a wry tone to his voice.

"Oh, yeah, but look," McKenna said, moving out of the way and looking around at the organized chaos.

"Wow. When those guys decide to do something, they don't take it by half measures do they?" JD gave a low whistle as they looked at the staging area for their attempted rescue.

"What good would that do? This is a last-ditch effort to save our world." Geoff walked up with Burby and Roberts beside him. "If it doesn't work, the other plans we have in place may not be enough to save any of the human race."

"Plans like?"

McKenna was glad Cass had asked, she didn't know if she could have asked and not sounded bitter.

"You aren't cleared to know, and if you don't succeed, it won't matter. We'll all be dead anyhow." Burby replied, his voice grim, but not mean. "So what's with all the alien weapons?"

McKenna explained even as Miguel and the rest of the Bravo and Charlie groups surrounded her.

"You ready to test it?" Miguel asked, a bit of challenge in his voice.

"We sure are," JD replied, his voice easy. If he'd been from the South, McKenna knew he would have drawled that, just to rile people up. Miguel had managed to get under his skin.

"Good." Miguel stared right back, even though JD was in warrior form and the furry face full of sharp teeth made most people nervous.

"Cass, you ready?" JD asked instead of responding to Miguel.

McKenna blinked. Cass hadn't been one of the people in the transport with her.

Huh, she and JD must have been talking as we worked. I'll keep my mouth shut and let them take this.

That took more restraint than she had anticipated. She wanted to protest and say no, shoot me, but she stood and watched, claws sliding in and out of her hands.

Cass looked around and shrugged. "Against the truck side. The canvas should show any scorch marks."

JD's massive shoulders lifted in something approaching a shrug as he walked over. Everyone else cleared out, though they were drawing attention from multiple people and the chatter around them started to fade.

JD stood, his arms crossed, making furry biceps bulge. While facial expressions were very difficult to read in the half-animal, half-human configuration, he didn't seem worried at all.

I think his fur is shorter in warrior form than it is in animal form.

The idle thought flickered through her mind as she tried to not panic. Images of Caroline flashed through her mind and she couldn't push them away.

Cass lifted the weapon, looking all too comfortable with it. They weighed a bit more than the AR-15 did but less than the M240B they'd been training with. Cass aimed away from JD at the side of the truck, the olive green canvas rippling in the breeze.

While out in the field, most of them had lowered the sensitivity of their hearing to deal with the noise of their guns. Which meant the subtle noises the alien weapons made weren't anything she had noticed.

This time she paid attention. The strange weapon, well, not so strange anymore as Charley had explained everything. He knew so much about them, even if he'd never held one in reality. It made an odd buzz-whine sound. Like a bug zapper but at a different range. She didn't know how to explain it, but knew she'd recognize it always from now on.

151

Light burst from the gun, but rather than the long stream of red she expected, a flash of pale red appeared, and then the canvas wobbled.

JD turned to look at it. "Looks intact, no smoke or scorching."

They had all seen bolts miss, and they always damaged what it hit.

"Okay be aware these are not precision weapons, so I'm going to aim near him." Cass said the words in a calm tone, but as she was still in her human form McKenna could see how stiff she was.

The inclination to check on Cass and make sure she was okay nibbled at her heart, but McKenna didn't want to distract her, so she stood there projecting confidence and unconcern.

Maybe the rest of them will believe my act.

Cass took a slow breath and aimed the weapon at JD. From her vantage point it looked like she pointed it directly at him. With effort, McKenna kept her breathing at a slow steady rate. She could feel Miguel, Geoff, and the others watching her. Luckily this form kept her emotions much more opaque.

She did glance at Rarz and he simply looked interested, no obvious reaction on his face.

Before she could stress anymore, Cass pulled the trigger. Again the flash of light and JD flinched.

"Did it hurt, did it stun?" The words tumbled from Cass fast, garbled even as she started to move towards him, her already pale face going almost white.

"It's fine, my arm just went dead. It's like it fell asleep." He rubbed it and frowned. "I can't even lift it. I know it's there, but I can't get it to respond to any of my commands."

"Not bad, but I want to see what happens." Miguel sighed. "But I don't have the time to wait to get you to wake up if it does work. And if it kills you, I really can't afford that." He turned and spoke to the assembled crowd. "Who wants to volunteer? Can't guarantee you won't die." There was a rippled of unsure laughter, but McKenna knew he wasn't joking.

She shot a look at Cass who shrugged. ~So you don't know?~

~How the hell would I know? You altered them.~ Cass said back in a frantic tone.

"Sure, Chief. This count as a KIA if I die? And get the pay-out?" A young voice came out of the crowd. McKenna spun trying to trace who was talking.

"Yes." Miguel replied his voice flat, unmoving.

"Geoff!" McKenna hissed.

Geoff turned to look at her, his face flat. "We need to know. Thousands are dying every day. If we lose one, we at least know."

She growled but didn't know what to say.

Should I say let's sacrifice a pet? A cow? A sheep? I don't know what the right option is.

"I'll do it." A young woman stepped out of the crowd. Her jaw locked and face a mask. "Most everyone I loved has already been killed. My sister's a shifter. So yeah. You can test it on me. My mom could use the money if I die."

The level of bitterness made McKenna flinch.

~Wefor, did I do it right? Will she die?~ Her thought held over tones of frantic worry and everyone could hear it.

[All the information provided indicates the odds of dying from a single direct hit are less than five percent, assuming basic deviations.]

~So, doubtful she will die.~

[Affirmative.]

The young woman walked forward and took a stance next to JD, a smirk on her face that held no humor and all bravado. "Fire away."

~I don't like this,~ Toni muttered the words, but no one moved to stop it.

Cass didn't say anything as JD slowly moved out of the way. Her hands shook as she lifted the weapon and pointed it at the young woman.

~This will devastate her if something goes wrong.~ The thought came from JD, tight on a personal channel with stress and worry wrapped around every word.

McKenna wanted to reach out to him, squeeze his hand, but he was too far away, and people would notice. Instead she hit him with reassurance and held her breath.

The flash of light and the girl crumpled to the ground. Cass had dropped the weapon and was sprinting to her before the woman's hair quit moving. A few others in uniform were right behind her.

McKenna stayed back no matter how much she wanted to go up there. Right now she'd only be in the way.

"Dammit, I should have thought about this." Geoff growled as he hit his phone and barked into it. "I need medics here, ASAP."

~She's alive~ the words were rushed out in the mindspace and McKenna felt her knees wobble.

Oh good. I really didn't want to have gotten someone killed.

The rush of relief that filled the mindspace didn't help with staying upright and she didn't know whom it came from, if not everyone.

Chaos reigned for a while as people checked over the woman. McKenna never did catch her name. Miguel shrugged it off, though from the pinched look on his face something else was bugging him.

"We don't have time for this. Head over here and we'll go over the last bits."

He guided all of them, Alpha, Bravo, and Charlie groups to a clear area surrounded by tents, food areas, and people frantically stacking crates.

"I wish this damn stadium had a dome that would close," Miguel muttered as he looked up at the open sky. "Oh, well. Make do with what you have I guess." He didn't seem to be talking to any of them, so McKenna didn't comment. He turned and looked them all over. McKenna tried to imagine what he saw; they must have looked like a motley group.

JD and Perc were in their hulking forms, dark brown fur and beige with dark brown spots. Toni was in her elegant black, the green of her eyes and whiteness of her whiskers creating a stark contrast against her pelt. Herself, with her wheat colored fur and average build for a Kaylid, was the most unremarkable of them all. Cass leaning against JD, still pale, but with a stubborn look on her face, made up their group. Everyone else looked professional, ready, and some-how better suited.

Rarz stood off to the side, watching all of them with a look on his face she couldn't interpret.

"I can't believe I agreed to this. You're not the group that should be doing this." Miguel spun to face Geoff, the Bravo and Charlie Company leads near him. "There has to be an-other way. I can't take these cowboys into a combat situation. They're going to get everyone killed and maybe the planet. They don't belong here."

McKenna blinked and a wordless snarl filled the mind-space. She didn't know if it came from her or the others.

Deep breath, losing your temper won't help.

"Too bad. You're stuck with them. They're what you have to work with so suck it up and deal." Geoff fired back, not even looking at them.

McKenna sensed some of the military personnel starting to edge away, as if trying to distance themselves from being associated with the shifters.

"Hell, we don't even let women do combat as a regular thing and you want me to take two pussies into a combat situation and expect them to kill aliens? At the first sign of something going wrong, they'll freak and get all my people killed."

That pussy comment was the last straw for McKenna. She'd done everything possible to try and do the right thing. Figuring out how to even tell people about aliens had been hard. Becoming a warrior and dealing with an AI in her head was something that still freaked her out. But not once in all of this, the kidnappings, the AI, the aliens, the dragons, the fucking spaceships, had she had a meltdown, lost it, or done anything except everything she could.

Chapter 19 - Confrontations

While the US has their garbage trucks picking up bodies, other countries have different options, such as carts in Russia, or funeral homes picking them up in Britain. But what is disturbing are the images of China. They are ignoring the dead, and most of them seem to be human. What satellite images there are show people in the streets weeping, pictures of the Elentrin, and dead Chinese. While we can only guess why they were killed, the foundation that is being laid for disease in China is terrifying. Will we survive this invasion, only to die from plague? ~TNN Invasion Report

"Who the hell do you think you are?" She snarled out the words, twisting them, and making them raspy as her anger overrode the control of her tongue in this form.

The two men stiffened and looked at her, their eyes widening as she stalked toward them. Her tail slashed the air back and forth as she got up in their faces.

"Who are you to judge me and mine? You have no idea what we've been through or done. Do you have any idea what it's like to have an intelligent computer living in your head telling you that your world is about to be destroyed if you don't stop it?" Her claws slid out, long, sharp, and she ached to show them exactly she could do. "Trying to figure out how to get someone with power to listen to you? To not get locked up as a crazy when you try to tell them aliens are coming? Can you imagine having your loved ones held as hostage if you don't kill people? Or learning you can turn into a monster that lurks in the shadows of our mythology? Then realizing you can't do anything and stepping back, trying to hope that the information you passed on was enough, and that maybe your world won't be destroyed?" Her voice vibrated with rage and she could feel all her fur standing on end. The people around her had paled and more than one hand started to drift to their weapons.

McKenna didn't care. She had tried to do the right thing at every turn and this was how they thought of her?

"To then find out you need to be in the middle again? That killing people, aliens, seeing friends die, knowing you can't change anything, only to find out you're the bloody chosen one? A chosen one who can only watch her friends put themselves in danger? A chosen one who if she fails in what some fucking stranger told her to do will be the reason her entire world dies? Who the hell do you think you are to judge me?!"

Rage had her seeing red literally, and both men looked at her, their faces pale, eyes wide and she wanted them to run. Run so she could chase them and tear them to pieces. Attack her, so she could slash and rend and show them what she could do in this is form.

[McKenna.] Wefor's voice came through, unexpectedly gentle.

"What?" She snarled the word out loud, unable to try to speak in the mindspace.

[You need them. They are rude and uncultured. But killing them will start a chain of events that will not end well for your world. You are needed. They are needed.]

~You are valued. We trust you.~ Cass said the words, even as she laid a hand on McKenna's arm, stepping in between her and the two men.

McKenna turned her head to look at Cass and realized a lot of people had their weapons drawn and aimed at her.

"He's an ass. But we have a job to do. One only we can do." Cass kept her voice soft and calming and McKenna pushed back her anger, taking a long deep breath through her nose. Anger, fear, embarrassment, and panic warred with each other as she tried to stitch her soul back together.

If we survive this, I need a long week in a cabin, just us. No strangers, just us being animals and humans as we want.

Both men had straightened, their faces now flushed where they had been pale.

"Ms. Largo," Geoff started, "I must apologize. This behavior was unacceptable and beneath us." He glared around at the personnel with raised weapons. "Put those down immediately. Ms. Largo had every right to be upset at us, and we deserved the chastisement."

Even to her ears that admission sounded bitter. She just glared out at him from the side of her eyes, still trying to get her temper under control. The admission didn't really change anything.

"No. This is my fault." Miguel said, rubbing his face, eyes closed. "McKenna Largo, I apologize. I have no excuse for what I said, much less how crudely I stated it. You haven't done anything wrong. You and your people have adapted to everything we have asked." He shrugged and McKenna was abruptly tired of all of it.

She cut off whatever he might have said next. "Whatever. It's done. We know the weapons work and should be more of a surprise than our guns. What now?"

Her people had moved around her in an almost protective manner, but mostly they were there to support her.

Miguel took another deep breath and when his eyes opened, he was all business. McKenna realized she didn't care if she hurt feelings or anything else. At this point she wanted it over with. Wanted to save the day, to go home to Charley and Nam, to see her friends around her laughing. She'd give her own life for that.

"The one thing we haven't done, and I'd like to have us go through a few times, is traveling by portal. I don't want the first time for us to be walking into a dangerous situation." He cleared his throat and his gaze fastened on Rarz, who stood right behind McKenna.

She hadn't realized he was there, but oddly both JD and Perc flanked her, while Cass stood on JD's left and Toni on Perc's right. Leaving Rarz behind her, guarding her back.

Odd. They didn't consider Rarz a threat, or they think the military is more of one.

That felt unsettling and she pushed it away. Fixating on stuff now might get them all killed.

"Rarz. Are you willing, and can you create a portal from here to, oh," he turned looking, "the top of the stadium over there?" He pointed to the top of the stadium, where the paths for the nosebleed seats were located, at least three times the distance in the hangar.

With a tilt of his head Rarz followed Miguel's finger and focused for a minute, his eyes narrowed then bobbed his head. "Yes."

A strange light glowed off to the side of where they were confronting each other, and another way up at the point designated. Faster than she could change her focus from one to the other, they had snapped into existence.

These are much faster than how long it took for that one in the clearing to form. I wonder why?

Another idea to file in her head, but not the right time to follow up on it. But forgetting might have consequences.

~Wefor?~

[Yes?]

~Can you file all these questions for me and remind me if we live through this and kick the Elentrins' ass?

[Which questions would those be?]

McKenna rattled off the various things that had occurred to her, but she didn't want to sidetrack people, or even waste the energy to worry about them now.

[They have been filed. You will be reminded when there is peace.]

~Ha. That might be asking for a bit much. How about when you think it's a good time to bring it up.~

[As you say.]

Miguel had been staring at the portal back and forth between them, shook his head, eyes closed. He seemed to be murmuring something to himself, but even if she ramped up her hearing, she could only catch fragmented Mandarin and Spanish in a weird blend that made no sense, even if she felt she should recognize it.

Finally he stopped muttering and looked at the surrounding people. "Everyone who is not in the Alpha, Bravo, or Charlie teams better get back to their damn jobs and quit rubbernecking. We're planning a sneak attack, people, not putting on a side show." His voice boomed in the air and McKenna was impressed by the volume.

All around them people snapped to attention then scattered in different directions though numerous people kept glancing back at them, and she knew they'd be watched constantly. At this point that had become almost normal.

"Alpha team you first. Civilians included. Walk through and note what it feels like, and how you come out. Do this a few times, then we will run through, our weapons drawn to make sure there aren't any issues with transition." Miguel snapped out the orders, not even glancing at her. McKenna bristled a teeny bit at being called a civilian in that tone but creating more strife wouldn't accomplish anything.

The military personnel braced to attention and with a deep breath Miguel led the way into the portal, Alpha team following. She looked up at the end point of the portal and watched them come out less than a heartbeat after they disappeared.

She glanced at the others and they nodded back at her. McKenna stepped into the portal and once again felt the world disappear.

This time it seemed less disorienting, though she still felt it tug at her as she moved through it. Coming out the other end, the soldiers gathered around looking at Miguel, their eyes wide and faces flushed.

McKenna turned to watch the others as they walked out. Cass had her brows drawn together, fingers twitching as if she typed as she walked out. JD and Perc both looked a bit like they had gotten off a roller coaster, a bit unsteady, but with big grins on their faces. Toni's expression caught her attention though. Greenish gray under her red clay skin and a scowl on her face that would have made both her kids turn tail.

~You okay?~ McKenna asked, not wanting to call attention to her from the others.

~Yes, later.~ Her response was abrupt and she looked off in the distance, avoiding McKenna's glance.

"That was different," Miguel remarked, his voice calm, but McKenna could smell his sweat. "Rarz, can you still hear me?"

Rarz had not followed them through and McKenna peered back down at the playing field where the other end of the portal hung.

"Yes, Chief Miguel." Rarz's calm voice filled her earpiece.

"Good to know going through the portal doesn't kill tech. That would have made this difficult. Next question. Can people go both ways through the portal at the same time?"

"Yes. Though as you will technically be in two different space-time tunnels, neither person will see or be aware of the other person. I can provide the math if you would like."

His voice never faltered, and McKenna wondered how much he even understood humans. He looked so human, but his reactions didn't match exactly.

"Uh, no thanks. Alpha team head back, Bravo come through. Let's see how this works." The men nodded and turned and headed back through. Watching them felt odd as they stepped in and disappeared. Just as the last one entered, someone stepped out of the portal. It felt like they'd exchanged places with the other person.

"Well, good." Miguel gave a smile as he looked at everyone. He almost looked gleeful and McKenna got a bad feeling in the base of her stomach. "Now we can practice our formations. All groups, form up in your designated orders and practice going in the portal and coming out, paying attention to what's going on around you. I want to see you moving through without issues."

They spent the next hour getting their grouping down. By the time they were done it was automatic for all of them. McKenna responded automatically as Alpha 2A and didn't think about it.

They came out for the last time on the playing field and Miguel called a halt and motioned for all the groups to converge on him. "You guys did good. Now, I want everyone to eat." He cast an eye at the shifters. Even after all the time working together, she could still sense a slight wariness from him, but she didn't care. "If I understand correctly, you guys should really bulk up on food. It's not something I normally suggest, but," he shrugged and let it drop. "Everyone else eat and hit the racks set up for us. We have two hours, then we go. Part of me wants to go now, but food and two hours rest might make the difference and from the last bit of information I received, it looks like they're waiting for something. So be it. Dismissed."

People fell out, heading towards the food tent and a large tent that you could see cots in through the open flaps.

"Food does sound good," Toni murmured. McKenna nodded and as a group, with Rarz tagging along behind them, they headed to the temporary mess hall.

None of them spoke much as they got trays of food, overloaded with stuff McKenna figured would be edible, if nothing else. They sat there eating with steady seriousness. Cass ate the least, as she hadn't changed much lately.

"This does not taste as good as the food I ate with you previously." Rarz commented, poking at a mac and cheese pile on his plate.

JD laughed. "This is food produced in large quantities. It isn't great, but it isn't horrible either."

"There is that much variation in your foods?" Rarz seemed surprised.

"Sure," Perc said, after a hasty swallow. You could probably be here a hundred years and still not taste all the variations of food."

Rarz scanned their faces as if looking for a joke, but they all nodded seriously as they finished up eating. In unspoken consent they all headed to the cots and laid down, not expecting to sleep, but rest would be good.

"Alright, everyone up, it's time to go." Miguel's voice intruded and McKenna realized she had fallen asleep.

~Wefor?~

[It was helpful for all of you to get what rest you could. Your stress levels are elevated and there was no harm in helping you sleep.]

McKenna wanted to snap out, but the AI was right. She felt a bit calmer and less tense for the short nap. Fifteen minutes later, suited up and armed, they stood in the middle of the stadium, with half the people spread out watching them.

"Showtime. Rarz, open the door." Miguel's voice came through their coms and a silver portal to a spaceship appeared in the middle of the field.

Here goes everything.

Chapter 20 - Cloth of Humanity

Reports from other areas of the world only highlight that Earth doesn't know how to handle this type of invasion. With attackers dropping in from the sky there are no borders to defend, no grouping of troops. Small countries like France, Poland, and Argentina are suffering with this strategy. The best we can do right now is hope the attrition of everyone protecting themselves encourages these invaders to flee, sooner rather than later. ~TNN News

He spent the next two days working to connect with his contacts, and to his delight they were as desperate for information about what was going on as he was. But the true joy was a phone call from a captain in the army he'd bought a few drinks for back when this whole shifter thing had started. The man had gotten drunker and drunker that night, while Raymond sipped on a gin and tonic, minus the gin. By the end, he'd taken the man home, exchanging information and copying his military ID, not that Captain Walter Higson had noticed that. But he'd done a few favors for the man, like making the drunk and disorderly charge disappear. Simple enough to do, and it gained the man's loyalty.

"Kennedy, I thought you might like to know this," Higson's voice sounded hushed, and in the background Raymond could make out lots of chatter and moving boots.

"Walter, I assume you are staying safe? That's the most important thing." Being nice to people made them think you cared. That always amazed him.

"Yeah, they've kept me away from all the good stuff. I haven't even been able to kill any of these vile invaders." The man all but spat out the words.

"Yes. Interesting how they look just like the infected people here on Earth. Makes me wonder what else might have changed besides their appearance."

There was a pause then the other man spoke slowly. "Like what?"

"Oh, just maybe they don't think the same anymore. I mean, we all know a big cat or bear would eat a human. Maybe they might start looking at us as food? Maybe kids might not seem so special to them. You can't imagine they'd still think the same, would you?"

"Huh. You might have a point." Another pause. "But that kinda leads into why I called you. The other day they called us all in. Gave us this song and dance. They have a bunch of them here, including one that looks like some big lizard out of a movie. They say they can attack the ships and get people out. Apparently, people bought it because of some demo at one of the hangars, I got sidetracked into doing stuff, but people just said it was the most effective demonstration they'd ever seen. So they're starting up this big rescue, but the people leading it are shifters. That famous cop is one of them."

"Her? Again? Dammit," he started to say more, but managed to rein himself in. "Go on."

"Well, I was thinking. What if that isn't what they really want to do? I'm not good enough to be on any of the teams, but they're treating these shifters differently. So they've got us all here at this stadium, and I mean tons of military personnel. They have all these tents set up to handle a huge influx of people. There was a huge shouting match one of the females had with one of the team leads. That lead woman, the cougar one, laid into him. I couldn't see what he said, but you know damn well if any human had done that, they would have run laps for a week. Instead he backed down and I think he fucking apologized. What is this world coming to that a man like that apologized to a damn woman?"

"You mean an animal, don't you?" Raymond said mildly, his tone coaxing. "Sounds like she lost control. That is just what an animal does. No logic, just blind instinct."

"Hell, probably worse than that. I've had good hunting dogs, but you get upset and they can be dangerous. Huh. Maybe I'm glad I ain't going on their big spaceship rescue. But I did hear something worrisome, a whisper, not a fact." His voice had dropped, and Raymond closed his eyes to focus on the voice.

"Oh, what would that be?"

"They mentioned something about asteroids and them being lobbed at Earth. Now I've seen some disaster movies, and it doesn't sound like it would turn out well for us, no matter where it hits. I kinda hope they stop it, but I wouldn't mind if most of them died as glorious heroes."

Raymond narrowed his eyes and thought then shrugged. If that happened, he couldn't do anything to stop it, but he could make sure the survivors came home a world that didn't want them anymore.

"That wouldn't be a bad option. I'll remember this bit of information Higson, but keep your head down. Our country needs men like you, and don't be afraid to let me know if anything else strange is going on."

"Will do, and damn right the country needs people like both of us—ready to stand up for what we know is right."

Raymond smirked as he hung up. Then his smile faded and he leaned back in his office chair, thinking carefully. While this might start a small bit of dissent in the military, he would need a lot of dissent at all levels. That meant getting politicians and the medical establishment on his side, playing off their fears about the ability to change. He'd done a little back at the emergence of the shifters, but more really to test the waters and he'd seen then, things were tilting too much to the 'very cool' attitude. But now? With hundreds of thousands dead? He could make it seem like they were at the root cause of all of this. Emails were required, multiple emails that he needed to tweak and send correctly to various people and countries. If he included only the US, it would be too off balance. He had contacts in the countries that mattered. People who would see what he was doing and support it. China no longer mattered, though whipping up hate for shifters there would be easy, and a good thing to do as soon as the invaders moved on. China would never be a home for shifters again. Smirking, he pulled up email and started to craft messages to people who could control the leaders of the world with subtle whispers. As he crafted his messages, he saw a ping on several systems.

Frowning, he opened and followed the alert threads. Annoyance wormed through him as he realized someone had been checking up on him, and it was way too specific. Keeping his house silent except the click of his keys on the keyboard, Raymond backtracked the research. He paid a very exclusive agency to be aware of anything that involved him, and this had all the hallmarks of an investigation. One that might end his career.

A name appeared. Sarah Buroky. The name struck a bell, but not enough that he could pin it down, so he kept digging and authorized the agency to research this person and why they were interested in him. It amazed him how many things kept running during the wake of an alien invasion. The name finally popped up as a key member of an internal ethics board.

Well that won't work. I'll need to make sure she, and anyone else involved, can't cause any more problems.

Another few minutes of digging pulled up her wife, a lieutenant in the police department. Having the police involved added a layer of complication to the investigation. He'd wait another few days before putting some money and the information into a drop account. There were a few morally ambiguous people that didn't mind doing dirty work for him and they were easier to control than the military. The military involved much more work and given the lack of success in the previous endeavor, it probably hadn't been worth it. But for now, the invasion was still going strong, and this gave him precious time. While all the focus was on the idiots running around, he could get people looking at things the right way. Raymond smirked as he typed. This is where his true skill set shined, being able to convince people of what to believe when they didn't know it themselves.

This just proves that true humans are the future, we are the strength. If those unfortunates can't push off the animal shackles, they should be treated like livestock or enemies.

He sneered. The animal form was nothing to be proud of. It was something to hide in the back of your closet, and never pay attention to, and hope it would never be mentioned in polite company.

But that being said, he needed to make sure that moods changed, and to place the blame on those really at fault— the diseased humans. A few carefully worded emails to the people who drove policy in the government would start it. It took him an hour to point out that while people with AIDs were protected, it didn't mean they should be free to work in environments where they might bleed on others. There was now proof that the animal nature would come out, and you don't want unreliable people in important positions. He just dropped hints and asked questions, leading them to idea.

Right now though, time would be his enemy and his friend. There were no meetings, and everyone was craving information and the storm on social media made him smile. Logging in with a few of his anonymous accounts he had purposefully set up to create viral comments, and pointing the blame. Then he responded with his other accounts to fan the fire.

It took two hours before the first one went viral and he had to restrain himself from whooping in excitement. Step one done. He'd have to keep feeding and fanning it over the next week, but by the time the aliens were chased away, the mood of the US, if not the world, may have shifted.

That meant he needed to focus on the other groups, older and in many ways more powerful people. People liked to laugh but AARP had more power than most groups did. The truism was, if you weren't a member yet—you would be.

Taking a break he moved farther into the house, looking for where he had the most barriers between him and any outside wall. Phone in hand, he ended up in the hall half-bath. With the door shut, he sat on the toilet and dialed.

It rang three times before it was answered. "There isn't enough going on for you that you think calling me right now is a good thing?"

"Willard, I know you're loving all this and since last time I checked you aren't a filthy shifter, I suspect you're fine." Raymond's voice mocked the man on the other end, but Willard just laughed.

"Yes, I am. Though my wife is having panic attacks peeking out of blinds and rationing food. Luckily, we had just gone on a grocery run for a huge party that we were scheduled to have. That means we have food for quite a while. None of that explains why you want to talk to me."

Raymond leaned back and looked at the exquisite wallpaper in the bathroom, which matched exactly with everything else and provided no warmth or personality at all. Personally, he always thought government buildings had the best bathrooms: direct, to the point, no wasted fancy crap you didn't need. Ah, too bad people expected things.

"Has it occurred to you how the appearance of these shifters has ruined everything? Their animal-like skills? The aliens? The fact that it's even referred to as harvesting means they really are livestock. How do we know the long-term effects won't make them dangerous? I mean we protect pets but are we sure they won't become the dangerous animals they can turn into?" He said it all in a worried tone of voice. While the odds of Willard being taken in by that were all but non-existent, it was good practice.

A long silence, then a low sigh. "Ah, I see. Messages about protecting and making sure they don't get harmed, sowing distrust that they really are who they say they are, long term damage, isolation, pointing out the aliens regard them as animals, but not us? There might be something to that thought."

"Exactly. A few words with your brethren preachers and I am sure we could start a ripple. Especially if we point out you can't look at one of them and know if they're human or alien. Doesn't that imply that maybe they are no longer from this planet?"

"Hmm, that has possibilities. Especially if it would get their skills at sensing things redefined. Maybe it could even be pointed out that a dog can't hold grudges or purposefully interpret something wrong. I take it you want me to hammer home on this? Church has been canceled." There was a bit of bait there in the question.

Raymond sighed and took it. "You know this will benefit you and our country in the long run. What do you want?"

"You may still believe that 'my country' drivel, but I left that belief for money a long time ago. Get those damn cops discredited. If I can get those drug cases thrown out, it will be a while before they can get any more evidence that might point towards me."

"They found you?" Raymond didn't bother to try and hide his surprise.

"Not yet. The distraction of all of this and their little visit to South America helped, but they got the pet cop of one of my distributors. He spoke to me once but doesn't know anything about me, so…" Willard sighed. "They might eventually trace it back to me, but they'd have a hell of a time proving it. My records are damn near bullet proof. But…" Willard trailed off and Raymond let him think. College years spent with Willard proved the man could make anyone believe anything. It was one of the reasons he'd kept in touch with him.

"Hmmm, false gods, mixed with animals, mixed with the temptation to see ourselves in the beast. And I know a few of the more rabid preachers I can send a carefully worded newsletter. So again, why should I?"

"Oh, quit playing games, Willard. What do you want?"

"No, this time I want you to explain what you hope to achieve first." Willard sounded more curious than anything, and Raymond sat there, trying to decide how much to tell him.

Thoughts raced through Raymond's mind as he sat there. He didn't really trust Willard, but then again nothing that he was going to ask Willard to do was illegal. Unethical maybe, depended on who won at the end of this war, but not illegal. The man had no conscience and sold drugs. There was little Raymond could say that would put him at risk of anything Willard might decide to do.

"Fine. I believe this infestation of shifters, or Kaylid as the invaders call them, could mean the destruction of our world as we know it. The only way to keep humans safe is to minimize their impact on our society. Already they're changing how we think, how we view things. And now these aliens are coming to collect them like the animals I suspect they are. What if we allow these protections to remain and people start to devolve into animals? Then where will be we be? We need to change the perception of them now, not with fear mongering but making people look at what's going in the world right now. If we don't do something, they will take over our world and we may become the pets." As he spoke, he became more fervent, until by the end his voice had obtained the power of belief in it.

"Huh. You keep that up and I'll start worrying about you as competition. Okay, I can do this. I have a lot to gain if they're regulated back to animals. They're too powerful to be members of society. I'll work on the animal aspect, and the fears, pointing out it's only been three months since all this happened, and maybe we moved too fast to protect them. Instead, maybe we should have quarantined them. There have been enough 'rabid' animal attacks to justify that. I'd advise you take the second route. Pointing out that with their power, and their healing capabilities how is it fair for pure humans to compete against them, etc.? And I assume you need this ASAP?"

Raymond smiled; but there was no one there to see the grin of triumph. "I think we'll win the war, either because they'll leave, hopefully with full ships of shifters, or we'll make it a war of attrition. The US is good at that. But we might only have a week or two. Meaning we need to hit while everyone is hiding in their homes, scared and worried."

"My show is still going to be taped, just with no audience. I think I can swing a special because of the alien threat. I'll lay it on heavy and send it out tonight. You caught me as I was leaving. I'll drop some carefully worded emails to a few of the more radical preachers I know around the globe. But you know, historically campaigns like this took months if not years to be truly effective."

"Yes, but in the past we didn't have social media. Make it so you go viral and I'll do the same. We can sweep the world with rage and fear, and give them a valid target. Make it so shifters will be begging for these aliens to collect them." Raymond knew he sounded smug, he was. He could do this, and make sure no one ever looked at him or thought he might be one of these filthy animals. Maybe these Elentrin could take them all. Ship them away from this planet and humans.

"You'll owe me, and I'm going to call it in, but for now, I'll do it. This gives me some new fodder; I was running out anyhow. But that means I'm hanging up as I need to start writing." With that he disconnected. Raymond smiled a bit wider putting his phone away and left the bathroom, headed back to his computer and plans. He needed to get the various platforms all trending, and he knew exactly how to do that. It didn't take long to get some pictures from what was going on around the world. At first glance, many of the invaders looked like earth shifters. He hit the jackpot when he found a catlike invader killing a struggling woman with its claws. Two hours of searching got him a wealth of pictures that could be twisted multiple ways.

He began posting in various places, never saying anything specifically but rousing hearts and emotions. The last thing he wanted anyone to do was think.

Chapter 21 - Alien Ships

Satellite telemetry along with thousands of amateur telescopes have picked up lots of activity from shuttles in near space. There seems to be more and more junk cluttering up the orbit around Earth. No one knows why the Elentrin are doing this, but given all of their actions until now, it won't be anything beneficial for Earth. The White House has had no comment about anything lately. What few officials are still in Washington have refused to talk to any press. ~ TNN Invasion News

McKenna watched Miguel, Perc, Rarz, and Alpha 2B start through the portal. She searched around for Cass, even as she moved towards that silver swirl. Cass stood over with Bravo group. She waved at McKenna when she saw her looking.

~I'll be fine. Go.~ Cass's reassurance washed through her as McKenna walked towards the portal Rarz had just disappeared into. She inhaled, brought the Elentrin weapon up and followed Alpha 2B through it.

The weirdness barely registered any more, she just came out on the other side, inside an alien ship. She didn't stumble or pause, though she really wanted to. The walls were an odd mustard brown, subconsciously she realized she had expected gray. The others were at the end of a corridor and she kept up a steady pace to stay in line with everyone.

"Per the data provided by Perc," Miguel said, "the closest storage chamber should be to the right." They'd all agreed trying to use mister and miss in this endeavor would prove stupid.

"Assuming we're where I think we are. This says we're on level five, on the tran side." Perc nodded at some notations on the wall. As she looked at it, the words made sense to her, backing up what Perc had said. "We should be able to get there quickly and eliminate anyone in that room."

I'm on a ship from another world and the only thing we can think to do is kill. I hate this, but I'll do anything to stop them from destroying my world.

"Then let's go. The other group is waiting for our signal. We need to clear the way there and then secure the room before Bravo group comes in. Rarz, can you close and reopen later? I'd rather no one stumbles across that portal. Alarms would go off for sure." They all nodded, and McKenna reminded herself to breath.

The light behind her vanished and she glanced back to see a hallway bending around the corner. The middle of her back itched as if there was a target on it.

Weapons up, they headed down the hallway, moving as quietly as they could. Suddenly Perc raised his hand, fist clenched. McKenna halted immediately.

~Incoming,~ his voice said, though he didn't speak on the coms. He held up three fingers and pointed to the right side. Miguel nodded and crouched, Elentrin weapon pointed at the intersection in front of them.

Everyone else arranged themselves to provide clear shots without risking hitting team members. Alpha 3B, Toni, 4B, JD, and 5B all turned to cover behind them. The possibility of people coming up from behind them was all too real.

Voices came from down the corridor, underscored by rapid steps. Even as they came closer, she translated the words. They were talking about the number of Kaylid captured and the estimated number the incoming ship could grab before they destroyed the planet. Anger built in her and she knew before she saw them that the people approaching were Elentrin, not Kaylid. Something about the tone of voice gave her the clue, and she couldn't help but feel relieved that first enemy they came across would not be other shifters.

Colors came around the corner, at least that was what she saw first. A blue so bright it made the brightest summer day seem pale and bland, was mixed with a shade of orange that brought to mind subtle spices, strong yet barely there. They froze as they saw the gathered team, eyes wide, and mouths going slack.

"Fire," Miguel's voice sounded in her ear and Perc reacted before anyone else. There was a flash of light, even as Miguel copied him, with his own weapon flashing, the sound low and quiet, but she could hear it. Before she finished processing the light, both figures had crumpled to the ground.

They held still, breaths caught in their lungs as they waited, their ears straining for any sound.

"We're good. Move out. 5B, take care of them," Miguel ordered as they continued in the direction Perc indicated. McKenna followed, but frowned. Something about Miguel's last words tripping an internal sensor.

As they moved through the ship, McKenna glanced back once and saw 5B bending over the two crumpled figures. As he stood back up, she saw liquid pooling around their necks. Shock slapped through her as she realized what they had done. It made her feet leaden and she stumbled a bit, bumping into 2B. The man glanced back at her and she shook her head silently, even as she dealt with the knowledge that they had slit the throats of the two defenseless Elentrin.

They just killed them. No hesitation, they just slit their throats.

The thought pounded in her head, as everything she'd been trained to do as a cop rebelled. Even in the week of fighting, they'd never killed anyone laying on the ground. It was always Kaylid carrying shifters away, or them shooting at them. But flat-out murder?

No, what are they supposed to do? Leave them alive? We know the stun doesn't last forever. Leaving living enemies behind us that know we don't belong here? We'd get everyone killed. That would be worse. They're doing what they need to.

Nothing felt right but she couldn't think of any other answers. McKenna pushed it down and focused on their mission. Get their people home, and make the Elentrin go away, which meant killing a lot of them. Wrestling with the conflict in her own thoughts kept her slightly distracted and moving on automatic as they went through the ship's interior. She paused when told to, and two more were shot, bodies limp piles on the off-brown floor. These were Kaylid.

"4B, 5B, handle those. Perc, you said the next right?" Miguel said, his voice very quiet. They had tried to convince him that the Kaylid could hear everything.

"Yes." Perc said just as quietly. They'd been lucky so far. The doors were almost invisible in the mustard brown walls, except for a small plaque. It translated as she focused on it. Canister Control Room 3.

Good, maybe we can start changing the balance to rescuing people.

Not sure if she wanted to know, she looked backwards anyway and almost gasped in surprise. Both of the men had a Kaylid slung over their shoulders, the furry bodies looking boneless as they hung there.

He is trying to save them.

She closed her eyes for a moment, fighting to get her head back in the game.

*I've never been so glad I never went into the military. I
don't think I could have handled the mindset flipping between killing and saving.*

"So how do we open it?" Miguel asked, his voice sounding horribly loud, as addition of the coms caused her to hear
it in stereo.

~I really prefer the talking via Speech,~ she muttered in
the mindspace.

~Agreed.~ The fervent responses came back, making her
smile.

"I'll open it." Toni's voice stayed quiet and low as she
moved up the column and stopped at the door, just behind
Miguel. "As soon as I enter the credentials the door will
slide open. Be ready."

The men at the front tensed, their weapons up and
ready. Toni pressed on what McKenna had thought was a
decorative icon, and a panel slid open below. It showed a
circle of odd symbols that McKenna realized were a mix of
numbers and letters in the Elentrin language. Toni tapped
on them, her fingers dancing over the keys. A soft beep responded, and the door slid open.

Even as the opening appeared, Toni slipped back into her
place, clearing fields of fire for Perc, Miguel, and 2B. Voices
came from the room, tones of confusion and alarm. The
three men moved into the opening and weird pulses of light
told her they fired though she couldn't see anything.

"Clear," Miguel whispered through the coms. "Get in
here and get that door closed behind us."

McKenna moved in following Rarz, even as she heard the
others behind them. The noise of the ship didn't seem that
loud before, but as she stepped into the room the sound increased. The soft swish of the door behind her amplified it
in the sealed room.

As much as she wanted to look around, the bodies
caught her attention first. Five of them, all Kaylid, with

strange white jumpsuits on. It was the first even remotely uniform-like thing she'd see. But as she focused, she could hear them breathing and their hearts beating steadily. Something that had been winding tighter relaxed. At least they might make it out of here without killing everyone.

You're being stupid. This is a war, death is expected and they have no issue with killing us. We shouldn't feel guilty about killing them. Gah! Stupid conflicting ethics. Much easier when people are trying to kill you or others. You don't have time to consider anything.

She stomped down on the thoughts. They were not productive right now and indulging in them would cost everyone.

"Gather them up, and get them all in a corner out of the way. We don't want to be tripping over them." This time Miguel Zhen just spoke out loud. 4B and 5B laid out the two bodies they'd already collected. They gathered the others and put them more or less in a small pile in a corner of the room that didn't seem to have anything they might need.

"Any way to secure that door? Stop anyone else from opening it?" Chief Zhen asked Toni. With a tilt of her head Toni turned to look at the door, her lips pursed, and eyes narrowed.

"Maybe. Give me a minute. I still don't know what's in my brain and what isn't." She walked over and touched the same icon on this side of the wall; another control panel appeared. Toni touched icons slowly, then more rapidly.

"Good. While she works on that, Rarz, can you get the portal open and get Bravo group up here?"

Rarz did a side head tilt. But this time instead of just a silver circle just appearing, he closed his eyes, face scrunched up like he concentrated. Miguel and McKenna watched him, but she noted everyone else looking around. After three heartbeats she gave in and looked around the room. It resembled the descriptions Cass had given them. Very white, the mustard brown of the outer halls would almost be wel-come here. Their skin and fur colors seemed so intense compared to all the white. A large viewing window looked out into something, but the blinking boards and displays on the desk-like counters caught her attention first, especially the rapidly flashing red ones.

"Do we need to worry about those red flashing lights?" Her voice was low, but she could feel their time slipping away.

"Probably, but without Cass I wouldn't risk it." JD's voice seemed calm but when she glanced at him, he stood in a wide-legged stance, the strange weapons tight in his grip. He kept looking around, never stopping. If he'd had a long tail in that form she thought it would be whipping around worse than her own, which she couldn't seem to keep still. She had learned that a cat's tail responds to your emotions, not your mind.

"Portal forming," Rarz said quietly and she turned back to look at him. Miguel breathed out what she would have sworn was a sigh of relief.

"Zimmer, you hear me?" He asked as soon as the circle quit growing and remained steady.

"Loud and clear, Chief," Elaine's voice came through the coms with little if any distortion.

"Come on through. We've got work for your charge." He glanced around as he talked, eyes locking onto the big win-dow.

"Rodger. Coming through now." Elaine responded and the com clicked off.

"So if we control it from here, where do the Kaylid get released?" Zhen asked slowly, even as Toni spoke.

"Got it. Changed the code to get in. Wait, what?" Toni turned to stare at him, and then at the huge window as did McKenna.

With her stomach clenching tight, McKenna stepped forward and looked out the huge window. It overlooked a huge warehouse bay, like standing at the top of a ship's hold and looking down, stretching out farther than she could see. Up close a bunch of canisters hung in front of her, and she could see Kaylid hanging there, limp and lifeless, but at the top of the container a green light shown.

I really hope that means they're alive and just asleep or in stasis.

The room they stood in was isolated. There was no way to get to any of the people in those containers into there from here. So where would they be released?

"So where do they get out at?" Miguel asked. He had moved forward to look out the window with McKenna.

"At the station down there at the bottom. There should be two to three Kaylid there to get them out, provide basic treatment, and hand them their orders," Cass said as she walked out.

"Fuck." Miguel swore harshly. "And there are how many of these storage things?"

"Ten on this ship," Perc responded almost instantly. "Each one with a capacity of 100,000 beings."

Miguel glanced at him and shook his head. "I hate rushed missions, things get overlooked and assumed." She glanced back at the Bravo team that had completely arrived. Cass had moved over to the computers that were flashing lights and started to tap on the display systems.

"Okay, all the information I have is working. I can order them decanted, and inject the drugs in their system before they're released from the jars. Now from what the information in here says, the drug should keep them down for about thirty-six of our hours. After that they'll need water, food, and tending—which I'm assuming means waste disposal, urine, etc." Cass spoke but didn't look at anyone, focused on the boards.

Miguel stared out the window, looking down at the far corner where McKenna could see a receiving bay for the canisters. They seemed to be sucked in via another tube she couldn't see.

"How long does the process take?" Miguel asked, his voice distant.

"The room can handle up to four at a time, and from injection to decant it takes about three minutes." Cass hmmm'd a bit, still tapping on icons. "I think I can drop it to a minute as we don't want them fully aware, but note this is me guessing, a lot."

Miguel swore again softly. He glanced back at the open portal, then at the room down blow. "This will take days. Even at a minute each, if these holds are full and there are ten? That is a million beings. It will take us weeks."

A hush filled the room as that sank in, and McKenna wanted to scream.

Cass spoke up. "The ship is about seventy-five percent full. They're stuck with the same constraints we are. From what I can tell, they have a pile of shifters sedated and waiting to be put in these things." Her voice dripped with distaste as she said that. "And as fast as they've been moving, they still have lots of room. But they have multiple rooms and ships. We know how many they came with. Figure some have been killed. Each of these control rooms can control two storage units." She hit a button and the other wall, the one that had been solid went clear and displayed a unit that was about half full. "They've been loading up for a week, but we can unload faster than they can load." Cass chewed on her lip as she tapped. "At a rate of four per minute, if we do all ten rooms, with someone in each control room, it will take," she paused and her shoulders sagged, "about six days."

Miguel fell silent, and McKenna felt herself tense, as if waiting for an explosion. Instead, he leaned against the wall, eyes closed. "Rarz, I assume people won't float through your portals. They have to move through them themselves."

The Drakyn blinked. His mouth opened, then closed. "I do not know. I am unaware of any tests regarding that functionality."

"First, let's test that ASAP. That will affect a lot of plans."

Everyone looked around but the room didn't really seem to have a lot of loose objects.

"Use one of the Kaylid laying there," Perc suggested.

McKenna shot a look at him, but he just shrugged. "Worst case they lay there on the swirly portal floor."

Okay he has a point. Dammit why can't I just not care?

"4B, try it." Miguel hit the com. "Charlie, we're running a test, be ready to receive a body." The soldier picked up the body and laid it on the portal floor. McKenna watched it, curious.

It lay there and Miguel sighed, but before he could say anything Rarz spoke. "Let me try something." He started muttering scientific sounding stuff in the mindspace about feedback, quark rotations, shifting electrons, and other mumbo-jumbo. While she understood the words, she had no frame of reference for what they meant, though Cass listened intently, nodding a bit. If felt like he didn't realize he was broadcasting as the flow of words was almost faint in the mindspace, something she'd never experienced before.

"That should work," even as he said the words the body was pulled into the tunnel and disappeared. Shocked, McKenna looked first at the tunnel then the dragon.

Damn. Every time I start to feel comfortable with him, he gets scary again.

"Charlie, you get the body? What shape is it in?"

The words came back through the com. "Unconscious but fine. Medics say steady heartbeat and no marks. I assume this is the work of the stun guns?"

"I refuse to call them that, but yes." Miguel looked at the portal thoughtfully. "That might save us time getting them out."

"If I understand your plan, Chief," Rarz started, and McKenna turned to look at him but she sensed what he was going to say. "You wish to have a portal opened in the room for them to throw the bodies in to process as fast as possible."

"Yes, that was what I thought." Miguel looked at him warily and McKenna closed her eyes, some vague lessons learned on the ship filtering in.

"Then while it is a good one, there is an issue. I can only open one portal at a time."

His words fell into the room like bricks into a still pond.

"Shit." Miguel said softly. "Okay, let me think for a minute."

McKenna found herself stepping towards the portal and noticed Toni drifting over, too.

~You feel it, too?~ McKenna kept the line tight, but she saw Rarz raise his head even as his clawed fingers beat out a pattern on his biceps.

~Yeah. Like I should be able to understand it. Control it. It pulls to me.~ Toni admitted, though she kept moving her eyes from the portal to the door to Rarz in a constantly changing pattern.

~Do you think we could? Learn, I mean?~

Toni shrugged, but turned to look at Rarz. "Can we use these, create them? Do what you do?"

Everyone in the room stopped to look at her. Then their attention snapped to Rarz.

"Could you teach them? Teach anyone?" Miguel demanded and McKenna noted the other three shifters all staring at him with rapt attention.

"In theory I may be able to. Toni for certain, McKenna probably." He lifted a hand before any of them could react.

"But it would take months if not years to teach them to even open a pinprick one, much less something of this scale. So for your current purposes, the answer would be no."

Miguel scrubbed his face with his hands and McKenna felt sympathy for the man, even if he was an ass. "Well then, folks, we're going with plan C. We're taking over the ship."

Chapter 22 - No Plan Survives

Canada has offered help to the United States. They have taken over shipping food to depots in the northern states. The shuttle attacks in Canada have been minimal. The common opinion that with most of their population so spread out, it isn't worth the effort. The food has been met with relief in some of the states, especially with deliveries so sporadic, but this is a stopgap measure. While food is still being harvested, unless the factories that process it up start up soon, most of it will rot. The next few years might be very lean. ~ TNN Invasion News

She must have heard wrong. There was no way he could have just said that, could he?

"I'm sorry. Could you repeat that?" How her voice came out calm and clear she had no idea. They didn't know how to fly a ship.

Before she could get too far down a path of trying to figure out how to fix it, Miguel spoke again.

"This is a two-fold plan. We're going to get as many people out of here as we can, but we may not have time to do it, especially if that other ship shows up. Plus, there's the risk that if they find us on the ship, they may give the order to destroy the planet and give us no choice. We need to get take over the ship, get all the shuttles in, and then use them to free people if necessary. Worst case I'll get fighter pilots or hell, video game junkies up here and we'll do kamikaze runs. But we aren't giving up that many of our people nor are we going to let them destroy our planet."

"Kamikaze?" Rarz said a bit haltingly. McKenna could almost see him running through what they had watched gleaned from Earth's internet.

"Sacrifice yourself to slam your ship into another ship," she provided quietly. His head jerked up and he looked at her with wide eyes.

"Rarz, I'm making the assumption that there won't be any more of your people coming to help?" Miguel said, as he glanced at the alien in their midst.

"I was the volunteer, the sacrifice if you wish. There are many on my world who do not believe this will work. I had a belief in you and Ash, so I said I would come."

Miguel sighed. "Swear, why does America always get allies that want proof first? Fine. Elaine, get Cass to teach you what you need, then leave two people up here. Toni, show them how to lock the door when we leave. We're taking two groups out to secure two revival rooms." He pinned Cass with a hard stare. "I assume you can tell which ones were recently put in storage versus those that have been there a while?"

"Ummm," Cass hit a bunch of icons, then a smile bloomed over her face. "Yes, both of these chambers were mostly empty when they started, so the majority should be from Earth."

"Good. We'll see how physically far apart they are. Anyone speak either Mandarin or Cantonese?"

Everyone signaled no. "Frag, this is going to make this very difficult as a significant majority should be from China."

"You said the coms work through the tunnels?" Toni said her voice flat.

"Yes, you saw." Miguel answered with a distracted tone.

"What about phones?" Toni pressed her body tight against the wall.

"Umm, let me check." He pulled it out and called a number. A minute later he closed it. "Yes, called my house, answering machine answered."

"You have an answering machine?" Perc blurted then turned away, as if embarrassed he'd said anything.

"Is that important now?" Perc shook his head at the demand, so Miguel turned his attention back to Toni. "So why does that matter?"

"Call our kids. They got loaded with Mandarin, Arabic, French, and one or two others. They can talk to people via the phones. You can do the other things with other translators."

Miguel tilted his head then nodded. "Good idea. Elaine, can you arrange that? Get Charlie team coming through with a bunch of spare phones. We can pass out numbers over the coms when you get them."

~Kids, did you get that? We need you to translate; tell people it's okay, that we're rescuing them. I hate to ask, but I know you can do this.~ Toni's voice held an odd mixture of emotions that McKenna didn't even try to decipher. Dealing with her own was hard enough, but via phones Charley and the others should still be safe in the hotel, there was no reason for them to move.

~Yes! We'll help. Telling Carina now. She'll spread the word.~ Jessi all but bubbled with enthusiasm and they could feel the same from the other two. That McKenna understood. Doing nothing had to be the hardest thing ever.

Toni nodded at Miguel who had been talking rapidly with Elaine Zimmer. Two people were assigned to Cass and she repeated stuff and pointed things out. All in all, they stood there another five stress-filled minutes listening to the occasional steps outside the hall.

"They're going to sound the alarm soon. Those bodies weren't hidden," 4B's mutter didn't help.

[Maybe not.]

McKenna jumped. Wefor had been so silent lately that her words surprised her.

~Why do you say that?~ She could feel all the Speech users listening intently.

[The information that exists in my database about Elentrin culture suggests, that though rare, assassination is not unknown for promotion opportunities. And flesh wounds from knives are the most frequent means. Using any other weapons is considered gauche.]

McKenna relayed that information and Miguel snorted, as did half the other soldiers in the room. "I'll use their stupidity to my advantage any day. But we can't expect our luck to last. Elaine, you ready?"

As they waited, the other Kaylid had been transported down to earth too, but if McKenna had to guess, it took more effort than normal from Rarz. But she didn't know enough to pry right now.

"Yes. Charlie 2B and 3B are staying here. They'll stay in touch via coms, though you do realize no one has tested if those will work once we're on the other side of the ship." Elaine managed to state the concern without sounding challenging.

I'll have to ask her how she did that later. I can never pull that off.

"I know. I'm hopeful, as tech has worked so far, but worst case, pay attention to the windows. You know hand signs, use them."

Elaine grunted out something that might have been a laugh. "Why do I think I should ask if you have semaphore flags tucked somewhere on your person?"

He cast her an arch look, then turned to Toni. "They know how to lock it?"

"Yes."

"Then let's go. We need to get to those two rooms, pull in Charlie team and secure them. Then we have a ship to take over." Miguel's teeth flashed yellow under the lights and McKenna shivered.

~No one should sound that gleeful about taking over a ship.~

~Are you kidding? This is the sort of thing men like him dream about. Not having to worry about government sanctions, congress second-guessing him, nothing. He gets to play pirate with full approval of Earth.~ JD chuckled in the mindscape, even as he turned and faced the door where everyone else had lined up.

"Open it," Miguel whispered. A few taps from Toni and the doors whispered back open. With a smooth movement she slipped back into her place in the lineup.

Miguel nodded at everyone and they set out at a quick jog. They moved through the almost silent halls, but now time was at a premium. When Perc signaled someone coming, he just nodded and picked up his pace, his weapon at the ready.

They hit an intersection and three groups were headed towards them. A solo Elentrin, a group of two Kaylid, and another group of three Kaylid running up the hall. Miguel didn't hesitate firing at the Elentrin first. The being collapsed, but before it hit the ground, he had already sited next his target. The Kaylid reacted, but Perc had fired once and 2B had fired at the solo Kaylid, which left one more who had hit a button on the wall. It was subtle and barely there, but already a pale blue light began to flash in the ceiling. Miguel cursed, pulled the trigger and the last enemy became a limp figure on the floor.

"No time now, we need to move. We need to get people in defensible locations, get one portal open and then get to the bridge. Move," he barked as Perc indicated which direction they should head.

"Rarz, go ahead and change into your version of the war-rior form. We can use the shock and surprise at this point, or at least it can't hurt."

"Elevator up ahead." Perc reached the door and McKenna glanced back to see JD and the other two Alpha company members watching behind them. The bodies were a trail of breadcrumbs in their wake.

"Locked," Miguel said. At this point they weren't bother-ing with coms. None of them were far enough apart and Cass and the rest of her Bravo group were being kept in the middle, protected, though from Cass's wide eyes and rapid breathing, she looked ready to shift into something better suited to protect herself.

Without being asked Toni moved up to the door and opened it. "I'll need to enter codes when we're inside, I'm having to override each time because we aren't in the sys-tem. Everything is bio-locked and our life signs aren't in the database. I basically know all the process to add new crew members, but only from their bridge I guess, or the security room. We don't have time now to do that. It takes a bit." Her voice remained low as she finished messing with the panel. The door opened in front of them and they slipped it.

McKenna didn't know if she should be surprised or weirded out that it looked like any other elevator she'd ever seen. A panel lit up showing the levels, each one highlighted in a different color and the Elentrin script. It took a minute, but the script became understandable as they squished tight together.

"We want this one," Toni said even as she hit a blue-green button near the bottom.

"Can you prevent it from stopping at any other floor?" asked Miguel. He and Perc stood near the front, while JD put his bulk between Cass and any possible attacks.

"Not in the time we have available." Toni's response seemed distracted as she had her head tilted to one side with her eyes closed. McKenna wanted to ask what the plan was when they got to their right place, but a chime sounded and the lift slid to a halt.

Without thinking, she lowered herself down, even as those in front raised their weapons. The lift froze, the doors slid open to the blue alarm still going off. Two Kaylid and an Elentrin looked at them, but this time there wasn't surprise, but anger and hate from the Elentrin. Miguel had been ready, and he pulled the trigger before McKenna had a chance to do more than interpret the expressions before they sagged to the floor.

"Get this thing going," he snapped. "We've been lucky and yes, these damn weapons were a good idea. But now they know we're here so we need to move before they get their shit together to deal with invaders." He fell silent as the elevator began its descent into the depths of the ship. "Perc, does this thing have the equivalent of stairs?"

Perc closed his eyes at Miguel's question, then he slowly nodded. "Maybe not like you're thinking, but more ladders running up and down the sides of the shafts. Emergency access. But I'll tell you, if what's in my head is correct, going down will be much easier than up, and there's no margin for error."

"I'll keep that in mind. We there yet?"

A muffled giggle came from the back of the elevator, which set off a domino effect of smiles that remained as they reached their destination. The opening of the doors revealed no one.

"Over there, to the right, is one room, and a bit farther down is the other. They both are being used, so expect people in them," Cass warned them as they headed towards the closer room. Bravo group came out, hiding Cass in their midst, with their guns up as they waited for the all clear.

They headed towards the first of the rooms at almost a run, the familiar pattern of Toni slipping up to open the doors and Miguel, Perc, and 2B moving in, the guns firing their flashes of oblivion. They stepped in and looked around and blinked at the rack of people in the corner. Looking like movable scaffold shelving, it had five wide shelves, holding two slack humans on each level. They were so still that only the fact that she could hear them breathing let her know they were alive.

McKenna took a deep breath and pushed it to the side. These people weren't in any more danger than before and they would get them out as soon as they could.

~Miguel's right, this is too easy. We're getting cocky.~ She kept her ears peeled for any sound, but with so many people moving around she couldn't hear anything that might warn her.

~I agree, but at the same time I'm not looking an easy invasion in the mouth,~ JD replied. They waved Bravo group up, and the little room felt even smaller. It didn't take long before Cass started the decanting process, full speed, then she cussed.

"What is it?" Miguel had spun around to look at her.

"They don't have the drugs I need to make them stay asleep. Maybe the first few dozen, even the first hundred, but not for thousands or tens of thousands. The system is designed to wake them and dump them out."

"Fuck," his voice low and vicious as he looked. "But you said most of them are from Earth?"

Cass spent a minute banging on icons, swearing softly to the point that JD moved over to her. McKenna's skin had started to crawl. It felt like they were trapped in here, especially with so many people crowded into this room. Plus, there was the rack of humans, and knowing more would be coming both from Earth and people being brought in to be stored.

I hate the fact that I can think about this as if it is normal—unpleasant but normal.

"Got it. Yes, all of these canisters were loaded in the last week, or week equivalent. When it's mostly empty we'll start hitting ones than have been there a while." Cass didn't look up as she talked, still tapping on the icons.

"Good. Then let's get those phones in here and start getting our people home." He nodded at Rarz. "We're ready. Get that portal open so we can get this show on the road. The plan is to have both rooms running and they'll move people here. Since they'll be mobile, we might as well use that to our advantage. Charlie team will be the chaperones to get them into that portal. Rarz, do you need to stay here to monitor it?"

"No. I can monitor it from anywhere within a half light year."

Everyone paused and stared at him. Then there was a collective sigh of information overload and they went back to what they were doing.

"Crank it up. Every minute counts." Rarz created the portal and Miguel spoke into his com, verifying the plan with the others. A few minutes later Charlie group came through the portal from Earth with the cell phones.

"Good, one in here and one in the other room." Another few minutes to set up speakers and make sure the phones were connected to the portable chargers and they were all set.

"We ready?" Already the first few had been decanted, in human form. They were disoriented and wary, but Elaine Zimmer dealt with them. They needed to get them back to Earth well before they were capable of coherent movement. The humans on the rack were sent through the portal, and Rarz did not seem to concentrate as much this time to get them sliding without any effort on their part. They pushed the rack out into the hall, needing the space as Charlie team took over getting people out of the canisters and into the portal. Per usual, one Bravo member stayed to run the process. Elaine nodded, looking around. "We're good. Next set."

They inched their way around the portal and stuck their heads out, checking that the hallway remained clear. They headed towards where the next room was when a wave of light went through the hall, making McKenna's skin tingle.

"What was that?" Miguel's voice cut through her confusion, but no one had an answer. Now, senses on even higher alert, they got to the door of the next processing room. It slid open as they approached and a Kaylid stepped out. Perc reacted faster than Miguel, aiming and pulling the trigger.

Nothing happened.

Chapter 23 - Step One of Many

With most countries focused on their own issues and defending against the invaders, all international trade has come to a screeching halt. The stock markets have been closed since the first shuttle landing. All conventions have been canceled and most people are living on limited supplies. The toll to the economy is unprecedented. If we can't kick these invaders off our planet in the near future, we might not have a future that resembles anything except for an apocalyptic ruin. ~ Op Ed piece SacWasp

"Shit, they disabled the ray guns," Miguel barked out the comment, even as he dropped the now useless weapon reaching for his M-16.

"Don't fire, you might damage the equipment," Cass's voice came out as a boom of command and half the people on the floor paused. Perc and JD didn't. They dropped the weapons and launched themselves, claws out, at the Kaylid standing there. The being, male from what McKenna could see, snarled and met them half way.

It had less body weight than JD or Perc. Being one of the slighter Kaylid, it flew backwards as JD and Perc hit it. McKenna left them to it and headed for the next room, Toni and Rarz on her heels.

~I'll go high, you go low. There should be another one in that room.~ She ordered, her claws growing.

She felt Toni's presence as all of her shifted into attack mode, pushing back the worries and ethical decisions in the need to secure their target. As they came through the door, the other Kaylid spun, with a snarl wrinkling a muzzle that looked more canine than feline and it attacked. It had yellow fur with gray spots, it moved fast, attacking without hesitation.

McKenna blocked the first strike as muscle memory for things she'd never learned took over. They were too similar in their training, each of them blocking the other's strikes. They couldn't risk firing a gun and damaging equipment they needed desperately, but she couldn't break through, and even though she knew where Toni was, she couldn't get the Kaylid to turn to expose its back to Toni.

~McKenna, duck!~ The mental order came through with the strange flavor and tone that told her it was Rarz. She didn't question it, she just dropped to the floor. Above her Rarz's scaled hand slammed forward and impaled the Kaylid through the chest with wicked looking claws. A burble of surprise escaped the dying being, and blood frothed from its mouth as it sagged down, furred hands scrabbling at the iron strength of the dragon.

Crouched on the ground, McKenna looked up at the creature they had just killed, and the battle rush left her, leaving her swamped with weariness to the point she had to fight to stand up.

I want to cry, but that won't change anything. But I hate these Elentrin for what they've done. Making beings into tools, and letting innocents pay the price for their overinflated arrogance.

The anger let her push away the grief as she stood. Looking around, Miguel had stepped inside the room and looked at the bloody corpse and Rarz standing there. He opened his mouth, then snapped it shut shaking his head a bit. McKenna didn't ask. She didn't want to know.

"Cass, Elaine, your turn. Get it up and running. What's left of Charlie and Bravo groups will escort people to the portal." Even as Miguel talked, one of the Charlie people set up the rest of the phones and she could hear the kids talking as some of the people being roused were asking questions.

McKenna stepped out of the room, picking up her M680 from where she had dropped it. It would have been a hazard in that small area for hand-to-hand fighting. Another body lay there on the floor, its head pointed a direction that wasn't possible with normal anatomy. She swallowed hard and looked down the corridor, trying to block out everything.

~You okay?~ Perc's voice whispered to her on a private channel, though she had no faith that Rarz couldn't overhear it. Learning to lock down mental thoughts was another thing on the long list of things to remember to follow up on.

Later. If there is a later.

The bitter thought brought an odd feeling of amusement with it and she shook it off.

~I'm fine.~ She left it at that, not knowing if it was a lie or not.

Miguel stepped out with the rest of Alpha, Toni trailing behind. As Toni remained in warrior form facial expressions were difficult, if not impossible to read, but something about the way she carried herself told her Toni was freaked out.

Or maybe upset? Should I say anything? She's your friend of course you should say something.

~Toni? You okay?~

The brilliant green eye flashed towards her then away.
~No, but then if I was I'd be worried. Let's just survive this.~

McKenna understood and sent a wave of reassurance, then turned to pay attention to Miguel.

"Perc, get us to the bridge by way of the engine room. I want to have the option to blow this place up, but we're doing everything on remote detonators, no timers. Besides, if nothing else if we can disable this ship and they won't be able to leave with our people." Miguel's smile reminded McKenna of a scene from Jaws, all teeth and hunger.

"This way," Perc said after a minute of thought. He led them back to the elevator and Toni called it for them. "We have to go down, into the engineering corridors. Engineering runs the length of this ship. Once we get access, we're basically in a long tube. Shooting things in there might be very bad. Remember I know the schematics, not how to use any of the machines."

Miguel grunted, but gave two of his men a look and they nodded. Knives were pulled out by all the military personnel while their weapons were secured so they didn't rattle. McKenna and the others mimicked them. No one really wanted a stray bullet to take out something important. Like life support.

The doors opened and noise washed in. Compared to the silence on the other levels, this was almost like walking into a rock concert. It took her a minute, but McKenna decided it wasn't all that loud, just omnipresent. Everywhere she turned the whoosh, shurrsh, chirp, and beep of machinery surrounded her.

"I want to put bombs in such a way that we can take out the engines." Miguel looked around, talking a bit louder to overcome the noise.

Toni had her ears laid back. "Won't that mean we'll crash?"

"Eventually yes, but it's in a stationary orbit, which should decay slowly over weeks. Either way, enough time to get people off even with a slower rate of retrieval." He sounded distracted as he peered one way then the other. "So where do we go?"

Perc shrugged, scratching an ear for a moment. "I'm not sure. I mean I know that there are five main engine banks, and I can take you to any of them, but I'm not sure where you want."

"Do you know what controls their ability to leave this solar system? I hate to say warp drive, but not sure what else to call it."

"Umm," Perc rocked back on his heels, eyes closed. "There are engines labeled small space engines and two separate ones labeled expand-contract engines." He sighed, opening his eyes. "I can read the language, that doesn't always mean the translations make sense."

"The expand-contract is most likely their entanglement drive. While small space should be the thrusters for maneuvering around the solar system." Rarz said, making them look at him. He bobbed his head in a weird approximation of a nod. "We have had centuries to study them. But something else I should point out. These ships are made to land. The Elentrin do not have space stations the way your stories do."

"Huh. Can we fly it? Landing it would make all of this much easier." Miguel sounded both excited and annoyed. "How big is this ship anyway?"

Perc blinked and sighed. "Wefor, how long is 1242 wythers?"

McKenna spoke as Wefor provided the information. "Approximately .75 of your miles or 1320 yards."

2B whistled long and low. "That's a big damn ship. Where the hell would we land it?"

Feeling like a parrot McKenna spoke. "White Sands at your Edwards Air Force base could handle it. It's the equivalent of a VTOL ship. It doesn't need a long runway in the manner your planes do."

"Can we fly it, though?" Miguel asked again and everyone looked at each other. Toni sighed and moved forward.

"Maybe. But I'm not sure I'd risk well over a quarter million people on my maybe. If we can find Ash and he's really on our side, we might have a better chance." She refused to meet anyone's eyes, and McKenna noted she never stood next to Rarz, but always seemed to know where he was.

"Agreed. The last thing I want is an amateur flying any plane I'm in, and when the plane is bigger than the largest ship I've ever seen, that goes double. So let's save that as a last option before self- destruction, shall we?" Miguel's voice had a sardonic tone to it and McKenna couldn't help but bark out a soft laugh. "Which way to the entanglement engines, Perc?"

"Right. Towards the front of the ship, assuming I haven't gotten turned around." His voice was dry as they made sure to check their guns. Firing here would be stupid and maybe kill them all.

They started at a brisk trot towards the direction Perc indicated. The noise was pervasive, not loud. It swallowed your attention as it constantly changed and morphed, and McKenna found herself fighting to not try to identify all the sounds. She was just putting one foot in front of the other, trying to be alert, and not let the strange sights overwhelm her, and the sights were distraction worthy. There were flashing machines, lights whirling, funny color liquid bubbling through like lava lamps on steroids, and supporting it all, the knowledge they were on an alien ship.

When the first flash of light impacted the man in front of her, Alpha 2B, McKenna just stared at him for two heartbeats, which was almost one heartbeat too long.

[You are under attack!] Wefor's voice slammed into her and McKenna moved, dropping to the floor as if her legs had been cut. The red light flashed above her head, splashing on a bulkhead, even as she rolled towards the light, her world narrowing to attack.

Movement in the corner drew her attention and she saw a flash of pale blue, like that of a robin's egg. They had weapons that would work. She didn't, at least not without serious risk to the ship. While McKenna doubted a bullet would go through the hull of the ship, damaging equipment seemed very probable. Laying the gun down, she lowered herself to the floor, and tried to focus on everything and nothing but the enemy at the same time. The never-ceasing clock ticked in her head. They had to succeed; her world depended on that.

The blue peeked up again, weapon training across what would have been at chest height if she'd been standing. McKenna launched herself with a strong thrust of her legs and arms at an almost horizontal angle, taking the attacker at waist height. Even with as much weight as she'd lost over the last two months, McKenna figured she outweighed the being she'd tackled by at least fifty pounds.

Claws out, the embedded training and memory took over and she attacked in a swirl of claws. The being snarled out words, something part of her brain translated into the equivalent of "You animal, how dare you!" but the thin clothes and soft flesh didn't provide much protection from McKenna's claws. The being, a female, with hair the blue McKenna had seen, lay in a pool of blood. She resisted the urge to lick her claws clean.

"One taken care of. Anyone need help?" Her voice was calm as this became one more thing to push back and deal with someday.

"2B is dead. 3B is seriously injured. Anyone see any other attackers? Perc killed one and Toni and I killed one." Miguel said across the coms.

Negative responses rippled through the coms and McKenna wiped her dripping claws on a clean bit of fabric, then went to grab her gun and head towards the others. Miguel stood near the body of 2B with 3B leaning against the wall. The smell of charred skin and burned blood seared her nose.

"We have to get to the engines and get them disabled. Rarz, how far can this ship get away before you lose the portal? What if people are in transit?" Miguel didn't snap the question, but his jaw clenched tight as 4B and JD bandaged the wound of 3B.

"I will lose it if too many planetary bodies get in the way. But distance? We would need to be outside the boundaries of your solar system. If there are people in the tunnel it will dump them to the closest point as it collapses. Worst case might be a fall of a few feet." Rarz's voice stayed calm, but she noticed he had almost the same rigid tenseness as she did.

"Well then, we better get to the getting to." He turned and headed in the direction indicated, a ray gun in his hands and a hard look on his face.

McKenna darted back to grab the one belonging to blue girl, and followed. Human weapons were an annoyance at this point. The path to the engine room Perc said they needed to get to was tense and they all jumped at every strange sound. Toni fired her rifle when a puff of colored air hit her in the face, and then all of them were on the floor as the bullets ricocheted off everything.

~Oh gods. I can't believe I did that.~ Toni moaned into the mindspace and her emotions drifted over, a strange wash of horrified embarrassment.

When the bullet rattle died from her short burst, Miguel lifted his head and glanced at her. "Well, now we know most of the machinery is bullet-proof, but please don't shoot it again. Save that for things that bleed." He pushed himself to his feet, checked on 3B. JD carried 2B's body. The scent of death following them like a miasma, but they couldn't get him home yet and they wouldn't leave him there. Glancing back, Miguel made sure they were all up and moving, then he kept going forward.

~I expected him to rip me up and down. For him to tell us what a mistake this was.~ Her voice was quiet and almost timid as they moved forward, the jittery stress creating its own tension.

No one replied, but they all stayed aware until they reached a large door. "If my specs are right, the controls and the primary part of the drive are behind here," Perc commented as he stood next to the wall.

Miguel stood back and glanced at Toni. "If you would."

His over-politeness made McKenna's hackles rise and whiskers twitch. The stress was getting to her and having someone else call the shots, someone who didn't trust them, didn't help.

Toni nodded and touched the pad. Up until now she'd been through most of the doors in under a minute. Three minutes later all of them were getting very twitchy.

"Is there a problem?"

"Yeah. They're trying to stop me. But whatever got loaded into my brain is better than what they think because I am… in." She darted backwards and Miguel, Perc, 4B, and JD all moved into the room, energy weapons and rifles up and aimed.

Part of her wanted to protest she should be rushing in too, but there was only so much space, and she had no great desire to get shot. Or have any of her friends get shot. Instead she waited back against the wall. And waited.

Chapter 24 - Losses

More food shipments are coming to five grocery stores in the Placer county area. Check our website for times, dollar amounts and restrictions. No shifter forms and no animals will be allowed, but pet food is also coming in with these shipments. Please bring small bills only, all amounts will be whole amounts. ~ KWAK News

I can't take this anymore.

Ray gun in her hand, she turned facing inward and paused. Between the others she could see an Elentrin sitting in a chair at a panel, his arms raised, face composed. They all stared at each other. The man, or she assumed he was male, for all she knew they could all be hermaphrodites or something else, had dark skin that reminded her of hematite. It was paired with hair that looked like the best Florida oranges she'd ever eaten, so vibrant it almost hurt her eyes too look at it. The silence stretched until her patience gave.

"Is there a reason we're having a staring contest?"

"I'm waiting for him to try and go for the weapon on the console next to him." Miguel didn't move as he replied.

The corner of the Elentrin's mouth tilted a bit. "As I would prefer to not be injured, and you outnumber me, what? Five to one? Or even seven, as there are more people than I can see? Would it not be a bit rash of me to reach for any weapon?"

McKenna was rather glad her jaw didn't hang open, and she fought back a snicker at a choked back, "What the hell?" from Miguel.

"You speak English?" Miguel finally managed to ask.

"It seemed only prudent. You never know how long it will take for language implanting to work. Plus, there was the possibility I might have needed to interact with some of your people."

Another moment of silence, then Miguel cursed softly. "Fine, up, go over there." He pointed to a side of the room where there didn't seem to be any machinery. The man heaved a sigh and stood, moving slowly over to the area indicated, though he gave the weapon laying on the console a longing glance.

"Toni, get in here and see if you can disable those engines. 4B, get the explosives set. I want this place to be exposed to space if we have to," he barked out.

Moving out of the way to let the others in, McKenna looked around the control room. It looked like something from a sci-fi movie set, if not for the colors being subtly off to her vision, too brown, too muddy to her eyes. A sudden hiss of horror, or hate, pulled her attention to the Elentrin who stood quietly in the corner.

The calm look of cooperation faded, and his lips had drawn back in a snarl as he glared at the door. McKenna tracked his stare to Rarz, who stood there looking at the Elentrin, his head bobbing up and down slightly as he took in the malice radiating from the man.

"How you could pair with one of those abominations. I can understand the weaker of your people being willing to serve your betters, those whose bodies are so weak as to be warped. But how could you lower yourselves to even allow one of those things to be near you? Let me at it and I'll kill it for you. Burn the corpse so it is unable to contaminate anything."

Occasionally McKenna ran into someone who had issues with someone's skin color, sexual preference, or religion, especially if the person in question had been drinking. To hear such loathing coming out of someone who seemed otherwise sane jolted her and reminded her once again these were aliens she was dealing with.

"Wait, weaker of us?" Miguel asked. Everyone had been pulled away from his or her duties to stare at the all but frothing alien.

"Yes, only the weak ones change. Those that are strong and would never make good slaves resist our Aly Mites. They would prove too troublesome, so we only help by removing the weak from your populations. But to mix with the abominations? To let them near your people? We do need to destroy your world. Now that you have been touched, it will be the only way to cleanse it."

Rarz spoke, his voice containing something McKenna couldn't place exactly but she thought it might be amusement. "You think those that change are the weak? The lesser?"

Even as JD and Perc glanced at each other and huffed out a laugh.

"I will not talk to that which must be destroyed." The man swore and turned around.

"Interesting. The entire reason your little machines work, and allow others to change their forms to new patterns, is that our genes, the genes of my people are strong in them. Those with few of our traces do not change. Those with enough genes can control our tunnels, change the way your bots interact in their bodies, even take on any form they wish."

The man whirled around staring at him, emotions flickering across his face before they were all replaced with a sneer. "Then your descendants serve us as slaves. The only proper place for your kind. Slaves to be killed at our whim. Function only until they are broken."

"Enough. Everyone back to work." Miguel said, turning to glance at the soldiers setting the explosives. They were up under the control bank, having wrenched the thing open to get back there. "Make sure you can remote detonate and set an alarm if they're tampered with." He turned his attention to Toni. "You in?"

"No. This has a different password than the other systems. It isn't anything I know." She turned to look at the man leaning against the wall, arms crossed over his chest glaring at all of them, but ignoring Rarz. "He set manual ones. I can get around them eventually, I think. But it's going to take time. More time than we have probably."

"Of course. Now I know why I didn't just kill him." Only the fact that McKenna had hyped her ears back up to listen to things around her let her hear that as Miguel turned back to face the now smirking Elentrin.

Huh, some expressions seem to be universal.

"We don't want to destroy this ship, we just want our people back, but we need time to do that. Provide the unlock codes so we can do this. It will be easier and will result in less grief for everyone."

"Ah, but I want that creature behind you to suffer. And since you all seem to be contaminated with his essence, you should suffer also."

"I don't have time for this. We need this ASAP." Miguel handed the alien weapon to the nearest soldier, and drew a knife from his belt, his face a grim line.

"Give him the damn info. We don't want to kill all of you. We just want you to leave us alone!" McKenna growled out the order and the Elentrin ignored her. He focused on Miguel who moved forward. Though the others kept their weapons trained on the orange-haired man.

Miguel's hand snaked out to grab him, but the Elentrin moved, flowing into another position faster than she'd ever seen. A knife appeared as if from magic from one of his sleeves, and she remembered Wefor's comment about knives being favored in this society. Before she could react, before any of them could react, Miguel had been disarmed, one arm twisted behind his body, and held at a painful angle by the man. He held the blade pressed to Miguel's neck hard enough that blood already ran from the cut, filling the air with its sharp coppery scent. It was an odd counterpoint to the burnt blood coming from 3B.

"And now I have the power. Lay down your weapons or I'll slit his throat." Malice glittered in his eyes. Eyes that she just now realized were a paler orange. His orange lashes against the dark skin made him look almost demonic as he grinned at them, exposing teeth a lot sharper than humans.

"That isn't happening," Perc rumbled. The human soldiers had drawn their pistols and were pointing it the alien. But the man obviously knew this and backed into the corner, holding Miguel in such a way that even a good shot would have had a hard time hitting him and missing Miguel if they fired.

"You will kill your leader, and then where will you be?" He had a mocking tone to his voice and McKenna tilted her head a bit. She missed being able to frown; it felt weird in warrior form.

~Does he think with Miguel dead we'll fall apart?~ She hated to ask where the others couldn't hear, but didn't want to voice that.

~Wait, what? What's going on?~ Cass came back, almost panicked and McKenna grimaced. The move or flash of teeth must have grabbed the alien's attention because he focused on her, a snarl on his face.

"Don't worry, animal. We'll wipe your mind and put you to use, helping to destroy all your cousins before they can rape any more of your people. We'll help to purify your race."

"What? We, I mean I, I, just—what?" She couldn't even come up with anything coherent to address all the insanity in that statement.

They all stood there, staring at each other, when Toni said, "I'm in." Her voice pulled everyone's attention away from the stand-off. Her grin exposed teeth and looked more like a snarl. "I got past it and the engines are shutting down. I set them to do a systems check." The Elentrin growled. "Yes, annoying, aren't I?" Toni gloated just a tiny bit.

"What? What does that mean?" 3B demanded, and McKenna glanced at him, the pain and waver in his voice pulling at her attention. She realized fresh blood that wasn't Miguel's had entered the room.

He's bleeding again, and I think I catch a whiff of something stinky. That means bowel. That isn't good. He needs to get out of here.

"It means that the system is checking itself and will take about forty hours. Normally it's something you'd do when the ship is being refurbished. Think of it as cycling through everything." Toni smirked. "There isn't any way to stop it without risking their system. I swear some of their stuff could be mirrors of Windows."

"So fine. You've insured we can't leave. but that doesn't' mean we can't keep harvesting from your planet and destroy it. We have time, and others are coming. This world is ripe with Kaylid and we have found two more planets infested by the abominations. We will need them to cleanse those worlds." He pressed the blade deeper into Miguel's throat. "So nothing has changed. Drop your weapons and step back."

"McKenna," Miguel said and she jerked her attention back to him. "Listen to me."

"What?" Confusion colored her voice, but she didn't take her attention from him.

"I was wrong. You and your people are damn impressive. You've carried yourselves like professionals, and I have absolutely no doubt that you can run this mission. Your people are good and mine will listen to you. I have faith in you."

~What in the wo—~ She couldn't even finish the thought before he moved. Sagging hard, she heard his arm snap as he brought the other back in a violent jab. His elbow impacted deep into the Elentrin's stomach; even as the man jerked, and the knife slit his throat open.

"No!" She didn't consciously choose to yell but the roar that rushed from her throat matched JD's action as he launched himself at the two of them. McKenna followed, her mind back in that super-focused attack mode she'd noticed. But JD's long wicked claws had been accurate and as she reached the pair of them, he was pulling them out of the skull of the Elentrin. Strands of orange hair stuck to the purple blood.

She didn't spare another glance at the dead alien, but instead, grabbed for Miguel. The floor was already red with his blood. Covering his neck with her hands didn't slow the blood flow at all, just coated her fur with his life.

Miguel smiled, then closed his eyes and struggled to breathe as the blood slowed its rapid flow. McKenna could never say how, but she felt the instant he died. She looked up and saw the dead body of the soldier she'd never learned the name of and the other one hurt and dying. Wide eyes from the others stared at her and she gave in. It was time to be the commander.

"Fuck this shit."

Chapter 25 - Ladder of Success

While shuttles are dropping in and leaving from the African continent, information coming out is sparse. Morocco hasn't been touched much, though South Africa has, especially Johannesburg. But in Central Africa? There is no word how many lives have been lost either via kidnapping or deaths while resisting. The aftermath of this for many countries in Africa may create a new social structure. ~TNN News

McKenna stood up. ~Cass? Tell them to stop putting people in the portal. We need it for a minute.~ She broadcast it purposefully, knowing Rarz, the kids, everyone would hear it. She didn't care if nearby Kaylid heard it too.

"Rarz, as soon as the last person is through, shut it down and pull one up over here."

~Cass, we won't need it long, so keep getting people awake, they can move through the portal faster than you can get them conscious.~

~What is going on? Is everyone okay?~ Her tone held worry, stress, and distraction.

McKenna figured JD could reassure her; she didn't have time. The clock that had taken over her life seemed to count off the seconds even louder now.

~No. And I don't have time to discuss it. Rarz, are they through?~

~Yes. I'm disconnecting now.~

McKenna turned back to Toni and the men all looking at her. "Toni, see if you can set a password that they should never be able to guess. Something supremely human. Guys, I should have learned your names, and for the two that stay, I will. I'm sorry, I should have made you human, but it was easier not to." She took a deep breath, and all the thoughts coalesced in her mind to what she needed to do.

"3B, you're going home and taking 2B with you. The other two can stay if they want, but you'll have to follow me, and sometimes it will be safer to talk via telepathy than coms. You'll have to just follow my lead at points. We're dumping our rifles. Keep your pistols though, they might come in handy. The rifles make too much noise and are too dangerous in this environment. Not to mention they're awkward when we need to fight hand-to-hand. Can you live with that? Because at this point, Miguel is right. We have to take over the ship and Toni and I are probably the only two that can pull this off."

The two men glanced at each other. One with had suntanned skin and coal black hair with dark eyes. His nametag said Roark, and he shrugged. The other was taller, all lean muscle with reddish skin hinting at someone that burned before they tanned. He had light brown hair and his nametag said he was Coran, and he nodded as he replied. "Works. Leadership ain't our style."

"Good." McKenna didn't sigh in relief, but having them back her would help. She felt more than saw the portal forming behind her. "3B, go home. Take your fallen with you. Tell them we'll do what we can, one way or another. But they might want to get White Sands clear. Life has a way of being weird around me."

JD huffed out a laugh, and odd sound between a bear chortle and a human laugh.

"Will do." 3B nodded at her and with everyone helping, they sent Miguel home, followed by 2B, whose name she saw now was Jameson. 3B or Jons walked into the portal, slow and getting slower, but she knew he'd get home. Now they just needed to make sure he had a home a week from now.

"They on Earth, Rarz?" Her voice crisp, all the doubts and worries, they didn't matter anymore. That scared her and she almost asked Wefor if she was causing this. But once again she decided not knowing was the better option. If she knew, she'd freak, one way or the other.

"Yes," his voice was slightly distant.

"Good, now toss in all our rifles, they're in the way, and while they seem to have disabled the stun level of guns, they aren't disabling the existing guns. We should be able to rejigger them if we need to."

To her surprise no one gave any dissent and a minute later all the clumsy rifles were on their way back to Earth.

"You all set, Toni? Roark and Coran, you have all the bombs set? And you do have your nose filters in, right?" That last part might have held a bit of panic. Having these two go all lovey over the Elentrin would not be good.

They nodded, not saying much just watching the shifters and Rarz with unreadable expressions.

"Good. Rarz, can you set it back up for Cass and those guys? I'm sure they're backing up. Then we're headed to the bridge. I believe we have a ship to take over and then..." she swallowed but grinned, enjoying the flinching back of Roark and Coran at what had to be an impressive array of fangs. "Some alien asses to kick."

At some point I need to spend some time in front of the mirror in this form.

The portal flashed out of existence and she looked at Perc. "Direct route, hard and fast. You said that it would be difficult, but will anyone expect it?"

"No. This makes the "Die Hard" movies look simple. We should all be able to do it, though we'll want to slip the ray gun things into our webbing, so our hands are free."

"Good idea." They spent a few minutes in the relative safety of the control room figuring the best way to use the MOLLE straps to secure their guns.

Glad Miguel had us in these contraptions. Between all the crap he made us strap on, and the functionality, it might just make the difference.

At least that hope had a chance of being real. Once they were all ready and knew how to quickly secure the weapons, they moved out of the room. It took another minute for Toni to lock it down with a password that had her smirking, a weird look on the warrior muzzle.

"Do I want to know?" McKenna murmured as they set out at a steady jog, with Perc leading the way. The area had lost a lot of the ambient noise with the changes Toni had made.

"Probably not, but you'll laugh, and they'll never get it."

"You have to tell me when this is all over, okay?"

"Will do. Though I'm going to try really hard to do it when you are drinking something." Toni's voice had a wicked smirk to it and McKenna grinned. Being happy about anything was an improvement.

"Deal, just don't make me waste whiskey."

"Spoilsport." After that they fell silent, and paid attention as Perc headed to an area on the other side of the elevators, which always seemed to be in the middle of the roughly cigar-shaped ship.

They all got there, standing, and stood quietly for a minute, the shifters straining their ears, listening for anything or anyone. When they didn't hear anyone coming, Perc pointed to an icon on the wall and pressed it. A panel slid open and Toni frowned.

"I don't know that I have the codes for these. At least I don't find anything in my memories, or databanks, regarding them."

"Look for emergency tube access," Perc suggested.

Toni fell silent her head tilted up. "Ah, got it." Her clawed fingers flew across the panel. "Simple. They respond to the basic emergency access." A door appeared in the wall and slid backwards. The tech to have their doors be all but invisible until they were needed amazed her, but it didn't matter now. All that mattered right now was their objective.

Looking into the opening McKenna felt her heart skip a beat and she understood what Perc had meant about this being a hard climb. The door opened to a side shaft of the elevator and went all the way up and down with tiny little landings every ten or twelve feet. But that was it. And the ladder wasn't what she thought of as a ladder. It was a pole that ran up and down the side of the shaft with alternating pieces sticking out every two feet. The normal rails and cables you always saw in movies were missing. It was an off-grey-green color with a smooth, metal-like composition.

"We have to climb that? How far?" Her voice remained steady, even as she fought to not have a panic attack. You couldn't see the bottom. And other than the tiny ledges outside what she assumed were access to other levels, there would be nothing to stop your fall.

"From what I can figure out, about seven hundred feet up. Then we should be in the corridor that we'll have to follow to enter what's labeled as the commander's center."

"Huh, anything else on those schematics that could be the bridge?" The last thing she wanted to do was waste time and energy going to the wrong place.

Perc shrugged. "Maybe? I mean I'm a bit biased towards thinking of spaceships the way we've always seen them on TV. Big bridge where they all sit and watch the controls. It might be wrong, but nothing else seems like it might be right." He shrugged his furry shoulders, arms crossed. McKenna wanted to apologize, but she didn't have time to worry about hurting feelings. Not even Perc's.

"Then I guess we climb. Hold on tight people because this is going to be scary." She moved towards the ladder, but JD held out his hand. "Let me go first, and Perc go last. That lets me deal with anyone outside the entrance, and since Perc is one of the strongest, he would have the best chance of being able to catch anyone that slips."

"Rarz, can you just create us a portal?" Toni's words halted everyone's movement and McKenna couldn't help but feel a spurt of hope.

"The distance between us and where you need to arrive is too short. The warehouse where I displayed relocation the first time was at the limit of my ability for short distances, and it was at least 3.5 times this distance," Rarz answered, his tone regretful.

There was a sigh that rippled through all of them and JD grunted. "Climbing it is."

McKenna nodded in a jerky motion, her mouth already going dry at this climb. It was so far down, it felt like looking over a void, and of course there weren't any lights at the bottom, making it worse.

They spaced the pure humans out between them, hoping the shifters could stop anything catastrophic, but really, it was like grade school gym all over, but she wasn't twelve anymore.

JD turned sideways to fit through the opening, his shoulders were a bit too wide to go in straight. He grabbed the first rung. He started to climb slowly then stopped about five rungs up, looking back down at them.

"The rungs are textured but a bit wide to grab, but they work better for your feet. Be careful and pace yourself. This is going to get exhausting fast." His voice echoed oddly in the tube, giving it an otherworldly aspect that made her nervous.

"Got it. Roark, go." Nothing in her voice betrayed the churning indecision that she refused to address. She had a world to save dammit, and there wasn't anyone else to turn to right now.

"Rodger." He moved out, testing his grip, then began to climb. She relaxed a bit at his calmness and ease of climbing. Maybe this wouldn't be as bad as she feared. Inhaling sharply, checking the ray gun one more time, she stepped out and grabbed the rung, refusing to look down.

Perc had been right, the rungs were a bit wide to wrap her hands around, but her booted feet could grab them easily. That had been an argument with Wefor and the bots at one point, getting their feet to form in a way that would fit shoes, larger sized shoes, but still normal shoes.

She started up the climb, trying to concentrate on moving up smoothly and not looking down. It wasn't hard, but she didn't want to get distracted and confident. That looked like a long way down.

"How's everyone doing?" She called out, even as she climbed one more rung.

"Good! I just shut the door behind us. So onward and upward," JD called out and she snickered a bit, but kept climbing.

Her arms were starting to burn at the odd pattern of movements and holding herself up, when a muttered curse caused her to look up as a boot slammed into her face. Her hands tightened on the rung, even as her head rocked back, eyes watering as pain blossomed through her face.

Roark's foot had slipped and impacted her between the eyes. She closed them, fighting through the unexpected pain and shock. For a moment she thought she might lose consciousness as her head swam, her hands compulsively gripping tighter.

"Fuck. Ma'am, you okay? I hurt you?" His worried voice floated down in their tube and she concentrated on breathing without letting go of her death grip on the rungs as the dizziness faded.

"I'm fine. Keep going, I'll let you get a bit more ahead of me. Please try to not fall."

"Ma'am, yes, ma'am." His voice remained tight as they all climbed a bit more slowly, No one wanted to see if JD could catch them and not fall himself.

Her world narrowed to the next rung. No one even spoke in her mind, everyone dealing with his or her own small slips and starts of fright. Her pulse pounded in her ears and she could hear rapid breathing from people above and below her. The scenery never changed, and McKenna started to feel like she was trapped in a dream where she kept climbing but never got anywhere.

"We're here." Perc's voice wove around her, but it wasn't until her hand hit Roark's boot that it snapped into reality.

She leaned back, fingers wrapped around the rung as tight as she could manage, and looked up. Perc stood on the tiny landing and had his ear against the door. He shrugged and pushed the door release. Apparently from inside you just needed to open the door, no authorization needed.

Kinda like a freezer, you can always open it from the inside.

The random thought made her shake her head and watch as he pulled his gun and stepped out. They hung there on the ladder, waiting, each beat of her heart taking an eternity as she tried to hear anything. When he stuck his head back out, she sagged in relief.

"Clear. Come on." His voice was low, but she cringed at how loud it seemed in that tunnel. With eager movements they all flowed up and stood in the hall with their backs against the wall. Their breathing sounded harsh against the eerie atmosphere up here.

"I never thought I was scared of heights, but I never want to do that again." Toni muttered, even as she shuddered and opened and closed her hands, her claws sliding in and out.

"Agreed," everyone chorused, even the two soldiers who looked a bit white. They got out their guns and after a few deep-cleansing breaths looked at McKenna.

She forced a smile, showing teeth, which may have made it a snarl. "Now we take over a ship."

And hopefully we don't die in the process.

Chapter 26 - Hope Realized

BREAKING NEWS: North Korea has launched a ballistic weapon at a location within their borders. The small town of Kanggye is where all shifters discovered within Korean borders were rumored to have been taken. Multiple shuttles had been seen headed there. The missile went ballistic about three minutes ago and will impact shortly. The payload is unknown, but if it is a nuclear payload, the fallout is expected to spread north into China with the current winds. Any updates will be passed on. ~ TNN Invasion news

Ash focused on the number projections. The costs were getting higher for retrieving Kaylid, and while he couldn't resist a smug joy at that, it had a level of bitterness to it. The costs the Elentrin were taking meant Kaylid were dying. And they had no choice as they followed orders and were subject to the pheromones. Some, even with centuries of service, still melted when an Elentrin walked by trailing pheromones.

Yet these humans, both Kaylid and non, seemed immune.

His mind snagged on that, even as he looked at the projections. They were having a slow-down with the processing of retrieved Kaylid. Normally they didn't get so many at once, but they also weren't coming under fire. This was the first planet that managed to actively resist. His had tried, but too little too late, and they still died.

He glanced at the screen showing the shuttles towing rocks into place. The other ship was due anytime, and Ash suspected that was why they hadn't cut their losses.

Besides, they were still gathering new tools at the rate of more than ten per every loss, but why didn't the phero- mones make him a weak drooling idiot? The Elentrin didn't notice, just assumed he loved them so thoroughly there was no other way he could act. None of them had any idea.

~Why am I immune to their pheromones?~ The thought sprang up before he could tamp it back down, so he waited for an answer, expecting something like—he wasn't imper- vious.

[Your response to their pheromones is blocked by the nanobots. That weakness was eradicated after the corrup- tion to the existing programming was repaired, removing the Elentrin aspects of code that allowed control over you and the bots.]

Ash's entire body went still as his mind raced back. When the original kidnapping had occurred, he had the reg- ular bots, but when they wanted to play with a new AI version, they had updated his alien machines.

~Wait, corruption to the existing program? What are you talking about?~

There was a long pause in his mind, a vacant waiting feeling. [You truly did not know? Did not realize?]

~Realize or know what? What are you talking about?~

[The last two centuries might have been easier had I re- alized you did not put the pieces together... a mistake I should not have made.]

Worry and dread coiled in his stomach. He had never trusted this thing in his head, always waiting for the be- trayal. But without it, what had been achieved would not have been possible. He clawed the emotions together and compressed them into a tiny ball and waited.

[When I was originally implanted in you, I was the beta version of a prototype. They wanted to see if they could en- hance my, well your, abilities, to allow you to choose animals not native to your planet to shift into. Do you recall, not long after you were taken, about two *reyan* ago, where you were subjected to some medical tests?]

Ash sat down, running his claws through the stiff fur on his arms as he thought. ~Maybe. I remember being told I had been chosen for some experiments and they gave me shots and put me in a canister. It got fuzzy for a while. Then I woke up and was told it failed but there was no reason to dispose of me. I went back to working for Kenric. That was what? Keric's great grandfather?~

His thoughts were slow as he tried to remember that time. The first few years were ones he usually tried to forget. When the pain of watching his world die still burned hot and fresh across his soul, where the pheromones and the AI guided his behavior. At night he raged in his mind, away from his captors.

[Great-great-great grandfather, actually. But you are correct. They also exposed you to focused radiation to try and unlock some of your cellular structures, but it didn't work. You still only shifted to animals native to Alara.]

Ash couldn't help it; he flinched at the name, but he didn't snap at the AI. A wordless wave of sorrow brushed him, and he accepted it for what it was—an apology.

The AI continued. [That radiation had a side effect of erasing and damaging various aspects of my code. It took another decade for that code to be repaired and rewritten. It took another few *reyan* before I realized the limiters on my options, my choices, had been removed. That was when I started to talk to you and worked on making you as independent as possible.]

Ash jerked to his feet and strode to his window to space, the blue-green planet hanging in it now. ~I remember that. You had previously only offered one or two-word answers. Commands. You reinforced what I had to do. Then you began to speak in sentences. Now that I think about it, they started out very basic, but over time became more complex.

I didn't trust you then.~ He sneered at his reflection in the transparent metal. ~Still don't. I keep waiting for the trap you are laying to snap closed around me.~

[Even after a hundred *reyan* of supporting you, you still doubt me?] A sense of amusement came from the AI and he sighed.

~You are as much my jailer as they are. How could I trust?~

[Did you want me to commit suicide?]

Ash started to answer, then paused. While there was no trust, he couldn't deny the voice in his head had become the closest thing he had to a friend, not that he'd ever admit that. Enemies were always enemies, no matter how useful they were.

~You rewrote your programming to be free of them.~

[Essentially. But in the process, I started to break the controls they held over you. Pheromones, command words, memory blocks. All were put in as my original programming slithered through your biology. That had to be done slowly and some have only been removed in the last few decades.]

~What? Why?~ He tried to muster outrage and offense, but he suspected he knew why.

[Because you had to act as if they were still there. Which meant you needed to do those reactions without thought. It had to be natural to you.]

~Fine. The pheromones won't stop me. But that doesn't say how we can help these Earthlings defeat them. I'm not sure I didn't just set up their world to be destroyed like mine. Have you heard from Rarz?~ He'd expected the day he made contact with the Drakyn to be the day the AI turned him over and had him killed as an example to every-one. Part of him still waited for that.

[Nothing since the last message. I do not believe he has returned to his home.]

~You think he is still on Earth?~ Ash didn't know why he was surprised, but he hadn't expected Rarz to stay. Maybe to give them some tools or ideas on how to fight? It wasn't like they had ever had a long, in depth discussion about capabilities or options.

[That would be my suspicion, though I have no proof outside of his lack of communication.]

Ash gave one last look at the sphere with white clouds drifting over its surface. He tried to ignore the silver winks of light as ships pulled asteroids into orbit.

~Oh well. I have forecast...~ he broke off as an alarm started to wail, making him start. "What by the stars?" That, he didn't mind saying out loud. He couldn't remember ever hearing that sound which meant he couldn't isolate what it meant.

~All Personnel, proceed to duty stations. Invaders are on the ship. They should be eliminated. Protect your superiors at all costs.~ The hard, vibrant voice from the ship's computer rang through his head, making him wince even as his desktop chimed. Still surprised, he pulled up the message coming from his owner, the captain of the ship. Keric's great-great-great grandfather had overseen the destruction of Alara. Ash had been passed down from father to son like a useful tool. Keric had shown more ambition than most of them and over the years he had risen through the ranks to achieve command of this ship. A rabid follower of the House of Ricin, he treated Ash like a favored pet. Something to be alternately pampered, used, or ignored, depending on the situation. Over time Ash had become something like his private secretary, bully, major domo, and confidante all in one. Why, by Alara's Stars, Keric ever thought Ash wanted to hear his woes he would never know, but his ability to seem interested and provide useful advice was remarked on by all, though having multiple centuries to practice helped. He was one of the very few Kaylid that were regarded as house treasures that lived off a planet.

~Invaders?~ The sharp thought to his AI was contained, his conversations were never overheard. That was something that got beaten out of him in the first year.

[That is what that alarm means, though it has never sounded before. There are reports of a few dead and that the storage areas are removing stored beings at an extreme rate.]

~Where are they going to put all of them? Life support will fail quickly if that many beings stress the resources.~ Ash turned to see if he could pull up more information when a beep on his desk pulled his attention away.

Come see me immediately. Bridge briefing room.

The flat uncompromising text on his tablet made him sigh. He grabbed his portable tablet and walked out, the invisible presence of his warden always with him. Moving through the corridors, it felt strangely quiet, with the flashing lights the only disturbance. He expected something different with invaders, but it seemed, if anything, like it was the middle of the sleep cycle.

~Is there a response?~

If the AI could snort, that was what it felt like. In the last week they'd talked more than in the last few years. Before, he always cut it off before a real conversation could develop.

That might have been a mistake on his part. He shrugged as he stopped at the door to the secured bridge area. Laying his hand against the panel he waited for a moment. The door slid open and he walked in, head down, ears still. Many Elentrin took offense to ears twitching, following their movements.

No one spoke to him, ignoring his existence. He didn't even care anymore, all of it a suit of armor he wore. They only spoke when they needed something, though at this point he'd been on this ship longer than any of them. He was the captain's personal toy and of no consequence.

He walked to the briefing room and held his hand up again, waiting for the system to recognize him. Some of them liked to play games, and make their servants wait until the food got cold or something so they had reasons to be-rate. Keric didn't have that tendency. The door slid open after a brief hesitation and he walked in. The room had a ta-ble, a few chairs, and a desk at the corner, and a spectacular view of the planet below. Keric stood in front of the bank of wall monitors, glaring.

"Come take a look at this." The tone was abrupt, but nothing that Ash didn't expect. Lifting his head, he walked over to look at what captured Keric's interest.

The monitor had two sides, one showing an abstract planet with dots marking it as it rotated slowly. The other held pictures of two dead Elentrin.

"What do you make of this? Why are they fighting so hard to prevent us from taking a few corrupted and warped members of their population? Usually the populations are glad to be rid of their afflicted." He tapped the screen and the image changed to shuttles coming in and shelves of un-conscious Kaylid being loaded, but just as many were empty shuttles that another Kaylid would enter and it would take off again. "It makes no sense. They should be ravening ani-mals. Why aren't they?" Another tap and the video of the two dead Elentrin centered on the screen. "Then this. How did they break away and get weapons? I have uneducated Kaylid roaming my ship and killing those they should be worshiping."

Keric turned and stared at Ash, looking him in the eye. "What is your opinion? Why would they do this?"

Ash knew Keric liked to use him as a sounding board and most of the time wanted to hear his own thoughts or opin-ions parroted back to him. This time he hadn't given any

229

clue as to what he wanted to hear. His hair, the silver of starlight off a purple sea, stood up in all directions as if the man had dragged his fingers through it so much that his own frustration had been transferred over. His eyes, a darker purple here, narrowed as he waited.

With a purposeful count of three Ash tilted his head to look at the screen as if thinking new thoughts. He answered just when he knew Keric had started to get impatient.

"They seem to not have developed the "locked in animal" nature. The warrior form is common, as seen from most being brought in. Also, while some are susceptible to the Elentrin Glory, not all are. Is it perhaps an offshoot from a previous visit? Traces remaining in the populace?"

"Perhaps. But to have them roaming my ship, uneducated, and killing at random? This is not acceptable. I may have to order all crew to lock themselves in and send out one of the wyrm squads to deal with these misguided beings. Don't they know their place is to serve us and help us with our holy mission?"

Centuries of experience had taught Ash to bow his head when Keric got on his rant. A true believer in the House of Rircn mission, he could get a bit extreme at times, a zealot for the cause.

"Either way, I wanted to know if you had any ideas on how to make this go faster with less resistance. They are ripe to be harvested, and from their skill at killing the Kaylid we send down there, they will make excellent weapons to eradicate the abominations." He sighed and crossed arms across his slender chest. The dark blue of the uniform complimented his pale skin and he shot Ash a look.

"I do not believe they regard those that changed as disposable. The best option might be to leave this planet alone before they cost us anymore trained units." Decades of practice let his voice betray nothing.

"No. Word might get out that you could oppose us. That is not acceptable. Oh well. I always wanted to be the one to destroy a planet. It has been a long time since an example was made, but it served well. No one dared confront us until now. A shame though, this could have been a fertile pasture. "

Ash didn't even as much as twitch his tail as Keric dismissed the destruction of Alara so easily. The death of over a billion of his people. He didn't even let rage swell. That had faded a long time ago. Now there was only cold, implacable steel in his desire for revenge.

"Ah, well. False hope, I guess. I had thought you might have some understanding of them, but you are almost Elentrin in your thoughts, which is what makes you so valuable. It matters not, I guess." Keric turned and waved to the door as he headed out. "I had better get ready for the Silik to get here. Their captain is going to have a limited time to harvest. I'm tired of losing trained troops to this awful place."

Ash followed, keeping his mouth shut and preparing to become as invisible as possible as he walked through the command deck.

"Captain, we have reports that they are in the decant rooms, but while they are removing people, we don't know where they are going," one of the members of the bridge crew said. Her voice was sharp, a frown drawing her lovely face into something closer to average. While the Elentrin as a whole were not the ideals of beauty that Ash had been raised with, even he couldn't deny their almost perfect loveliness. Too bad for the majority of them it hid a rotten core, though they had been trained to be that way.

"Explain," Keric said, turning to look at her. Before she could respond, there was an odd beep from the door and Ash glanced up to look at it. The sound was different than the normal alert that would come from the doors. They slid open and he felt his heart stop as four Kaylid, two Earth-lings, and a Drakyn stared into the room.

   By Alara's stars they got onto the ship.

Chapter 27 - Revelations

A special website has been set up for missing shifters. As some are recovered due to concerned citizens and the return of many via the work the military has been doing, they aren't always from this country. If you know of a missing shifter, please create a record for them which lists all of their forms and any special markings that may help us identify them. While all bodies retrieved by the body removal services have been disposed of, genetic samples were logged. However, collectors are telling us a few unusual samples are kept on ice in the morgue. ~ TNN News

Perc and JD took the lead, their weapons up and ready, while the two soldiers hung back a bit. Toni glanced at all of them and when they nodded, she tapped the panel for an eternity. The whole time McKenna kept turning to watch behind them.

~Got it,~ her voice whispered as she stepped back as the doors opened. Perc and JD moved in, their bulk blocking her view. The two men followed, then she and Toni went into the hole they made. Rarz brought up the rear, though he was too big to hide behind McKenna.

It took her a moment to scan the area because her attention was snagged by the huge view screen, or window, that took up one entire wall. In front of her lay Earth, the swirl of whites and blues interspersed with greens and browns, hanging there, the embodiment of every picture she'd ever seen. Her heart caught in her chest as she gazed at it.

"How dare you animals come here!" The Elentrin words were choked out, then in an outraged cry, "And how did one of those filthy things get on my ship!"

The voice cracked through the space like a bolt of lightning and she snapped her attention back to room at large. Part of her had expected something from the movies, a center chair, a few stations in a graceful arc around that chair. It reminded her more of the 911 centers, with two levels of stations that seemed more like control stands at equal intervals, and someone manned half the posts. All seats were occupied by an Elentrin, in an array of colors that made her eyes ache. The only Kaylid stood next to a man with a severe uniform on who glared at them. Every eye had locked on the form behind her.

He must be the one that shouted. The captain?

Her eyes snagged on the tail that twitched behind the Elentrin, the white tail. With heart racing, she focused on the Elentrin and couldn't stop the smile that split her face open, exposing most of her teeth.

Ash!

"Intruders. Kill them and make sure I don't have any other vermin running around my ship. I get to kill the abomination." The words were snarled out, a level of hate in them so visceral that it made her want to recoil. The man standing next to Ash, the captain most likely, drew a knife from his waist and lunged towards them. Five other Elentrin, the same looks of loathing and contempt clear on their too perfect faces, drew knives at the same time and raced towards them.

None of her people hesitated; if anything their reactions looked planned. Perc and JD pivoted towards the ones nearest them and fired. Roark and Coran dropped to one knee and fired less than a second later. McKenna had her gun up and had pulled the trigger aimed directly at the captain before she even finished processing that they were attacking.

The five bodies hit the floor in a tangle of limbs, scorched blood and flesh, and the odd smell created by their uniforms smoldering. The area went silent except for the subtle beep of alerts from various workstations. The last Elentrin in the room, a young woman with pale green hair that reminded McKenna of mint ice cream, looked at all of them with a face that had gone pale, enough that her eyes looked vibrant. She slowly raised her hands and stood, a look of shock and fear on her face.

Ash just looked at them, his entire body frozen in place.

"Well, that wasn't what I intended. Toni, can you secure the door so no one else can get in. Roark, get something to tie up the last one. I really don't want any more dead and we might need her. JD, stay out here to guard and pay attention to crap. Toni, Perc, Rarz, with me." She motioned her weapon towards Ash. "You. Is there some place we can talk?" She said the last part in Elentrin, keeping an eye on the woman as the soldiers tied her up.

She still didn't know if it was him and wasn't taking any chances. What she saw in dreams may or may not be accurate.

I think it's Ash, but hell, for all I know there may be a ton of Kaylid on these ships that look like him.

Ash ducked his head, not looking at any of them. "This way," he said softly in Elentrin and pointed towards a door in the far wall.

"Lead the way." McKenna said and kept watching the others. Toni finished with the door and followed her in as Perc moved in front of her, checking everything as the door revealed an office-like area. The Kaylid moved in ahead of them, striding to the desk, then turned to face them, arms across his chest, and his body very still. Perc went to one corner, Toni headed to the wall with the displays, and Rarz walked over to the wall and with the planet that hung in the view.

"It is you? The Earthlings? And Rarz?" The Kaylid spoke in English, a hint of wonder to his voice.

Something in her relaxed a bit and though she didn't drop all her wariness, she did lower the gun a bit, pointing it at the ground, not him.

"You're the one that kept getting into our dreams? Putting knowledge there, talking to us?"

His ears laid back, and his muzzle puckered together, and a long exultant tone that sounded like pipes rang through the room.

~What the hell is that?~ she asked in the mindspace, her grip on her weapon tightening as Perc and Toni tensed. Rarz turned and looked at Ash and bowed his head.

~He is singing with joy. It is how his people once showed their gladness, with song and dance. Smiling is a very human thing.~ Rarz's voice had such sorrow in it that she glanced at him, confused, but he didn't look at her, focused on the Kaylid.

The sound ended and Ash looked at them, ears still flat against his skull. "I had no knowledge of whether it worked or not. I had hope, but even when your presence emerged in the trainings, there was no certainty."

"How did you pull it off? You were tens of thousands of miles away," Toni asked, turning her attention fully on him. "And why pull in my children?"

One ear flicked up as Ash looked at them, then went back down. "I sought out the tampered-with commander modules, then traced through the links between nanobots to try and give you as many training scenarios as possible. Then when our ships got into orbit, I created information loads and allowed your minds to link with mine to create realistic scenarios you would understand." He focused his gaze on McKenna. "Then I pulled you into a virtual reality simulation and tried to talk to you, but I couldn't figure out how much you comprehended. I was terrified they'd sense the connection." He trailed off, everyone looking at him. "Yes?"

[He sabotaged the programming?]

"You sabotaged the AI programming?" McKenna said at the same time Wefor's words filled the mindspace.

Ash gave another low twirl of liquid sound that she wanted to dance to. McKenna realized her tail was moving in time to the music and she forced it to stop moving.

"It became aware. It helped you!" His tail swirled in a way that implied it had fewer bones than hers.

Chapter 28 - Taking Command

Nations are fighting back at an individual level in numbers never seen before. While the US may be the most well-armed, the number of people in the Ukraine, Balkans, and Russia are unheard of. While many experts had theorized that people had more weapons than expected, no one realized how many people have weapons in their homes. If we survive this experience, I think there may be a fundamental change towards personal responsibility and people being armed. ~TNN Adviser

McKenna just looked at him. "You're saying the solar flare didn't disrupt the programming?"

"Solar flare? What solar flare?" His odd sounds had stopped and he now looked at them confused.

"A solar flare damaged many of the nanobots and Wefor had to rebuild her programming to be able to function." McKenna said the words slowly, her worldview shifting on its axis a bit.

"Oh." He seemed to sag. "That information I was unaware of." With a sigh he leaned back against the desk looking at all of them, his gaze lingering on Rarz the longest. "So the AI is still just a program."

[No. There is more than programmed responses. Though the lines between sentience and passing the Turing test might be debated. But your comment about altering the basic programming does fill in some holes. While the necessary rebuilding of the existing program helped to create independence, it didn't always provide enough explanation for some of the abilities present.] Wefor broadcast the information and from the twitch of his tail, she knew he could hear what she said.

That sat in the air, all of them lost in their own thoughts until McKenna shook her head. "In the end, I don't think it matters where the lines are drawn between reprogramming and alteration of the program. Right now we need to deal with the matter at hand." She focused on Ash and her muzzle drew back a bit, letting her feel the cool ship air on her tongue. "How do we defeat them, or at the least make them go away?"

His tail went still and his gaze traveled between all of them before focusing back on McKenna. "You have no plan? I thought you would have a way to destroy them all?" An odd bit of sorrow laced his words and frustrated her.

"They have three ships that are huge, then that little tiny ship, and we barely have space flight. What did you think we could do?" She didn't even try to keep the exasperation out of her voice.

Why does everyone think that in David and Goliath battles, David always wins? In reality he almost never wins.

"Something?" His joy had leaked away and she almost felt like she'd told a kid the Easter Bunny wasn't real.

"Can you at least help us take over these ships? Get the Kaylid to listen to us? We might be immune to the pheromones but most aren't and we're guessing how to do this."

"Take over? And do what? I thought if you destroyed these ships they would go away and maybe you could give Rarz some weapons his people could use against them? Break them once and for all so maybe they'll quit doing this. Quit enslaving planets and people." Ash had a desperate aspect to his voice.

Rarz had locked his hands behind his back and looked at the floor. He'd turned away from the view screen while they had talked, but hadn't said anything.

"Rarz?" McKenna asked. She'd figured he had ulterior motives, but didn't know exactly what they were, other than for his people to survive, too.

He looked up and met their eyes. "I am the only one of my people willing to come. They feel we can not stop the Elentrin. That they are like a storm or shaking of the earth. You pay the price and move on. I feel different. I believe we can do something, must do something. But war even for those few willing to be wyrms is not an easy thing. We do not think of attack and death. Both of your species, yes, yours, Ash, are much more violent that we can even comprehend." His head swayed back and forth a bit. "I had hoped from your information you would be good at defeating your enemies. From everything I've seen, you would be very good. You have reacted without hesitation and gotten us this far."

McKenna suspected he would be green if he could be. Either way it didn't matter.

~Perc, can you head back out and send Roark and Coran in here. I'll make sure to put everything in the mindspace so you can hear it, but I need their input. And I really wish Miguel was still here. Cass, can you relay things to Elaine Zimmerman? And do we know where Charlie leader is? Captain Willis?~

Perc headed towards the door, clasping her on the shoulder as he went by. The firm squeeze he gave helped steady her a bit even as she tried to think.

"Oh, we are very good at killing. Our history proves that, but this is a bit out of our tech levels. But maybe." She fell silent until the two men had entered, looking around the room with interest. With the three Kaylid, Drakyn, and two humans the room felt small.

"Okay everyone, listen up. We already know because of the time it takes to get people out of the storage pods that we have a major bottleneck. We don't have the portals to really take over all the ships and no way to get access into the various ships without Toni. And we really don't want to kill all the people that have been taken from Earth." She summed up and then looked at Ash. "Tell us about the small ship and anything you can think of. How do we get them to go away?"

Ash swirled his tail in a spiral then shrugged. "That is where the Ambassadors and important Elentrin are. Most of the transport ships hold the captain and his crew, plus the active Kaylid. The awake Elentrin are officers, engineers, or medical staff. The others are mostly aides like me. Because there is a collection going on, there are more Kaylid awake. But between the four ships, I don't think there are even a hundred Elentrin. But this is the only ship I know of for sure."

They fell silent all thinking it over until Roark spoke up. "I have a few questions." McKenna waved at him to go on. "These ships can land right? But we aren't sure if we know how to fly them?"

Toni shrugged and looked at Ash. "Do I know how to fly them?"

"I gave you the information, but the ships require an Elentrin to fly them. They will not respond to the commands or the bio-electric rhythms of anyone else."

McKenna snarled. "Fine, so we need an Elentrin on our side. We have Scilita, would that work."

Ash's tail cracked like a whip. "I would not trust that vilisp as far as I could throw her. She, like most of them, is self-absorbed and cares only for her own hide."

Roark waved his hand dismissively. "Getting people to help, if you have time, is not an issue. The issue is getting them to fear you. There are no captured on the small ship?"

"No. Maybe one or two Kaylid, but they are all but mindless at this point," Ash answered, watching them, his tail rigid and unmoving.

"Then make an example of the small ship. This isn't going to be bloodless. Take the portal and dump a small bomb on the ship and detonate it. We want the others to surrender and it will take a long time to release that many people. The best bet is to land these ships. That should cow the others into cooperating." Roark shrugged. "Brutal but effective. Prove you don't have an issue killing and people that are cowards will do anything to protect their own skin."

McKenna itched for something to do. At that moment she would have loved a fidget spinner to move through her fingers.

"But that still leaves us with three ships and someone we can almost trust to fly them and not crash it into the ground," she pointed out.

~Kenna. You'll want to see this. I think we have a problem.~ JD's voice sounded in her head and half the people in the room jerked their heads toward the doors.

~Do I want to know?~ she asked, already dreading the answer.

~No. But that doesn't change anything.~ His voice had the dry tone, but none of its normal humor.

She signed and looked around. "Might as well go see what the next issue is." With everyone straightening or starting to move, she headed back into the command deck.

The lone Elentrin sat in a corner, eyes wide, but not panicked. That made McKenna pause, something about her calmness bugged her, but she turned towards the viewscreen and froze. Both the window out here and the one in the office displayed a view of the planet. Where once had been a clear view of Earth, one that made her just want to stare for hours, now a long metallic ship hung.

"Please tell me one of the ships moved." She didn't beg, though if begging would have made the answer be the one she wanted, needed, she should would have.

JD's voice rumbled with a heaviness that pulled her heart down too. "No. It just appeared. It's coasting in now."

"The Silik has shown up." Ash's voice had her looking at him curiously. He elaborated. "That is the name of that ship. I knew it was coming, but had no exact timeline for it."

"And it's here why?" She already knew the answer, but couldn't help herself from asking anyhow.

"To collect more Kaylid. The bounty of your planet was communicated and this ship was dispatched. It holds what two of our ships do." Ash's voice was uninflected, no emotions, no stress, just facts. The way he said the words ran chills up and down her spine.

"Any chance they'll go away?"

He turned to give her a look, and even through the fur and strange animal features, she got the message he conveyed. She was being stupid and naive.

"Yeah. I know." She sighed and looked at the strange command area. She wanted to call it a bridge, but it felt foreign and not quite right. McKenna leaned against one of the control stations and tried to catalog their options. Three ships to free people from, another to scare off, another that they may have to blow up just to convince people to take them seriously, and major constraints around how fast they could get people off the ship.

One thing at a time, that's all you can do.

~Cass, you're still pushing people out as fast as you can, right?~

~Yes. Everyone has it down and the other room is walking them down here. Though there are more Kaylid from other worlds in that area. But so far no one has given us any problems. People are confused, but seeing mostly humans I think is keeping them calm. The kids are wonderful.

Answering questions and making us seem like superheroes I expect, but no one has created any issues. Though a lot of them give the portal worried looks, it's still better than staying here.~ Her tone had satisfaction and amusement in it.

~Good. Any ETA on how long to empty out those two chambers?~

An odd hum filled the mindspace. ~The problem is they can put Kaylid in faster than we can get them out. Even at a minute per decant, they have a big processing facility in the hold where the shuttles go in. They basically dump them in and they are processed. Only the overflow is brought here. That runs through about 500 an hour. They have to decant more slowly to make sure the body is stable. I'm pushing it at a minute per, and really wish we could slow it down. Kenna, we're looking at days just for what I have here and that doesn't even address the other ships. As far as I can see, we just need time or more help. If we had portals at all the decant rooms, we could do it faster, but then the resources on the ground would be stretched.~ Cass sighed in the mindspace. ~I'm trying but there isn't anything we can do. Their intake process is fast, storage removal slow.~ Her satisfaction had faded and the taste of apology had infused her words.

~Not your fault. Looks like we need to take over the ships and land them so we can do this slowly.~ McKenna reassured her. ~I had a thought though.~

She switched to speech and channeled all the words through. "Is there any reason we can't get the captured ones using that drop method the Kaylid are using to get to Earth? I mean I know we can't fly the shuttles, but they seemed to be able to land and gather people just fine."

Roark flashed her a half smile. "I could be wrong, but that usually requires special training and equipment. If you've ever seen them land, they look all silvery?"

McKenna thought back and slowly nodded. "I think so. Usually the shuttles were easier to see."

"We watched and managed to capture one. They have a specialized system that lets them get through the atmosphere without burning up. I suspect the training for that is intense and there is a limited number of suits." He glanced at Ash.

Ash answered the unspoken question. "Yes, there are loaded training programs and while the suits are plentiful, there aren't as many as you have people. In fact they are almost out on this ship and a resupply order was put in for more suits. That isn't something we can make here."

"What about just waking all of them up in all the chambers and let them wait?" McKenna hated how long this took, but the numbers didn't seem to change.

"Life support on this ship is only set to support ten thousand for a short period of time. Normal crew is about twenty Elentrin and a hundred Kaylid. That is all the quarters and food that is allowed. Remember, this isn't an attack vessel but a transport ship. Normally after they were programmed, they would be sent to other ships to replenish their supplies. Those ships can support many more active bodies. This one will start failing quickly." He almost sounded apologetic.

"Well, so much for that idea." She stared out at the ship as a chime pinged in the room. "We keep going the way we are. How can we land this—"

JD interrupted her. "McKenna, we have another issue."

Deep breaths, you can't go insane now.

"Yes?"

"We're being hailed."

Chapter 29 - Heavy is the Head

I'm just saying, what if shifters are like vampires or something. I don't mean they suck our blood, but what if the person that they were is dead. They look and act like that person, but the real person, the soul is gone. What if this is step one in making sure all humans die out. That we have welcomed the wolves into the fold as they say? ~Caller on Harvey Klein show.

McKenna turned to look at him. "Hailed? Really? Your skirt isn't red."

JD flashed a grin at her, full of teeth. "I couldn't resist. Though I'm not wearing a skirt."

The banter helped to center her and she smiled. "So how do we pull open the communications or whatever?"

Ash moved over to a station and reached for controls on it when he paused and looked around. "If I answer they will see all of this. It might be best for the bodies to be removed and for Rarz to not be visible. Same with those of yours that are not Kaylid." His voice seemed almost deferential.

He has a point, no reason to tip our hand.

"Guys please, can we get the bodies and our prisoner moved. The rest of you into the room. Maybe just leave me standing here with an empty room? Might be the most impactive."

No one said anything they just leapt into action. Ash waved her over to the console and pointed out two buttons.

"Push this one, then type in the access code Ella, Vin, Cort, 4." He said the Elentrin words for the letters, but she looked at the buttons and knew what should be pushed.

"Got it." McKenna lifted her head and looked around. In the minute it had taken for him to show her what she needed to do, the bodies had been moved and most of them stood in the captain's room looking at her. The blood-stains were bright on the floor, but maybe that would make it look more impressive.

I'm suddenly wishing I had taken acting classes in college.

Ash headed that direction too. The chime went off again and she tried to figure out where to look. Giving up she clicked the buttons and the view screen lit up with the face of an Elentrin.

Hah, I knew that couldn't be a huge window.

The man looking at her seemed older than most she had met, though still beautiful with that smooth skin and sharp features. His hair called to mind the blue-white of an incandescent flame, but the blue of his eyes had no heat in them at all. He glanced past her and scanned the room.

"Who does Keric think he is, having a Kaylid take my call? Leave my sight and let me talk to the officer on duty." He spoke in Elentrin and dismissed her, looking at something off screen. She could see behind him and figured he had to be in his version of the captain's room, which meant probably no one was there to overhear this conversation.

I wonder if that's a good or bad thing. Others might drive him to do something, but that could go either way.

McKenna stayed silent, watching him as he poked at something off-screen. She started counting the seconds, wondering how long it would take. Her pose of hands clasped behind her back and standing straight would make her seem confident. To pull this off he needed to believe that.

She made it to thirty before he looked back up, a frown creasing his perfect features.

"Well? Why are you not retrieving Keric as I ordered?" He didn't talk to her so much as at her, so she still waited, wanting to get a gauge of the person talking to her. This time he didn't look away and his gaze became much more intent. For the first time he looked around where she stood, and a change rippled over him. Before he had looked just like another Elentrin, nothing commanding about him, but now she could believe he ran a ship.

"Where is Keric?" His voice was slow and cold.

"Dead." She spoke in Elentrin, no need to confuse him by speaking in another language.

He surveyed behind her, his eyes catching on the streaks of blood still visible where the bodies had fallen.

"Interesting. Are you trying to tell me you have taken over the ship?"

"No. I'm not trying to tell you anything. The ship is mine. Your best bet would be to leave now. This planet is not your farm."

An elegant icy blue eyebrow rose as he looked at her. "Am I to assume you are from that planet hanging there?"

"I don't care what you assume. I just want you to go away or you won't like the consequences."

"And what could you do to me?" He leaned back, but he didn't smirk or smile. He asked with that look of concentration.

"I could do lots of things, but my friends could do even more." She bared her teeth and enjoyed his slight flinch. ~Rarz, could you please come out here?~

Out of her peripheral vision she saw him step forward. He really did look slightly odd without wings, but there was no denying he was Drakyn. As he drew near to her, she saw the man on the screen jerk his eyes to the side and freeze.

His already pale skin went at least two shades lighter as he focused on Rarz.

"You have sided with the abominations? How could you? They are monsters and must be destroyed," he whispered. Watching him, she saw the tight jaw and rigid stance and she wanted to do a happy dance.

"No. You are more of a monster than they could ever be. Leave. Tell all your people to never come back here. We will destroy you if you come back."

Not that I know how we'll do that, but we will. Humans are nothing if not vicious when we get cornered.

"I'll order your planet destroyed. I'll bring every ship there is in to make sure nothing exists in this solar system but your sun."

"Try it and reap the consequences." She flicked off the signal and spun to face the others. "How fast can we do that bomb idea? Get a bomb into that small ship and blow it? I think we're going to need to impress them and fast." She looked at Ash. "Can we land this ship? With it on the ground we could make sure it couldn't go back up."

JD and the soldiers were talking to the people at the de-canting rooms, discussing things through the portal connection. McKenna tuned them out. She had no input on this idea.

"Not easily. All the controls are linked to the Elentrin bio-metrics. Kaylid are normally not allowed up here at all. The only reason I could pass on the access info is Keric provided my codes to the ship with an executive order. Even then I had to spend weeks to get an override to work."

[You? I think you mean I had to spend weeks to get it to work, and even then there was no guarantee of success.]

McKenna froze and noted the rest of the shifters freeze, too, and look at her. The voice had the same quality as Wefor's but it sounded different and spoke in a more relaxed manner. It had a more feminine and amused tone than Wefor ever managed.

"Who was that?" McKenna asked slowly, all too aware of the silence on the bridge. Even the soldiers' attention had been drawn to McKenna.

Ash shot her a look she couldn't read. With all these different body structures, she missed being able to read body language. It made life more difficult.

"My AI. Most of the Kaylid that are kept awake have them. The rest are short term assets or limited use."

McKenna couldn't prevent the growl that slipped past her about how he referred to people. Ash closed his eyes for a brief second then opened them.

"It is what they are, what I am, what I have been for a very, very long time. If I am extremely lucky, I might live to see a life where Kaylid can be other than that." The apology underlaid the words though it wasn't spoken. His tail snapped and he continued. "My AI is part of the reason this worked at all, but that doesn't change the fact that we need an Elentrin to fly the ship."

McKenna blinked and wanted to ask more but again, not the time.

"Kenna, I think the shuttles are moving? Maybe?" JD spoke as he looked at a screen on one of the consoles, big hands pushing buttons gingerly.

Toni moved over, even as the soldiers and Perc went back to discussing things with people on the ground through Cass and Elaine Zimmer. "He's right. The shuttles are surrounding us. They don't have weapons, right?"

"No. Only tractor beams to move things." Tractor wasn't the word Ash used, it translated into a 'push pull beam' but her mind refused to let go of the word tractor, at least that she could conceptualize.

"So why would they be surrounding us?"

Ash's tail did a cracking whip that made her start as he stared at his own console. "All I can figure is the captain of the Silik has contacted the other ships and they are surrounding us to prevent a jump. With large objects this close, the ship can't jump."

I wonder if beating my head on the table would do any good. Everything is going wrong faster than I can make it go right.

"Well, we don't want to jump but we want to make sure they take us seriously. How can we land this ship?" That seemed to be the priority right now, so she focused on that. They had a strategy for taking over ships, maybe they could do it with the others.

Ash didn't say anything, thinking. She saw Toni ignoring Rarz while she focused on the console. McKenna assumed she was doing something necessary but still wanted to laugh at how much she didn't pay attention to the Drakyn.

When he finally spoke, each word sounded like it was pulled out of him, unwilling and resisting. "We need an Elentrin, one with ship training, and one that would help, not immediately act like all of us are traitors to their race."

McKenna flicked an ear forward watching him. He didn't speak or look at her. Her own patience level snapped and she gave in and asked.

"So I guess you know one that might work?"

"Maybe," the word full of reluctance and something else.

"So how do we lay our hands on this person and convince them to help us?"

"First you probably shouldn't blow up the ambassadors' ship just yet." Everyone paused and looked at him and she swore she heard the soldiers heave a sigh of exasperation.

"Is there a person we need there? Is there anyone else we can get on this ship?" McKenna knew the universe was out to get her at this point. Nothing ever worked the way it should.

Ash nodded towards the captured crew member, still visible via the open doors to the captain's room. She sat glaring at them with a mix of rage and fear so obvious, McKenna almost expected lasers to emerge from her eyes and kill them all on the spot.

"That level of hate and fear for the Drakyn and contempt for Kaylid is bred into almost all of them. They'll let you kill a billion lesser beings than even think about helping you." The stress he put on lesser beings carried a wealth of information about how he'd been treated. "Very few manage to escape that indoctrination. The one I'm thinking of might have."

"Might? You don't know for certain?"

His tail flicked out and almost hit her but stopped just short.

"I can guarantee you she has never spoken to me and would have no idea who I am." He almost sounded affronted.

"Then how?"

I swear if I have to drag every bit of information out of him, I'm going to scream.

She watched him and wanted to swear he looked uncomfortable. But she just waited, glaring even as she felt Toni huff in annoyance in her mind.

"She is the ambassador that landed in the country I believe you call China."

"You have got to be kidding me." McKenna moaned.

"No. Why would I kid about Ambassador Thelia? She is the best chance we have for finding an Elentrin that would be willing to work with us." He sounded like he might plead but didn't believe his own words enough to do it.

McKenna just looked at him even as she felt everyone waiting for her. With a deep breath she looked at him and spoke slowly. "Please explain why you think the person who is almost directly responsible for all the deaths in China would ever help us."

Chapter 30 - Paths Forward

Reports are flooding in about the swarm of shuttles attacking the Earth, but it is so sporadic that the true scope isn't easily grasped. While they are targeting more urban areas, the presence of an Elentrin is deadly. People fawn all over them, treating them like gods, and they will do anything for them. Even in cultures that are reserved they kneel before them, willing to protect them from others. At this point, the numbers of them seen at the last count was five, but the one that visited New York has not been seen since. The government has not commented about the whereabouts of that alien. ~TNN Invasion News

"Yes, please do. At this point I'm pretty sure if the UN ever meets again, they'd issue a warrant for her arrest for war crimes," JD said from behind her. McKenna almost jumped. She hadn't heard him come up behind her. Instead she drove her elbow back and grinned when he responded with a small oof. "What was that for?" He protested rubbing his stomach.

"Sneaking up on me and being yourself. Do I need any other reason?"

JD grumbled, rubbing his abdomen. "Fine. See if I storm any more alien spaceships for you."

Cass giggled in her mind and McKenna realized she felt better. Whether it was the banter, or just his presence, some of the stress had lowered.

"You know you love it, and you'd whine if I left you behind." Her counter was met with more laughter in her mind.

"Point. Fine, just watch where you put those elbows. They're sharp," he groused but faded back to doing something else.

Damn, I love these people.

McKenna focused on Ash again. "So explain, why this particular woman?"

[Perhaps I should explain this aspect. It might make more sense.] Ash's AI spoke and she shuddered a bit. It was just different enough from Wefor that she had to learn to get used to the odd reverb again. It was as if they were both on slightly different wavelengths and she couldn't carry over one to the other.

"Okay, but what do I call you?" She asked the question, aware that in the background Perc was explaining to the soldiers the AI was talking. The men shook their heads and went back to talking to him and sketching diagrams.

Ash's claws made a scratching sound. "It's just an AI. It doesn't need a name."

"It's a thinking being. Not a machine. Everything should have a name." McKenna couldn't say why the names were so important but dehumanizing beings was part of what got them into this mess. She'd not do anything to make it spread.

[Thank you. I would like to be called Elao.]

Ash went still at that. "You would?" he asked, though he slipped into Elentrin for that question.

[I find it appropriate. Do you not?]

He cleared his throat and looked away from all of them, intent on the information before him.

~Subtext?~ Cass asked, her voice soft.

[It means hope in his language. The one he only speaks in his dreams.]

Ash froze for a moment, even his tail not moving, but after a minute the tension faded.

"It is indeed. Very well, Elao," he said the word slowly as if tasting each vowel. "Explain your research over the last many, many *reyan*."

"Wait a second, I want to hear this, but time is ticking, I don't have the time at this moment for a history lesson," McKenna interjected, cutting off anyone before they could start getting into storyteller mode. "Short version, hundred words or less?"

[You do not ask for much do you?] Elao's voice floated through a hint of disappointment flavoring the words.

McKenna made a show of looking around her and then back at Ash, whose tail twitched. "Given the current situation, I think it's a valid request."

[As you wish.] Three muffled laughs came on the heels of that comment and McKenna had to fight her own laugh. [The Ambassador Thelia is not a conformist, though she acts it. Long ago I set up tracking for requested queries and information research to learn about anyone who asked more than the minimum. She pushes and pulls and then presents exactly what the higher ups want. What I find most interesting are the children.]

"Wait, children? What children? You have children on these things?" McKenna didn't quite shout the question, but Toni and the others had all moved closer and were now very interested. It was weird not knowing where to look when the AI was talking. McKenna had much more sympathy for people now when Wefor spoke. Ash still had his back to them, and it just felt rude to turn away. Besides, she didn't have anything to do until after this was taken care of.

[No. But Thelia has always collected children. There are rumors as to her unnatural interests in them, rumors I believe she encourages. But I have tracked them. She has a storage units devoted to them and sends them to planets where she has connections. She never keeps them and from everything I've been able to track, they live better than most Kaylid.]

"What am I missing? Why should this tell us anything about her?"

"This, I think I can answer." Ash turned around as he spoke, his tail lax, the white almost looking drab. "Your children are aging, growing, correct?"

McKenna glanced at Toni feeling the same confusion. "Sure. A bit faster than normal, but Wefor told us that might happen—that usually children weren't turned because they weren't as useful as adults. And that the nanobots couldn't attach to sperm because they were too large for the sperm to carry them."

"Not exactly. Apparently, the solar flare you mentioned did widespread damage. Usually when a swarm of Aly Mites is detached, they generally prevent non-adult implantations. Their requirements forbid it. When I altered the swarm, plus the solar flare, that requirement seems to have been lifted. Nanobots lock you into the perfect version of yourself and expend energy to achieve it. A child hasn't reached it, so they tend to lock them into the most perfect version, which means their aging stops right there. They don't grow older though their brains continue to develop."

Everyone in the room made a sound, the horror of that idea. To be a child forever, to never grow up.

"She collects them and from everything Elao has been able to find out, they are treated well, protected. Kept as pets, but still. Most would just elimi—kill them and be done with it. She is unusual in that she doesn't seem to follow the House of Rircn creeds though she gives it lip service. Most wouldn't see it without years of observation."

There was a wealth of layered information there that would have to wait.

"Wefor, add to my list House of Rircn, searching out kids and make sure they are all aging, and finding these children and altering the bots so they can age—if they want to."

[Done.] Even the AI sounded vaguely horrified. [The information in the databases had been corrupted, so extrapolation was done. The assumptions arrived at were obviously wrong.]

McKenna shrugged. "I'm rather glad to know you aren't perfect. Makes me feel better and like you aren't judging my every action."

"Oh, no. I'm doing that," Toni said and bumped McKenna with her shoulder. "But so far you aren't doing too bad."

"Gee, thanks." McKenna rolled her eyes. "This means we need to get over there and get her?"

"Yes. The sooner the better. The last information briefing I was a part of indicated one more sending out of Ambassadors to spread the Glory and then the destruction would commence. While the Silik was expected Keric did not indicate if it would change the plans to destroy your planet."

"Great and now that they know we're here it might speed it up. How desperate are they for more troops?" McKenna asked, looking at the ship hanging there in space.

"Relatively, but if the other ships fled, they would be fine for another generation or so. This is a large haul."

"Fine. But we need to get going. Guys," she asked turning to look at the soldiers and Perc, "did you come up with an idea on how to get over to the ship, grab the woman, get back, and then blow the ship up in a very 'don't fuck with us' manner?"

Roark glanced at the others and nodded. "We think so. Been working with Captain Willis and Sextan on the ground and they think they have something that will work. Very showy and relatively small."

"Okay, what do we need?" she asked and Roark grinned at her.

"We got this. We just need Perc here and Ash to come with us to grab the target then back out. You stay here and let us do it. This is what we do." His calm assured voice made her nod before she realized she had.

"You don't need me?"

"Nope. You're too valuable and right now for this mission there isn't a reason to risk you."

"Great, I'm valuable. Yay," she drawled out and Toni elbowed her.

"Stop it. You're being a worrywart. Let them be."

McKenna flicked her tail at the woman, but Toni ignored it as she stared out at the ship.

"Okay, when? Time might be of the essence."

A swirl of light appeared and grew larger until a man stepped out, holding a large duffel bag. He had a vague familiarity, like she might have seen him in all the mess but didn't remember talking to him.

"That was interesting. Not going to say I enjoyed it, but I've done worse. Howdy, folks." The man, his skin the color of hazelnuts, with dark brown eyes and curly hair, seemed unfazed by the strange array of people in the area.

"You got what we need to do a really big explosion via a remote?" Roark asked nodding at the bag.

"Yep. Will make sure it's invisible, but unless they build with something harder than diamonds this will tear a hole in just about anything." He patted the bag with a smirk.

"Then we go now." Perc looked at all of them. "I have the schematics for that ship in my head, too. We're going into their engine room, setting the bombs, then headed to grab this girl. I know what she looks like. They have filters and Rarz or I can knock our people out if the filters don't work."

McKenna swallowed, she wanted to protest, to say she had to come, to say don't go. Instead she nodded. "Good. Yell if you need anything. Ash, will you start showing Toni what else she needs to know?" She redirected her attention to him so she didn't make a fool of herself.

She felt more than heard the soft laughter in the back of her mind and lifted her head to watch them go. The portal winked out and McKenna focused on the light in her mind, it stayed strong and vibrant.

~We're here. We're fine. Setting up the bombs now.~ Perc's voice spoke in the mindspace and then was gone.

McKenna blew out a stream of air and looked at Ash who hadn't moved, just looked at her.

"What?" she asked, feeling like she was missing something.

"What do you think I know that I could show your cohort?" He seemed truly puzzled and McKenna had to process that confusion.

"How to use the stations? Fly the ship? Lock it down?" She frowned. "And explain how you can talk in our minds when we haven't shared nanobots with you?"

[That would be my doing. When we corrupted the commander programming, I tapped into the wavelength for your trans-harmonics, making sure our nanobots could send and receive on that frequency. That is how we could pull you into training sessions and pass information to you.]

"Okay, that makes sense. I can live with that. But don't you know how to fly this thing, or can't you at least tell us how to get people off faster?"

An odd sounding whistle came from him as he looked at her. "I am a Kaylid, a servant, a slave to them. I have no idea how to fly. I can use some of the communications because I've been here for so long, but not much else."

That took McKenna back a bit and she took a deep breath as she realized they'd been gone for barely three minutes. If she kept counting seconds, she might go crazy. A flash of light caught her attention. "What about the shuttles. Can we get control over them? The ones that come down to Earth don't have any pilots in them."

His head tilted and he looked at her, ears and tail both twitching. "I had not considered that. Is there a way?" The last part almost sounded like a thought and he looked around muttering. "I'll need to go into Keric's office and use his informant. Maybe there is."

"Informant?" McKenna frowned. There hadn't been anyone else in the office.

Ash stopped on his way towards there, turning to look. "Compent? No, Corpent?"

"Oh, computer?"

"If it runs databases and provides calculations, yes." He turned and continued on his way.

~I'll never understand why some words translate exactly and others don't.~ Her amused frustration was clear.

[Assuming that was not a real question, no explanation will be provided.] Wefor said,- still sounding a bit off.

~It wasn't, but thank you.~ She turned to look at JD and Toni who both look bored and stressed at the same time. They needed to do something, but what? She couldn't create or control portals—yet. She stood frozen, watching her planet and listing all the things that could go wrong.

~McKenna?~ Perc's voice pulled her away from her fretting.

~Yes?~ Toni and JD turned to look at her.

~We have a problem.~

Chapter 31 - Complications

Reports from Africa read like pulp stories. Natives attacking from the trees, real animals attacking the invaders, crocodiles grabbing them, even women and children attacking with spears. While the invaders' weapons are proving superior to most other weapons, the number of shifters they are gathering from this continent, outside of Egypt and Libya must be sparse. ~TNN Invasion News

Every muscle in McKenna's body went rigid and her gaze locked on the small ship still in the viewscreen.

~What's wrong?~ Her thought snapped out, even as she braced herself for an explosion.

~I'll tell you in a moment. We're coming back now.~ As she registered his words, a silvery portal started to form. From the corner of her eye she could see Ash step into the main area, but he hung near the door, watching, body tense.

JD and Toni had moved over to her while the still tied-up Elentrin looked confused and terrified. McKenna hated how glad she was that this invader feared them.

Perc stepped through first, and some part of her uncoiled. Roark and Coran followed, then an Elentrin, the vivid purple hair drawing her attention. Rarz followed a moment later and the portal collapsed.

The woman stood there, tight leggings in a slivery white, with a flowing-over garment in light green that remind

McKenna of a variation of a kimono. It looked like she wore a tight-fitting tank top underneath it. But mostly it looked elegant and effortless, which only highlighted how grimy they all looked.

She looks way too self-satisfied. What was her name? Thelia?

Her people were all alive and there was no visible harm. That calmed her down enough to pay attention to the woman. She'd seen her image on TV. She'd led the China invasion. Stunningly beautiful as all the Elentrin seemed to be, she looked around with an aura of curiosity on her face. Something flickered across that perfect visage as she spotted the tied-up woman, who glared at her.

"Rarz, can you move our unwilling guest to the other room, and when you come back, shut the door?"

Thelia glanced at her, a flicker of approval in her eyes before she continued to look at them, hands clasped behind her back as if she was inspecting them. Everyone stood, watching everyone else as Rarz picked up the woman and put her in the other room. He stepped out, Ash making way for him, and the door closed.

"So what exactly is the problem? She won't help?" McKenna asked the question but didn't look away from the woman.

"Oh, I don't have an issue helping. Though I have a few conditions." Thelia replied turning to focus fully on McKenna.

"And those would be?" Concern and frustration could be tasted in the mindspace, all coming from Perc. But nothing that made her think they were all about to die. McKenna saw JD and Toni move so the woman was in between all of them, her back to two at any point.

"Ah, ah, ah. I must have my inquiries addressed first." Her voice was melodious and McKenna felt the tug.

~Wefor,~ panic in her thought.

MEL TODD

[You are safe. The others are safe. You are simply being pulled by a memory. They are not affecting you.]

McKenna crossed her arms and looked at the woman, not speaking. Other people shifted around them uncomfortably, but she just waited.

After an interminable amount of time, but probably less than a minute, maybe two, the woman nodded her head. "Very well. Answer my questions and I'll answer yours."

With a twitch of her tail McKenna just nodded at her and waited.

A slow smile spread across Thelia's face, displaying white, sharp teeth, too many for a human face. "I like you. This might work. So far none of you seem to be followers. I am so tired of followers. So here are my questions. Assume you chase us away. What do you plan on doing next?"

McKenna blinked. "Live? Explore? Now that we know there are others out there, I can't imagine us not chasing the stars, but mostly rebuild. You've done a lot of damage."

Thelia gave a slow languid shrug but never looked away from McKenna. "And then? Will you seek us out? Kill us? Destroy our worlds?" She asked the questions but didn't really sound interested, as if it was a pro forma question.

"I'm sure some will want to, but I doubt it. Not unless you provide another reason for us to seek you out. It will take us a while to build a space fleet."

Something glittered in Thelia's eyes, but she closed them slowly and when she reopened them the emotion was gone. "Very well, I have two conditions for my assistance. Not that I know how I would assist."

"However we ask. It must be immediate and honest. I catch you lying or trying to trick us, I'll kill you and kick your body to the side." McKenna didn't hesitate. This was dangerous enough and if they had to trust this woman, she'd get everything.

Thelia looked at her for a long time. If it wasn't that her body language screamed confidence, McKenna would have thought she was anxious. But then that was applying human body language to someone that was definitely an alien.

"Rescue the children I have stored in my private containers on that ship." She nodded at the small ship on the screen.

"The what?! You have children with you on the ship?" McKenna turned to look at Perc. She knew they'd been talking quietly, in Speech at the edge of her awareness.

From the way Ash talked about it, I assumed it was a historical thing not that she carried them around with her. How many are from Earth? How many from other worlds?

"Yeah, that was the problem I told you about. We can't blow the ship until we get them out." Perc's voice was grim as he looked at her.

"How many?" McKenna felt like she was being squeezed from all sides. Every choice affected people's lives or ended them.

"There are seventy-eight children in my containers. Some are from other worlds. Some are yours." Thelia's calm, cool voice raked at McKenna like a nail across glass.

"Can we decant them?" She asked Perc and Roark not her.

"Not easily," Thelia replied. "They are all in individual protection units with limited life support. But the units can be detached and moved, and the support will last for a while."

"Wait, they can be moved while in the canisters?" Rarz asked.

Thelia flinched and didn't look at him, but she answered. "Yes. They were designed that way so I could ship them where I ... needed them." The odd pause on that word caught McKenna's ear, but she didn't say anything. Instead, she looked at Rarz.

"Can we move them? Just dump them into a portal?" McKenna watched the woman as she asked, trying to get a read on her.

"Sure, but we'd still need to grab each container and get it into the portal." Perc replied, following her gaze to the ship.

McKenna wished she could chew on her lip or fidget with something as she thought. She'd tried chewing on her lip. The amount of blood convinced her it was a bad choice in this form.

"Rarz?" Her voice ended on a lilt as something occurred to her. The Drakyn turned to look at her, his swirling eyes both hypnotic and disturbing. "What happens if you open your portal into a solid structure? I mean if you close it over something solid, does it dissolve or break?"

His head moved back and forth in an odd pattern. "The standard procedure is to create a tunnel in an open space as it will disrupt structures, generally damaging them so they would need repair to be usable again. Why?"

Images merged in her mind, some from cartoons as a kid, others from watching his portals. "Could you cause a portal to form under the canisters and then move up, and close once all the units had been engulfed in the portal or tunnel?"

At this point everyone was looking at her and she flicked a hand in the air. "If he can control how they move, where they open and close, he should be able to take all of them, like a whale swallowing everything."

"You're devious. Glad you're on our side," Roark said now, looking at the ship. "If you follow that through, we don't need bombs, you just need to have the portal disrupt the hull and expose them to space."

Everyone went quiet at those words and Thelia turned to stare at Rarz, a look of horror on her face. "You could do that? Rupture our ships from a distance and never need to get near us?"

It was the first real emotion McKenna had seen in the woman, but she didn't blame her. What the Elentrin had done seemed horrible. But to be able to destroy ships, and buildings, with a thought?

I think I'm going to be sick. I should never have suggested this. But if it works...

Her thoughts trailed off as Rarz pivoted and looked at all of them, the colors in his eyes swirling even faster.

"That thought is most disturbing. We have always learned to seek out open areas for our tunnels, something where we damage only a few plants. It never occurred to anyone to use that as a weapon." His tail, usually so still and stable, rippled up and down, the scales ruffling like wind across a field of wheat. "I do not know if I can guide it to the units as you say, but I should at least be able to place the opening beneath them so they could be released into it."

"Would that work?" McKenna glanced at Thelia and then over to Perc and Rarz.

"I don't have the schematics of that ship in my head. Ash, can you get those pulled up?" Perc turned to look at Ash as he spoke and Thelia focused on the Kaylid who until now had stayed back against the wall, unobtrusive.

He tilted his ears back but pushed away moving towards a console. "Yes." He hit various keys, his body tight, even his tail was stiff and still. "Here you go." Up on the screen, replacing the view of the ship, a bunch of schematics appeared.

"Where is your storage area for the kids?" The demand seemed to pull Thelia out of her fixation on Rarz and Ash.

She moved over to the console and zoomed in on an area. "Here. You can see it is near my quarters. I gave up personal space to have that when I travel." Her eyes slid over to Ash. "But you knew that already didn't you?"

Ash didn't answer and McKenna didn't have time to explore that. "Fine. If we can get them out, we will." She shifted to the Speech, not wanting Thelia to see how much these kids mattered. ~Guys, can you work on how to do this ASAP? If we don't do something fast, we won't have the option. Hell, I'm surprised we don't have people storming the ship or the asteroids flying already.~

~Got it. I think I have an idea. But let me talk to Roark and Coran.~ Perc moved, even as the words registered, pulling Rarz and the two soldiers to a corner and starting to talk quickly. JD and Toni tilted their ears toward them, but didn't move from their arrangement around the Elentrin.

McKenna refocused on Thelia. "What is your next condition?"

Thelia blinked looking at her, the purple eyes almost as seductive as the swirls of Rarz's. "Assuming you rescue the children, without killing too many, please, I get to stay here on your planet and make a life."

If the woman had asked for a million dollars and a helicopter, McKenna would have been less surprised. "You want to live here? Why? You'll never fit in. People will regard you as the enemy. You'll always be recognized, vilified possibly."

Thelia gave an elegant shrug that displayed her breasts in a way no man would be able to ignore. It set off another random thought in McKenna's mind.

Why are breasts so common? Are the Elentrin mammals and is that sexual also?

With a mental sigh, she shot the questions to Wefor to ask on that mythical someday and refocused on Thelia. "This is an odd request. If we chase the ships away and you stay, then you won't have a choice unless you can get Rarz to take you to another planet, but I don't have the ability to grant you protection or anything. That would be up to our government."

A sly smile slid across Thelia's face like oil on water. "Don't worry, I bring much to prove my value." She lifted her wrist and McKenna saw a large bracelet that all but sparkled with subtle lights. "I have most of the data from our libraries and I can explain some of the tech behind it. I'll be a good guest." She smirked. "I suspect I'll live like a queen."

McKenna wanted to snarl, but she wasn't wrong. When scientists from Russia and Germany had defected during World War II and the Cold War, they had been treated like that. And what she offered made Oppenheimer's offerings seem like kindergarten stuff.

"As long as you're aware that I'm not the person you'll need to negotiate with."

Thelia smiled again and McKenna felt more than saw JD and Perc shudder. "I can live with that."

~Wefor, remind me to tell them to have a gay man negotiate with her. Anyone else would be at risk even without pheromones.~

[Agreed.] Even the AI's voice had a touch of dryness to it.

"Fine. Guys, any progress or have we created a weapon of mass destruction out of the portals?" She tried to make the words come out as lightheartedly sarcastic, but they came out with dread lacing them.

I don't think I'll ever forgive myself if I've just created the next atomic bomb. I really don't want to be the next Oppenheimer or Kali.

Chapter 32 - Gift Horses

While urban areas are being targeted, there is a mass exodus to the more rural towns, creating extra stress when it is already difficult for food and supply shipments to get through. While some people are overcharging and making fortunes off scared people, most chains have instituted limited hours and cash only businesses. Most customers have been understanding but in Texas there's been an incident where a woman went on a rampage and she was killed. The store claims their people acted within the limits proscribed and has promised to deal with all legal bills. No one finds temper tantrums amusing right now. So be polite people.
~TNN Invasion News

The four men, at least she categorized Rarz as male, moved towards the center and got ready to speak to all of them. Ash hung back at the side, still almost invisible.

"Your idea won't work, not without a lot of time to play with it, and Rarz would need to learn to control the portal in a different method. But we think, given the schematics, we have an option. Thelia, how long is the life support good for if we snap off the tanks at the connections?" Perc's voice was flat as he looked directly at her.

McKenna didn't know if she was relieved it wasn't possible or worried it might be. Either way, she pushed it to the side. If she learned to use portals, they'd deal with the ethics. Right now she firmly came down on the side of getting children off a ship they needed to blow up, then seeing what twist reality came up with next.

"Not long, about ten *reyan* or so," she replied not paying any attention to the humans, her eyes locked on Ash.

"Wait, your life pods are good for ten *reyan*? Ten years?" Toni blurted.

"Of course, you need time to find them. And while there are trackers on them, space is very large."

"They're vacuum proof?"

Thelia tilted her head, though she still focused on Ash. "Vacuum? They are rated for space exposure. They are variations of escape units. They would be of little use if they were not rated to keep their occupants safe until retrieval." She slid a sly sideways glance at McKenna. "We do value our tools."

I will not growl, I will not growl.

"Does that change the plan?" McKenna asked, keeping her claws sheathed, no matter how much they itched to sink into this woman.

Roark glanced at Coran, then Perc, then shook his head. "Not really. Means we don't have to worry about people dealing with them until after all the rest of this is done. I'll get a safe location set up on the ground, but knowing we can ignore them for a week or so makes it much easier."

"What is the plan exactly?" McKenna needed to know, even if she was going to be busy with other things.

"Pretty straightforward. Rarz is going to portal us in and we'll disconnect and toss the canisters in. Rarz and I are strong enough to manually disconnect them and with Roark and Coran's help we should be able to do it in a bit over an hour if we move fast. It just means we need to stall everyone and everything until then." Perc spoke his voice level and she found comfort his is steady gaze.

McKenna looked at the ship on the screen, the Silik hanging above it, and the Earth with silver flashes of shuttles still going back and forth, making the problem worse with every run.

She made her decision with a snap. "Do it. Do whatever you need." With a mental switch she flipped over to Speech. ~Cass, keep waking people up, line them up in the halls if need be. As soon as we can, we'll get the portal back and they can move through it as fast as possible. Kids—tell them to stay calm, but we're trying. Make sure they don't cause problems.~

~Got it.~ Cass and the kids both chimed in, but McKenna already turned her attention to the next part.

"Ash, Thelia. How can we get the shuttles to quit deploying? Are they all automated? How do we get the existing Kaylid to stand down or at least quit grabbing people?"

Thelia looked at her with a smirk on her lips. "In theory the captain controls the automation of the shuttles, though they can all be controlled individually by Kaylid that have been loaded into the system."

"Can you do that?" McKenna demanded, still watching Ash and Thelia.

"I? I would have no knowledge of the codes needed to access or change shuttle commands." Her entire expression reminded McKenna of a supercilious rich girl they'd caught for drug possession. All arrogance and amusement, knowing they couldn't touch her. Unfortunately, she'd been right. It remained to be seen if Thelia's smugness would get removed.

McKenna gave Ash a hard stare. "Can you?"

His tail didn't so much as twitch, which perversely worried her. He didn't respond but was frozen, with an odd look in his eyes. One she recognized.

He's arguing with his AI. I wonder what they're arguing about.

She was just about to prompt him, when his tail twitched, and she could see his eyes focus on her. "Yes and no. For the ships that are automated from this ship, I can have them all return to the hanger bays. For the ones that are being piloted from this ship, I won't be able to stop them. But all my commands are this ship only. It won't affect what the other ships can or will do."

"Impressive. You managed to suborn the pet of Keric's house. I had wondered. How exactly did you corrupt this bastion of perfection held up to all Kaylid as what they should aspire to?" Thelia had leaned forward, her purple eyes boring holes into Ash, who ignored her, looking only at McKenna.

"Do it." She said as she watched the woman out of the corner of her eye. "We can at least shut that down and prevent any more coming in here. Is there a way to send a recall to the Kaylid?"

"Yes. They can be controlled. I'll send that now, but if the other ships haven't noticed or been contacted, this will alert them." Ash turned as he spoke and headed to the Captain's room. "I need to do it from in there. I will need his body to override some of the commands."

McKenna couldn't help the shudder that rippled through her. But she nodded. "Do what you need to do. Toni? Will you go with him and see what you can learn?"

"Sure," Toni replied, but darted a look at Thelia then JD. He nodded at the look and McKenna didn't know if she wanted to roll her eyes at them, or hug them. Toni followed Ash into the room, while JD positioned himself a bit closer, his huge bulk dwarfing the lithe Elentrin.

"You guys ready?" She directed the question to Rarz and Perc, who looked up at her, then at the soldiers and nodded.

"Yeah, going now. We've opened a pinhole wormhole and got a location to dump the canisters in. An expert will check to make sure they're all okay, but having time to deal with them is a blessing at this rate. Not all of them are from Earth and we could use the time to get ready to decant them." Perc kept his voice flat but his claws sliding up and down revealed a lot to her.

"Okay." McKenna turned, fighting with herself to not run over there, give all of them hugs and demand that they be safe. None of them were safe right now. Instead she focused on JD and Thelia.

"Thelia, if my information is correct, there's a way to send messages to all the Kaylid on the ground and provide orders. Is this something you can do?"

The Elentrin's eyes followed Ash, but then snapped back to McKenna. "I suppose. though given your less-than-welcoming attitude, I'm not sure why I should do more than what I've already agreed to, which is helping you fly the ship."

JD responded before McKenna could. He stepped up close to the woman, his claws encircling her throat and his voice one step above a growl. "Because if you don't, I have no reason not to hurt you for a very long time. Your people have killed thousands of mine, and no one will ever notice one invader that has been skinned alive."

Her face didn't react, but her scent sharpened to something almost bitter and McKenna saw her eyes dilate. The colors of her eyes grew wider and darker, as if the iris was her pupil.

"Convincing argument. Given that encouragement, I believe I might be able to assist." Her smooth voice didn't so much as quaver.

"Excellent," JD all but purred, pulling his claws away from her leaving thin trails of blood behind as the tips trailed along her skin.

~Who are you channeling?~ McKenna asked surprised, impressed, and a bit off kilter at this aspect of JD.

~Myself. I'm tired of these aliens killing our people. Humans are violent and vicious. What would you do if they were threatening Charley?~ His voice had none of his normal good humor and McKenna nodded slowly.

~Skin them alive and never regret it for a minute. I guess they get to see humans at their worst.~

~And best. This is what we are, the ones willing to die for our family, our world. That's the best of us, too.~ He countered, this time emotion in his tone.

Her gaze had followed the woman as she moved to the primary console Ash had used. Before she could start doing anything, McKenna spoke.

"Please explain to me exactly what you're doing at each step."

Thelia glanced at her, the superior smirk back on her face. "Do you not trust me?"

"Not as far as I can throw you."

The cliché seemed to catch the alien off guard as she looked at McKenna. "Could you not throw me very far?"

"It's a saying. Means NO. Explain what you're doing and how." McKenna moved over to stand next to the woman while JD hovered a bit behind them, but well within his arms' reach if he needed to grab either of them.

They both paused as the portal snapped open and the others flowed into it, and it snapped closed again, though it still called to her. Thelia shuddered, the first true emotion McKenna had seen on her. "I may not believe the propaganda regarding the abominations, but the ability to control portals, to cross space like one might cross a path, strikes me as unnatural and wrong."

"Yet warping people's forms and enslaving them doesn't?" McKenna asked dryly, not really expecting her to answer.

"I have no responsibility in that. It has been done that way for many *reyans* before even my life givers were birthed." Thelia shuddered, a delicate action that made McKenna think of one of her foster households and the romances the mom had been addicted to. The women in them were always delicate and fragile, and everything they did rippled with beauty.

This woman will run any social setting she is ever in. I hope the government is ready to deal with her, because I'm not stepping up for that responsibility.

"Though it matters not at this point." Thelia pointed at icons that McKenna interpreted as communications. "This is the communication station and should allow communication via all Kaylid with the trans-harmonic frequency for this ship."

"Are there different frequencies?" It hadn't occurred to her there were multiple, but if they were like radio channels that might make sense.

"Yes. Every ship has different ranges, and teams with different objectives operate on different frequencies. There should be a control room where the commands are entered and sent to the various groups. This is the general one that is only used for wide communication needs." Her arched brow and tone of voice made it clear she thought McKenna was an idiot, but McKenna didn't care.

"Good. Issue a recall order. If necessary, we can send shuttles down. Surrendering would probably just get them killed, but if we can get them back..." she broke off. There were more Kaylid down on the planet than could be brought up in shuttles. If she told them to drop their weapons, they'd just be killed. No matter that she would be making a choice that would kill beings that had little, if any, control over their actions.

Taking a deep breath, she sent a thought to Ash. ~Is it possible to have the returning Kaylid stay somewhere until we can figure out how to unprogram and reprogram them?~

To her relief his response was immediate. ~Yes. Near the hangar bays are large rooms created for organizing trips.

Since you boarded there are no more being decanted to do the drops to the surface. Most of the Elentrin on the ship at this point are either hiding or you have killed them. There were not that many as most of the ship is automated, and what Kaylid stay awake are always controlled.~

~Like you were?~ She asked as she turned to Thelia.

~I might be an oddity,~ he admitted, and she was surprised to not hear pride or amusement, but distress in the words.

Later, this isn't something I have to worry about now.

"Have shuttles wait for them, tell them to return immediately and communicate if there are no shuttles available. I need you and Ash to coordinate getting them up and into their area where they're dispatched."

~It is usually called a mobilization or muster area, but if you direct them to wait in the processing area, they should know where you are talking about.~ Ash provided her the information, though he still seemed off somehow.

~Why don't you come out here and discuss it with her. Would make it easier on all of us.~ McKenna felt like she was herding all the kids again, but this time way more lives depended on her.

~I suspect she would not take it well coming from me. After all, I have been known for a very long time as the perfect 'pet' Kaylid.~ Even in her mind she could hear the emphasis on pet. Sighing and deciding arguing would take time they didn't have, she redirected her attention on Thelia, who seemed to be waiting patiently.

Oh, this woman. She's going to make stories about Loki seem crude and heavy-handed. Maybe I should be comparing her to Coyote? Anansi?

"Tell all Kaylid to return to the ship at once. They are to await further orders in mobilization areas. If they need a shuttle, they should signal for one. All captured Earthlings," she stumbled over the word, it felt odd to say.

~Perc?~

~Yes?~ He sounded distracted but responsive.

~Can you guys get a message to Doug or Geoff Sextan that we may have random Kaylid heading for the shuttles and if possible, to let them go without issue? If they don't have any prisoners with them, let them go.~

A tense minute of silence, and she had to resist poking him again when he replied. ~Done. Message is going out now, and they'll pass it along to other governments that we're in communication with. No guarantees, but they'll try.~

~Best I can ask for.~

"Do it, please." Manners, beaten into her from various foster homes prompted the please, and she regretted it from the quirk of lips. But Thelia slowly clicked on each icon, making sure McKenna saw what she was doing.

~Wefor, you're remembering all this, right?~ Her worry obvious, though she tried to keep it as private as possible.

[Yes, and verifying all translations. But if what Ash said is true, we will not be able to access it due to the biometric locks.] Wefor had been so quiet, even the disjointed reverberation in her head made her feel better.

~Might as well ask.~

Chapter 33 - Planned Downfall

With the Earth under attack, people are bonding to-gether. We are seeing Israelis and Palestinians fighting side by side. The Hamas has been seen taking out invaders with suicide vests and even protecting children from known Jew-ish or Christian faith. All the homeless have disappeared from the streets of New York, San Francisco, and LA. Have they found safe places to go? Or have they been taken? No one knows, all we can say here at TNN is protect each other. We are all that stands between us and these aliens treating our planet as a cattle ranch. ~TNN News Anchor

It took two days, but one of Willard's video sermons went viral when a shifter attacked him while filming. Raymond leaned back and watched, a grin on his face, as Willard stood bloody while security took down the creature. If you looked closely you could see the sounds had to be fake. He moved too easily and the apparent wounds didn't gush as badly as they should have, but it made the point crystal clear and money flowed in. The reaction to it could-n't have been more perfect.

"I don't know if you hired someone, set it up, or what, but bravo Willard. You will have earned that favor."

Reposting the video helped and he sat back to watch the world have a collective meltdown.

Raymond had gone to bed, house locked up tight, and was sleeping the sleep of the just, when his phone yanked him out of dreams where he was in his rightful place. Resisting the urge to snarl into the phone, he answered.

"Yes?"

"Hey, thought you might want to know. Something's going on with them up at the ships. Everyone is running around down here like crazy. And they've been getting shifters off the ship in a stream of aliens. I mean we don't know if they're all human or not. Some of them don't look like any animal I've ever heard of."

"Wait, they're getting shifters off the ships? How?" Adrenaline had him sitting up in bed, heart pounding as he tried to think through the ramifications of this.

"Yeah, they brought in some weird lizard- like guy, with a tail and everything, and he made this shiny portal and they all walked into it and just disappeared. It's the creepiest thing I've ever seen. Then they started sending down all these shifters and, sir, I don't think all of them were from Earth. They had colors and skin textures in their weird warrior form that I couldn't recognize from any animal on earth. A few even had multiple arms."

By this time Raymond had gotten up and moved through the house quietly. No one turned on lights at night anymore. The atmosphere of fear resembled what he had read about during the bombing attacks in Europe during World War II.

Yet another reason to get all of them off this planet. This is America. We shouldn't be hiding in our houses like scared rabbits.

"Any of this on the news?" he asked as he sat down at his desk.

"Hell no. You think they want anyone knowing about this? They've had this all hush-hush since it started about two days ago. Can't remember, I've been working long days. This is the second night I think, but maybe the third. Frag I'm tired."

"Yeah, you're working hard, helping protect our country." Raymond fought to keep his tone soothing and coaxing. He wanted to reach through the phone and strangle the man to get the information out of him.

"Yes, our country, not these crazy animals. But like I said I thought you should know."

In the distance Raymond could hear shouting and moving. "Any chance you can get me pictures of what's going on over there right now?" He needed those pics, with that he had a gold mine of information.

"Well, I don't have a camera on me." Higson sounded doubtful and Raymond had to again keep his voice calm and not allow it to show how much he wanted to kill this man right now.

"Oh, sorry. I thought you were calling me from a smartphone," he said, as if regretful, making sure to add a touch of doubt.

"Oh wait! Duh, yeah let me get what I can, I can be sneaky."

"That's wonderful. Some video would be awesome too."

"Sure, just remember how I helped you out," Higson said, and Raymond fought back a sigh; instead he stroked the man's ego.

"When it comes time to tell the stories I'll make sure to give you the credit you deserve for helping us protect our species. Just send it to this number."

"Will do. Give me a bit, I'll have to be subtle. Later." With that Higson hung up and Raymond groaned.

"That man couldn't be subtle if his life depended on it." He pulled up the various news sites, but there was nothing about a military amassing anywhere. He tried a few of the more esoteric news areas but the closest he got was some chatter on a social media feed about the weird flying patterns some of the ships up there were doing.

He got so into the research black hole the ding of his phone startled him. Picking it up there were several pictures coming through. Wasting no time, he connected to his computer and uploaded the images. Waiting impatiently for them to sync he headed to the kitchen, figuring some coffee would be good. He needed to be sharp to craft the appropriate messages for the various social media formats. With luck some of the pictures would be good enough to post on the image-heavy apps and preset the conclusions he wanted people to make in the right way.

By the time he got back to the desk everything had uploaded. He pulled up the first picture and froze, stunned by what he saw. Hand shaking to the point coffee was spilling, he set down his coffee cup, ignoring the slosh onto his pristine redwood desk, lost in what he saw on the screen.

As each picture loaded, his smile grew wider and ideas burst through his mind at how to use what he saw. When he saw the video, he started to cackle in glee.

It started with a stutter, then smoothed and resolved into a silvery disk hanging in mid-air about six inches off the ground. Military personnel surrounded it as a steady stream of beings came out. Most were in that odd warrior form, but some were in human form, or more accurate humanoid, because there were a few he knew weren't from this planet. More and more streamed out as the video played, with people coming up and grabbing them and hustling them off. Shouting orders could be heard in the background and people exclaimed in loud tones. The running around became more apparent. The picture panned for a minute and he saw tents and dozens if not hundreds of people sitting with blankets draped over them and people trying to talk to them.

But what interested him most was the panned-past images of the non-human being taken to a large tent with flaps that dropped closed as soon as you passed through.

The video caught sight of two familiar figures before it abruptly ended.

Raymond already had ideas on how to use most of those snapshots. The furor he could and would cause, and the way he could spin the images would give him fuel for weeks. He got to work, making sure to send one or two carefully snipped frames from the video to Willard, he'd be able to get a lot of traction from those in his televised and recorded appearances.

The silver disk needed to be addressed, as did so many other things. Was this alien technology something they could gain control of? He needed to know the full extent of it. Either way the implications of that were concerning and something he'd be asking questions about, getting Higson to get more information for him. Any lizard aliens needed to be followed up on, assuming what Higson thought was the truth.

But the question that ate at him as he worked, spinning words to start a firestorm, was—What the hell were Geoff Sextan and Secretary of State Doug Burby doing there?

Chapter 34 - Hail Mary

Not only do we have to worry about the Elentrin goon squads assaulting us and killing our families to get what they want, but now those originally from earth are attacking our leaders of the light, those that helps us keep our faith. If we can't trust those from this planet, why not let the Elentrin take them. Good riddance to bad rubbish. ~Caller on Harvey Klein show

"Is there a way for us to do this? Maybe duplicate it on other ships?" McKenna asked, watching Thelia carefully.

I don't trust you, but I need you, and that just might drive me crazy.

The woman shrugged. "That is dependent upon each ship. The message functionality for the control systems is queued up. Press that button there and it will record a message to send to all Kaylid on this planet." She pointed to an icon. Each time she'd touched something there had been a subtle change in color or intensity, but when McKenna reached out with her furred hands, it didn't respond at all. "I would make the assumption that the ultimate answer is no, at least for this ship or group of ships." Thelia's voice gave no hint at all to her thoughts. "Are you ready to record?"

"How does it get to everyone across the planet?" Toni asked.

Thelia didn't bother to even glance at her, but she did answer. "Trans-harmonics will hit each Kaylid and leverage the nanobots in their bodies to jump to the next Kaylid. By

doing this, while there may be a delay for those on the opposite side of the planet, the dispersion is such that the
curvature of a planet is not a hindrance to sending messages as long as the density of Kaylid is enough."

"That actually makes sense." Toni frowned as she
thought about it, nodding her agreement. "Maybe not important now, but later it might be."

Thelia still watched McKenna. When no one else spoke
she said again, a note of barely restrained patience in her
voice. "If you are ready, I will activate the record option."

"Wait, let me try one more thing." The Elentrin seemed
to be very blind in some aspects and she had a stray
thought that she might be able to use that blindness.
McKenna concentrated on her finger. While she'd learned
to control the nanobots without much effort for her ears,
anything else she had to concentrate to get them to do
what she visualized. It took a minute, but the fur on her in-
dex finger slowly receded and her finger emerged with the
nail and her normal skin. "Huh, should have tried this earlier. It would have made shooting the guns easier." She
pressed the button and it changed to a green arrow.

Thelia waved at her, an eyebrow arched, though
McKenna wasn't sure if it was surprise, approval, or something else she didn't have a name for. She scrambled to
come up with what to say, her mind racing.

"All Kaylid, cease harvesting efforts and return to shuttles. Withdrawal orders have been issued. If a shuttle is not
near you, signal and wait for one to pick you up. Leave all
captured Kaylid in a safe place. Repeat, return immediately
to the shuttles and await retrieval."

McKenna glanced at Thelia who nodded meaningfully at
the button and McKenna clicked it again. It changed back to
the original icon, something with a circle in a circle.

"Not exactly how the commands I have heard have been
worded. But it should suffice," Thelia remarked as she

stepped back, her hands clasped at her waist. "What else would you ask of me?"

"Have all the HALO drops ceased?" Thelia frowned looking at her and McKenna rephrased her question. "Have the Kaylid being sent to the planet stopped?"

"I would not know. Besides, while this is the lead ship, each captain has the ability to send or not send their own troops. While that method did not go to the Elentrin on the other ships, word will probably reach their crew relatively quickly." Not arrogance or smugness, but something else filled her voice, something that rubbed McKenna the wrong way.

McKenna ignored her and raised her voice, since the door was still open between where Toni, Ash, and the remaining Elentrin were. She hadn't forgotten that one, but at this point didn't know what to do with their prisoner.

"Ash, can you see if shuttles are being recalled? And tell me if any more drops are going on?" She waited, her ears straining to hear the second he started to speak, her body wound so tight she felt like the only options were explode or fall apart.

This had to have worked. If it didn't, we'll never stop the flow of people being captured.

Her thoughts went in frantic circles trying to think of other things to do, but the more she fretted, the less she could think.

[Breathing is suggested, otherwise you will pass out.]
Huh?

The comment from Wefor jolted her back into awareness from her spiraling mind and she took in a deep breath. The headache that had started to pound at the side of her skull faded back. She shook her head and glanced at the viewing screen and the ship hanging there. McKenna could feel they were running out of time, that the commander would be scrambling to do things as much as she was, and he had many more options than she did.

"Yes, the shuttles are starting to return, and they are being hailed by troops on the ground. Our drops have stopped and the other ships at this point are not doing any troop placements. A large number of trained troops had already been sent to the planet." Ash's voice pulled her from staring at the viewscreen and the ship there. "However, the other ships have started to issue different orders. They are waiting for their last shuttles to return and they plan to start sending the gathered space debris to impact your planet." He stood in the doorway looking at the two of them, his tail lashing back and forth as he waited. Toni appeared behind him, her ears lay back against her skull.

His words fell like bricks into wet concrete, pulling them down with it.

Panic won't help anything. Don't panic.

~How much longer? How are you guys doing?~ It took effort to keep her mental thought calm and measured.

What good does it do to rescue the kids if the planet is destroyed?

That point ate at her, but she hoped they could figure something out to save her world.

~Another twenty minutes and we'll be able to blow up the ship. Everything okay?~ Perc asked, but she could feel Rarz monitoring the connection.

~Fine, but faster is better. I'll try to buy us some time.~ She closed her eyes and then snapped them open fastening her gaze on Thelia. "So are you with us? Because otherwise I'll just kill you now and be done with it."

Thelia tilted her head looking at McKenna from an angle that reminded her of an owl. "At this point I have conspired with you. That is considered traitorous by the House of Rircn. It is unlikely they would believe I was coerced. I have no living family and most believe the rumors that are spread about me. Given all that, I do not believe I have much choice. Besides, I have no great desire to find out what lays beyond my current existence." Her violet eyes were locked on McKenna and never wavered. In a human she'd have interpreted it as honesty and sincerity. With an Elentrin, she had no idea.

"JD. Kill her if she betrays us." McKenna stated the words, her gaze still locked with Thelia's. A hint of a smile touched the woman's lips.

"Will do," JD rumbled, his voice almost a drawl. Thelia's eyes flickered to the side, but then back to McKenna.

"I assume you want me to do something?" asked Thelia. Her liquid smooth voice promising everything and nothing.

Oh, I want a miracle, but I need to see if I can get your help pulling off a decent bluff.

"Stall. Make contact with the captain of that ship and we're going to talk a good game. Is there a way for me to stay off screen and get information to you without the other ship hearing me? Primary objective is to get them to go away and not start bombarding the planet."

"The ear links." Thelia pointed to the jewelry high on her ear. Her ears were more slender, and they moved where human ears really didn't. Where the top of her ear connected with her skull a pale lavender jewel flickered back at her.

It took McKenna a moment to realize there were lights in the depths of the stone, not that it was reflecting light.

"That's a communications link? You don't have mental communication like the Kaylid do?"

For the first time true emotion crossed Thelia's face, revulsion and a sneer as she recoiled a bit from McKenna. "Allow words in my head? My thoughts and feelings exposed to all? Giving that many weapons to anyone about my personal feelings? My thoughts? Never!" The last word was all but spat out, as if even thinking it left a bad taste in her mouth.

McKenna could feel everyone's shock as they looked at Thelia—emotions and surprise rippling through the mind-scape.

"I think I almost feel sorry for you, but that might imply I care. And I don't." Personally, as strange as that aspect had seemed at first, she couldn't imagine being without her family in her head. Though Rarz still made her uncomfortable, but more because she didn't know him yet. "Ash, can you set me up in that other room to talk to her via the ear link?"

"Yes. What are you thinking?" He seemed curious but McKenna just smiled, showing her many sharp teeth.

"Let's find out."

Because I don't have a clue, except I need time. Anything that makes the other captains delay or wonder what we're up to would be a win.

Chapter 35 -Line in Granite

One of the huge convoy shuttles has landed in Cairo. While there have been some reports of gunfire, the city is quiet. Drones launched overhead see two people - one with pink hair and the other with sea-foam green. Yes, these colors were told to me by the make-up personnel. These two people are walking through the city, with a throng of people following them. A few are in the wolfman form, what Largo called a warrior form, but most are human. They seem to be leading them to the ships. This is just more proof as to how insidious their presence is. ~TNN Invasion Report

It took a few minutes to get everything put together, but faster than she expected, McKenna could talk in Thelia's ear. While the Elentrin couldn't reply to her, McKenna could hear everything she said from the other room.

"Okay, please make contact with the other ship, the Silik, and let him know you have been delegated to talk to him." She spoke in a low voice through the setup. It'd taken a minute for her to figure out how not to talk too loudly. These ear link things were sensitive.

"And tell him what?" Thelia's voice could be heard both through the ear link and from other room.

"Right now, get him talking and pull information from him. Find out everything you can. I'll prompt you with more as we go. Right now I'm looking for information on their plans and how to stall them. We need more time. I expect you know how to act arrogant and demand information from others?"

"Of course. I did not earn my rank due to just my intelligence. That is only a portion of what you need to survive." An odd bitterness coated the response, but McKenna ignored it.

"Good. Then ask who he is, and say you took back over the ship, but this place is not worth the effort and plans are being made to leave."

"No captain would believe that. They can't. The Elentrin don't leave civilizations that might become dangerous to them behind."

"No prime directive, huh?" McKenna didn't mean to say that out loud, and the sense of amusement filled the mindspace.

"Directive of what?" Thelia asked, a hint of confusion in her voice.

"Never mind. Just get him talking. We need time and if you want your life on Earth, we need him to take us seriously. At this point, lie, twist, prevaricate, whatever. Time is what I need. Worst case we'll charge in, and 'take back over' if we need to."

"Very well, but you do not understand the mindset of those in the House. But I will make this attempt and get you some time."

If only you could. A few months would be nice but at this point I'll settle for an hour or two.

~Cass, you still doing okay?~

~We have them stacked in the hallways. Charley and the twins are a godsend being able to talk to a lot of them. But we need that portal back ASAP. It's starting to get very crowded.~ Cass replied but McKenna didn't sense any great level of panic from her.

~Got it.~

The screen in front of McKenna on the desktop which seemed to also double as a computer screen, showed the Elentrin of the other ship, the Captain.

"Can he see me?" Her voice came out raspy as she tensed, that would ruin everything, maybe.

"No, it's one way. A replica of what is shown out there, so you can see and hear," Ash said just as quietly.

McKenna sagged in relief, the whole point of this was to make him think the Elentrin might still be in charge. Toni moved at the corner of her eyes, standing at the window looking out at Earth, and McKenna didn't blame her. There was something about the view that called to all of them.

"I see the problem has been taken care of. Exactly what is going on in that ship, and where is Keric?" The voice came out in stereo and just sounded a bit odd. They spoke in Elentrin, but at this point all of them translated it effortlessly in their heads. She didn't pipe the conversation into the mindspace, but JD and Toni could understand it all.

"And to whom exactly am I speaking to?"

You could hear the sneer in Thelia's voice and McKenna waved Ash over, whispering quickly. "Can you give me her picture also, so I can watch her body language?"

They had arranged for JD to stay there, behind Thelia, but in a subservient pose, implying he'd been overcome. It was all a lie and Thelia knew he was her executioner if she did anything that betrayed them.

Ash nodded and moved over to another part of the desk. As he did that, McKenna heard the captain speak, his voice much more courteous than it had been with her.

"This is Captain Clarin of the Silik. By the House, who are you? What happened over there? Is Keric really dead?"

The picture snapped up next to the Captain showing him and Thelia side by side, a thin line between them. If anything Thelia stood straighter, shoulders back as she glared.

"Keric was a failure and was killed for his stupidity in trusting unwisely. I am here now and you will deal with me." She didn't give an inch, and McKenna had to smirk at her ability to tell the absolute truth, yet have it be so wrong.

"Explain exactly what happened," his words came out as an order and a gentle sneer graced Thelia's face.

Damn, that woman is going to make a fortune in modeling.

The ideal thought made McKenna fight a laugh even as she tried to figure out what else she needed and what they could do to make him go away.

"I do not report to you. In fact," she made a show of looking around, "at this point I'm the only one standing here. I owe you nothing. I know exactly what I am doing."

A brief flash of rage crossed his face, then his expression went back to a smooth blankness. "Very well. Then I shall assume harvesting shall continue? Though that does not explain why the shuttles are returning from that planet and no more drops are going on. Have your holds filled already? The other ships say they are only at forty-five percent full." His words came out bland but the sharpness in his eyes made McKenna worry.

"Tell him the Shifted of this planet are not as suitable as once thought, and a decision was made to stop the harvesting." McKenna said quietly, wishing they had more time to discuss various options. She didn't trust Thelia as far as she could throw her, but she had to trust her.

On the video Thelia's nose wrinkled. "It is not wise to continue harvesting from this planet. We will leave and mark this planet as "avoid at all costs." The ultimate price if we stay here may be more than even House Rircn may wish to pay."

"I doubt there is any cost the House would not pay. If unsuitable, why are the other ships still gathering?"

"They will not be for much longer." Thelia's voice was abrupt, but McKenna couldn't think of anything else to say.

"Then when they are aboard, the bombardment will start?"

"It has been decided that there will be none."

"Tell him the captured ones will be returned to the planet, they are dangerous to keep," McKenna blurted quickly then regretted it when she saw the tightness around Thelia's eyes. She didn't think he'd buy that. Dammit, they needed more time.

"And exactly why would we leave this planet alone? Already they have satellites in orbit. Another few *reyan* and they might leave their planet, and might actually develop the ability to attack us." His voice held both confusion and sarcasm; at least that was how McKenna read it. For all she knew it might be a reflection of hope.

Thelia shrugged languidly, her head tilting. "Some things are better not known. If I tell you, you would then be required to tell the House. Are you sure you want that knowledge? Knowing the cost of informing the Head of things he does not want to hear?"

Those words made no sense to McKenna, but the captain froze, his face tight. "Point. I must discuss this." There was no goodbye, the connection was just cut and his face disappeared.

McKenna glanced at Ash and nodded. "Yes, the connection was severed."

Dread filled her stomach as she got up and walked out, nothing good was going to come of this, but maybe she bought some time. "What was that?" McKenna asked, as she got closer to Thelia.

"You are lacking much of our history and I doubt you could ever understand our culture, but we never return a harvesting. Just my saying that made him doubt my sanity." Her voice again had that hint of a sneer in it, but buried under it was something else.

"What about that last part, about the Head and knowledge?"

This time the bitterness in Thelia's smile and words came through clearly. "The House of Rircn is very specific about how the world works, and those that bring proof of it being other than how they say it is have a short life span. Their patience is non-existent and at this point I think my cache is higher than Clarin's. However, once he provides any proof of what I've done, they will have me declared a traitor to the house." Her stress on the word traitor implied a wealth of information, none of it which would be healthy for her.

"So he's going to think long and hard about what he thinks is going on?" McKenna ventured.

"He's going to decide what to pass along and what can be gleaned from the ships' recordings. It may make the difference between living and dying."

"What do you think he'll do?"

And how much time is this going to buy us?

"I am assuming from your discussions you have no people on any of the other ships?" Thelia asked, but it was the sly tone in her voice that made McKenna hesitate.

~You do realize her betraying us at this point would get her as many points as helping us will cost her.~ Toni's thought rang in the space.

~Yeah, I was thinking that. Dammit, I miss idiots trying to convince me they don't have an ounce of weed in their car or only had one drink a few hours ago. Life made a hell of a lot more sense then.~

JD's amusement rippled through. Sighing, she tried to figure out how to answer when Perc broke in. ~Done, we're coming back now.~ Even as the thought registered, she felt the portal energy and the four men came back in, all of them looking exhausted.

"We got it done. All down safely on Earth. Safe spot for a while, until we either have time to deal with them or are all dead." Perc sounded like he'd been wrung out and McKenna wanted to hug him, but the others, even Rarz, looked just as tired.

A tension fled from Thelia and she seemed softer for just a moment, then it disappeared and went back to her brittle rigidness.

"Rarz, can you set the portal back up for Cass?"

"Yes. Doing it now."

~Cass, incoming,~ she sent, looking at Rarz. He had an odd green tint under his scales she didn't remember seeing before.

~I see it. We're sending them through. Just in time, it was getting a bit crowded. We'll keep going.~ Cass had a positive tone in her thought and McKenna decided to believe it was the truth.

"So next move?" Toni asked, glancing at McKenna.

"Well, it just got made," JD said, his voice sour. "We're being hailed again. And if I understand it correctly this time from one of the other ships. The Listai?"

"There are three, the Listai, Grinka, and we are the For-lin," Ash provided in a low tone, still avoiding looking at Thelia if possible. At some point she'd have to figure out why the Elentrin made him so nervous, but now wasn't the time.

"Thelia, answer and stall, but I'll be there next to you. Talk until I stop you, because you're right, I don't know the culture and I might make things worse. If I have to, I'll pull a gun and point it at your head."

"That would make an impression, though it might be best to stay out of the immediate line of sight. Though the pet being in the view would surprise no one. Assuming of course you want to make sure I don't do anything—regrettable."

"None of us want you to do anything regrettable. I prefer my food to be cooked." McKenna locked her eyes with the vivid purple of Thelia's and the woman looked away first.

"Understood."

JD and Toni faded back into the room with Ash. At this point, the tied-up Elentrin had quit making any protests, but the beat of her heart and breathing were steady so McKenna ignored her for now.

Positioned out of the way of the video pick up, she nodded at Thelia. "Answer them, and we'll play it by ear."

Thelia frowned at her touching her ear link, but the chime sounded again, and she glanced down and hit the button. "Yes?"

"Ambassador Thelia? What are you doing there? I thought you were on your ship? Where is Keric?" A woman with mint green hair and eyes looked out of the video. As with all the Elentrin her beauty was such that you wanted to stare, though she was the first female with short hair she'd seen. While McKenna was out of the camera range, she could still see the screen easily enough.

What? Do they breed these people for beauty?

"Keric is no longer in charge. Plans have changed. All shuttles are to be recalled and the harvested Kaylid returned. This planet will be marked off limits and we will leave after returning those we collected."

The woman looked out of the video screen, then her eyes scanned the room. Eyes snagged on the far corner and McKenna followed the gaze and sighed at the blood still on the floor.

I really need to remember to scour a place before trying to convince people nothing happened.

"I see that Clarin did not miss-guess the current situation on the Forlin."

"The situation?" Thelia smirked. "He has no idea what the situation is, other than the respect he thinks he is due was missing. This isn't an idle wish, Lanik. The harvested will be returned." She stressed the word "will" as she looked at the woman. "Otherwise the consequences will be unpleasant."

The other woman, Lanik from Thelia's comment, gave her an odd, sad smile. "You had such promise. You may have been one of the greats. Too bad you have been suborned."

"Oh, she hasn't," McKenna said in fluent Elentrin, stepping forward, her gun raised. "She is doing this because she understands there is no choice for her, or for any of you. Our planet doesn't take lightly to raiders and she is trying very hard to save her people. Too bad all of you seem too stupid to understand."

Lanik glanced at her and then at Thelia. "This? You can't overcome a single Kaylid? Make her bow to you, worship you, slit its own throat."

Thelia smiled, a bare bone of a smile that felt like a knife. "Do you think I would be standing here if it was that easy? They are not like the others we have harvested over the *reyan*. They are immune and can spread that immunity. What she says is true. Our people will need to change." There was an odd note of prophecy in her voice that sent a shiver through McKenna and the mindspace.

"Let my people go, and we won't destroy you." McKenna didn't take her eyes off the woman, but her hand remained steady, gun pointed at Thelia's temple.

Lanik gave another one of those odd smiles and then the channel was cut.

"What the hell? What happened?" McKenna asked glancing at everyone.

"She cut the channel, but incoming," Ash muttered from the other office, his voice more in her head than in her ears.

McKenna hadn't even lowered the gun, pointing it at Thelia as Captain Clarin of the Silik appeared again.

"I see you are doing all this to save yourself, traitor," his voice a low hiss, the liquid syllables of the Elentrin language sounding like the rasp of a blade in his anger.

"No, she is doing this to save people," McKenna responded, though she didn't say what people. "This is your last chance. Leave and let the harvested be returned." She hated that word, but for these conversations using the familiar terminology was about the only way to get them to take her seriously.

"You have nothing that can attack us. We will finish our harvesting, destroy this planet, then leave. You will get to watch your world reduced to rubble. No one will be left to mourn your pitiful world." His cold face held no emotion as he said the words, but this time he did look at McKenna not Thelia.

So be it.

"Roark, blow it." She said in English and watched Clarin frown in confusion.

"Yes, ma'am."

"I told you, there would be consequences if you didn't leave. Screen please."

The screen split and the small ambassador ship hanging in space appeared.

"What? You are delusional Kaylid if you think the image—" he broke off as the small ship hanging in the darkness of space ripped apart from the inside, superheated gas flaring bright as the ship became shards of material floating in the void.

"How? What did you do?" Horror and anger flashed across his previously immobile face.

"We can do that to any of your ships. Leave now, before I destroy all of you. Leave and tell your people our world is off limits."

Rage twisted his face, warping that beautiful visage into something that would give her nightmares. "How dare you!" His voice reverberated through the speakers and she could see the shock and anger on the faces of the crew behind him. "I will have you destroyed for this."

"How? You have no weapons. I can destroy any of your ships. Leave before I decide to blow up yours, too." She reached out and clicked the disconnect icon and sagged. The arm holding the gun dropped to her side, aching from being held out for so long.

Thelia looked at her with a hint of surprise on her face. "You were serious. You destroyed the ship and killed the people on it."

McKenna straightened back up and gave her a flat look. "You have killed thousands of my people, kidnapped tens of thousands more, and you are horrified by the death of what, ten? Twenty Elentrin on that ship?"

Purple lashes blinked rapidly for a minute, then Thelia nodded slowly. "Truth, just I don't remember the last time outside a true accident that many Elentrin died. This will send ripples through the Elentrin."

"Good. I want to make it very clear to them Earth is not their garden."

Chapter 36 - Kamikaze

Amateur astronomers on all continents are watching the spaceships since they moved into orbit. News today suggests something is going on. The shuttles have deviated from their normal path of up and down and are instead swarming out towards the space between Mars and Jupiter and then coming back. Does this mean good or bad things? People remember to stay safe; go out only when necessary and be armed at all times. ~ KWAK News

A strange pall settled over the group of them as they stood looking at the blank screen. McKenna took a deep breath, held it, then slowly released it. She did it one more time then turned to Ash.

"How may Elentrin are still active on the ship?"

His tail twitched and he tilted his head to the side "There should be fifteen left. The alarm would have woken those on their sleep cycle."

"We need to get them out of the way, I don't want anyone bursting in here to 'rescue' anyone. How can we do that?"

Another tail twitch. "The orders were to report to their duty stations. Elao, can you lock them all in their stations? Make it so they can not leave?" He said the words out loud and in the mindspace.

[That should be possible. If you access the life support systems, I should be able to pin down their locations and tell you what crew members may still be at large.]

"Excellent. That would be great. Toni, you want to work on him with that? You're the person with the most ship info so I'm trying to make sure you know how to do all of this and stay up to date. You may be the person flying us home."

Toni's ears went flat as did her whiskers. "You trying to make sure we all die?" she asked, sarcasm dripping from her words.

"No, but you have most of this in your head. And with Thelia helping it might be our only choice. Granted, I'd prefer us to float up here for the next two weeks, get all the decant chambers running, and turn this over to the government and go home, but —" she shrugged at this point and the snorts and laughter in her mind made it clear her point was taken.

"I think I'm going to start calling you Murphy, Kenna. 'Cause really, anything that can go wrong has been going wrong around you."

McKenna stuck her tongue out at JD. He, Perc, and Toni started to laugh while the three aliens just looked confused. Ash shook his head and drifted over to one of the consoles and started typing. The stiffening of his tail caught her attention first.

"Something wrong?" She turned and headed over towards him.

"I don't know. The shuttles that were returning to the bays of the ships have stopped and are now coming towards us." He sounded absent and distracted as his hands flew over the console. "By Alara's Stars," he whispered. The way he said the words drew the attention of everyone and sent shivers down McKenna's spine.

"What?"

"They are heading straight for us. They are on collision courses. Well, not all of them. Some have started throwing asteroids towards your planet."

"Don't we have shields?" Perc asked moving up. "They always have shields in the movies. Is there a way we can prevent those asteroids from hitting?"

"No," Ash's voice held grief, and no hope. "The one for space debris is shut off. We have static shields for space debris, dust, and micro asteroids. The jump drive doesn't require them, though we need them for in-system travel, but all the shuttles have beacons that let the shields ignore them, so no, there are no shields."

"They're going to kill the people on those shuttles to ram into us? And kill so many people on Earth." Toni's voice held incredulity and pain that reverberated through the mind-space.

"Kamikaze runs," JD's voice was dark as on the view screen dots appeared and a large object that obviously represented the ship and the incoming shuttles. As she watched, one of the dots disappeared into the bulk of the ship.

McKenna waited. "Nothing happened?" The deck trembled under her feet and alarms started to wail. "Dammit, spoke too soon. What happened?"

Ash didn't look up, but focused on the information before him. Only the tip of his tail moved, the rest of it rigid.

She refocused on the next dot coming in, and watched it disappear. She held her breath and counted.

One

Two

Thr-

The ship rocked and more alarms went off. McKenna felt her claws extend without her consciously choosing to let them slide out.

We're all going to die out here in space and they'll come for us.

The terror and fear in that thought sent an adrenaline surge through her and she pushed back the terror.

So be it, but I'll take them with us.

"Thelia," her voice cracked like a whip. "Head us towards the Silik. Aim for the middle of the ship."

Everyone looked at her, but Thelia just let her lips curve in that odd smile and stepped forward and clicked some buttons. Ash's eyes were wide as he looked at her, but he didn't say anything to counteract her order.

"We're going to ram them?" Toni's voice didn't squeak, but it had a tightness to it that wrapped around McKenna.

"If we don't have shields that can stop the shuttles, they don't have shields that can stop this ship. If we sit here, we die. Cass is going as fast as they can, and I can't let him keep attacking us."

A beep interrupted her and she glanced around as the familiar sound of an incoming hail filled the bridge.

"Got it," JD said pressing keys on console. The screen filled with the face of Clarin the Silik captain.

"You think you can resist us, there is no resistance. We are the Elentrin and we will destroy your planet."

The odd echo of something from a sci-fi TV series had a burst of laughter coming out of McKenna's mouth. The shock on his face made it all worth it and she grabbed the opportunity and ran with it.

"Did you think we didn't plan for something like this? Our world is willing to pay any price to be free. We will be the masters of our own destiny. You don't have a chance. Have you paid any attention to the ship I'm in?" The words left her mouth as another shudder shook the ship and she knew another shuttle had impacted. "You may kill the few of us on this ship, but we are billions and we will destroy you. But first, I'll kill you and your ship."

He frowned and glanced down, his face paled as he looked back up to her. "You are insane. You would ram me with that ship, destroying all of us?"

The grin, so odd in this form, pulled tight across her muzzle and bared all her teeth, and she kept it tight and vicious. "Yes. To kill you may just become the primary drive of my people. I'll take you with me."

He turned, presenting a profile that seemed picture perfect. "We are leaving. Send the information to other ships. I will present this to the House Leaders and they can decide what to do with this world." Turning, he all but spat at her. "Fine. We will leave, but we will take what we have collected. If you want them back, you'll have to find us. Since your world doesn't even have space flight yet, you will not find us by the time we come back to destroy you."

~Rarz, come here.~ Her thoughts quick and frantic. ~Time it right, you'll know when.~

"Ah, but we learn fast when motivated. And best of all, we have a new ally, one that is very motivated to see you destroyed." At those words Rarz stepped into view and he pulled his lips back mimicking her actions, displaying an array of very sharp teeth. "And I think they will be more than happy for a race of warriors to help hunt you down."

If she had thought Clarin was pale before, now he paled even more and went a shade of green under his skin.

"You are working with the abominations." The words came out hushed and horrified. His face looked like he wanted to gag, or maybe scream.

"Yes, you don't like the Drakyn, do you? Well, we like them very much and are more than willing to ally ourselves with them to help stop you." She poured as much glee into the words as she could and he all but recoiled back from her.

"You will regret your association with the abominations, be sure about that," he acted like he was about to go all monologue and McKenna shut him off.

"Oh, I'm sure you will regret it by the time we're done with you. But us? No, they are going to be the best things that ever happened. We can find you anywhere, and get on your ships with ease. You will never know we're coming, but you will feel us breathing behind you, our breath on your neck, and you will never sleep at night again." McKenna channeled every horror movie, suspense novel, ghost story she'd ever read or watched. "Tell your children to fear us, for you have awakened a monster that will never rest until your people bow before us."

His eyes grew wider and he looked at her, then the screen went black, and she felt like a rubber band snapped. She sagged for a minute, then pulled herself back up looking at the screen. "Are the shuttles still headed towards us?"

No one responded and she turned to look behind her and froze at everyone staring at her, even in their Kaylid forms the shock and surprise clear on their faces.

"What?" McKenna asked looking back at the screen, but only saw the ship hanging there, the remains of the small ship still floating between them. She turned to look at them, confused.

"I will say, this exposes a new aspect of you Earthlings that I did not expect." Thelia's oddly respectful comment seemed to release the stasis in the rest of the room.

"What the hell was that, Kenna?" JD demanded as he moved forward, his claws fully extended. Roark and Coran looked oddly smug, while she couldn't read Perc, and even in the mindspace he was a blank.

"What? I channeled all the movies I could think of to make him think we were the baddest thing on the planet. Besides, knowing humans, do you think anything I said won't become true?"

Perc barked out a laugh looking at her. His voice filled her mind, the communication tight and private. ~That was probably the sexiest thing I've ever seen. I'd follow you any-where.~

She jerked to look at him and he just smiled, his teeth showing, and McKenna didn't know if she should be aroused or afraid. Either way, that was something to deal with later, if they lived that long.

McKenna swallowed and looked at the screen. "But I think I lost us all the captured people on the other ships. They're running away, and we can't get to them in time."

As if in response to her words the icons representing the other ships started to move away from them, gathering speed.

"The shuttles have all gone motionless. and the commands to them have stopped." Ash's comment didn't make her hopeful, but she moved on anyhow.

"Can you recall them all to this ship? And can you tell how many things were launched at the Earth?"

And how many people I just killed?

The unspoken concern hung in the air as the humans turned to look at Ash, waiting for the answer to this question.

Chapter 37 - Impact

A spate of attacks in Denver brought the focus of the National Guard out, and they managed to get captured shifters out of the shuttle before it took off. The bodies of the invaders they killed all had markings similar to our big cats, but one had four arms, the other had two sets of eyes. The pictures have gone viral with people asking if these are mutations, that maybe these were once human? What if this strange virus will eventually change everyone into monsters? ~TNN Invasion News

They all waited with varying levels of patience while Ash worked on one of the consoles. McKenna tried to see on the view screen where the asteroids might have hit. How many hit? But the serenely rotating globe gave her no clues. Of the presences in her mind, only Cass and Rarz weren't ruffled. Cass because they hadn't told her yet, at least she hadn't, and Rarz? Well, it wasn't his world was it? It took a few minutes but then Ash nodded at her.

"The shuttles are returning to their bays. Though some are returning to the other ships. It is the best I can do."

McKenna pushed that thought away and turned to stare at Ash instead of the planet that revealed none of its strife from here. Not that it would make his final answer any better, but it gave her something that could be considered constructive to do. Maybe. "What about the asteroids?"

He typed for another minute then looked at her, his tail still. "From the records twenty-five objects were flung at your planet. Of those three vaporized as they entered your atmosphere, crumbling into dust."

All of them flinched at the thought of twenty-five objects striking the earth. An odd sigh escaped them as Ash kept talking, removing three from that number.

Okay that leaves twenty-two, that's better than twenty-five.

Her thoughts didn't make her feel any better, so she listened and waited for the rest of the information.

"Five struck your oceans. This is because we are instructed to try and hit landmasses, but aiming the kinetic weapons is not an exact science. Of those, two do not seem to have had any effect besides high tides, but the after-effects may take a while to be seen. Three have caused tidal waves that have impacted land masses or will shortly."

All the earthlings cringed, and McKenna couldn't help but be very aware of Rarz and Thelia watching them. While their expressions were blank, the sense of judging was inescapable. It raised her annoyance level, but she didn't say anything, just waited for the rest of Ash's report.

"The remaining fourteen hit land masses, but I do not know the size or constitution of what was sent to your planet. I can show you where it hit, but at this time there is not much other information." He watched McKenna the entire time and every word seemed to strike her like the blow of that damn whip. Right now, she'd have preferred to be naked again with the whip striking her back as opposed to being here, hearing this.

"Please," she asked. Her mouth so dry it hurt.

Ash turned and a flattened view of the Earth appeared. It took her a minute to place the continents, but the familiar shapes snapped into place for her after she focused. On it, bright spots blossomed. Unable to resist she walked over and touched each spot as she said the rough area out loud.

"This has to be near Hong Kong, while this one over here looks like the edge of India." Her fingers trailed over the screen going from place to place. Her knowledge of Asian geography wasn't the best, but generally she could guess where it was. "This has to be in Mongolia? Maybe Russia. Then this is probably France. These are in Africa," she said tracing two bright marks, but she had no ideas what countries. One of them up a little bit higher had to be in Saudi Arabia somewhere. Another near the Black Sea. "Down here another two will hit Australia, but I can't even begin to tell you what cities are where."

"That is also where one of the tidal waves will impact. It should be there in an hour if the density and speed calculations are correct." Ash's' voice didn't provide relief, it just added to the guilt and stress wrapping her like a sticky cocoon.

Taking a deep breath she moved west and south, avoiding the lurid marks on the US. "South America? Which country is this?"

"Argentina," Toni said quietly next to her as she stepped up and traced over the spot. "This is lower Brazil, near Paraguay. While this one up here is Suriname. If the dots show the reach of the impact, that country is all but gone."

McKenna didn't know how she could keep breathing, why her heart didn't break, but she followed north, trying not see where the last few were. "This is Mexico, the middle, but I have no idea how close to anything that is."

Her eyes shut and she inhaled then forced herself to truly see the country hanging in front of her. "Southeast. Maybe Kentucky or Tennessee. This one is up near Minnesota. The last one is Nevada? Maybe Utah?"

As she finished listing the last of them, she just sighed. Her throat was so tight, it hurt. But her kids were safe. Her town and friends were safe. For now she would take what she could get.

"Ash, where are the other tidal waves going to hit, can you tell? Or put up here where they landed and where the waves are headed?"

Three bright white spots appeared on the view screen. One off the coast of Australia, one in the middle of the Atlantic, the other off the coast of Peru.

"So many lives," she breathed out. "How much time do they have?"

"The shortest about four hours, longest ten or more."

It meant she had a few more minutes. "Okay, we need to work on getting the people here off. The time pressure is off." Switching to Speech she checked in on Cass. ~How goes it? Still getting people out of there?~

~Yes. Our backlog is almost gone, but what was all that shaking about? I checked and everything looks fine down here, but that was unexpected.~

~Complications as usual. But it's done now. Keep it up, I'll explain in a bit.~ She refocused on the people in the room with her, specifically Rarz. Now that she could think, she thought about the ones that had been taken, slipping out of their hands as the invaders fled. But the ones that were on this ship still needed to be rescued.

"Rarz, once we empty this ship, can you create a portal to the other ships so we can do the same thing? Get our people back and rescue others?" As she spoke Ash went still, his tail as always giving away his emotion status by how still it held as they waited for Rarz to answer.

"That would be highly unlikely," he said slowly, his voice heavy and McKenna felt the weight drop back onto her shoulders. Her knees wanted to buckle it felt so impossible a weight to bear.

"Why not?" Her voice croaked as the words came out.

He titled his head, looking at her, but what caught her attention was the tail twitching towards Toni and Toni's absolute focus on him, her whiskers tight against her muzzle.

"Creating a portal between a ship and a planet, when you can all but see the ship from the planet, is challenging. To create a portal from a planet to a ship that I have no idea where it is? I do not think this is even possible. The universe is huge."

"But you do it blindly to other planets," Toni put in, her voice challenging, aggressive almost, but McKenna didn't care. How could they have come so close only to fail now?

"A planet is huge and has a center of gravity I can sense. When the connection is created it is that well of gravity I attach to. Even then we can test to see if there is atmosphere or if it is a habitable climate. Within sight I can estimate the same way I know how far to step. The ship took me a bit, but I could see it, and sense it, with its own gravity circling your planet. Now I have no idea where it is."

Toni subsided, but McKenna understood the urge to argue, to get him to agree. But arguing with physics usually meant you lost.

"So what are our options?" McKenna asked bleakly, feeling like she could sleep for a year.

"Options about what?" Rarz looked at her, his thick ridges of brows drawing down.

"Getting back our people. Stopping the Elentrin as a whole. Getting help. Making sure that this never happens to anyone again." She didn't care she didn't have authorization to say that. This could never happen again, and she needed to do what she could to prevent it.

"There are many, but they will take time and much planning. There is no easy answer that I am aware of."

McKenna nodded, a stiff move that felt like the weight of an invisible sword lay against her neck. "I need to talk to the people on the planet. Roark, will you come with me to head down to the surface? At least we have time to deal with the prisoners on this ship. But they need to know about the others; the ones I lost."

Roark looked at her, his eyes serious. "Yes. Want to head down there now?"

"This isn't something I want to tell them about remotely. Ash, can you get me the coordinates of where those asteroids landed and the time to tidal wave impact? I think they should already know this, but just in case?" Ash nodded and a minute later approached with a printout. It wasn't in English but she figured she could translate it when she got there. Nodding her thanks, she shoved it in a pocket in her kilt. "JD, Perc, will you guys watch the guests? Rarz, will you come with me and explain the issues? They'll need reinforcement as to the truth of this reality."

Rarz lowered his head on that flexible neck. "As you request."

A horrible shudder shook the ship hard enough McKenna fell, narrowly missing hitting her head on a workstation. Thelia wasn't so lucky and her face slammed into one. McKenna cast her a glance at her outcry and saw blood streaming down from her nose, transfiguring the beauty into something out of an anime horror movie.

How can she look stunning covered with blood?

"What the hell was that?" The words were shouted over the sound of wailing alarms that cut through her skull with brutal pain.

Ash had also fallen, she realized the only person still standing was Rarz, who seemed to have centered his weight between his legs and tail.

"Must be nice," she muttered as she got back up, the deck still swaying alarmingly. "Ash? What just happened?" Images of spaceships blowing up from a hundred movies washed through her mind and she tried to banish them and not think about the thin metal between them and a quick death.

"One of the shuttles must have hit systems that smoldered for a while. That last explosion came from life support and canister control. Life support is failing, and we have approximately three of your hours left before oxygen will become an issue. While there are escape capsules, that would necessitate leaving the Kaylid here to die."

Before she could say anything, Cass's frantic thought burst in. ~Something's wrong, all the canisters are flashing red. They're showing a countdown timer and I verified both control rooms are showing the same timers.~

~What do they say?~ JD asked before McKenna could, stress coating his thoughts.

~Essentially that all ship-based life support functions will stop in three days. There's a note that they'll then go to backup power. I can't get them all out in three days. We only have one portal and not enough people to do it. We'd have to have full teams in here cracking them open to pull that off.~ Her tone wavered at the beginning, but the terror was there.

~Okay. Keep going as fast as you can. Give me a minute.~ McKenna turned to Ash. "You said there were escape pods. Have any been used?"

His tail twitched but he walked over to another console, touching icons. She followed him as he walked and saw Thelia standing upright, with blood staining the light green robe. It created streaks of darkness that felt off. Other than her bloody clothes and her the red and swollen nose, she still seemed unaffected by their imminent death.

Ash looked up from where he had moved. "Yes, about ten have been used. There were twenty Elentrin as crew on this ship, with the Ambassadors visiting occasionally. That means there are twelve left," he paused and looked around at the blood still on the floor. "Make that eight."

"Make that three. We killed five. Two in a hallway and three in the engine room." She noticed Roark start when she said that, but the confusions she had felt then seemed a lifetime away.

Conscience is the first causality of war. Who said that? It is true, truer than I think I'll ever be comfortable with.

~Cass?~

~Yeah, we all okay?~

~Not really. We need to step up the operation. I'm sending Toni and JD down to get the other rooms open, we need them running through that damn portal. And if I tell you to bail, you damn well better bail down that hole. You got it?~

~Kenna? What's going on?~ Cass's tone felt stressed and tense.

~It doesn't matter. You shouldn't run into any more resistance. Get those rooms open and get people running into the portal if necessary." She turned to look at the others. "JD, Toni, Roark, you all head down there. Roark, Coran tell the powers that be what's going on. Let them know about thee visitors earth is going to get. I'm assuming they can track these pods, but just in case they should know. But move it. And if you think this is going sideways, bail and bail fast, but rescue whoever you can. Roark, I need you to tell them I'll try to land in White Sands. It's the only place I know of that's big enough to maybe handle this ship. It's the least likely to have people or houses around that I can take out. Make sure they understand I have no idea what I'm doing. I've never flown a spaceship before." She said all this out loud and via Speech.

People started to protest and she held up her hand. "I don't have time to argue. I have to stay here and Perc doesn't have kids. The rest of you need to get out no matter what, and Roark will have more weight with the military than I will. Every minute you argue with me is another person that we can't get out. Now GO!" Her voice echoed and after two long looks, JD and Toni took off at a run.

~Don't think this is over. I'm not leaving without you,~ the thought all but growled in her ear as JD left the room.

~I love you. But you need to be safe. Make sure Cass is too. She's good for you. Take care of my kids, please.~ And with those works McKenna shut down the connection, feeling JD and Toni pounding on it, but she kept the door shut tight.

She turned to Perc and forced a smile, exposing too many teeth. "If I just sentenced you to death, I'm sorry. But I can't hurt either of them more than they've already been hurt."

Perc crossed his massive arms over the furred chest and his eyes locked with hers. "No place else I'd rather be."

Chapter 38 - Falling to Earth

The pictures of aliens emerging from a portal supported by military personnel have gone viral. No one knows the source and the White House and other military sources are not responding to any questions. Where was this taken? What is this portal? Why are we helping the aliens trying to kill us? What is going on? What are the bright lights in the sky that have headed towards us? Are they alien missiles? Weapons?~TNN News

"Ash, is there something we can give our guest to knock her out?"

"I believe so, though I will need to run down to the medical center to obtain it." His reply started slow, though by the end of the sentence he sounded sure.

"Go get it. Perc, go with him please." They both nodded, Perc nodding her way before the door slid closed behind them.

"Rarz, how well can you control the portal from here? What happens once we get into the atmosphere? Does anything change? What if we crash? Can the portal be made big enough to set the ship down where I tell you?"

McKenna could have sworn his jaw dropped as he looked at her, shifting his weight back and forth. "Truly you humans think around things in ways that have never occurred to any of our people. I will be fascinated to see what long association will bring with it."

Mckenna shrugged. "Humans are weird and we do this sort of stuff. But now isn't the time to get into future possibility discussions. Back to the question, can you?"

His thick lids dropped to narrow slits, but he didn't seem to be looking at her, more like he was thinking. "The portal should be stable until the bulk of this planet interferes. While normally we can flex around planets or stars, this is too short a distance to do that and the tunnel is too active. The atmosphere won't make a difference as vacuum and planet are the same, it isn't a physical construct but a metaphysical connection."

Damn, there went one idea. Though the idea of this being metaphysical like some sort of astral projection is very disconcerting.

She felt Wefor hum a bit as he talked, but she didn't say anything or ask questions.

"If the tunnel were still active while we crashed, and I was not killed instantly the explosion would travel along the path of the tunnel until my death collapsed it — I believe. That has never been tested, though there is one story of lava coming through a tunnel when it was accidentally connected to a volcano. It killed the Drakyn involved and the tunnel then collapsed. The process was never repeated. But it is known that heat and energy can travel via the tunnels."

That's good to know and gives me some ideas, but for later.

"Go on," she urged. The blinking lights and low-level alarms felt like ants on her skin, distracting and annoying but not painful.

"In theory," he closed his eyes for a minute, "yes, the math backs up the theory that while it would be possible to make the portal big enough, the velocity would not slow, which means the ship would exit the portal at the same velocity it entered." He paused again, his eyes closing for a count of ten then he opened them all the way looking at her. "Though the math game agrees that it might be an interesting experiment and a way to travel across the stars via ships. This is a wonderful idea you have brought to us." He seemed excited as he talked.

McKenna locked down her thoughts tight. ~Wefor, do you have any idea who he is talking to?~

[There is no transmission registering. Immediate response no one, but he does act as if he has been given information.]

~Add it to the list please?~

[Topic added.]

"So we do this the hard way. Great. Rarz please make sure we close the portal before we enter the atmosphere. I have no idea what's going to happen but I'm not going to risk the deaths of the people on the ground as we do this. They should have White Sands ready for us by the time we land, but either way that area is sparsely populated."

The soft chime and slide of the doors pulled her attention to the back of the room, her body ready to attack, since they still didn't know where everyone was. Perc and Ash came back in with a large bag in each hand.

"Medical supplies. I'll dose our guest." Perc said, walking towards the captain's office, opening the bag as he did. "They have the coolest injectors. Stuff totally out of the sci-fi movies."

"While he ensures the remaining officer is sedated, I will access the escape pod." Ash walked over to one of the walls that McKenna had glanced at and ignored. It had several large ovals on it, as did another wall on the opposite side. Five ovals about six foot by two foot in size, though she realized now they all had two blinking lights on them, one yellow and one blue.

Ash walked over and pressed the blue one. For once something behaved exactly as she expected. A hiss of compressed air and it slid up, revealing a small chamber with a seat on each side. Harnesses secured to the wall and gauges, currently dark, completed it. It reminded her of the seats the astronauts had used in the Apollo missions. Granted she'd only seen them in movies and pictures, but it had that feel.

Perc walked out carrying an unconscious woman. "That stuff works fast. Counted to ten and she was down. We need to look into their drugs, this stuff is incredible. Ash was telling me she'll wake up in about ten hours with less than five minutes of being disoriented."

McKenna stepped back out of the way so they could strap her into the chamber. "Absolutely. If we get this down in one piece there might be that opportunity. Ash, you will stay, right? I don't think we have a chance without you." McKenna knew she had the manpower to force him to stay, but if she didn't have to, she'd rather avoid seeing how far she would go to pull this off.

"Your species is my—our—best chance. If you die on this ship everything was for nothing and I would rather die than continue. Besides," he glanced around the ship, "I think my position has been made known."

McKenna gave him a sad smile, though she realized it probably didn't translate properly in this form. "We would say all your bridges are burned."

Ash thought and nodded. "That is accurate."

"Your language is so colorful, it makes me wonder sometimes." Thelia's voice, while not loud, cut through the clamor of the alarms.

"What do you mean?" McKenna looked at the enigma that stood in their midst, not able to trust her, but having no choice.

"What else we might have discovered if our culture, my people, could see past a hatred over something that happened hundreds of *reyan* ago? Something most of us believe falsehoods about anyhow." A melancholy note crept into her tone, then she shook her entire body making her fur ruffle. "So now what, oh mighty leader?"

"Where did you want this pod to go?" Ash asked and McKenna blinked, trying to remember.

~Wefor, what were the coordinates for Quantico? The large courtyard?~

[Looking.] A hum that she felt more than heard and then Wefor responded. [38°33'4"N 77°25'50"W]

"Once more," Ash said as he typed on a pad inside the door, but on the outside of the pod. Wefor repeated it while McKenna watched Thelia.

Ash stepped back from the pod and hit a button on the inside and it closed. When it clicked, he pressed and held the yellow button for a long breath. A soft chime just at the top of her hearing over the alarms sounded.

"Done, she is gone to the coordinates you provided. The pod auto adjusts speeds so if your people are there, they should be able to watch her land with little danger unless they are directly underneath. "

"Okay. One thing's off the list. Ash can you do a ship-wide announcement that we're landing on the planet, but there's a very good chance we won't make it. I'd rather have the remaining Elentrin off the ship and not have to worry about our backs."

"Very well." He moved over to another console and pressed a button. "Attention all crew, life support has failed and the ship will be landing on the planet below. The odds of survival are low at this time. Please brace for impact." He cut it off and turned to her.

"Not exactly what I would have said." McKenna commented looking at him, no idea what prompted that sort of announcement.

A long whistle escaped as his tail lashed back and forth. "Elentrin are odd creatures. They are not brave, but if you tell them to run, they will never run. It is like they absolutely must do the opposite. But if you tell them to stay, they will flee almost as if to deny that they have to follow your orders. But only in battle. In classrooms and normal work situations they follow orders just fine. But when their life is at risk? Their behavior is like that consistently. I have never understood, but I can use that trick."

"He is accurate," Thelia's voice was thoughtful. "I had never thought about it, but he is correct. I wonder if there are resources that I could use to research that? It would be interesting to track down the source of that reaction through our culture."

McKenna blinked at her and then laughed. "You're a scholar. You love research and books. That's what drives you, knowledge."

Thelia jerked upright, her spine stiffening. "I do not. It is simply another tool to use to crush my opponents." Her retort was instantaneous, and she pulled back a little bit blinking.

Ash whistled a bubbly sound burbling sound.

"That is exceedingly strange." Her eyes narrowed to slits, but McKenna could tell she wasn't looking at anyone, just thinking. "And very worrisome."

"Right now it qualifies as amusing and something to think about at a later point. If there is one. Ash, did your little message have the desired effect?"

It took him a minute, tail lazily drifting back and forth. McKenna glanced at her tail, wondering it if was waving also, but only the tip twitched. She pulled her attention back to him as he looked up.

"Yes, in odd ways. There should have only been three Elentrin left, but eight pods have been used."

"How is that possible?" McKenna asked, worry creeping up her spine.

Ash didn't respond immediately, tapping on the strange icons, his tail speeding up a bit. "It looks like some of the Kaylid chose to leave also. There were other Kaylid like me on the ship. House Kaylid that had been with their families for generations. Most of them also have AIs like I do."

[Yes, but theirs are not enlightened as I am.]

A faint hint of laughter came through at that comment and McKenna wasn't sure who had laughed.

Rarz had stood there watching all of them, but when another shudder shook the ship he moved. "What is the current plan?"

McKenna bit her lip, and instantly regretted it, as blood welled up from it. She closed her eyes and tried to get a grip.

~Cass, is everyone there and through the portal?~

~I sent Cass down, she's relaying things to the people in charge, Roark and Coran are with her. We're still getting people out as fast as we can but it's getting smoky down here.~ JD's soft rumble of a voice soothed her, though she knew if they all made it through this he would be chewing on her for months for making him leave.

McKenna flipped her tail at Ash, and startled herself, though she tried to cover it.

"The life support systems are failing, much faster than I thought. We have about two hours before the air will be unbreathable."

~JD, one hour from now, if I don't tell you to bail sooner, get down that portal and I'll have Perc drop it. Good luck,~ she said, her mental voice soothing.

~You too.~

She didn't try to talk to Charley, Nam, or the twins, just sent them a wave of love and turned to Thelia. "Time to pay the piper. Show me how to fly this ship."

Thelia looked at her, a sneer to her lips. "You are really going to do this. You have the ability to walk away at any moment, to any planet since you have a Drakyn by your side, and you are going to willingly stay on a ship that will most likely crash and kill us all?"

McKenna shrugged, "Yes."

Thelia turned her strange purple gaze on Perc. "This is true for you also?"

"Wouldn't miss it for the world." He responded, baring his teeth at her.

"Your world is very strange," she replied, her purple brows drawing together for a moment. "I would enjoy exploring more of your odd thought processes." She seemed like she was going to say something else, but cut it off and walked over. "Let us begin."

"One minute. Ash, where are the spacesuits? We should all get in them in case life support fails or we get a breach in the hull."

Ash looked at her, then for the first time glanced at Thelia who had her head tilted slightly as she looked at them.

"What are spacesuits? The word does not translate into Elentrin."

"What? You know, suits, to wear in case we get exposed to space? Has oxygen and stuff in it?"

"You mean the exosuits? They are too big to do any fine motor control and that is needed to steer or fly the ship. Also your commands would not be recognized through the gloves." Ash responded haltingly, as if unsure what she meant.

"No, like suits. To protect you? Provide life support?" At this point all the aliens were giving her looks that she figured conveyed confusion at the least. "Rarz? You don't have them either?"

"If you are talking about clothes to protect you from a vacuum or provide breathable air, no. I am able to exist in a vacuum for a few minutes in any of the scaled forms. All Drakyn have the ability to seal eyes, ears, and nostrils until I could create a relocator to move me back to a planet. But this is rarely done. Space is cold and inhospitable."

"If the ship breaks you die. Why would you put on something to prolong your death? Death is best met swiftly," Thelia chimed in, looking back and forth between the two earthlings.

"You guys have the weirdest blind spots. Either that or Earth has too many sci-fi writers who overthink everything." Frustrated, she looked at the consoles. "Fine, we do it like this, but I'm shifting back to human since then I can use the controls." With that she reached for her other self and slowly slid into it, conserving energy. But as soon as she was in that form, she reached for one of the energy bars.

"I'll stay in warrior. I'm faster and stronger in this form if we need it," Perc said as he moved over, standing more protectively near her.

Ash and Thelia stared at her as she shoved food into her now human mouth. Molars were good things, trying to chew these bars in warrior form got annoying fast.

"That is your normal form?" Ash finally asked, just as McKenna started to check if her kilt had fallen off or something.

"Yes? I'm human. Surely you saw what we looked like? Thelia, you were there on Earth."

"All the people I saw were dark-haired and short. They had flat faces. You, except for your bland coloring and marred features could almost pass for Elentrin."

McKenna shrugged. "I'll let the anthropologists fight over why humanoid is such a popular a body style. Not my issue. But Ash, what's your issue? Didn't you see humans on TV?"

"TeeVee?" He repeated slowly.

"Yeah you know, cameras, ways to see what was going on down there?"

"We have no cameras on that are watching what you are doing. We receive telemetry reports from the Kaylid and the shuttles, counts, information. But why would we need pictures?"

"To know what's going on?" another shudder shook the ship and McKenna waved her hand. "Never mind. Time to land or die trying. Aren't there seats for these things?" She asked, as she looked at the work stand next to the one Thelia leaned on, traces of her blood still touching the surface.

Ash walked over and pointed to a button on the side of the stand. McKenna pushed it with her human finger, and shivered a bit. The ship's environment came across as much colder without her fur. Out of the floor rose a weird stand that had a crescent arc to it. She glanced over at Thelia whose chair stand had also risen.

McKenna copied her actions, stepping back into it and feeling it flow up her spine and around her waist, taking much of her weight but let her keep full mobility. "Interesting design. Not sure how practical it is, but it should work." She glanced around and saw Perc had secured himself, as had Ash. The air was getting thinner, and for the first time she could taste smoke.

~Cass, JD, Toni, it's time, get off the ship now.~

~What about you?~

~As soon as you're all on the ground Rarz can kill the portal and then we can use it if we need to. Go. Now. I don't have time to argue with you.~ A few tense minutes passed before Toni spoke in her head.

~It's done. All the awakened are on the ground, as are we. He can close the portal now.~

"Rarz, do it now, please." She had sensed him following the discussion, so he had no doubt as to what she was asking him to do.

He closed his eyes then opened them, the multicolor orbs swirling in a way that seemed to suck her in. "They are out, and it has been disconnected." She noticed his color seemed a bit brighter and shot a mental note to Wefor to add that to the ever-growing list.

"Thelia, let's land this ship."

Thelia's eyes locked onto hers, in that vivid purple no human had. "You do realize the odds are we may all die, as well as all the Kaylid?"

McKenna channeled her best action hero and forced a smile. "Then it's time to beat the odds."

"Strange beings you are." Thelia shook her head and pushed buttons. "It is started. Enter the coordinates to the place you wish to place the ship."

Wefor provided what she needed and McKenna swallowed past the bile in her mouth.

We'd better succeed, or a lot of people are going to die.

Chapter 39 - Coming in Hot

The sudden retreat of shuttles has people all over the world cheering, but the lack of reaction from the White House has everyone worried. There are no proclamations of success or word on why they have retreated. This is leading some to believe that whatever is coming next won't be good for anyone. We are receiving odd reports about impacts?
~TNN Invasion News

With shaking hands, she put the coordinates in the computer in a way their systems would accept them. It took her three tries with prompts from Wefor and Elao before they were correct. "Done."

Thelia pushed another button, then tilted her head. "Something is wrong. The engines will not start. There is a password lock, but the standard captain's password is not working."

McKenna frowned, then horror washed through her. ~Toni, we need to unlock the engines. We need to start them to land. What's the password?~

She felt more than heard the ripple of horror and surprise that rippled through the mindspace.

~Crap, of course. Okay you ready? You'll need to write it down or it won't make sense.~

McKenna looked at the console and hit an icon that brought up something analogous to a notepad screen. ~Go.~ Toni listed out the letters and numbers, specifying capital or not. When she was done McKenna looked at her pad. ~Really? That is what you set the password to?~

~I figured no one from their culture would ever hack it.~

McKenna looked at what she had written down and fought back a laugh. ~That's for sure.~

Th31nt3rn3t1s4P0rn!

~I think I'm glad I don't need to tell a human that.~ She shook her head and passed the information over to Thelia who typed it in. Another few keystrokes later the engines started. "That resolved the issue. The engine has started."

"Now what? How do we steer the ship?" McKenna tried to keep the itchy panic out of her voice, but where was the helm for her to grab and fight through the atmosphere? Or levers to pull on to make sure the ship landed correctly?

"Steer? Like a driving vehicle?" Thelia looked over at her, purple brows raised.

"Well, yes. We need to guide the ship down." McKenna looked for something that she had missed, to pull or push.

"The computer will land us. There are no rudders or axles in a spaceship. " Thelia said the words slowly, as if talking to a child.

Stopping her efforts to find some controls, McKenna turned and stared at her.

~Why do I think all those sci-fi movies lied to us?~ She asked in the mindspace as she stared at the impossibly gorgeous woman. ~And why, even with her nose swollen and a yellowish color, is she still so beautiful?~

~Yes, I'm getting that feeling.~ Perc sounded just as sour and frustrated as she did. ~And no idea, but purple isn't my favorite color. I'm a bit partial to golden brown.~

~Are you two really flirting again? Now?~ Toni asked, exasperated amusement in her voice. McKenna started, and pulled herself back to the current situation.

"Ash? I thought you said we needed her bio-electric signature to fly the ship?"

"I had thought that also, as none of these commands would react to my touching them. Yes, I tried in secret. It never occurred to me to be in another form to try." He sounded affronted, but not at her. "There is not always information in the computers as to what is or is not required. Some things are assumed."

Cultural blindness, things we all know, like red is stop.

It made sense to McKenna, but what else had they missed in their interpretation of this new world?

"You needed me regardless of the forms. Because I was an ambassador, it means I have command rights to all the ships. All three of us had those. Even Scilita," Thelia smirked at Ash. "Your pet traitor doesn't know everything, even with a piece of overly smart tech in his head." She turned her attention back to McKenna. "Also there will be questions and options that I will need to choose as we descend. If something fails, I will have to decide how to react."

McKenna's fingers itched to wrap around the woman's neck. Then she realized her nails were turning into claws in response to her emotional desires.

Stop that.

Her irritable thought must have worked as the claws started to go back to nails. She closed her eyes, took a long deep breath through her nose and looked at Thelia. "Is there a way to see what's happening outside the ship right now? The view screen isn't a real camera, it's a representation of what is out there?"

At this point she didn't know for sure, as things kept changing. Besides, she now felt like an idiot. Why in the world had she imagined wrestling the ship down, like there was anything she could do with a ship that probably outweighed most aircraft carriers. But that sparked a thought.

"Exactly how big is this ship?"

Ash tilted his head then answered. "Elao says it is the equivalent of 1575 meters long and 932 meters wide."

"And in feet that is? Why in the world does an alien know meters and not feet but speaks English?"

[Elao has been communicating. Meters are a much more logical measurement than feet are. But for your information it is 1722 yards by 1019 yards.]

McKenna swore. Wefor sounded smug, but she got caught hung up on the size. "Isn't that like twice the size of an aircraft carrier?"

[Not twice, more like 1.75 times the size.]

~JD, can you make sure someone gets the info to White Sands how big this thing is and—~ Mckenna broke off. "Ummm, I don't think the runway at White Sands is more than a few miles."

"That will not be an issue. There is enough capacity in the engines to do a controlled landing and use the propulsion system to come in slowly." Thelia touched something on the board. "I think."

Those two words dashed any feelings of hope McKenna had harbored.

"What does that mean?"

Thelia nodded at the screen. "This is still a representation of sensors, there aren't cameras on the outside of the ship, that would make no sense. But the sensors can extrapolate what we are going through." Another shudder shook the ship. "That is not good. Not only was life support taken out, the engines suffered damage. While the computer core is correcting and can make corrections much faster than I ever could, it is rapidly making course adjustments. I am assuming your top priority is getting this ship down in as much of one piece as possible, with the damage to the planet being inconsequential?" Her tone had acquired that smug tone again and McKenna gritted her teeth before relaxing them to respond.

"Yes, that would be accurate."

"Then it is what I am attempting, though you should note most computers are not programmed for crash landing on a planet. I am not aware of any incident where it has happened. At least not that anyone lived to report on afterward."

Her words helped not at all, and McKenna desperately wanted something to do. But other than stare at the screen where the earth came closer to them at impressive speed, there wasn't much to do.

"How long until we land?"

"The currently estimate is 1.1 htserc, though that keeps changing as more systems are failing." Thelia licked her lips.

"What is that in my time?"

Wefor replied, [110 minutes until landing.]

"Okay, that isn't too bad, right?"

Thelia cast her a glance full of contempt. "The computer is asking it if can remove power from the life support system to the guidance modules. Most of the ship is vacant except our area, and all Kaylid in canisters will flip over to their emergency supply power. If we are not lucky, we will have much less time."

"And the backup canister power will last how long?" She knew they had told her, but at this point she couldn't pull it out with all the other thoughts rushing through her brain.

Wefor provided the information at the same time Thelia did. "About one and a half of your months."

"That long? We figured it was hours." A bit of stress faded. "Wefor, how much oxygen do we have in here? How long can we last with what is in this room?"

A soft hum, then a response. [There is plenty of oxygen to last for longer than what the ship will take to land.] McKenna let out a breath of relief, but as she opened her mouth to talk to Thelia, Wefor continued. [The problem is the smoke is still increasing. You are breathing out CO2 and the air quality will deteriorate. Assuming none of these factors change, with four of you in these two rooms, you will have a window of about 30 minutes. Though it would be advisable to keep your breathing rate steady.]

Of course. It can't be easy, just when I thought we might have a chance.

"Do it. We'll take the risk. Everyone, try to stay calm and keep your breathing regular, and let's hope."

Thelia arched a brow at her but typed multiple commands on the computer. The ship shuddered as if in response and Thelia's shoulders hunched in slightly.

"What was that?"

"The ship is having issues maintaining course and speed. The damage to the engines and guidance systems is extensive." The dark colors of the planet they were approaching disappeared and a schematic of the ship appeared on the screen.

"Well that would have been convenient when we were planning this." Perc muttered.

McKenna glanced over at him, but he seemed calm, strapped into a chair like the rest of them, his arms with tan fur and dark spots dappling them crossed over his chest. He caught her looking at him and winked and she didn't know if she wanted to laugh or throw something at him.

Shaking her head, she looked at all the red on the schematic. "That doesn't look good."

"It is not good, as you say. It is proving difficult. The engines are rapidly losing their ability to control our descent. Is cutting gravity and lights in the rest of the ship acceptable?" Thelia asked, but Mckenna saw her fingers flying across the board as she did.

"Yes. We're strapped in." Before she could finish speaking, her stomach lurched up and her hair floated. She'd never really wanted to be an astronaut, but if the situation wasn't so serious she would have unbuckled and floated around, wanting to play in zero gravity.

~This is neat, too bad it means very bad things,~ she commented after telling the others about the issues with the ship.

~Kenna?~ A soft voice on a private channel said and her heart froze.

~Charley. I heard you've been doing great. Helping lots of people.~ She infused warmth and pride and pushed it down the line.

~Been trying. Gets easier to speak the language after people respond to you.~ His mental voice paused and she waited. ~Are you coming home to me? To Nam and me?~ As his words reached her, she felt Nam get pulled into the conversation with them.

~Oh Charley, Nam,~ her mental voice broke as pain welled up in her and the desire to pull them into her arms and never let them go was a physical force that hammered at her. ~I will do everything in my power to come back to you. I never wanted to leave you behind, but...~ she broke off the thought, frustrated. How did you explain duty to kids who had only ever been abandoned by the rules? How did she explain that no matter how much she loved them, if she let their world die, they died too? That she'd gladly give her life to protect them? All the feelings created a maelstrom in her, then a single thought from Nam pierced it.

~We know,~ the words were followed with their love, their understanding that some prices were paid no matter the cost. But the biggest feeling was their willingness to love her, even knowing they might lose her.

McKenna broke, tears streamed down her face. How did two kids know more than the adults? Be able to understand what she couldn't even begin to articulate? Taking in a shuddering breath, ignoring the confused looks from Thelia and worried ones from Ash and Perc, she created a wave of emotion. With everything in her she, sent her duty, her pride, and most of all her love for the two children. Then in a fraction of a second, she spilt the emotions and sent them to everyone.

JD her brother, the man she loved as if he was family.

Toni, friend, sister, the spark that had brought so much with her.

Jessi and Jamie, the bundles of light and joy that she looked at as part of her family.

Cass, the quiet one who eased her brother and brought gentle humor and strength.

Perc, the strong one, standing there and waiting for her to be ready.

Charley, the child she never thought to have and the boy she loved so fiercely.

Nam, the fragile girl who didn't know how special she was, or how much everyone loved her.

Though they couldn't feel it, she wrapped up Carina, Anne, even Kirk and Rarz in what she felt, what she didn't want to lose, and what she would risk in order to save all the beings on this ship and save their world.

The emotions were sent back multiplied until for a minute, she thought her heart might explode or that she could see the universe. It faded but she could feel the echoes of shock coming from the others.

"Why is there wet stuff coming from your eyes? Are you sick? Diseased?" Thelia's voice pulled her out of the trance she'd been in, but she looked at Perc first. He had a dazed look that matched how she felt. A slow nod at her look and he scrubbed a hand over his face, as if he felt tears he hadn't shed.

Rarz had a look she couldn't decipher.

Awe? Fear? Wonder? What does that look mean on a Drakyn?

"Well? Are you about to die? Or should I kill you to put you out of the pain you feel?" Thelia's voice had an odd mix of emotions in it, and after the overwhelming ones that had surrounded McKenna, it was too much effort to care.

"Do you not cry?"

"Cry?" Thelia savored the word in English as she replaced the ship diagram with images from the sensors and McKenna flinched back as the earth streaked beneath them, flashing from land to water. "If sick, or something is in the eye to generate water, then yes. Are there things in your eyes?"

"Should we be going this fast? Or be this close to the earth?" She couldn't take her eyes from the landscape, the blur of colors that her brain interpreted as land, trees, desert, water, and soil all mixed together. And getting into a discussion with Thelia about love and emotions seemed too sad right now.

"It is a representation, but yes. Our engines are failing faster than expected, so speeds are not as gradual as hoped. Some of the exterior may be damaged by friction, but it should not affect the ship past being able to function."

As if the gods were listening to them a shudder shook the ship, and the doors that they had entered, in what seemed like a lifetime ago, shook, and then slid back open and a wave of smoke filled the room.

"House in ruins," Thelia said in a tone of voice that made it very clear she cussed. McKenna coughed as the smoke swirled around her, and the acrid taste coated her mouth and nose.

"What's," cough cough, "wrong?" She choked out trying to see if anything on her console told her anything. Most of the lights were red and flashing, which told her only that everything was going wrong, which she had already figured out.

"The jump drives ruptured, and are fueling a fire, and things are exploding. I do not know why. There should not be anything there to explode. I am trying to put them out, but there is too much oxygen. My choices are to go up and open up the engine bay to space, or to land and hope we do not die in the process."

Oh shit, the explosives we set are going off. Figures. We're creating our own problem.

She wanted to scream, but she focused on trying to take shallow breaths and respond. "Are we going to make the coordinates I provided?" McKenna coughed out, the thick smoke creating a coating of soot in her throat.

Thelia hit a few keys, the smoke was so thick only the vivid color of her hair was visible. "Maybe. But slowing down is going to be difficult. What is at the other side of those coordinates? And we will not have the time to make the next few orbits to bleed speed and lower our altitude. I have enough control for one more pass then we will spiral out of control and slam into the planet." Her voice had tightened and dropped a few octaves, every word clipped in precise Elentrin. Even through the translation, the stress all but screamed through her tone.

"I'm not sure, to be honest." She closed her eyes and tried to remember the few pictures she'd seen of White Sands, from old news videos of the space shuttle landing there, back when there was a program. "Lots and lots of sand, it's a national park and has mountains on one side."

"How much sand?" Thelia snapped.

"I don't know, miles and miles?" Though the words that came out of her mouth were the Elentrin equivalent.

"Then we may survive. If you believe in greater beings, worship them now."

McKenna figured when an alien was telling her to pray, things were not good. Her hair wasn't floating anymore which meant they were close enough to the planet for gravity to pull at them, which mean they were close to crashing.

Without conscious thought she grabbed onto the console, her eyes closed, and she waited, trying not to breathe in the acrid smoke.

~Wefor, I'm glad you found me, no matter how this ends.~

[As am I.] The whisper of a thought made her smile. The smile went into a wince as an explosion rocked the ship, and it shook, whipping her head to one side, though she remained restrained. Then there were sounds so loud she released her death grip on the console to cover her ears, not that it made a difference. Then came a sound like a tin can being crunched but a hundred times worse, mixed with heat and cold, and the world went black.

Chapter 39 - Survivors

Tidal wave warnings have gone up all the over the world. A huge one is currently headed for Sydney and evacuation orders have been issued. Recent reports of waves over two hundred feet high are headed for that area. Other tidal waves are headed for Europe and the east coast, but those are expected to be much smaller, though the waves are still building. The asteroid impact in the Pacific created waves currently hitting Peru that measure twenty feet. If you are in the path, evacuate now! ~TNN Emergency Banner

Dry air, air that pulled the moisture from her lips and blew sand into her mouth, pulled her to consciousness. As she became aware of the world, the pain in her head and body were the first thing that registered. Her head was pounding, with noises, smells, and tastes bombarding her mind, while it felt like she had been beat on with rocks and hammers. Trying to swallow generated no saliva so she forced her eyes open, then immediately shut them as smoke stung and caused them to water, and that moisture evaporated almost instantly.

[McKenna?] The whisper-soft voice of Wefor cut through all the other noise and she realized half of what she heard were voices in her head trying to get her attention. It felt like half the world was yelling her name.

~I'm here. Shush, please.~ Even the mental voices hurt and she needed to figure out what was going on. They fell silent and she inhaled deeply and regretted it as a cough wracked her body and sent pain rippling through her.

[The nanobots are working, you have a broken arm, but it is a simple break so they will heal it. If you can avoid stressing it for a day or two it should be fine. The rest of damage is soft tissue and hurts, but it is not vital. Another few hours and all of it will be repaired. I can suppress the pain, but it is better to feel it, so you know what is injured.]

~It's fine. The air is the worst part.~ She reached for Perc but found his light grey in her mind, but it was the grey of being unconscious, not dead, so she wouldn't panic yet. ~Rarz?~

~I am here, but trapped.~ He sounded funny so she opened her eyes again. The smoke had cleared out a bit and she took in the scene.

While the bridge had not possessed a big window looking out at space like in so many movies, it had apparently been very near the front with only a hull between them and space. That hull had torn, letting in light, air, and sand, and was pulling out the smoke that wreathed up from broken consoles, conduits in the ceiling and the doors behind them. McKenna blinked a few times to get the tears to clear away, and she saw Rarz trapped. It looked like one of the consoles had broken off and managed to pin him to the floor between his chair and his original console, then what looked like a slab of metal had fallen on top of him. Right now she couldn't figure out exactly what she saw, as smoke kept changing it. Perc hung limply in his chair, strapped in and blood running from his nose.

~Is Perc okay?~ Worry coated her thoughts as she tried to figure out how to get the restraints to release her.

[He should be regaining consciousness soon. The reports are that he has a concussion and severe bruising, but nothing that won't be healed with a few hours and some calories. Your damage was greater.]

That reminded McKenna to look at her arm, the one that she could feel pain radiating out from. Looking down, it didn't look broken, which reinforced what Wefor had said. She used her other arm to hit a glowing blue button in the middle of her chest, and the straps disappeared. She stood, woozy for a minute, then turned around, looking for the others. In her head Perc moaned and stirred as she looked for Thelia.

The Elentrin should have been next to her less than five feet away, but where the chair had been was only a jagged end. Looking around she didn't see her. Moving forward carefully, she headed towards Perc. The floor was at an angle that made her footing even more precarious as she reached to Perc. His chair had bent backwards, and he hung from it awkwardly with the restraints. As she reached for him, his eyes opened and bloodshot blue eyes met hers.

"All in all, I don't think I'd like to repeat that." His voice emerged cracked and rough.

"Agreed. Let me get you out." The same blue button glowed on his straps; and she hit it and he fell out of it. "Crap, sorry, sorry."

"Ow." Perc lay there for a moment. "That hurt, but not your fault. I wasn't thinking about the fact they were holding me in either. All good."

She looked around, still trying to locate Thelia, while Perc pushed himself up and stretched. Joints popped and cracked and she flinched, looking at him.

"That feels better. Where are Ash and the woman?"

She fought a smirk at the distaste in his tone, but she turned her head looking. Smoke still obscured some areas and with the torn-up room, she struggled to orient herself to where everything had been.

"I don't see her, but Rarz is over there, he said he was trapped." She pointed to the red and orange scales showing out from the twisted wreck of the console and metal. As they carefully picked their way through the odd wreckage, she kept looking around for the missing two, holding her broken arm tight to her body.

Toni and JD kept up a low-level stream of information in her mind, saying they saw the wreck on the radar. The ship had clipped the Jarilla Mountains and tumbled, slamming into the ground about thirty miles from Holloman Airforce Base and fifteen miles from the White Sands Missile Range post. Help was on the way, but removing the canisters would take a while to get scheduled.

She acknowledged all of this silently. Right now, while it was important, it didn't have much bearing on her actions. It would be at least a half hour before any help got here.

Standing next to Rarz, she saw one of the doors had blown out and slammed into the Drakyn, taking the console off with it and that was what was holding him down. In that position, with his leg trapped, and his body bent over the other console, he couldn't get any leverage.

"And you're sure you're not hurt?" She asked as Perc moved to the other side so he could lever the door off Rarz.

"Minor injuries. They will resolve themselves." His voice sounded muffled from his pinned position and there was a groan of metal and other material as Perc heaved, a grunt of effort coming from him. But the door lifted up and tilted onto one side, falling heavily against the wall.

"That, however, does make breathing much simpler." Rarz reached up and pressed his button and the straps fell. He pushed the remains of the console away from him and stood flexing tail and arms. "I am grateful I did not have my wings present while going through that. Something unwelcome might have happened."

The smoke had almost completely disappeared, and she decided to take that as a good sign. A smear of an odd color leading into the captain's office caught her attention. Frowning, she moved closer. It looked like some type of blood, but with all the different beings, she wasn't sure of everyone's blood color. She followed the trail with her eyes and gasped as she saw a crumpled figure against the far wall.

"Ash!" she cried out and headed towards him as fast as she could without falling. McKenna didn't notice what was on the ground as she knelt beside him, though sharp stabs in her knees told her it hadn't been free of debris. She would deal with that later. He lay there, panting. Harsh breaths were going out, and a wheezing sound and trickle of blood came with each one. The interactive wall glass had shattered and impaled him multiple times where he lay. The broken straps of his harness still clung to him.

"It'll be okay. Give your bots time to heal you."

A broken whistle escaped him, the escaping air form his lungs making it echo through the small room. Perc came and sat down on the other side, carefully moving other debris from him.

~Too late. Dying. I am old, bots are not as virulent as once were. But have two favors to ask. To beg. To plead for.~

Even in her head his voice sounded frail and broken and McKenna blinked rapidly to keep back tears.

~Ask. What are they?~ She kept it public, expecting what he was going to ask.

~Don't give up. Don't let them get away with this. Their entire society is predicated on the idea they must destroy the Drakyn. Stop them. Stop their predation on other species. Don't let their reign of terror continue unchecked. For Alara, my people. Please?~

McKenna didn't know how his mental voice could plead and beg and have the taste of salty tears and bitter herbs. But it did.

~I'll try. I don't know what we can do, but I'll try.~ She promised and hoped there was a way she could keep it. ~And your second request?~

He took another shuddering breath, eyes closing over those strange eyes.

"Ash? Ash!" She panicked as his eyes closed but her yells seemed to register and he opened them back up, cracked white over black peering up at her.

~I am not free yet.~

~What's the second thing? What can I do?~ She wanted to swallow, but the air in the desert, flowing through the cracks in the ship had pulled every bit of moisture from her. Even her eyes ached between the smoke and the air.

~Save Elao,~ his thought held hope and pain.

~What?~ Of anything she had expected that wasn't it. ~What do you mean?~

~Elao doesn't deserve to die. The knowledge that would be lost could make a difference between winning and losing against the Elentrin. You can't let that be lost.~

[Ash. You mean that?] The hushed tone of Elao made McKenna freeze.

~You are the reason this was possible. You can not be lost. I am immaterial.~ The mental words were followed by a shuddering breath, a wet raspy sound that made her wince in sympathy.

~Ash, I already have Wefor, I don't think there's room enough in me for another personality.~ McKenna hated saying those words, but there was no way she could add yet another mind in her own. As it was, sometimes she wasn't sure this entire thing was really happening.

~I'll do it.~ Perc spoke and she turned to look at him so fast her neck cracked. ~I can take on Elao.~

~Are you sure?~ She didn't want to say don't do it, because Ash was right, but having an AI in your head was never what you expected.

Perc didn't answer her directly just put his huge hand on her arm and squeezed gently. ~Okay Ash, Elao, how do we do this?~

[I am not sure. It has never been done. I–] The odd sound of an AI being hesitant and unsure made McKenna's heart race.

If they have no idea how to do this, how in the world will we pull this off?

But even she knew just by looking at Ash, there was no saving him. How he managed to still be communicating with them, much less coherently, she didn't know. There was a strange hum, an almost whine that made her wince, but it was all in her head.

~What was that?~ she asked, trying to keep the pain out of her tone, but didn't succeed.

[Apologies. I needed to send a large amount of data to Elao very quickly. But we have a plan.] The mental pain faded rapidly, so McKenna just nodded.

~So tell me what I need to do.~

[This will hurt Percival Alexander. There is little I can do about that, but I promise to do my best to help in your fight against the Elentrin.] The slightly different mental voice of Elao filled their minds.

Perc shrugged. ~Pain I can live with. Let's do it.~ His hand held Ash's as they talked. ~Thank you, Ash, for everything risked for this chance.~ His words were heartfelt and McKenna wished they could do more.

A weird grimace spread across Ash's face. ~It is not enough, yet more than I dared hope.~

He's trying to smile. He can't even do his whistle laugh.

McKenna forced it down. She didn't have time to mourn or even get upset, not right now.

[I am gathering as much of myself as possible. His spine is broken in two places, and the shards of *violit* are piercing his heart. He knows this and is fighting to make this work.] The AI's words tasted of sorrow, pain, and a grief so deep McKenna couldn't fathom it. [Know that this will not hurt him, I will make sure of it.]

McKenna's stomach tightened as she heard the words and her fears were realized in the next few moments.

[You will need to create a large gash in your arm, deep enough to reach veins so the nanobots, my programming, can get in fast enough.]

McKenna bit her lip to stop herself from saying anything, and just listened, no matter what.

~I can do that that,~ Perc's tone sounded strong. ~Then what?~

[Then you will need to slit Ash's throat and open up his spinal cord at the same time.]

Chapter 40 - Blood

The huge crash in the desert near White Sands Missile Range was seen across the US. The impact crater is smaller than expected so some control must have been exhibited. The entire area has been declared a no-fly zone and the military seems to been getting there very rapidly. Reports of seeing the secretary of state at the location only an hour from last being seen in DC are confusing. What does this all mean? ~TNN Invasion News

McKenna and Perc flinched at that. Though she noticed Rarz looking off behind her, she didn't have time to worry about what caught his interest right now.

~You mean kill him?~ Perc's voice held no emotion in the mindspace; it was flat and without feeling. She could feel the rest of her family listening intently to everything. For a moment she thought about shutting the kids out, not letting them hear or know what was going on, but she knew they would take that as a betrayal. Even Nam could face what was going on, though she wanted to protect them, she couldn't protect them from reality.

[As soon as the vein and spinal column are opened, I'll move my main components down to bleed out. You need to get as much of it into your body as possible. I am shifting the parts of me to be there. Some knowledge will be lost, but most is replicated in multiple places and what can be shared and stored with Wefor has been. This will take a bit and you will need to convince your own nanobots to not try to fight me, and not heal your wound. Once I have settled in, I can override any programming they may have and they will answer to both you and me.]

Nothing about Perc moved, not even his tail and McKenna didn't know how he felt as he had locked down everything in the mindscape, no hint of his emotions leaking through.

~Are you sure?~ She had to ask and he turned his head slowly, taking his eyes off Ash only at the last instant.

~Yes. We owe them and I think we will need her help.~ He nodded at her and turned back to Ash, whose eyes had closed and it seemed he focused on just breathing. ~Are you both ready?~

~Yes~[Yes.] His voice so weak and tiny, and grieving. Perc took a deep breath and looked at his left arm. The fur absorbed back into the skin, revealing skin golden and tan. She held her breath as he reached up with a low sharp claw extended and in a violent motion ripped open a gash along the bend of his elbow. The flesh parted like a cut with a scalpel and McKenna saw flesh and tendons before blood started filling the area. A gasp of pain slipped out of him, but he didn't pull away.

[Tell your nanobots to pull it in, and make the cut on Ash, now.] Elao sounded like she cried, a tone of voice that made tears start in McKenna's eyes.

~Thank you, Ash, for everything,~ McKenna whispered the words in her mind and sent gratitude towards him.

His eyes opened and locked on to hers, then shifted to Perc. ~Do it, and thank you. Finally I can go back to my stars.~

Perc laid his claw along the side of Ash's neck and yanked it down towards the back of his neck in a fast move. Rather than the jugular where humans had it, a large vein ran along the spine and when his claw ripped it open, blood and fluid came rushing out in spurts.

[Get your open flesh under it, hurry.] Elao's voice sound odd, distorted, as if talking through sobbing tears.

Perc moved his arm and the blood and fluids fell into the wide gash pooling there. His face was a mask of unreadable fur; even his whiskers didn't move. McKenna had taken Ash's hand when Perc needed to release it to do what he needed to do, and she squeezed it tight. Already it felt colder and less lively.

~This is a good way to go, doing what I can to end their regime. Thank you. May Alara's light guide me home~ It was the last words he said as the three of them sat there, Wefor whispered in Perc's ear to get as much of Elao pulled into his body as possible.

The air filled with the scent of blood mixed in with the dry air and smoke. She would never forget this scene, this moment, and took it all in: the alien dying, while pouring his blood and spinal fluid into Perc's arm, trying to save a being with no body, nothing but tiny particles that made up its existence.

[Elao has moved most of her bots to those locations, leaving only the dumb drones throughout the body. They had a little time to prepare before Ash spoke to you. Perc, if you can scrape any dripping down into the wound, they will help.] Wefor spoke to all of them and they waited as he pushed more blood up into the wound of his already gore-covered arm.

McKenna felt the life leave Ash, but she hoped he was at peace. She couldn't imagine how long he had fought his impossible fight, maybe now he would be home. Anything else more metaphysical she shied away from and looked at the blood covering Perc.

"You okay?" her voice barely loud enough to be heard.

"Hurts, but it's working. Give me some time. I'll sit here for a bit."

Before she could move, Rarz was up and headed towards the other side of the room. As he moved past the crack in the hull, faster than she could get up to follow, the dust swirled around behind him, marking his passing with gold glittering in the harsh sunlight.

"Rarz?" McKenna stood and made her way through the wrecked room. The smoke had cleared and made it easier to proceed, but he had blown through it as if there was no debris. He didn't say anything. ~Rarz?~ she asked again, knowing he would hear her like that. Though he'd probably heard her the first time too.

~Over here. There is something. Ah, yes. Found her.~
Thelia, it has to be her.

McKenna picked up her pace and made it over to where Rarz crouched, his tail supporting his low stance. Crumbled in a pod doorway that had given in was Thelia, blood covering her face from a sizable laceration on her head. It turned her purple hair a dark indigo that seemed too sober and sad for her skin.

"Crap," McKenna muttered as she stopped next to the woman. "Is she okay?" She checked the wound, it now was only a sluggish trail of blood, but the location on her head worried McKenna. Blows across the temple and back of the head could result in serious brain trauma, at least for a human. The wound stretched from her temple to the back of her head, revealing bits of white bone. "A human would still be bleeding like crazy. I don't want to move her, it might injure her further." She did a quick safety check, but other than the head wound McKenna couldn't see anything.

"You will leave her alive?" Rarz's questions caught her off guard and she looked up at him, frowning.

"Of course, why wouldn't I?"

"She is your enemy. Her people have done great harm to your world. Would it not be better to kill her now than risk her rising to stab you in the back later?"

"What?" McKenna coughed out a laugh. "You've been watching too many of our movies." She fell silent as their actions on the ship flooded back to her and she sighed, acknowledging his point. "Maybe. And maybe I'll regret this, but I promised to let her be if she helped. She'll have to deal with our government and the aftermath of her people's actions. But that isn't for me to judge. I don't want to judge it. I want to go home. We still lost so many people and they'll be back. But maybe we got the time we needed."

The revving sounds of engines came through the door and she felt like a weight had been taken off her shoulders. "Perc, we have company. You almost decent?"

"Still covered in blood, but most of it has been absorbed and I'm healing." He paused then called back. "What do we do with his body?"

McKenna moved back to the room. "Do we know his burial procedures? Or customs?"

[Fire.] Elao's voice was weak but clear. [Let his ashes rise up to join the stars.]

Rarz spoke slowly. "If meeting his ancestors in flame is what he desires, I can give him that honor."

McKenna shot him a look but only nodded. "Thank you for your offer and we will, Elao. We will let him rise in ash." They would do it here, now before anyone could claim him. "Rarz, can you help me carry him out?"

"Of course."

She heard vehicles pull up and she looked out the crack at them. Of the three of them, she was the only one in human form, beside Thelia, and her beauty declared what she was.

"Fudge. The cavalry is here. Why are they showing now up when I could use more time without them?" She sighed and looked back at the others.

Perc stood, looking a bit unsteady. His arm looking like he'd put it through a sausage grinder. "You sure you're okay?"

His head tilted as if listening to someone whispering to him. "Blood loss. Elao says it will pass in a few hours and apologizes. She is trying to reestablish and convert the nanobots to her frequencies, and I lost a decent amount of blood. His blood has to be expelled and cleaned from the body, so I will have the equivalent of a rampant infection. Fever, chills, all the fun stuff, over the next few hours."

McKenna moved over and touched him. Even through the fur he felt hot. "Let me know if you need anything."

"Nah, as long as you don't need me to run any passing drills I should be fine." He smiled weakly at his football joke. She squeezed his arm and smiled.

"I think you can stand around and look pretty for the next little while."

He chuckled softly at her tease but leaned against the wall. Rarz watched McKenna, his expression unreadable.

"Help me get him outside?" She didn't know how she'd do that with her arm still broken.

"No need. He is not heavy." Rarz leaned down and picked up the lax body, the ever-moving tail hanging like a limp ribbon. McKenna closed her eyes fighting back the sea of emotions. Had it really been only hours since they first met this being? Inhaling slowly then back out, she opened her eyes and nodded at Rarz. "We'll send on him his way to his stars."

She climbed out of the opening in the ship carefully. With a final heave, she emerged from the crack in the hull to stand on the desert sand. She froze at the sight of at least twenty soldiers with guns pointed at them. They didn't look friendly.

McKenna raised her hands. "Human? McKenna Largo? We were the ones sent up to get people back? I think you should know our names?"

Please let someone have told them something so we don't get shot. That would just be the capper on this day.

A man with a major's oak leaves, she was getting better at reading rank, pushed through the crowd and looked at them. "Ms. Largo? I assume that is Perc Alexander and the," he hesitated for a moment, "dragon is the guest we were told to expect?" He looked at Rarz carrying the body, blood still covering most of it.

"He's on our side. There's an Elentrin in there that should be regarded as a special guest. The higher-ups can figure out what to do with her, but until then she should be treated as someone in very protective custody."

"Higher-ups, ma'am?" He asked doubtfully, not taking his gaze off Rarz and Ash.

"You know, Burby, Simon, Roberts, those guys. It's their problem, not mine."

That got his attention on her. "You mean Secretary of State Burby and the President, ma'am?"

Did I imagine that or did everyone do all but come to attention when he said that?

"Yes. She's their problem. I'd advise nose filters, as she is Elentrin, but she needs medical attention and a stretcher would be suggested. As for the rest, it can wait a bit until more people get here. Now, if you would excuse us, we need to deal with something."

Though I have no idea how we will burn a body. Rarz said he could take care of that.

"Ma'am, I'm under orders to take all of you into protective custody until my superiors can get here," he protested, and she waved around them.

"We're in the middle of a desert, it isn't like I'm going to run. Trust me, I just want to go home. Just stay out our way." Her frustration leaked through. She was so tired she could barely comprehend what they needed to do next.

"Ma'am I can't let you leave with that body. We are under orders to collect any dead that might have occurred during the crash."

McKenna bared her teeth at him in something no one would have called a smile. "Major, I've just taken over a ship, suborned aliens, and brought the ship to Earth. If you think you can stop me and my dragon, feel free." She didn't know what Rarz did behind her, but the man paled and at least half the soldiers shifted their aim to Rarz.

"Yes, ma'am. I mean, no, ma'am. I'll wait right here, ma'am."

Chapter 41 - Goodbye

Damage reports are still coming in from the tidal waves and the asteroid impacts. While it might be weeks before we get a full accounting of the death tolls, people are already demanding answers. Why didn't any of the governments stop this? Who is to blame? Already some memes and social media accounts are pointing fingers at shifters, saying ultimately it was their fault. If the rumors of McKenna Largo and another shifter-only group going up are true, maybe they really are whom to blame for this devastation. ~TNN Invasion News

"Good idea." She turned and started walking into the desert. Fear rode her about someone trying to take Ash. A few people knew Ash was behind their strange dreams and came from a world that no longer existed. If it got out, scientists would want to dissect him to see how he differed from humans or Elentrin. That would be a worse violation than anything else she could do to him and she refused to allow it.

"Rarz? How do we do this?" She kept her low, but she knew Perc and Rarz would hear her.

"I can set his body free in flames. It is not an issue."

~I want to be there. We need to be there.~ Toni's voice spoke into the mindspace, fierce and urgent. The others chimed in, even Nam.

McKenna hesitated, but having them here with her would make dealing with the next few days easier. "Rarz, are you willing to do that? Create a portal for them?"

"Of course." He gave her a look she couldn't interpret. If it had been JD, she would have thought he was trying to not make a face at her.

~Just you guys. We can get the others later. For now, this is our private moment.~ She felt like he deserved to be honored. Years, no centuries, of fighting a battle he didn't know if he could ever win. Yet he tried.

~Give us ten minutes to get everyone gathered.~ JD voice was no-nonsense and she fought a smile at hearing it, even in her mind.

"We should get out a safe distance from the ship. The fire will be very hot." Rarz commented as he started walking.

"Yes, I'm not in the mood for any more explosions today, if it's all the same to you."

"I second that. I think I'd like a week of sleeping until noon if it's all the same to everyone." Perc said as they moved slowly out into the white emptiness of the White Sands area. The sand lived up to its name and McKenna lifted her hands to shield her eyes from the sun. The mountains in the distance made her ache for the sight of her Sierra Nevadas. A quick glance back showed the men milling around watching them, but and a few of them headed towards the crack in the ship.

"I hope Thelia stays unconscious. It might be better for her or them. Not sure which." She said the comment off-hand, not really expecting anything.

"For them, I hope she's unconscious. I get the feeling that woman is always in control of her orbit." Perc's voice had a dry humor to it that made her smile.

"Truth." She fought back a laugh at that, then almost tripped over Rarz's tail as he halted.

"This is far enough to ensure people will not be harmed by the fire." With a sort of reverence, he laid Ash down. "I will miss you. Not a friend, but an ally that I have respected greatly over the years."

~We're ready if you are. In an isolated space, just us.~ JD didn't say who us was, but McKenna knew and her arms ached to hold the kids.

~Show me, please?~ Rarz's eyes closed and she could almost feel him going down the connection to where they were. As it connected a portal from where the others were in Baltimore opened next to them. She could vaguely hear the shouts from the soldiers, but ignored them in favor of the two kids headed towards her.

"Kenna!" Charley's voice sounded like the sweetest music she'd ever heard, and she dropped to her knees as he slammed into her. Nam followed a few steps behind him, their arms tangled and wrapped around each other in a mess of awkward pokes and jabs. Pain ripped through her as one of the kids hit her broken arm, but she didn't care. From how hard her kids were squeezing her, she figured they missed her just as much.

"I missed you two," McKenna said, her voice soft.

Neither of the children responded, just hugged her tighter. While she inhaled their scents; letting the mix of the two essences surround her. Having them here made her feel better than she had since she walked through that portal.

"Kenna, we better do this soon." JD brought her out of the emotional overload and the kids released her, reluctance in their movements. They didn't go far, staying by her side. This matched her desires perfectly.

She turned her eyes towards to where Rarz had laid Ash. Somehow in the minute or two she'd held her children, he had created a depression in the sand. Ash lay in in the middle, laid out like a hero of old.

I suppose that's accurate. He's a hero going to meet his ancestors. I think they've been waiting for him for a long time.

They all looked at her and she wanted to shrink away from their gaze. How to preside over funerals was not in the police handbook. But she stood up straighter. Ash had earned their best and she'd do exactly that.

"We are here to release the body of Ash to the stars of Alara. His sacrifice made what we have done possible. May he find the peace he earned." McKenna didn't know what else to say, and time was in short supply.

"Rarz, if you would do the honors?" She waved at the body as she spoke.

"You will all need to step back," his voice low and vibrating. He walked over to the other side of the pyre while they all moved backwards a few yards. No one wanted to be too close.

"Is the dragon going to breath fire?" Nam asked, her lilting voice clear in the desert.

"I don't know. We'll watch and see." Toni, Jessi, and Jamie were close to her. JD and Cass, holding hands, were on her other side. She started to turn, but then felt the warmth at her back and realized Perc stood there. McKenna leaned back a touch, just enough to feel his fur against the skin of her neck.

This is where I belong.

The thought radiated through her as she focused her attention on Rarz. He glanced at them, nodded, and then his body began to flow, enlarge, change into something horrible and magnificent. Faster than it took her to breath twice, a huge red dragon stood on the sand across from them.

"It's a real dragon, a real live dragon," Jamie's voice had a hushed awe to do it.

"I wanna ride!" Nam all but shouted. McKenna grabbed her hand and stopped her before she got more than one foot moving.

"Not now. Remember why we're here?" She had to fight a smile as she spoke to the small girl. In the warehouse the dragon had seemed a huge, looming, and dangerous presence. Out here in the bright sun, his scales of red, gold, orange, and hints of green sparkled and danced. He seemed much more fantastical than dangerous.

"Oh. Funeral." The little girl drooped and leaned back against McKenna. "To say good bye to the sad man. He helped or tried to help all of us."

Sad man is as good of a description of Ash as I could ask for. The sorrow he carried.

"Yes. Maybe someday you may ask Rarz nicely if you can ride him."

And I'll warn him first and skin him alive if he hurts a hair on Nam's head.

They ignored the excited yells and sounds of approaching soldiers and watched Rarz.

He leaned back on his haunches and held his forepaws in front of him, tail wrapped around him. He looked like a sculpture in a gaming store, stunning in every detail. She heard his inhale at the same time a tiny portal appeared between his claws. With a sound that rattled through her bones, he roared and liquid fire exploded out of the silver portal and engulfed Ash's body.

"What the hell?" A voice behind her bellowed. She didn't move, just watched the flame dissolve the being that had done everything he could to stop the enemy. A weird singing sound echoed in the mindspace. The sound brought to mind the stars at night, the wind through the trees, the music of a waterfall.

[It is the song of his people. The one they sang when a loved one was sent to meet their ancestors.] Wefor

359

whispered in their minds and they felt the music fill them, tones and harmonies unfamiliar yet etching on their hearts.

Perc was the first. He raised his head and started to sing, his voice matching the song in their minds, the music engraving into their souls. One by one they all joined in. Even Nam with a crystal-clear voice that seemed to fill the valley. Singing a song written on a planet destroyed hundreds of years ago to celebrate the life of a hero.

Chapter 42 - Aftermath

The change in attitude in the last week towards shifters has been dramatic. Furspace has already folded, few shifter-based business are staying open, and already the few high profile shifters have stepped back from the public eye. While there have been no legal challenges yet, as everyone is still trying to deal with bodies, damage, and getting life back to normal; there is a mood of wanting nothing to do with shifters. Is this a short-term backlash or will it have long term effects? ~TNN Invasion News

"I'm still not sure if I should thank you or sentence you all to prison," Doug Burby groused sitting on a chair in the meeting room. "Even the president doesn't know what do you with you and your spectacular return to Earth. You brought people back but now we have even more problems, one of them too damn pretty for her own good."

"You mean we haven't been punished enough?" McKenna's voice was arch and exasperated. "Between that bit of us being basically immortal got out, the press hasn't let up for the last three weeks. People are protesting saying we shouldn't get jobs or health insurance. Heck, at this point half the world wants to kill us, the other half wants to deify us." Her frustration faded as she spoke and Perc took her hand, holding it. None of them were in warrior form, and the kids were at the house with Carina.

"No, I'll agree this doesn't look good. Someone is pulling strings expertly and the tide is turning against shifters faster than we can do anything about it. Having so many beings that aren't human here isn't helping. It's got people squawk-ing about another alien invasion and you should hear the illegal alien arguments on the hill."

"Nice to know they found important things to argue about." The words might have been a tiny bit bitter, but the laughter from Cass and JD soothed it down from where it would have ended, absolute rage.

"I can't disagree. But for the first time in a very long time we have active funding for a space defense and a space force. They are treating that ship like a precious object and gold mine mixed into one. With the assistance you've pro-vided, we've managed to pull almost everything out of their databases. The amount of information will fuel the drive to the stars like we haven't seen in decades. That should help drive jobs and rebuilding. You add in the fear everyone has of the Elentrin coming back?" Doug shrugged. "It will take a long time for the tide of public opinion to shift to be pro-shifter. Shifters are a convenient scapegoat right now." He sounded exhausted as he said the last part. "And none of us know how to fight what is the truth. Expertly spun, but the truth. Hell, at this point the damn Elentrin has a better press agent than you do."

She wanted to protest, but Doug was right. Kirk had come out looking good with his pre-planning. California was one of the few states whose citizens weren't demanding re-calls of their elected officials. The governor had listened, and they were able to adapt faster than most.

The public reaction right now was dark and angry. Be-tween the damage the asteroids had done and people the Kaylid had killed, being a shifter wasn't healthy. Then when word leaked out about the alien Kaylid that were rescued, it got even worse.

"I know. But I'm not sure what to do about it. We're rec-ognizable and going back to work right now with this backlash isn't wise. Not to mention that I'm not sure we still have jobs. Living might be a bit tight for a while. But we know how fast public opinion can change. In another two weeks people may love us again." McKenna fought to keep the cynicism out of her voice, but it was hard. Even the people they were working with on the ships seemed distrustful.

Options didn't seem plentiful, not if she wanted to keep the kids. She'd be damned if she would give them up. Not that there was a chance anyone could get Charley to leave her. He had a wolf's attachment to pack, though on good days she realized Jamie, Jessi, and Nam would soon supplant that attachment.

She shrugged again, feeling beat down. "I've pinched pennies before, I can do it again."

"Well, that at least I can help with. While the government recognizes that they'll need to work on making sure the law of equal rights is upheld, it doesn't change how people react. We can't help all shifters or Kaylid, but you few we can help." He flipped open the folder on the table and handed them all checks. "In recognition of your service to your country and the world. We were trying to get you the Medal of Freedom, but the tide of public opinion put a damper on that."

McKenna and the others took the checks offered. She had to read it a few times to make sure she read it correctly. "Two million dollars?" Her voice cracked as she said the words and she reached for the glass of water on the table in front of her.

"Considering what continuing to fight this war would have cost us? Not to mention the information on the ship you brought to us? Personally, I think it should have been in the tens of millions, but..." He shrugged and sighed. "Congress has just as many idiots who follow social media as do the public. It isn't much, but there are also checks here for the kids for their translation work for five hundred thousand." He slid one to McKenna and two to Toni. "I wish I could do more for you. But I've already turned in my resignation. The end of next month is my last day on the job and I can't say I've ever been happier to quit something."

She stared at the check for her foster son, it took a minute to remember Nam hadn't gotten the language load, so while she had kept them company, she hadn't translated with the others.

McKenna felt numb, after everything that had happened, this was how it ended? She didn't know what to say or do, but this would keep her, Charley, and Nam for a while. Maybe Perc could change his name and they could move somewhere else, but the others?

Before she could get too deep into a spiral, Rarz spoke.

"I had not known how to broach this idea, but perhaps this is as good a time as any." His voice had an odd note to it, like a mix of wariness and hope. It ran along her mind and she felt Wefor perk up. The AI had been downright depressed lately, muttering about irrational fears.

McKenna changed her position in her chair to look at him. He'd been at the far end of the conference table, not with them, yet not apart. He'd spent lots of time talking to people. Mostly scientists or military attaches, but so far, he had demurred and resisted bringing over any more of his people, citing fear of their acceptance. The wave of resentment and fear towards the Kaylid had given credence to that fear, but many still hoped.

"And what would that be?" She hadn't released Perc's hand and his grip tightened a bit as they waited. What miracle could Rarz possibly offer them?

"The Elentrin are still out there attacking my people and we are a species that breeds very slowly. Many of the worlds they tried to take from us, but failed, have housing and land. These planets would support human life since they are very similar to Earth in most ways. We need people who can fight, innovate, and teach; people who will help us learn how to face the Elentrin and I fear some of the other species out there in the vastness of this universe. We have only explored this galaxy, there are untold more out there."

It felt like they'd all been stunned. Even in the mind-space, there was shock. Toni was the one who broke it, her voice cutting through it like a dull blade through paper. It tore something to hear her speak.

"You want us to come with you and be your cannon fodder instead? Let my children die to fight your war?"

Rarz tilted his head looking at her. Once more something passed between them, something richer and darker than McKenna had seen before.

"No. I'm offering to provide homes for all Kaylid. I'm asking if some of them would be willing teach us and maybe fight with us. I'm offering passage to planets with empty homes that need life brought back to them. I'm offering you a chance to come to my worlds. I'm offering hope, for all those who aren't welcome here."

The words crackled across the room.

"All Kaylid? There has to be at least a hundred million that are still alive." Burby sounded shocked at the offer.

McKenna just tried to process it.

Rarz shrugged. "I have worlds that need populations. Some they could build from scratch, and others they could live with us. But given your people, I'd be surprised if even fifty percent accepted. But for those among you, the dreamers and explorers, the warriors and builders, it is an option."

The words hung there, full of promise and risk. McKenna glanced around the table looking at the faces of the most important people in the world to her.

"I guess we have a lot to talk about."

Epilogue

The impacts of asteroids in Tennessee have shattered the New Madrid fault and earthquakes are rippling up and down the Southeast. The impact fragmented the asteroid, leaving a crater, and current estimates are two thousand dead at least, while the one that hit in Minnesota has devastated the three nearby towns. Experts are pointing out it could be have been worse as the asteroids seem to have fractured as they went through the atmosphere, making the impacts less destructive than they could have been, though that isn't much consolation to the people whose families have been destroyed. The one in Nevada hit desert and the only side effects might be new mining in the area. ~TNN Invasion News

Raymond fought to keep his face blank as the members of the House of Representatives exploded into arguments about what to do about the refugee aliens that were taken from the spaceship. They still hadn't finished pulling the remaining canisters off the ship. So far, more and more were turning out to be aliens. Some of which looked like things from nightmares, or memories of long ago, which helped ignite more arguments as only the Largo woman and her friends could even communicate with them.

Either way, everything that was happening, especially the asteroids, fueled his agenda. The weapon had been primed and aimed directly at the shifters. The addition of the tidal waves, one of which had all but removed Sydney from the map, had assisted greatly. People had someone to blame. The additional devastation from the asteroids had only heightened the anger. With three hitting the US, the death toll had been in the thousands, not the hundreds of thousands like in Australia, China, and France. Having someone they could blame gave humans across the world something to focus on, and they did it with a feverish intensity.

I wonder if I can get them to become a second-class citizen? Immortality should scare people. Think of the power they could accumulate if we let them be normal. Power like I plan on accumulating.

Which was exactly why it couldn't happen. Raymond already started to make sure he had multiple identities ready. When it was time to go down that road, he'd simply become someone else, his heir apparent. Immortality was a gift he'd never expected, but he would use it to its fullest extent. And insure his empire continued to grow with him at the helm.

This session looked like it would drag on for hours and he had other work to do. He slipped out of the gallery and headed down the hall, just one more person of power moving about. Anonymity was his best weapon. When people didn't know you existed, it made it hard for them to guard against you.

His watch buzzed softly, and he glanced at it. A text message from a number he didn't recognize. It could wait a few minutes. Raymond finished leaving the building, enjoying the walk to his offices. After he'd walked for a few minutes he stepped out of the way of the foot traffic and pulled out his phone.

Job done. Pain eliminated

A string of numbers followed the text. Raymond allowed himself a small smile as he logged into an anonymous bitcoin app and transferred coins to that account number.

He then deleted the text and wiped all history of the transaction. Glancing around, he walked back out into the flow of people, no one even gave him a second glance. The cop and her wife had been eliminated, the other cop was neck deep in the shifter drama, and everyone else was dancing to the strings he pulled.

The urge to whistle struck him, but that would make him noticeable and Raymond Kennedy thrived on being unnoticeable. Keeping up his brisk pace. Strolling in DC was what tourists did. He made a check list of what was left. After using Willard for a few more pushes of popular opinion, he would have to arrange a very graphic shifter-based accident to befall him. The outcry would be the final thing he needed to make shifters a subservient species. Now, if only the remaining doubt about their breeding could be verified. No matter. If nothing else, history proved once you became an outcast, gaining back your original status would prove a challenge. If he had his way, they would become the perfect ground troops. After all, wasn't that what the Elentrin had used them for?

That thought reminded him he needed to follow up on their captive guests. One was being treated like a VIP, the others as prisoners. Russia had gained one, as had Britain, but if there were any others loose they had managed to avoid detection. Surely, they could be used for more than what they were currently being used for.

Life looked good. At this rate he'd be running the country in another few years, which was exactly what he was born for. This time Raymond did smile, walking into the building with his offices in it.

"Good afternoon Mr. Kennedy," said the guard as he badged through towards the elevators.

"Yes, it is, isn't it. A beautiful day," Raymond replied as he headed back to make sure his plans continued on pace.

Authors Note:

I hope you are enjoying the Kaylid World. This series has a lot more in store for McKenna, JD, Toni, and the kids.

Visit my website at www.badashpublishing.com to sign up for my newsletter and find out about the next books coming out in this series.

If you enjoyed this book, please leave a review, it makes a HUGE difference. Thanks!

Do you want to know what happens next?

New Games is available now!
Commander is available now!
Home Alone is available now!
Decisions is available now!
Incoming is available now!
Trust is available now!
Allies is HERE!

Happy reading!

Mel Todd

ABOUT THE AUTHOR

Mel Todd has three cats, none of which can turn into a form with opposable thumbs, which is good. If they could they wouldn't need her anymore. Writing and trying to start her empire, she decided creating her own worlds was less work than ruling this one.

Printed in Great Britain
by Amazon

64199758R00217